THE
GAME

Also by Linda Calvey

The Locksmith

THE
GAME

LINDA CALVEY

WELBECK

Published in 2022 by Welbeck Fiction Limited, an imprint of Welbeck
Publishing Group Based in London and Sydney.
www.welbeckpublishing.com

A CIP catalogue record for this book is available from the British Library

Hardback ISBN: 978-1-78739-943-3
Ebook ISBN: 978-1-78739-942-6
Trade Paperback ISBN: 978-1-78739-944-0

Printed and bound by CPI Group (UK) Ltd, Croydon, CR0 4YY

10 9 8 7 6 5 4 3 2 1

to my great grandchildren:
Michael, James, Theo, Remilia and Marnie

PROLOGUE

Marbella Region, Spain, 2011

'Get your fucking hands off me, I know nothing about the stolen gear!' The Russian, a livid scar sliced across his cheek, struggled against his bonds as he was pushed into the deserted warehouse.

Ruby, a tall, elegant woman in Louboutin heels and a Chanel suit, waited inside. She turned, raised her eyebrows, and stepped over to the man. She smoothed back her jet-black hair, still glossy and sleek though she was forty years old and the mother of an eighteen-year-old daughter, and ran her emerald eyes over the captured man.

Several kilos of cocaine had disappeared from a drug run bound for London from South America. Her sources told her this man, who now cursed and swore in Russian as he struggled against his captor, was one of those responsible. She wanted to know everything: who was in on it, how they did it, and more importantly how they got away with it. And where was the missing shipment now? She had no doubt this snivelling traitor would talk. Alfie, her dead husband's twin, would make sure of it. And when she had the answers, she would take her revenge.

Alfie, his designer Westwood suit in stark contrast to the aura of menace he exuded, held the man still. His wiry build and arms filled with tattoos were covered from view by the finest virgin wool, though his stare was hard as he kept the man in his grip. He watched Ruby assess their prisoner, her cool gaze sizing up the man who'd thought he could get one over them, and smiled unpleasantly. He knew Ruby wouldn't back down until she got the answers she sought. He understood that underneath the polished exterior of a wealthy, classy lady was a woman who had stopped at nothing, including murder, to get to where she was today: the head of a drug cartel that spanned half of South America, Europe and Russia. He saw a woman who had worked her way up from nothing, from a poverty-stricken background in East London, who had faced hardened criminals without blinking, a woman to be reckoned with.

Formidable she may have been – ruthless, too – but her instincts were as sharp as the steel blade that once marked the crook they interrogated, a man who waited for her to speak, his face a picture of terror as he realised there was no escape from her. Ruby's reputation preceded her. She had killed before and wouldn't hesitate to do so again, if required.

'Oh, but ya do know about them drugs that disappeared between Cartagena and London,' Ruby said slowly, dropping her voice almost to a whisper.

'We know you was at the dock the day they vanished,' Alfie said. 'You was seen talkin' to some of the men just before the heist, the men who also disappeared with our goods. Now, tell us everythin' you know or you're a dead man.' He shoved the terrified crook down onto a chair, then pulled out his gun and pointed it at the man's head.

'No one can 'ear ya scream out 'ere, son, so spit it out . . .' he snarled.

The man had been seized at the Glasgow dock where the shipment had gone missing. Beaten and roughly handled, he'd been brought half-conscious via car boots and private air strips to this disused warehouse an hour's drive from Malaga, the city where Ruby's empire was now based. He was ready to talk.

'Shit, shit, OK, don't shoot me. Listen, I can help you. I know something about the robbery, the death of your husband. Please, listen to me . . .' The man was wide-eyed with fear now. He stared at Ruby. She glanced at Alfie.

'What d'ya mean, you *know* somethin'? Alfie sneered. 'He's lyin' to ya, hopin' the cavalry will arrive. I've got news for ya, mate, there ain't no cavalry. It's just us, and we've got all the time in the world.'

Ruby paused. She saw his fear, that was obvious, but her gut told her there was something else at play. If there was anything she'd learned in the life of crime she'd led, it was to trust her instincts. She knew people would say anything to save themselves, but it seemed strange the man

3

had mentioned the robbery in which her husband Archie had been murdered when he was caught for a different crime.

'No, Alfie, let's 'ear him. Go on, speak,' she commanded. Alfie walked round to face the Russian, and pointed the end of the gun into the frightened man's face. The man gabbled now, his words falling over themselves as horror overtook him.

'I mean it, I know what he did to you. I was too afraid to tell you, but I know something about your husband's death, I know who ordered it . . .'

Alfie glanced swiftly back at Ruby.

'He?' she said pointedly. 'Who are ya talkin' about? If ya know anythin' about my Archie's killin' then tell us now.'

'Spill the fuckin' beans, you cunt, and ya might just live,' Alfie added, but it was Ruby who was in charge. She walked slowly up to the man, who quaked and sweated. Her heels clicked on the cold, hard surface in the dark space. The nearest village was half an hour's drive away. They were alone.

'We buried my husband two days ago, so tell me, his grievin' widow, what do ya know, Micha? What could ya possibly know about that robbery?' Suddenly, out of nowhere, there came the sound of a car driving wildly towards the warehouse and then screeching to a halt. Ruby looked up quizzically. No one else knew about this place, where interrogations like this occurred, where those who thought they could do over Ruby and her cartel learned otherwise.

Despite the sound, the man opened his mouth, but before he could speak, the warehouse door slammed open.

'Jesus fuckin' Christ, what the fuck's goin' on?' Alfie yelled. They recognised the man marching in as one of their henchmen, another Russian employed by their business associate, drug baron Vladimir Ivanov. The man – a bearded, tall, burly guy wearing a black coat – strode into the warehouse, gun in hand.

'What the fuck—' Alfie started to say again but the man, who held a large rifle, ignored him. Before Ruby could say anything, the henchman raised his weapon.

'You caught the scum that took the coke. Good.' He turned to the captured man. 'My boss Mr Ivanov sends you this.'

He pulled the trigger: BANG! The sound ricocheted off the walls. In a mess of gristle and bone, blood splattered across the concrete floor as the Russian shot his countryman at point-blank range. Alfie leaped out of the way but was sprayed with blood. He pointed his gun at the henchman. Ruby stood still, half-wondering if the gun would be turned on her. It wouldn't be the first time she'd stared down the barrel of a weapon that could kill her in a millisecond.

'It is done. I will inform my boss.'

The man barely acknowledged them. He turned to leave but Ruby stopped him.

'*I'm* your fuckin' boss and you just shot a man who had information about my Archie's murder,' she said coldly. 'You can tell *Mr Ivanov* I'll be in touch. This won't ever happen again.'

She nodded to Alfie, who looked like he wanted to kill the man, and she walked out, her brother-in-law beside her, her head held high though anger burned through her.

'And you can clean that body up,' Ruby called back.

PART 1
REVENGE
Marbella, Spain, 2011

CHAPTER 1

'Cathy, darlin', I need to 'ave a word with ya,' Ruby called up to her daughter, who was in her bedroom in the plush villa they shared in an exclusive Spanish resort.

The palatial home was a long way from the place Ruby and her brother Bobby grew up in many years ago: a squat, terraced Victorian house in Star Lane, East London. In the intervening years, Ruby, helped by Bobby and her husband Archie, had created a criminal empire, from safe-breaking to drug-running, which had afforded them a life of luxury – and a life of continual danger too. The danger seemed no more present to them than now, a week after Ruby's beloved husband Archie was shot by robbers attempting to steal money from their safes in front of the two women, his wife and their daughter Cathy.

Ruby had been blissfully happy with Archie, the only man she'd ever given her heart to, and the man who helped propel her into the big time. His father, Lloyd, ran a large drug cartel which Ruby had been only too happy to join – and spearhead – with her sharp instincts and razor-like mind, and her skills in negotiation surpassing all others. She'd spent years fronting up the company, entering into a partnership with a Russian drug baron, and dealing with some of Europe's most dangerous and brutal crooks. Yet, it had all led to this, the death of Archie, and the proof that their life was one of immeasurable risk. Ruby knew now, more than ever, that one false move, one hesitation, could be the death of them all. Which was why even now, after she'd buried her husband and was consumed by grief, she had to carry on; she had to make her family safe.

She had watched the priest as he read the funeral liturgy, hardly able to believe it was Archie in the coffin that lay in front of her, covered in flowers; the white lilies he liked to buy her, and never would again. There had been crowds of people, all shady characters, big names in the underworld, who'd paid their respects, lavishing large sums of money on the new widow and paying tribute to Archie, a boy who came from nothing. Archie had been a ruthless businessman but he was a gentle husband and a loving father, while Alfie, his twin, dealt with the dangerous end of the business sourcing cocaine and bribing officials in South America, the home of the cartels they bought drugs from. Alfie, who looked so like Archie yet was hardened in a way his twin never had been, had wept openly at the funeral despite his tough man image.

In contrast, Ruby hadn't shed a tear. She knew they would call her cold, with a heart of ice, and that suited her image. She must appear strong, without even a chink in her defences, and so she had to do what she'd done since she was a young woman starting out in the under-world: she needed to bury her feelings as deep as they'd dug her beloved husband's coffin that day. Perhaps one day she would allow them to resurface so she could grieve properly, but on the day of the funeral she was being watched by the most dangerous men in the business, and so it had not been the day. She had learned the hard way to show no emotion, give nothing away. Life was too dangerous, too fragile to let her opponents see any sign of weakness, even when in the depths of grief. Somehow, she got through that day, supporting Cathy, comfort-ing Alfie and Lloyd, and never, ever showing anyone her pain. Now she had to do it again, because she knew deep down that she had to send her daughter away from her at the exact moment her daughter needed her love the most. The wrenching sensation was almost physical.

Ruby, an elegant, slim, still-beautiful woman, knew it was the only way she could protect Cathy, give her the time to grieve her dad, and put her somewhere she knew she'd be safe from the crooks, criminals, henchmen, drug-pushers and cartel bosses who circled Ruby like sharks. The decision brought Ruby no joy. She regretted that she couldn't give her only child a place to grieve – it hurt her deeply on top of the loss of the man that meant so much to both of them. Ruby had shot both gunmen dead, but she had been seconds too late to save Archie from the same fate. Loss piled upon loss. Ruby had lost so many people over the years: her beloved mum Cathy and dad Louie who would be horrified by her life of crime and by this life she had created; her little brother George; her best friends Charlie and Maureen Beaumont who had mentored her as she'd established herself as a tough negotiator, a woman to be reckoned with in the criminal world; and now her adored husband, the man of her life. Ruby became a crook to provide for her family when she, her brother Bobby and little George became orphans. They'd seen no other way to keep a roof over their heads and food on the table. They had much more than that now; their life was worlds away from their small ambitions back then. And yet the price of her success was high. Would she have paid it knowing how things would turn out? It was too late to ask. This was her life. And she had to stay on top. Or, like a house of cards, it would all come tumbling down.

Knowing she had to act quickly after the funeral, Ruby had set in motion the next course of events.

'Darlin', come down, will ya? I really need to talk to ya.'

When there was no response, Ruby sighed and headed up the stairs, feeling the soft white carpet under her stiletto heels and holding onto the sweeping balustrade as she went, inwardly still marvelling at the luxury which was now hers. For a moment, in her mind's eye, she saw the rickety wooden staircase, bare of carpet, in her old family home. It was meticulously clean, her mum Cathy had real pride in cleanliness, but no amount of scrubbing could make the stairs, or the floors, or the surfaces, appear anything other than shabby. So much had changed. So much more would, now that Archie was gone and she had to find some way of living without him.

Ruby tapped on Cathy's door.

'Listen, Cathy, I need to speak to ya. Couldn't ya hear me?'

Ruby walked in softly, but caught Cathy wiping away tears.

'Oh, darlin', it's OK to cry. You miss yer dad, it's natural to grieve for him,' she said, her voice low as if talking to a frightened child, though Cathy was almost a woman.

'Why did Dad have to get killed?' Cathy said, turning to face her mum, her eyes red-raw from crying. Ruby's heart skipped a beat at the sight of her, though Cathy was still so pretty with long dark blonde hair like her dad's and those green eyes inherited from Ruby. Was there an accusation in Cathy's words? Did she think her mum could've done more?

Ruby went over that evening at the villa in her mind every night as she lay in bed not sleeping, going through every detail obsessively, trying to see what she might've done differently, wondering if anything might've stopped the worst from occurring. She searched every second of the events, but in vain. She and Cathy had returned from a day of pampering to find Archie tied up in the lounge and two scruffy balaclava-clad robbers holding him at gun-point. The villa security guards were nowhere to be seen and the three of them were alone as the men demanded Ruby open the safe and give them the cash stashed inside. What the robbers didn't know was that Ruby always kept a gun in each of their safes. As soon as she clicked the safe open and put her hand on the gun, they shot her Archie, and she reacted by pulling the trigger on both crooks, killing them stone dead. It happened in a blur of seconds. Time stood still as Archie's blood mingled with that of the robbers, deep red on the white marble floors. Then Ruby awoke as if from a nightmare, and ran to her husband, cradling him in her arms, knowing he was lost to her, as Cathy screamed and screamed. What else could she have done? Did Cathy blame her for her dad's death?

'What d'ya mean darlin'? Dad got killed because them robbers were bastards who shot him and then were goin' to kill us all as soon as the safe was open. If I hadn't had that gun inside, we'd all be dead.'

Cathy looked up at her. Until that moment of the robbery, Cathy hadn't known about the true nature of the family business. Ruby and Archie had preferred to keep her protected, and had sent her to an exclusive international school where she'd been oblivious of their trade. Of course, Cathy had known they'd built up a business importing and exporting products but, amazing as it seemed to Ruby now, Cathy had never asked what the products were, and Ruby had never told. Cathy was an innocent, or had been until the murder of her dad and, before that, the horrible events with her uncle George, who had stolen her innocence properly. He'd raped her when she was just a child when high on the drugs he was trying to sell. Archie and Alfie had hunted him down, and would've tortured him, so horrified were they by his actions. It had been Ruby who'd stepped in, who'd done what needed to be done that night. It seemed she'd made a habit of that. She knew now though that there were no thanks for this – and her actions that night created fallout all through the family.

Ruby shuddered. So many secrets. So many lies, and so much death. And in all this, Cathy had turned to Belle, taking comfort from her rather than her own mother. That's how Ruby knew she was making the right decision, though it hurt her to do it. She had to get her daughter away from this life, back to England where Uncle Bobby and his wife Aunt Belle could take care of her. Ruby had always been jealous of the bond that had grown between Cathy and Belle, but right now, when the criminal underworld might sense the new vulnerability of Ruby and her family, it was best to use that relationship and get Cathy away.

'You've been through so much, Cathy,' Ruby murmured, stroking her daughter's honey-coloured hair and pushing a tendril back from her face.

'I wish it'd been me, not Dad, that was killed. I'd give anything to have him back.' Her daughter's voice broke and the tears came again.

Cathy's accent was a world away from Ruby's. The young woman had been to an expensive school and spoke with a vaguely European-sounding accent that was hard to pin down, interspersed with cut-glass English expressions. Ruby still spoke like the cockney she was, never leaving her roots behind though she was now a wealthy woman living an international jet-setting life, clad in designer labels and drinking only the best champagne.

'Don't say that, darlin'. I can't bear to 'ear ya say that. I'd give anythin' for your dad to be 'ere but he ain't, baby. He's gone and somehow we 'ave to try and find a way to manage. That's why I wanted to speak to ya.' Ruby had pulled her daughter close but now she sat back upright and held Cathy at arm's length, staring into those innocent eyes that were almost as green as her mum's.

'I've been doin' a lot of thinkin' and I want what's best for ya. If I'm honest, then I don't know if we're safe 'ere. With your dad's death, the businessmen I deal with—'

'The dealers and pushers, you mean . . .' Cathy interjected, her expression hardening with disapproval.

'Yes, love, the pushers and dealers, the hard men and cartel bosses around Europe, well, they'll all be expectin' me to collapse, to lose my edge because of my grief, and they'll be sniffin' around tryin' to take our territories and our contacts. I 'ave to be 'ere to stop them and show them, at least on the outside, that it's business as usual. I know that sounds harsh.'

Cathy nodded. 'Yes it does,' she said, pulling her cardie around her and moving back from her mum.

Ruby looked down at her hands. She still wore her engagement ring, a diamond solitaire that winked up at her. She gained strength from the hardness of this rock that had withstood millions of years of compression – the sheer power and beauty of it. Sometimes she knew how that stone felt: being squeezed from all angles, being made hard and brilliant by the pressure.

She breathed in and said, 'I'll come straight out with it, Cathy. I'm goin' to send ya to England to live with Aunt Belle and Uncle Bobby. It ain't safe for ya 'ere and there's too many memories. I know how close you are to Belle,' and here Ruby had to stop as emotion welled up inside her. It pained her to see how much Belle has become a maternal figure to Cathy, and how this seemed to shine a light on Ruby's failings as a mother. Ruby was a fierce negotiator, a cunning businesswoman, an adoring wife, but somehow, she never got it right with the daughter she loved so much. Perhaps she wasn't the maternal type? Perhaps Cathy would've been better off with Belle for a mum rather than Ruby, and the thought of that gave her fresh grief. Ruby looked away from the daughter she loved yet couldn't quite reach, and said, 'I know I haven't been the best mother to ya. I know you'd be happier if I'd stayed at home and baked cakes, but that's never been me. It don't mean I don't love ya, though, please remember that.'

A tear slid down Cathy's face but eventually she nodded.

'I'm scared for you, Mum. I'm scared for all of us. I had no idea our lives were in so much danger. I knew we were rich, that was obvious, and I feel so stupid now for never asking how we got to be like this.'

It was Ruby's turn to nod.

'Darlin', I would never 'ave told ya. Some things are best left unsaid. Those robbers won't be back, so don't worry about me. I'll get everythin' ship-shape 'ere and then I'll be over. Listen, I've booked you onto a flight tomorrow morning, first class. You can make a fresh start, a new beginning in England, away from this place and the horrors 'ere. I'll help ya pack if ya want . . .'

'No. Thanks, Mum, but I'd rather sort my stuff alone.'

Ruby blinked, trying not to break down. She hadn't told Cathy that she was convinced the robbery had been a set-up, and had almost had proof of it. Some things couldn't be shared with a girl as vulnerable as her daughter.

Ruby tried to smile, to reassure her.

'All right, darlin'. Just let me know if ya need anythin'. I'll be over to see ya once things are clearer 'ere, I promise.'

It broke Ruby's heart to see her gentle daughter nod then turn away from her, leaving her to get up off Cathy's bed where they'd been sitting, and make her way back downstairs. Ruby could've wept at the thought of her daughter's obvious coldness, the hurt and fear underneath it. *I'm doin' the right thing by her*, Ruby thought, though she wondered if she was merely convincing herself.

*

The next morning, Cathy stepped into the chauffeured limousine, which had blacked-out bulletproof windows. Two silent minders sat either side of her in the car, both carrying guns. Any pretence that they were a normal family was gone now. Cathy had politely refused her mum's request to come to the airport and see her off, so Ruby, respecting her wishes, was consigned to standing at the villa's main entrance, underneath an archway of orange trees. She blew her daughter a kiss as the car rolled off the driveway, the engine murmuring low as it took her Cathy away from her.

'I'll be over soon, I promise ya. I love ya, Cathy,' Ruby whispered, her smile never faltering. She carried on waving even though the car had swept out of the driveway, leaving her standing alone. In the time it took for a heart to beat, she was taken over by the desire to unleash her feelings, to crumple with the sheer weight of the loss of her daughter. She breathed in, taking in the scent of oranges in the warm morning sunshine, then she looked at the entrance, her force of will triumphing over her emotions.

'Shut those gates,' she ordered the security guards, who were now posted twenty-four hours a day along the length of the villa's estate. She turned, breathing in another long, deep breath, then stalked inside, her heels clicking on the marble floors, her head whirring with all the things unsaid between them. Her heart felt like it was breaking all over again at this new loss, that of her daughter, as Cathy flew out to be comforted by another woman.

CHAPTER 2

'You don't ever send your men in to override my decisions!' Ruby thumped the table as she emphasised her complaint. She was fuming. Vladimir Ivanov sat opposite her at the oval glass-topped table in her office, with Lloyd and Alfie on either side of him. She was standing, then pacing, so furious was she by what had happened.

Ruby had called the meeting a few days later, after Cathy had gone. The sun shone through the huge floor-to-ceiling glass window that looked over the small bay beneath them. The ocean was grey-blue and the waves choppier than their usual hazy calm, signalling a storm out at sea. It wasn't just the Mediterranean that was stormy.

'Don't ever think of doin' that to me again. We're business partners, but your henchman seemed to think you were the boss. Well, I hate to break it to ya, Vladimir, but you ain't.'

Lloyd, a good-looking man in his sixties, with streaks of silver grey in his immaculately trimmed hair, looked up at her, and without having to say anything, he signalled with his eyes that she should steady herself, rein in her fiery temper. It wasn't often Ruby lost her cool in business, but this was something else. She saw the killing as an attack on her authority, her power base, and no one, not even a billionaire Russian drug baron, would take that away from her. Her emotions were running high after Cathy had left for England. Even though she was convinced she had done the right thing, the departure of her daughter, and the knowledge that she couldn't comfort her the way she needed, had upset Ruby more than she cared to acknowledge.

Ruby breathed in and out, standing and clutching the back of her chair, and locked eyes with Vladimir, who had stayed silent until now. The Russian waited for Ruby to calm herself before he spoke, his voice like treacle.

'My dear lady, I can see I have offended you greatly. I apologise for the distress I have caused you. My man acted without authority, no matter what he said to you at the time, and as a consequence, I have let him go. A mistake was made. We are all only human – even in business.'

Vladimir smiled, but his eyes glinted cold and blue. Ruby's heart still pummelled in her chest though any onlooker would think she was quite serene by now. She'd had so much practise at mastering her feelings. She looked at the man they had invited into their empire, and knew that his denial would not stop her instincts nagging at her.

She was convinced there was more to the shooting than he was making out, yet she could say nothing, outwardly, at least, in the face of Vladimir's words. She knew she should let this drop for now, but she found she couldn't.

'Listen, the man, Micha, almost gave us a confession. He was about to tell us more about the robbery and Archie's murder and your man killed him before he could speak. How dare ya do that?'

'Ruby, I think you've said enough,' warned Lloyd. 'Let's please get to the business at hand, we 'ave the missin' coke to discuss. We need to find a new, reliable, supplier, or someone else'll muscle in on us.' Ruby had never questioned her father-in-law's authority before – nor he hers. The atmosphere in the room was tense. Vladimir looked down at his gold Rolex and then spoke, his voice as calm as the sea was now choppy.

'What can I do to make up for this . . . this lapse of judgement on my associate's behalf, a man who has paid for it with his livelihood? Should he pay with his life too?'

Ruby shook her head, but didn't speak. Lloyd was the first to reply. Alfie was silent, though the veins in his neck twitched, showing his agitation. None of them were buying Vladimir's explanation, but as he was their partner, and a powerful ally, it would've been suicide to call him out for lying to their faces.

'As ya know, Vladimir, we've always felt two chancers wouldn't 'ave the balls to mastermind gettin' into the villa,' Lloyd sighed. 'It takes money, proper money, to buy off security guards who know they'd be hunted down afterwards, if anyone survived. They can't 'ave been actin' alone. Someone else, someone with access to money and weapons, and who wanted us dead, had to be behind this.'

He leaned back in his chair, his handsome face lined now, looking like the grieving father he was. Ruby almost broke down at the sight of him. No parent should have to bear the death of a child.

In the drama of the events surrounding the robbery, funeral, and shooting of this possible lead who might've unravelled the secret they all wanted to know, she'd hardly had a moment to check in with Lloyd. She saw the grief raw and brutal on his face, and for a moment she felt like she couldn't breathe. It made her contemplate something else, a question that had been in her mind since the day Archie died. How long could they stay in this game and survive? All of their lives were at risk. Every moment of the day they had to rely on their guards doing their job, the bulletproof glass doing its job, the bribes and back-handers doing their work too.

The thought that perhaps they should wind up the company, get out while they were still ahead, had crept into her thoughts each night as she waited for the sleep that wouldn't come. She hated seeing her father-in-law suffer. He was the steady hand at the helm, the one who'd seen his cartel grow from a small seed to a giant oak tree. She had come on board and proved to be a natural leader, but it was Lloyd who was at the heart of their empire. He looked beaten, and it was the first time Ruby had ever seen him this way. He'd been a blagger – a bank robber – when he was in England, pulling off some of the UK's largest heists until, finally, he'd been caught and banged up.

He'd taken prison in his stride, even making lifelong partnerships with people like Charlie Beaumont, who'd become Ruby's mentor and friend. Lloyd had also brought up Archie and Alfie single-handed before he did time, and afterwards he'd moved them all lock, stock and barrel to Spain. *Better climate, better villains*, Lloyd would laugh, and he was right. Within ten years he'd set up the family business and money poured in as they expanded their trade from London into the rest of Europe and South America. Yet it was only now that he looked like the burdens he carried, the lifestyle he led, weighed heavily upon him.

Vladimir stood up abruptly. Still no one else said a word.

'I have spoken to all my contacts here, and I know everyone, my dear friends, but no one knows these men who killed your husband. They just got lucky. You have to try and move on.' He walked over to Ruby, adjusting his gold cufflinks, signalling that he was ready to leave this meeting though they hadn't discussed the actual business of the day: securing the new supplier.

'This man who says he knew something was lying to you. I'm sorry, but he was trying to save his skin.'

The Russian crime boss touched Ruby's arm lightly. Something about the gesture made her recoil, but she didn't show it. Instead, she stared up into his eyes and murmured her thanks, gesturing for him to sit down and finish their business.

'It seems I've spoken out of turn, please forgive me, Vladimir.' He nodded his head to signal his acceptance of her apology but stayed standing, gripping the white leather back of one of Ruby's designer chairs.

'We 'ave important business to talk about and we need your presence – and your contacts – as our supplier is now suspect. If Lloyd is right, if those men who broke into my villa were workin' for someone, I want to know about it. That won't ever change, and I won't ever apologise for it.'

Alfie coughed, showing his approval, though it flew in the face of the formal niceties of their meeting. Almost without thinking, Ruby took a small step closer to Vladimir. She held his gaze as she spoke.

'I promise all of ya that if we find who was responsible, then I want to kill him myself.'

Vladimir held Ruby's gaze, steady and direct, which sent a shiver down her back. She glanced away, feeling her intuition stirring. When she looked back, the Russian had a bland smile on his face and whatever it was she'd sensed evaporated in the sunshine that had broken through the storm clouds.

'Now, gentlemen, let's get back to business. Vladimir, you 'ave a new contact in Bolivia? I'd like ya to talk us through your proposal, and how much of the product we can expect . . .'

There was a brief silence, and after only a short pause, the Russian sat back down and the meeting recommenced; all the while Lloyd looked over at Ruby, who had taken her place, sitting at the head of the table, sensing her apprenticeship in crime was over. Ruby, once an office girl who longed for a designer handbag, was now the true head of an enterprise that stretched from the Pacific Ocean all the way to the edge of Siberia

An hour later, a plan was in place for Alfie to return to South America with free rein to bribe anyone and everyone they needed, however powerful or rich, so that their supply of cocaine to Europe wasn't interrupted in future.

'Get rid of every man who worked on that last shipment. We might've caught one but there'll be others who can't be trusted. Get rid of them all, and I also want you to put the word out everywhere. Someone was behind Archie's murder. They wanted him – and me – dead. I want every contact in every country we deal with to hunt the truth down. And when we find him, I want him alive – for now.'

Ruby swept her eyes around the room to each man in turn, finally resting on Vladimir. He bowed his head, his eyes cast down, his agreement secured. Ruby's gaze lingered on him a second longer before she stood up, saying, 'Thank you, gentlemen, I know you're all busy people and I won't keep ya a moment longer.'

She walked out of the room, closing the double doors behind her as the men continued talking. She pulled her phone from her handbag, a glossy Prada crocodile-skin clutch. The real deal. Just like Ruby.

'Bobby, how is she?' Ruby walked to the infinity pool and, sitting at the edge, took off her stiletto heels and dipped her feet into the cool water. She gazed at the grey-blue of the sea on the horizon, the palm trees waving gently in the breeze. Sometimes she had to pinch herself to believe all this was real. She was surrounded by beauty: marble floors, sweeping staircases, pots of white lilies, maids, chefs, chauffeur-driven cars, designer clothes and shoes and even a yacht, yet she knew she'd give up the lot in a heartbeat if she could see Archie one last time. She missed the sincerity in his gaze, the way he used to kiss her lightly on the lips and pull her towards him. His instincts were always to protect her. For a moment, she imagined nuzzling into his chest, listening to his heart beating steadily, the familiar sound of her beloved husband, and she felt utterly bereft. All the memories hovered there, just out of reach, which is where Ruby felt they were safest. If she let herself remember him, really remember him and how he made her feel, she'd break down completely.

'Hello sis, yeah she's OK, but she's grievin'. She'll be all right, she's safe 'ere with us. Did ya want to speak to her?' Bobby replied, ever the pacifier. He was her older brother by a year but he was always the soft-hearted one. Bobby didn't have a ruthless bone in his body, and he'd taken a lot of convincing to become a crooked locksmith, using his keys, or twirls, as robbers called them, to break into safes and steal cash or paintings worth thousands, sometimes millions, of pounds. It was only because they couldn't make ends meet while their mum was dying, only months after their dad was killed in an accident at work in the scrapyard, that Bobby reluctantly left behind his apprenticeship and first sold his skills for the cash they desperately needed. He had wanted it to be a one-off, but the money began to roll in, and they had no other option. Their survival depended upon these earnings.

Growing up surrounded by crooks and villains in the East End, it was hardly a surprise that two young people, Ruby and Bobby, would leave their straight life behind, but it had never been their intention. They'd been brought up to live an honest life, however impoverished, but in the end it was the only way they could bring up their orphaned baby brother George and keep a roof over their heads and food on the table. The shame of giving their father a nine o'clock trot, or pauper's burial, sat with Ruby even now. After a lifetime of working in the scrapyard and bringing up his family, Louie had nothing: no money, no savings, nothing stashed under the mattress. He'd died young, only forty-one years old the day a faulty crane dropped its load of twisted, mangled metal parts onto him, killing him instantly. The nine o'clock trot was the council-organised funeral; the body taken to the cemetery early, before the paying punters, for a short ceremony and a quick burial in a cheap coffin.

Afterwards, Ruby and Bobby hadn't even been able to afford to put money behind the bar for the wake, and the few visitors that came had to buy their own drinks. The humiliation had seared into Ruby's soul, and she'd vowed on that day never to be in that position again. She'd decided to do whatever it took to have money in her purse. Bobby, her sweet, gentle older brother, had not shared her ruthless intentions. He'd always wanted a simple, honest life, like their parents had made, but it was a choice they couldn't afford to make.

Ruby reflected on this, and the love she felt for Bobby, knowing she owed him more than anyone.

Ruby heard muffled footsteps and then Bobby's apologetic voice.

'Sorry, Rube, she's gone out shopping with Belle. Thought I might've caught them before they left . . .'

Ruby felt a tear prick the corner of her eye, which she batted away furiously.

'That's absolutely fine, Bobby. I'm glad Cathy is gettin' out and about. It must be doin' her the world of good to be with ya both,' she managed to say.

'Another time, Rube. Give her a ring in a couple of days, yeah?'

'Course I will Bobby, give her my love, won't ya. Tell her I miss her.'

CHAPTER 3

Two days later, after a fitful night's sleep, Ruby rang England early so she'd catch her daughter. 'Cathy, darlin', how are ya? I'm so glad you felt well enough to go out shoppin',' she said, hoping her tone was lighter than she felt.

'I'm OK, Mum, it's lovely being with Belle and Bobby, they're taking good care of me. We did go out yesterday and I'm sorry I wasn't at home to speak to you, but it was really nice just doing something normal,' Cathy replied. She sounded calmer, less distraught, more 'normal'. Ruby paused for a moment as her words sank in, particularly the mention of 'home' being her aunt and uncle's house.

This closeness between Belle and Cathy was like a physical pain to Ruby, yet she knew she had to be grateful that her daughter was living away from the danger of the world she'd created. For a second, Ruby shut her eyes and imagined giving it all up, becoming a 'normal' straight person again and being with her daughter rather than heading up a drug empire. The thought of it almost made her dizzy, yet she knew herself well enough to understand that something still drove her on, even with these thoughts nudging her. Ambition? Perhaps. Fear? Sometimes. Or maybe, by now, she didn't know any other way to be. She knew they'd have to give up eventually, retire as most crooks did to make way for the young blood following hard behind them, but in her heart she knew she couldn't do that yet.

'Mum? Are you there?'

'Sorry, darlin', I'm tired, still not sleepin',' Ruby replied. The thought of failing her daughter was what kept her awake each night, along with her longing for Archie. It seemed that every time she turned off the lights at night, her worries, all the things she'd buried during the day, showed up to haunt her, robbing her of sleep. Every night she saw Archie's face: his blue eyes that looked at her so intimately, his dark blond hair with its first streaks of silver, his high cheekbones and full mouth. The thought he would never kiss her again, hold her or make love to her was unbearable, yet what frightened her most was thinking of the day his face would fade, when the memories would become foggy, less clear. This thought terrified her because when that happened it would feel he'd truly left her.

A silence settled between Cathy and Ruby. Ruby searched her mind but couldn't think of what else to say. She wanted to ask Cathy if she was OK, without being trite. She wanted to tell her that she loved her deeply and it was a wrench not to be able to comfort her. Yet, the pause in their conversation seemed to drift on. Perhaps there was too much to say.

'Darlin', keep yerself safe. I'll call again tomorrow. I just want ya to be happy, that's all,' Ruby said awkwardly.

'Thanks Mum, and you. I hope you're OK too.' Cathy seemed just as stiff, just as unable to express herself. Ruby put it down to exhaustion, and the emotional whirlwind she and her daughter had been through in past years. Her daughter had been raped, then held at gunpoint in a robbery where her father was killed. It was enough for any person to deal with, yet strangely, instead of drawing them closer, it felt as if there was a new gap opening up between them. Ruby hoped it was only temporary.

The next call was from Vladimir.

'Dear lady, we need to have a meeting right away, it's urgent. I have some very important information for you all. I'm on my way to you now in my helicopter.'

Ruby headed through the house to the office where Alfie was making last-minute preparations for his flight to Bolivia and Lloyd was calling one of their network in London, promising that the new supply of coke would be flown in within days.

'It's Vladimir, he just rang. He's on his way 'ere sayin' it's urgent, so urgent that he's flyin' in . . .'

Lloyd and Alfie looked up at her, eyebrows arched.

'What can be so important that he gets in his helicopter and flies 150 miles here?' Lloyd said.

Vladimir had been meeting a Bolivian official who was taking a vacation, staying at a very exclusive hotel in Seville, courtesy of their cartel, and promising to cast a blind eye over their products as they left customs in South America – for a huge fee, of course.

An hour later, the sound of the helicopter's blades cutting through the sky alerted them to the Russian's arrival. From the window, they watched as the chopper landed safely on the villa's helicopter pad and the wind created by the spinning steel tore through the palm trees nearby. Two armed guards ran over to escort the businessman inside. Vladimir stepped out, his suit immaculate, his short hair barely moving as the air swirled around him. He walked swiftly towards the villa, acknowledging the three of them briefly with a small wave before entering via a door at the back of the building.

He marched into the office, and without a formal greeting, got straight to the point. 'I found him. I found the man responsible for your husband's death. It was a former associate of mine from Russia who has been trying to take over our business.'

Everyone stared back at the Russian.

'Someone encroachin' on our territory?' Alfie responded, glancing swiftly at Ruby who stood stock still, waiting for whatever was coming next.

Vladimir's eyes darted around the room.

'So, you're tellin' us that you discovered there *was* a plot against us?' Lloyd said.

'Yes, that is right. Your dead man, Micha, was correct. The robbery was a set-up. There was someone behind the terrible events of that day. Your deaths were meant to appear as part of the robbery when, in fact, they were arranged so that Alec could muscle in on the empire you have created.'

'So, where is this associate of yours, Vladimir?' Ruby said, getting straight to the point, 'I want to meet him.'

'Ah. Dear lady, he is dead,' Vladimir said, adjusting his cufflinks. 'He would've killed me, I had only one option. He had to die.'

There was a moment's silence as the news they'd all waited to hear was digested. They should've been celebrating, yet something about this didn't feel right, not to Ruby, anyway. She felt a prickling sensation on her skin, like a form of warning.

'What d'ya mean he's dead?' she snapped. 'I told ya I wanted to be the one who killed whoever was responsible for my Archie's murder. You're now tellin' us that not only did ya find him, but ya got rid of him as well? And all of this in two days, without sayin' a word to any of us?'

Vladimir nodded, though he didn't quite meet Ruby's gaze as he replied.

'I apologise for not telling you. I thought I would sort this out myself as it was a countryman of mine. I went to see him alone. He was an old KGB colleague, Alec Rumanov, a man I knew well in Moscow. I realised this was a mistake when he pulled a gun on me. I had no choice. I shot him before he killed me. That's all there is to say. It's dealt with, dear lady. We move forward now.'

It sounded plausible enough. Alfie shrugged, accepting the news, but Ruby's mind was whirring.

'Why 'ave I never 'eard of him, then? This Alec Rumanov must be a big player to try and barge in on our business. So why 'aven't we met him before?' Ruby asked. She was like a Rottweiler with a rat between her teeth, she couldn't let go of it. She hesitated when she saw the frown on Lloyd's face. Again, she was questioning Vladimir's word, and this went against the code of honour among their kind. They were business partners, and so their word to each other mattered. If Vladimir was saying this is what happened, then again, at least outwardly, she had to agree. Otherwise, she risked him losing face, and the consequences might be serious. Upsetting the Russian, with his extensive networks, contacts, henchmen and killers at his heel, was not the way to sort this. She knew she had stepped over a line, but something about all this still didn't make sense to her.

'Vladimir's explained what 'appened. He's right, we 'ave to move forward. Ruby, why don't ya take a breather. We'll sort the Bolivia deal.' Lloyd was all charm as he spoke.

Ruby nodded.

'I'm fine to stay 'ere. Vladimir, I didn't mean no offence to ya. On behalf of all of us, I thank you for sorting out my husband's killer. I'm only sorry I weren't there to see it.' Her face was now as calm and professional as it would be with any other transaction between them.

'Run through the details of Alfie's trip again. Can we guarantee the border crossings will go smoothly?' She sat down at the oval table and gestured for the men to join her, nothing in her manner suggesting how agitated she felt underneath her now-serene exterior.

After Vladimir had flown back to Seville, Ruby poured Lloyd and Alfie whisky, preferring vodka for herself.

'Keep an eye on him,' Ruby murmured, keeping her voice low in case any of their considerable number of staff were in Vladimir's pay.

'Find out what ya can about that Russian who Vladimir says was behind it. My hunch is . . .'

Ruby didn't have time to finish her sentence as the housekeeper, a stern Spanish woman, entered the lounge to announce dinner was served.

'Hold that thought, Rube. We'll do what ya ask, now let's eat,' said Lloyd, his hand on her back as they walked into the palatial dining room which was filled with the white lilies Ruby adored.

Later, Ruby sat by her pool, the cicadas sounding all around her, the heat slowly leeching from the day. She could do nothing to challenge Vladimir openly. She thought about Archie, what advice he would've given her, how he would've settled her, telling her she had to trust someone. She thought about her parents, Cathy and Louie, those simple souls who believed in the goodness of people despite growing up in Canning Town where there was plenty of evidence to the contrary. They would've washed their hands of her and her life, preferring to know nothing about it. Their love for her, Bobby and George wouldn't have changed, but they'd have hated the path their children had chosen. Finally, she remembered her beloved friends Charlie and Maureen. She'd inherited the palatial villa they were based in from them, as well as a considerable fortune, propelling her into millionairess status. Charlie had been her crime mentor, the big boss of the underworld who took her under his wing before his untimely death in a car crash. He'd been faithful to his wife Maureen, who was Ruby's closest friend, and she'd died alongside him as they'd rushed back to help her when Bobby was nicked by armed Flying Squad officers who had forced their way into their Chigwell home. That was the legacy of Freddie Harris, a low-life crook who'd mugged them off – a legacy she'd repaid in murder. Archie, who was Ruby's boyfriend at the time, and Alfie, had hunted Freddie down like an animal and butchered him. His remains were fed to pigs, his teeth and nails thrown into the Thames. She'd blamed Freddie for her friends' deaths as they drove to try to get Bobby out of the charges of robbery levelled against him.

She knew revenge, which is why she distrusted Vladimir's words. She knew about killing, about what drives people to vengeance, and in that deep, primal knowledge, she couldn't find the passion behind Archie's killing. She couldn't trace the scent of the killer back to this Russian, Alec, though it was only a hunch. Charlie's face swam in front of her eyes. He'd had blue eyes that seemed to see into someone's heart and mind. He would've known if he was being lied to. She could almost hear his voice saying to her, 'Trust no one.'

CHAPTER 4

'Come with us, sis, we know ya miss Cathy,' Alfie said as Ruby pulled the Range Rover up at the private airstrip. Lloyd and her brother-in-law were flying to the UK, then Alfie would head straight to Bolivia from London. They'd purchased a private jet, making their movements less traceable. Ruby stopped the car and turned to face the man who looked so much like the husband she'd adored. Grief marked his features, which were more drawn than usual. He had a hint of stubble on his chin and though his hair was expensively cut, none of it could mask the sorrow that still consumed him.

Ruby smiled sadly and shook her head.

'I won't come, yet, Alfie. I need to be 'ere to make sure everythin' runs smoothly. I'll come one day, though, I promise. You're right, I miss Cathy more than I can say but she's better off where she is – and same with me 'ere, for now. Keep an eye on her for me. Tell her I love her, won't ya?'

'Course we will, Rube,' Lloyd said. He checked his Rolex. 'Come on, son, we've a plane to catch. I need to make some calls before we take off.'

They all looked at the landing strip where the plane, a light jet that carried up to six passengers, meaning it could land at remote or mountainous destinations, waited for them. The pilot stood by the plane, the steps down, ready for them to climb on board.

'Can ya believe it? A private jet. That's somethin', ain't it?' Ruby said almost dreamily. Then, snapping out of her reverie, she turned to Lloyd. 'I mean it, take care of my girl, make sure she's got everythin' she needs. Keep her safe for me . . .'

Lloyd kissed her on the cheek, leaving the scent of his cologne before he got out of the car and gestured for Alfie to follow him.

'Take care, sis. Don't forget ya need to look after yerself while we're away. We're vulnerable now that Archie's gone, and they know it.'

'They?' Ruby smiled.

'All of 'em. All the scumbags that want to hustle in on our game. Keep safe.' With that, Alfie winked at her, picked up his expensive Italian leather holdall and joined Lloyd on the runway. Ruby watched as the two men walked over to the plane, shook the pilot's outstretched hand and climbed inside. She stayed there until the sleek jet started to move, taxiing nimbly along the runway. Then, light as a bird, with engines low and powerful, it roared into flight.

Ruby felt reluctant to return to her villa alone. It was as if the ghosts of those that had passed were suddenly threatening to climb out of the walls, to engulf her. With a deep purr of her car's engine, Ruby started the journey back. Instead of Archie filling her thoughts in the silence of the drive, her little brother George's face seemed to haunt her: the endless hassle he gave them as a teenager, his moods, his anger. Somehow, somewhere, he had lost himself. Ruby ached for him, ached to hold him once more, to rewind time to when he was a lovely little boy. How had it all gone so wrong? She put the radio on to try to distract herself, but switched it off again almost immediately, preferring the quiet to the manic Spanish presenter and upbeat pop music which seemed to be the only offering.

I'm sorry, George, I'ad to do it . . . she thought to herself as his sweet baby face kept surfacing while she drove. She wasn't remembering him as a truculent teenager now, a troubled boy who was expelled from four private schools for dealing weed, and who kicked off at the slightest thing. No, it was an image of George playing in the sunlit garden of her home in Chigwell, the place Bobby and Belle lived in now, the first real home she'd made for herself and her two siblings as the crooked work took off. Instead of the drug-ravaged face he presented to her seconds before she killed him with a bullet from her own handgun, she saw the blond curls and blue eyes of a cheeky toddler, waddling about on the lawn, pushing his toy trike and giggling as he went. Tears began to stream down her face.

I didn't want to kill ya, George, but you left me no choice, she pleaded to the ghost that filled her mind.

My Archie and his twin would've made ya suffer for what ya did to my Cathy. They were deranged, far beyond reason or forgiveness. Archie was out for yer blood that night, but he would've taken it slowly, torturing ya no doubt for raping his precious girl, an innocent in this world but, because of you, an innocent no longer. I couldn't let them do that to ya, George, despite what you'd done. You knew the score. In the under-world, there ain't no coppers called, no Old Bill involved. We sort things ourselves, no matter the consequences. You had no chance, George, no chance at all.

Despite her words, she could see him as he leaned up to kiss her, a bubble of spit on his mouth, his little teeth pearly white as he then grinned and ran away shrieking with delight. That little boy who so delighted his sister and older brother Bobby had disappeared, and in his place had been a teenager bent on self-destruction, taking drugs, smoking weed at school, lashing out at family and friends.

How did we all go so wrong, eh, George? Ruby asked herself. In truth she didn't have a clue. They'd all had to deal with being orphaned, though George had been only a babe-in-arms.

It was harder on ya, George, I understand that, but it don't justify what ya did. That was unforgiveable.

Ruby and Bobby had been like parents to George. Ruby had to give up her straight work in a West End office to care for him while Bobby's wages as an apprentice locksmith, even one who was particularly skilled, didn't stretch far enough to keep them all fed. They'd been faced with that choice: sink or swim, stay straight or move into the shady world around them where crooks and thieves rubbed shoulders with bank robbers and criminal bosses. Ruby wondered again, had she made the right choice? Should they have starved or lost their home instead?

She arrived at the villa and the security guards signalled for her to drive in.

All that they had in this world came from that moment in time, that decision to cross over into crooked work, breaking into safes or pinching artworks to order. Everything she'd lost also came from that decision. Had it been worth it? She'd asked herself this question so many times recently. She searched her feelings. She felt no remorse for killing her little brother. She knew in doing so, she'd saved him from a fate worse than death. The underworld had its rules. From the minute George had pounced upon Cathy, pinning her down, taking her virginity, he'd crossed a line. There was no going back. He was a dead man walking.

Archie and Alfie had hunted him like prey that night, eventually pulling him out of his mate's flat as he tried to take more crack. Shivering, puking, knowing he was facing retribution from the man who'd helped raise him as Ruby's husband, he begged for mercy. He got it, all right, but at Ruby's hands, by Ruby's methods. The only mercy he could have was a swift death, and so she delivered it, like an angel of death, wearing a silk dress and sliding her gun from her Louis Vuitton handbag. She'd never been taught to use a gun but she found it came naturally. One breath, one slight hesitation and then it was done, and she was a mess of gore and blood as his body slumped on the floor.

Ruby knew she'd saved him from a fate worse than death, but her grief had been real and lasting.

She'd never told Cathy what she'd done. She'd fought Belle over it, as her and Bobby knew, but she was convinced Cathy was better off thinking George had been sent away to America. Belle vehemently disagreed but Ruby had overruled her, demanding her secret stay hidden.

Cathy had asked and asked after George in the following days and weeks, but in time, she'd stopped, and resignation had set in. Then her dad was killed and she had a whole new trauma to deal with and so George's disappearance had slipped to the shadows, where his memory belonged.

Ruby pulled into the driveway. One of her guards came over to the black Range Rover, his gun held aloft, to escort her inside. She didn't take any chances these days, not after the robbery that had ended in tragedy. She'd replaced every member of staff, sacked them all, with large pay-offs. She hadn't wanted to fuel any new revenge plots against her and her dwindling family. She'd recruited some of the hardest men in their trade and paid them twice the going rate. Protection was everything. Charlie had always told her, 'Make sure you've got good men around ya. You'll never know when you'll need them, and if ya don't 'ave 'em, it's already too late.' She'd learned that the hard way, and there was no way anyone could bribe her guards now. They were all her men.

'Shut the gates. Don't let anyone in today,' she commanded, stepping out of her car and throwing the keys to a second guard who stood nearby.

'Yes, madam,' he replied, and for a brief moment she relished the authority she now wielded.

Bodies lined her route to power, yet she could not afford to have regrets, despite the tears coursing down her face. She ducked her head down as she entered the villa, her sunglasses shading her eyes, not wanting anyone to see her pain. Ruby walked into the lounge but there was already someone there, someone she thought had stayed in Seville. Vladimir walked straight over to her, his face a picture of concern. She was too surprised by his presence to wipe away the tear stains. Kissing her on the cheek, Vladimir lingered a second too long. She smelled his exclusive cologne, one made up for him and him alone by his perfumier in Paris. It was a sharp lemon scent with amber notes, a fragrance that spoke of understated wealth and privilege.

'Don't cry, Ruby, I'm here now,' he said, holding her face in his hands, his blue eyes staring into hers as if he could see every thought she'd ever had.

CHAPTER 5

Ruby stepped aboard Vladimir's yacht, which was moored in a nearby hot spot, a harbour town that boasted exclusive restaurants and boutiques between Cannes and the Italian Riviera – a billionaire's playground for the summer. The winter sun was still warm, the sea was a bright aquamarine blue, the same colour as the sky, and there was a slight breeze.

'Shall we sail today? The conditions are perfect, though perhaps a little cooler than we'd like, and it will be our first trip together on my little boat,' Vladimir said, handing her a pink cocktail embellished with extravagant sculpted fruit. She accepted it, murmuring her thanks, and looked around. One of their first meetings had been aboard Vladimir's last yacht, and both Archie and Lloyd had been there. She'd felt entirely at ease doing business in such plush surroundings with her two men beside her. This time she was alone, though thankfully it was a different yacht, so she wasn't confronted yet again with memories of Archie.

'I'd hardly call this small, Vladimir, it's a palace in the form of a ship,' Ruby smiled, though something about this made her feel uncomfortable. She realised she didn't really want to go for a cruise away from shore. She had no control over the journey they would take, and she was starting to think that Vladimir was coming on to her rather than supporting her as a business partner. It had been barely two months since Archie's funeral and Ruby's grief was almost untouched. It lay in her heart, waiting for the right moment to surface, but that was where she needed it to stay. If she let it come, she feared it might break her completely.

'It is not often I can mix business with pleasure, as I do with you, Ruby,' the Russian said, smiling too as he sipped his own drink, a whisky on the rocks.

'Unfortunately, we must set pleasure aside, Vladimir, as we 'ave urgent business matters to discuss, which is why I'd prefer it if we concentrated on that rather than a trip, if ya don't mind?' Ruby said, sipping the drink, which was ice cold and sweet. She placed the cocktail down on a glass table beside the luxurious seating – rounded sofas that spun round to look at the view – and looked at the man who now loomed so large in her life. He was an attractive man, with high cheekbones and piercing blue eyes. Everything about him spoke of money: his manicured hands, his expensively handmade shoes, his scent and bespoke designer suits. He was every inch a Russian oligarch, and Ruby should've been congratulating herself for bringing him on board, but something about him rankled.

He was too perfect, perhaps; too groomed and charming. She knew he wouldn't have got to where he was by just smooth-talking. He was a ruthless, dangerous man, yet to her, he was the perfect gentleman – and it made her wary. Over the years, Ruby had learned to trust her instincts, which her dad said came from her Romany heritage. Her grandmother had been a Gypsy, with a gift for understanding people. Ruby had inherited her grandmother's name – and perhaps her strange gifts as well.

'You look beautiful, dear Ruby, simply elegant. How can I concentrate with such a woman on my yacht?' Vladimir smiled, showing his white teeth, which had an almost canine effect. Ruby decided she had to dampen this ardour, even if it was just flattery.

'As ever, you are too kind to me, Vladimir, but I know a man as sharp and professional as yerself won't be distracted from talkin' business. Shall we get to work? We have much to discuss, and I 'ave a new proposal to put to ya, a new supplier in Mexico who Alfie may be bringin' on board – if you agree, of course,' she murmured, taking another sip and watching the Russian from behind her Prada sunglasses. He was physically perfect, so like Archie in many ways, with a lean athletic build and year-round suntan, yet she couldn't have felt more differently about the two men. Archie, she'd trusted with her life. Vladimir was a slippery character: composed, assured, yet she knew she could never afford him that level of trust. He smiled, leaned back against his seat and, with a magnanimous gesture, signalled for Ruby to continue. She nodded her head.

'My brother-in-law Alfie has sent word back from South America that we 'ave an opportunity to expand into Mexico. He has met with some contacts who assure him they can supply top grade product without any problems with customs. We all know that we need new suppliers. The risk of goods bein' stolen, the risk of local wars breakin' out and bein' caught up in gang retributions is always an occupational hazard. Alfie says if we agree on a deal for new supplies from both countries then we're covered. The Mexico cartel can fly over a hundred kilos this week, with more the followin' week. Has to be worth us checkin' it out?' Ruby took another sip of the delicious cocktail. It seemed light and fruity but already her head was spinning a little. It was obviously stronger than it appeared. Vladimir gestured to a silent waiter who stood nearby.

'Another for the lady,' he said before Ruby could protest.

'These are all excellent suggestions. It is imperative that we find a trustworthy supply chain as another robbery of a shipment would make us look weak – and cost us many hundreds of thousands of dollars in lost sales. We've dealt swiftly with the people who thought they could betray us and steal our drugs, but it won't deter others in the future. There is too much at stake. If, as you say, Alfie has found a supplier in Mexico as well as Bolivia then we should make arrangements for the product to be tested before we transport it to London.'

Ruby nodded. She could see the wisdom in checking if their suppliers were producing good product. Years ago, they relied on tasting it, but times had changed and Ruby now had a team of chemists who worked for them, checking everything before it was bought in bulk.

'Then it is settled, we will expand into Mexico, if the product is right. Our supply chain will be shored up. I think this calls for a celebration.' Vladimir turned to the same waiter who stood away from the pair. As soon as Vladimir gestured to him, he moved off and came back a few seconds later with a bottle of Krug Grande Cuvée Brut. With a reassuringly smooth pop, the bottle was opened and the first bubbles poured into two crystal champagne glasses. Vladimir handed one to Ruby, who, unable to refuse, knowing she would cause offence, took it and held it, waiting for the Russian to toast them.

'To us, dear lady,' he said eventually.

'To us . . .' she said softly in reply, taking only the smallest of sips before putting the glass back down on the table. Ruby loved the taste of champagne, Krug especially, but she wanted to keep her senses alert.

'I don't know if I've told you much about my background, Ruby. We all know about your meteoric rise from the dark streets of inner London, but did I ever tell you that my path to success was just as treacherous, and unlikely, as yours?'

'No, ya didn't,' replied Ruby, at once more interested in what Vladimir was saying. She'd had people look into his background before they sealed the deal on their partnership. It would've been foolish business practice not to. She liked to know as much about people as possible so she could try and guess at their motives, and their likely actions. Knowledge was power, or so she'd been told a thousand times by Charlie Beaumont. She'd never let Vladimir know she'd done this, but then again, she presumed he'd done the same to her when the talk of a partnership between their empires was first raised. They couldn't take chances in their world.

'Do tell me, I'm fascinated by how ya came to own all this.' Ruby smiled as she spoke. She sipped her champagne again and for the first time since stepping onto the yacht, she started to relax.

'Dear lady, I was not born to all this, but I'm sure you know that . . .' Vladimir grinned wolfishly, well aware that she'd done some digging into his past.

'Why don't you tell me what you know already and I will . . . elaborate.' Ruby giggled, the bubbles definitely starting to take effect. 'Well, naturally, when our partnership was first discussed, I had my men make a few enquiries. Beyond all the usual facts about your business prowess, the deals you'd made and the people who worked for you, well, we could find very little about ya . . .'

'And that didn't bother you?' Vladimir asked pleasantly, as if this was a perfectly normal chat over drinks.

Ruby hesitated before replying.

'I was intrigued, if ya must know. I liked the fact you had a mysterious past. Though one thing we did find, you've never been married. We couldn't unearth even one ex-girlfriend, no one from your background or past at all. It was as if you'd sprung from nowhere.'

For a moment, Ruby wondered if she'd gone too far, said too much. Eventually, Vladimir took a gulp of champagne and nodded.

'As ever, dear Ruby, you are right. There are no relationships cluttering up my path. You won't find any abused wives or neglected girlfriends. I simply decided as a young man that I would put business before everything. Except, of course, if I ever met the right woman. That would be an entirely different matter. Nothing would stop me from pursuing her.' At this point he lifted his eyes to Ruby's and held her gaze, his eyes boring into hers. Ruby swallowed. Was he implying what she thought he was?

'So, I vowed that I would become the biggest, most powerful player on the Moscow scene,' he continued, 'I came from great poverty – and there is nothing like a hungry stomach to feed ambition. Dear lady, I'm sure you'd agree.'

Ruby murmured her answer and took another sip. She wanted him to keep talking, keep revealing himself. She didn't know why but it felt important to know more about this mysterious figure.

'Yes, Bobby and I grew up in poverty too. Ours was a respectable kind. Both my parents worked night and day, my mum in a shop and my dad in a scrapyard. When they died, they left us with nothing.'

Vladimir nodded.

'My mother was widowed when I was a small boy, barely out of the cradle. My father, Dmitri, was killed in a terrible accident on the railways. He worked fixing the lines, but one day the wrong signal was given and he was crushed by a train. A terrible tragedy. I don't think my mother ever got over it.' He paused for a moment, sucking in the warm air. Ruby stayed silent, listening, hoping he would keep going. Her patience was rewarded.

'We lived in a small flat like everyone else's in a Moscow suburb where the mafia would meet wearing dark glasses and black suits. Each night we heard the rumbling of large trucks as they were driven into their warehouses and garages close by, hidden under darkness. We pretended we saw nothing. Mother would draw the curtains and refuse to answer my questions, saying some things were not for our ears. Power cables hung down from the ceilings, cockroaches swarmed out from the old gas cooker – which was all we had to cook on, shared with four other families on our floor. My mother Galina worked sweeping the Moscow Metro stations. Her job gave us enough to live on – just. I remember hunting for dropped onions or potatoes at Trubnaya Market, or stealing kindling and firewood from the dachas just outside of the city. We scraped by.

'Sometimes we didn't eat, most of the time we did, but hunger was never far away. A couple of times we missed dinners so Mother could buy tickets to the Bolshoi Ballet. As you know, back then, the ballet was for the people, and citizens could get tickets for a few roubles. Only foreigners paid the extortionate prices to watch the marvels of our great culture. It was seeing the Nutcracker performed at the Kremlin one year, I must have been seven years old, when I realised there was a whole world out there beyond manual work and cabbage soup and dark rye bread that could break your teeth. I will never forget that night. The colours seemed to glow, the dancers to fly. I feel like I held my breath – not wanting to miss a moment of its beauty in the act of even breathing. I don't think I've exhaled yet. If I do, perhaps I will lose everything: the money, the yachts, the villas and furs, the cars, diamonds, all of it.' Vladimir stopped speaking. His face gave away some internal struggle. He turned his head away and stared out into the bay. Ruby, captivated by his story, hadn't said a word as she took in the exotic sights and sounds of the Russia this man had left behind.

'So, how did ya do it? How did ya become one of the most powerful men in Russia?' she said eventually, her voice like a gentle caress. Seeming to come back to himself, Vladimir turned to her, took a long swig of champagne and laughed.

'By sheer hard work, my darling Ruby. I asked a lot of questions, found out who ran things. I asked to work for him, and then his boss, and then his, and before I knew it I was running my own deals, taking on my own men, sourcing my own products from all over the world.'

'And the KGB? You worked for them, ya said?' Ruby said softly, not wanting to break the spell and knowing it was a risk to ask, but her thirst for knowledge was almost palpable. She felt like a dog who could smell a buried bone. Vladimir put down his glass, and cleared his throat.

'Perhaps these tales are becoming mawkish. There is much in my past, and yes, that includes working for Soviet Intelligence, but I am unable to discuss that role, dear lady.' He clapped his hands and, as if by magic, two waiters appeared with white towels and yet more champagne.

'Now, I think our pursuits must be directed towards pleasure. Ruby, would you care to join me in the heated pool?' Though Vladimir asked a question, Ruby saw she would be unable to refuse without offending him. She also realised he was deflecting questions about his past – assuming, that was, his links to Russian state security were indeed in the past. She felt sharp disappointment, know-ing she'd gone too far with her questions.

'Of course, I'd love to,' Ruby murmured, hoping to regain his confidence, sensing some window of oppor-tunity had briefly opened to her and then shut just as quickly. Vladimir ushered her onwards to the front of the enormous yacht where an infinity pool lay on the lower deck. Slipping into the water, she experienced the pleas-ure of warm water on her skin as the air was almost chilly outside of the pool, but the questions still buzzed in her brain. Did Vladimir work for the Russian state now? Was he more dangerous than she'd previously thought? She might never know the answer.

Ruby smiled at him as she kicked off and swam to the far end. Leaning against the side, she gazed out to sea, trying to fathom who this man was, and what his intentions towards her could possibly be. Suddenly she felt a jolt of grief, a swooping feeling in her stomach that almost floored her. She wanted to be with Archie. She wanted him to hold her and tell her she was safe. She wanted his caress, his familiar scent, his whispered reassurances. Vladimir raised his glass to her and she took hold of hers, forcing herself to smile and look enchanted by the luxury and opulence around her, but all she really wanted was one hour with her man, one hour where the rest of the world, including Vladimir and his shady past, vanished.

The next day, rattled by the conversation with Vladimir, Ruby booked a first-class flight back to London. She'd been separated from Cathy for two months now and knew it was best if she disappeared for a few days and caught up with her precious girl.

Stepping out of the aircraft, Ruby walked through the VIP checks and straight out into the arrivals lounge where her chauffeur was waiting. The hour or so in the car gave her time to gather her thoughts. Perhaps she'd overplayed her hand on the yacht. Perhaps Vladimir was overstating his too. He had connections, of course. You didn't run a drug cartel as powerful as his without having the right political contacts, but she'd seen nothing so far to suggest there was anything more sinister than that going on. It was time to pull her focus back to her daughter, to put the Russian out of her mind and concentrate on what was really important, making sure her girl was OK.

'Where to, madam?' the driver said.

'Chigwell,' she answered, feeling that strange mix of sadness and joy, anticipating being close to her remaining family, but in a place with many memories to haunt her.

Cathy was standing at the door of Bobby and Belle's home, which lifted Ruby's heart. As she stepped out of the car, Belle appeared by Cathy's side. Ruby almost held out her arms, expecting her daughter to run into them the way she did when she was a little girl, but Cathy didn't move. She waited for her mother to approach, her aunt's arm around her protectively, looking for all the world like Belle's daughter.

CHAPTER 6

'Mum, look, this is where we have live music – jazz, mostly – and this is where the performers get ready. They make such a fuss, wanting expensive beer or snacks before they play, and you should see what some of them get up to!' Cathy giggled as she showed her mum the back rooms of the bar that Ruby owned. Ruby and Lloyd had bought a string of old pubs or rundown venues across Essex and the East End to transform into high class clubs and bars, which Bobby now oversaw. They were all fronts for money laundering, of course, though things were becoming increasingly difficult these days as the government tightened up the laws. Luckily, Ruby had kept on Charlie's dodgy accountant, a man with all the right connections, and the right accent, so they were still getting away with it, and likely to continue doing so. He was very 'creative' with his figures, and knew all the loopholes, and if Charlie had trusted him, then so would Ruby. She knew they had to be as sharp, if not sharper, than the law, and this accountant was the best at what he did.

'And if you come down to the cellar, you'll see we've got a huge walk-in fridge with some of the best brands of champagne, each one more expensive than the next!' Cathy beamed with pride. Ruby stepped carefully down the steep stairs into the basement of the bar in Chigwell. She looked around at the crates of pricey beer and the bottles of wine and nodded.

'You've certainly done wonders for the place,' Ruby said, smiling. It was good to see her daughter happy at last. She was grateful Cathy could work for her uncle and he could keep an eye on her. It looked like she was competent at managing the bar as well. The stock lists were neat and the bar was thriving. It raked in money, and each night it was crowded with local celebrities, crooks and television personalities.

'How is it, workin' for Uncle Bobby? Is he a good boss?' Ruby grinned as they walked back up to the bar, and slipped her Louis Vuitton handbag under the bar stool she then perched upon. Cathy laughed.

'He's the best, Mum. He lets me get on with the day-to-day running of the place, but if there are any problems then he steps in. Perfect, really.'

Ruby watched Cathy as she spoke. She was asking lots of questions, keeping her daughter talking while she scanned her face, trying to see how she really was. When Cathy had finished answering, there was a brief silence as Ruby chose her words carefully.

'And how are ya, darlin'? How are ya copin'? You've been through so much.'

Cathy looked up at her and then down at the tea towel she was holding, her hands twisting it as she fidgeted.

'I'm OK. I miss him so much . . .' Her voice choked as she spoke. 'But you must be missing Dad too. You've been through a lot too, Mum, and I'm sorry I'm not helping you.'

Ruby's heart swooped into her belly.

'The last thing I want is for you to worry about me! If you are copin' then I'm as happy as I can be. Yes, I miss your dad. I miss him every minute of every day, but my first thought is always for you, my darlin' girl. I hope I did the right thing sendin' ya back 'ere, to England?' Cathy nodded, though she kept her head down. Ruby saw a single tear drop onto the material she was clutching.

'It's funny. At the time, I was angry with you for sending me away, as if you didn't care for me, but I do now see that it has to be like this,' Cathy said quietly. She flashed her mum a glance to see what impact her words would have upon her. Ruby swallowed, composing herself. She'd rather speak plain, speak the truth, than be lied to, but it was also painful to hear that truth sometimes.

'I know, darlin'. It wasn't an easy decision. I didn't know if there would be repercussions, reprisals, even. Everythin' felt unsafe and uncertain. My instincts told me to get you as far away from that mess, that trouble in Spain, as I could. I don't know myself if that was the right thing to do, but I had my reasons, and I tell ya now, it weren't for lack of love for ya.' Ruby realised she sounded almost defensive. That wasn't how she wanted to appear at all.

She searched for something else to say, something softer, but already Cathy had turned away from her.

'I understand, I just wish . . .'

'What, love?'

Cathy opened her mouth to answer, then paused, seeming to change her mind.

'Nothing, Mum. Look, it's almost opening time, I'd better get on. I'll see you back at Aunt Belle's later tonight.' And with that, Cathy turned away and started to polish the wine glasses, ending the conversation. Ruby picked up her bag, feeling its glossy luxury, and smoothed back her hair.

'All right, darlin', I'll let ya get on with things, you're very busy.' Her voice sounded calm and steady, but it was all a disguise. She walked out of the bar, stepped inside her limo and it wasn't until the car moved away that she let her tears fall. Something had broken between Cathy and her, and she had no idea how to fix it.

'You're back early, is everything OK?' Belle said as Ruby walked back into their home. Ruby stopped and looked around for a moment. It was the first house she'd ever bought, the first move upwards as their criminal enterprise began to take off. Now, it looked like the modest three-bedroom family home it was, but to her and Bobby back then, it had felt like a palace. Belle's taste in furnishings was vastly different to Ruby's. Instead of the elegant, crushed velvet sofas and glass-topped tables covered with vases of pure white lilies, there were colourful scarves, incense sticks burning and every surface was covered with pens, paints, books or papers. Despite the clutter, it was cosy and welcoming. Ruby had gifted the pair the house after their wedding, insisting they should have it as their home, as by then she'd inherited Charlie and Maureen's mansion a few streets away. She'd decided against opening up that house on this visit as she'd wanted to stay close to Cathy, but already she was wondering if she'd made the right decision. At least there she'd be able to examine her thoughts and feelings away from prying eyes, have some peace from the undercurrents that swam through her family. Belle watched Ruby's gaze.

'I'm sure it isn't as pristine as it was when you lived here, Ruby; you always have such refined homes and furnishings,' Belle said softly.

'It's lovely, Belle, I mean it,' Ruby replied quickly. 'I was just rememberin' how it was when Bobby and I lived 'ere with . . .'

Ruby had been about to mention their little brother George's name, but she caught herself just in time. Despite this, the atmosphere changed suddenly, as Belle picked up on the missing name. The elephant in the room was always George: his murder and his disappearance. Belle's smile vanished and was replaced by a frown. Neither of them said anything to break the awkward silence. Eventually, Belle beckoned Ruby to join her in the lounge. She picked up a few books about art that were scattered on the sofa and gestured for Ruby to sit.

'It's probably time we had a proper conversation about Cathy,' Belle began, though Ruby wondered whether this was all linked to their fierce disagreement about keeping George's death a secret from Cathy. Belle was fiercely protective of Cathy, and hated lying to her. Ruby was just as protective and so wanted to keep the truth of his death from her daughter, not wanting to add trauma upon grief. Everything between her and her sister-in-law always seemed to come down to this, even indirectly.

Ruby felt suddenly bone-weary, as if she'd had enough talking for one night. Her time with her daughter had been soured and she was in no mood to handle any more difficult exchanges. In her own home, she might dismiss this and go to her bedroom, get away from the aggro she knew was coming, but she couldn't do that here, not while she was a guest of Belle's. Ruby pulled her hand through her thick black locks and sat back heavily. She didn't want another confrontation, but it seemed she was unable to avoid it.

'You coming here, well, it unsettles Cathy,' Belle said, her opening shot striking Ruby exactly where intended, in the heart.

'I'm not sure what ya mean, Belle. Cathy's my daughter, and if I choose to see her, and she chooses to see me, then I can't see what the problem would be . . . for you.' Ruby, her head tilted to one side now, stared back at Belle. She was dog-tired, had the start of a headache, but she couldn't let this go. 'I am Cathy's *mother*, Belle,'

Ruby added, emphasising the word 'mother'. It felt like she was facing a rival, and perhaps she was. Belle was a rival for her daughter's affections, but she had to be told. Ruby was beholden to no one when it came to her daughter, and anything that went between them was her business, and hers alone.

Belle's face flushed. 'I know you're Cathy's mother, that's why we're having this chat!' Her voice sounded brittle, her words stinging. 'You left her with us,' Belle continued, 'you didn't let the poor girl grieve with you, so what do you expect? Do you expect her to run into your arms, grateful that she was sent away? Surely you can't be so naive, Ruby.'

Ruby looked over at her brother's wife. The years had not been kind to Belle. She had grey streaks running through her curly hennaed hair and though she wore bright clothes, the effect was to make her skin look older. Ruby and Belle were like chalk and cheese, but that shouldn't matter, not if they both had Cathy's best interests at heart. The only problem was, they both had very different views on what those interests might be. Ruby tried to calm herself, but she was tired and Belle's words hit home hard.

'Poor girl? My daughter may be many things, but she definitely isn't a "poor girl". The sacrifices I've had to make over the years putting business before motherhood to make sure she wasn't poor, makin' sure she had the best of everythin', weren't easy for either of us,' Ruby retorted. Belle laughed, but there was no mirth in it.

'Sacrifices? From where I'm sitting, you *chose* to put business before your daughter, and now you're upset at what's happened; Cathy is happier here with Bobby and me, and you don't want to admit it. You chose to send her here, so let her be here. Leave her to grieve in peace – and maybe one day she'll forgive you for abandoning her.'

'I did not abandon my child!' Ruby retorted, stung by her sister-in-law's harsh words, 'you want Cathy to be more your daughter now than mine!' She stood up, furious at Belle's savage judgement of her. How dare she lecture her about the best way to look after her own daughter! How dare she presume to know more about Cathy than she did! If there was truth in Belle's words, Ruby ignored it, not wanting to hear any more. Just then, Bobby's voice interrupted the quarrel, which was fast growing nasty.

'Stop, please. Rube. Belle. Listen, ya both love Cathy, stop fightin'. It don't do no one any good to be at logger'eads like this.'

Both women swivelled round to see Bobby standing in the doorway. Behind him was Cathy, who had been silent until this point.

'Mum, I think you should go. Go back to Spain. I'm fine here. I'm safe with Aunt Belle and Uncle Bobby. I'm sorry if that hurts you but it's how I feel. I don't ever want to go back to Spain. My future is here.'

Stunned into silence, Ruby saw that she'd lost something – someone – deeply important to her. The battle, now she knew there'd been one, was over, and she was left broken on the battlefield. She couldn't say for sure when it had happened, but her daughter had slipped away. There was nothing she could say. She looked at her daughter sadly. All her fury at Belle had vanished.

'All right, darlin', I'm sorry, I didn't mean to upset you or Aunt Belle. I'm glad you've found peace 'ere, love. It's what I wanted for ya.'

Cathy looked back at her, her face a picture of sadness. In that moment, Ruby saw that they might never again be the mother and daughter to each other they wanted to be.

CHAPTER 7

The next morning, Ruby was packing her suitcase, getting ready to fly back to Spain that day.

'When are you going to tell Cathy?' Belle said from the open doorway, making Ruby jump. She hesitated, and for a second considered ignoring her sister-in-law. Ruby knew the pair of them weren't done yet, so she turned round, a smile hastily planted on her face.

'I think you've said enough, Belle. Leave it.' Ruby turned back to carry on folding her silk pyjamas, but Belle didn't budge.

'I don't mean to start on you, Ruby. None of this is personal, but we didn't manage to finish our talk last night. When are you going to tell her about George and what really happened? You know as well as I do that she needs to know.' If Belle was intimidated by her sister-in-law, a woman who headed up a drug cartel, she didn't show it. She'd faced some tough men in prison and knew how to stand her ground too. Teaching art in prison was how she'd met Bobby.

'It was a talk, was it? I thought it was an argument. I'm guessin' Cathy is out, as I'm sure ya wouldn't be so direct if she was in the house?' Ruby shot back, turning back to her packing, carrying on, folding the exquisite bedwear, deep red silk that whispered against the skin of her hands as she laid it down inside the suitcase.

'You can't ignore this for ever, Ruby!' Belle's voice sounded high-pitched and frantic now. She was losing her cool, which only made Ruby feel calmer, more in control.

'Oh, but I can, Belle. I can ignore this for as long as I want, because as I reminded ya last night, *I'm* Cathy's mum. And as I've *told* you, I don't think she needs to know.' Ruby's voice was dangerously low. She put down the camisole she had picked up, walked over to Belle and stood directly in front of her, sizing her up.

'What is it exactly ya want me to tell Cathy? That I killed her beloved uncle, the one who'd raped her that night? D'ya want me to tell her that her Uncle Alfie chopped up his body, pulled out his teeth and fed his miserable flesh to the pigs? Or perhaps ya want me to tell her that it was her own father who took George's jewellery, teeth and finger-nails and threw 'em off the Woolwich Ferry? Would that satisfy ya? Would that make Cathy feel better? I don't think so, do you?' Ruby stepped forward again. Her face was inches from Belle's, who cowered back against the wall, her courage failing her.

'Belle, I need ya to know this, so listen good. I will *never* tell Cathy, and neither will you. We've said everythin' we need to say about this. Killin' George is *my* secret, mine, and I'll take it to my grave. I've told ya this, and I won't tell ya again.'

Ruby stared hard at the woman Cathy was so fond of, who held her daughter's peace of mind in her hands, however much it pained Ruby to acknowledge it.

Suddenly Belle broke down. She sank to the ground, her face in her hands.

'I can't bear lying to her, and I hate you for making me.'

Ruby, still standing, nodded again.

'I know that, Belle, but it is what we all must do,' she said coldly. 'You, me, Bobby, Alfie and Lloyd. We must all keep up the pretence because if we don't, Cathy will never forgive us.'

'Forgive you, more like!' Belle sobbed. She clawed her way up to standing again. 'You're a monster, Ruby, and I want you out of my house.'

Tears streaming down her face, Belle turned and ran to her bedroom.

Ruby picked up her phone, called Lloyd and said, 'Meet me in an hour. Usual place.'

An hour later, Ruby sat outside Debbie's Fish Stall wearing her Prada sunshades and waiting for Lloyd and Alfie. She'd picked this spot to meet, knowing the clientele – a mix of crooks, yuppies, glamorous youngsters and travellers – were the safest backdrop to the conversations she might have here. It was like that saying, 'hiding in plain sight'. It was one of Ruby's favourites because it worked, it always worked.

'We need to talk before I leave,' she said.

'Alfie, get the coffees.' Lloyd replied and pulled up a chair beside her.

'Belle is pushin' for me to tell Cathy about George. We both know that can never 'appen. I'm worried she'll say somethin'; she's close to spillin' our secret.'

'Don't worry, Rube, I'll 'ave a word with Bob and get him to speak to Belle. She has to realise tellin' Cathy ain't a possibility. It would kill her – and she'd hate us. That girl really is a saint. Who else would forgive their rapist, would want him to come back to the family?'

Ruby sighed as Alfie returned with the drinks.

She watched as her brother-in-law tore open a sachet of sugar and poured it into the creamy coffee. He stirred it and sipped the drink, which left a trace of milk froth around his mouth.

'What's so bloody funny?' he said, wiping his mouth.

Ruby looked at Lloyd, who was already smirking, then back at the sight of Alfie with his milk moustache and they both burst out laughing.

'Well, that's the first time I've properly had a giggle since I've been back in England,' Ruby said, wiping her eyes.

She put her sunglasses back on her nose and turned to Lloyd, all businesslike again. It felt good to have a moment of light relief, but serious issues needed to be addressed, and not just the secret they kept from Cathy.

'Now, we need to discuss the Bolivia deal. I've got an hour before I have to leave for the flight back to Spain. What can ya tell me?' Ruby commanded.

Ruby told her driver to take a detour on the way to the airport. 'Just stop 'ere, thanks. Wait for me, I won't be long.'

She pushed open the bar door, though it still said 'closed', and called, 'Cathy? Bobby? Anyone 'ere?'

'Mum!' Cathy came into the room carrying a jar of olives. 'Let me 'elp ya,' Ruby said, stepping over and taking the jar. 'I thought you'd have left by now ...' she said hesitantly.

'I am leavin', but there's no way I was goin' to go without sayin' goodbye to ya. There's somethin' else I wanted to say too, love ...'

'Oh yeah, Mum, what's that?' the young woman replied, tipping olives out into small bowls and placing them along the counter. She had her head down and wouldn't catch Ruby's eye.

'I want to tell ya that I'm sorry.'

Cathy looked up.

'I truly am. I'm sorry I put the business before you. I'm sorry I've been such a bad mother to ya. I'm sorry I sent ya away, then upset ya last night. I'm sorry for everythin',' Ruby said simply.

Cathy didn't say a word. She stood staring at her mother, a woman who looked half the age she was, immaculate from head to toe, but who now wore a pleading expression.

'Belle was right. Business always came first. The stakes are so high, the game so dangerous, that I've allowed myself to be swept away by it for a long time now. In doin' that, I've sacrificed you and my love for ya. I don't expect ya to forgive me but I wanted ya to know. I won't be back for a while, my darlin', so look after yerself, and if there's anythin' ya need, you only 'ave to ask.'

Cathy moved quickly. She walked round the bar straight to her mother and put her arms around her. Ruby, shocked by this display of emotion, let Cathy embrace her, then tentatively, as if she couldn't believe it was happening, she folded her arms around her daughter, holding her carefully as if she'd bolt away in fright. They held each other close for a long time. By the time Cathy started to pull away, both women were crying, their tears proof of their love for each other.

'I love ya, Cathy.'

'I love you too, Mum.'

Ruby eased her daughter's arms from her. 'If ya don't let go I might not 'ave the courage to go back, and then we'd all be in a mess. I 'ave to go, my darlin'.' She wiped the mascara from her eyes, which were streaming now. How often had she hidden her tears in the back of her limo recently? Now they seemed to be spilling out of that private zone, and it wasn't a bad thing. For too long, Ruby had had to contain her feelings, but these days it seemed like she was always close to breaking down.

She slid inside the car, the chauffeur shutting her door, and as the vehicle pulled away from her daughter, she didn't look back, though Cathy was standing on the pavement, looking at the car, watching her mother leave yet again.

This time it felt different, like they'd resolved something she wasn't even aware of.

For Ruby, there was only the future now. She had to move forward. There were deals to arrange, contacts to bribe, cocaine to move into Europe. There were secrets to keep hidden, buried deep inside her heart, glittering like jewels, brilliant and hard.

The flight to Spain gave Ruby a chance to reflect. She waved away the air hostesses offering first-class passengers champagne and nibbles. She wanted a clear head to think through everything that had happened in England. She hoped Bobby would be able to keep Belle in check. Everything depended upon her not squealing. If she told Cathy, Ruby knew it would destroy their relationship for good. It just couldn't happen.

Then there was Vladimir. Who was this ex-KGB guy he'd killed? Why hadn't they heard of him before, if he was enough of a threat to destroy their business? Ruby decided to call Lloyd the next day to see what he'd discovered about this Alec Rumanov, and whether there was any way they could trace his and Vladimir's connections with the KGB. She needed answers. Her gut told her there was more to all this than they'd been told. It was just a feeling, but she knew to listen to her instincts.

Stepping out of the aircraft, Ruby was expecting to see her usual driver, a man thoroughly vetted and trustworthy, in her usual limo, a white Mercedes. Instead, a sleek silver Rolls-Royce pulled up, its engine purring. The door opened and Vladimir stepped out, tanned and relaxed in a white linen shirt, chinos and slip-on leather shoes, looking for a brief moment just like her dead husband. Ruby gasped, then recovered herself immediately. She wasn't some foolish schoolgirl, swept away by a man's charm and money. She'd had the real deal with Archie, true love, and though this Russian bore a striking resemblance to him, he wasn't him. That was cruelly clear.

'I wasn't expectin' to see ya, Vladimir,' she said demurely, despite the flurry of emotions she'd shut down expertly.

The Russian smiled and then stepped back, sweeping his arms around in a flourish to indicate that the car was for her use.

'Your carriage awaits, madam,' he smiled, his blue eyes looking into hers.

She felt a sudden urge to run, then, confusingly, to draw closer. What was going on? This man confounded her, and it was rare that anyone did that. Ruby was a sharp judge of character, she had to be. She could sniff out the wheelers and dealers, the sharks and the punters, the generals from the ground troops. She had a talent for seeing people's motives even when they thought they'd hidden them well. It had got her a long way, but this man, charming though he was, somehow remained a mystery to her.

'Why thank you, good sir.' She smiled and allowed herself to be led to the front passenger seat. Vladimir opened the door and she stepped in, elegantly. She noted a small nod of approval from him before he put on his shades and settled into the driver's seat.

'Ya didn't need to do this,' Ruby started to say but Vladimir cut in.

'It is my pleasure, dear Ruby. I hope your trip was . . . successful?'

Ruby didn't turn her head. She stared out the window at the large billboards that lined the road out of the airport as she replied. 'It was, thank you, Vladimir, though I'm 'appy to be back in Spain.'

Then, Ruby realised that the Russian had taken a different road, leading away from the villa, not towards it.

'Where are we goin'?' she said, calmly, though her heart had begun to beat a little faster.

Vladimir smiled. 'It's a surprise,' he murmured and carried on driving.

Ruby blinked. She hated surprises, especially when they meant being in a car with a dangerous man, one who ran drug operations to the borders of Afghanistan and all the way across to Mongolia and Korea.

'A surprise,' she echoed, giving no indication of her feelings.

The car moved silently, eating up the miles as the sun shone. Ruby's bag was at her feet. She usually carried a gun but because of the flight, she'd left it in the villa rather than try and smuggle it into Britain. Was this a decision she was going to regret?

Eventually, the car pulled into the grounds of an exclusive hotel. The gravel crunched beneath the tyres, and palm trees lined the driveway. A uniformed attendant stepped out of the grand entrance to greet them. Vladimir stopped the car, stepped out and opened Ruby's door. She gazed up at the façade, a classical building with a fountain out front surrounded by exquisite planting. Lush pink and red flowers sat among prickly cacti. It was beautiful, but was she safe? Ruby had no idea. Her heart pounding now, she smiled to hide her fear, and stepped out. She was alone with this man. Anything could happen.

They walked into the entrance and straight through to the restaurant which was situated at the back of the hotel in a large orangery.

'I've heard of this place but never been. It's beautiful,' she whispered.

Vladimir smiled again. 'I thought you would like it. Now please, let's eat together.'

He pulled out a chair which she sat down upon, scanning the space as discreetly as possible. There were three exits, the open doors to the gardens and pool, the main way they'd come in and a side door which probably led to the kitchens. Her senses were on high alert, though perhaps she'd read this wrong, perhaps this was just a nice meal. Why did Vladimir always make her so suspicious? It wasn't as if he'd ever screwed them over, to her knowledge at least.

'The menu, madam,' said a waiter who was hovering by her elbow. She gave him the quick once-over, scanning. He looked like a real waiter, but who knew? Was she safe? She glanced around the place, and suddenly realised why she felt so out of sorts: there was nobody else there. Only two waiters glided seamlessly between the kitchen and front of house.

'Vladimir?' she said, but before she could finish, the Russian leaned across the white linen tablecloth and took one of her hands. Again, she almost recoiled even though he was a handsome man. Why did she feel so . . . repulsed by him?

'Dear Ruby, you have seen through my ruse. I have lured you here and we are entirely alone . . .'

Ruby almost snatched back her hand. Should she run? Would he shoot her if she tried?

Yet Vladimir's face had softened.

He reached for something in his pocket, and Ruby instantly sat up, pulling her hand back. Ready to flee if needed.

Instead, a small red velvet box was placed on the table.

'What's this?' Ruby asked, though her head was buzz-ing. She already knew what was happening, yet something made her play along, play dumb, so she could buy herself time to think.

'My dear lady, you cannot say you have not noticed how I feel about you. I know it is very soon after your husband's death, but I could not wait a moment longer. I know you feel the same way, so please, Ruby, make me the happiest man alive and marry me . . .'

Ruby sat in stunned silence.

She'd realised he was proposing, but the thought of it was so ridiculous, so badly timed, so thoughtless that she hadn't wanted to see it. Her thoughts still battered against her brain, and she found she couldn't utter a word.

'At least open it, dear Ruby,' the Russian said softly.

As if in a daze, she took hold of the exquisite box and opened it. Inside sat an emerald and diamond ring, an engagement ring, with a solitaire as fat as her fingernail. She knew it must have cost thousands, perhaps hundreds of thousands of pounds, yet the sight of it distressed her beyond words.

Quickly, she snapped the box shut.

'Ruby, listen to me, I know so far it has just been business between us, but we both know it could be more. Be my wife, Ruby. There is no other woman in the world I would want to stand by my side. We are made for each other. Can't you see it?'

Ruby stood up so fast her chair almost clattered to the ground. 'Stop, Vladimir. I'm sorry, but stop. Archie was buried a couple of months ago; this, this is just too much. I'm sorry but I cannot marry you.'

Her words seemed to hover in the refined air between them. The fountain kept on with its tinkling water, the cicadas outside were beginning their afternoon song, but everything else seemed to have stopped dead.

'Please take me home,' Ruby said at last.

Vladimir hadn't said a word. If he was offended or upset he didn't show it except for a muscle in the side of his neck that was twitching. His smile seemed to have frozen on his face, but he dropped his gaze and said, 'Of course, dear lady, I should have known it was soon, far too soon. Please forgive my impatience.'

He turned and snapped his fingers at the waiter.

'My car,' he ordered.

Escorting Ruby out to the front, Vladimir's hand did not stray from her lower back. It was a gentlemanly gesture, yet Ruby felt there was something of possession in his touch, something that said, 'This is my woman, or will be my woman.'

Confused, with a headache beginning to throb above her eyes, Ruby turned to him once they were on the road.

'Please forgive my reaction. It was so . . . unexpected.' She had to make this better. His good will was essential to their business enterprise, and she didn't want to make an enemy of this man. 'I am deeply flattered, and I thank you for your proposal. I hope you understand that

I could not think to meet or marry anyone else. I'm so sorry, Vladimir.'

She hoped it was enough. Silence stretched between them. Eventually he replied, gruffly.

'It is me who should apologise. Of course, it is far too soon. We'll say nothing more about this, but please know you have my undying respect and admiration,' he said, taking hold of Ruby's hand and planting a gentle kiss there.

'Thank you,' she said. 'I'm honoured by your attention, but I'm not ready, I don't know if I ever will be.' Ruby pulled her hand back, hoping the Russian hadn't seen how hard she had to fight not to recoil from his touch.

Neither spoke during the drive back to the villa. Vladimir dropped Ruby inside the heavily guarded entrance, and, without another word, he swept away in his Rolls-Royce. Ruby stood and watched him go, narrowing her eyes against the sun. How would this play out? Had she offended him so much he might seek retribution? Or had he really meant his words? If she was honest, she hadn't a clue.

CHAPTER 8

'So, you couldn't find out nuthin' about this Alec Rumanov? Was he even operatin' business in Spain?' Ruby said, looking out over her view from the office. It was a cool winter's morning, though the sun was still shining, its rays bouncing off the ocean below her.

She was frowning as she spoke to Lloyd, who was still in London overseeing the network of contacts who were selling the new product from Mexico. In the time she'd been back in Marbella, they'd experienced some small hitches: a bad batch of coke, which had almost ended the deal, and a kilo here and there that had gone missing. Lloyd had sorted it all, finding new runners and reassuring the shady guys in the county lines that the new batch was kosher.

'Rube, I've put the word out, and nuthin'. No one's 'eard of him, no one's seen him. It don't mean he didn't exist but we don't know nuthin' about whether or not he was on our tail.'

Ruby took in the words, instinct stirring in her belly.

'But do we know any Russians who would talk to us? Surely they're all in Vladimir's pocket?'

'That's the problem, Rube. We can't go askin' too many questions, because if they came to Vladimir's ears then we'd lose face, and piss him off, which, believe me, we don't want to do,' Lloyd answered.

'Keep puttin' the word out. Carry on bein' discreet. It's all we can do. There ain't no other way of gettin' to the truth. Those ex-KGB men are secretive. They don't want anyone comin' after them; they know they're probably under surveillance anyway, or they're the ones in charge of seekin' out others, even now. We're on to a loser with this one, I can feel it,' Ruby said, despondently.

'You might be right. Though, Rube, it's fishy and ya know it. If there was a big ex-KBG guy who wanted to make things dangerous for us, we'd 'ave 'eard of him.'

Lloyd put the phone down, leaving Ruby deep in thought. Why would Vladimir concoct this story, if it was a story? Why go to the trouble? If this Alec Rumanov was a red herring, then what motive could Vladimir possibly have for concocting it?

Ruby knew these were dangerous thoughts.

Two months later, Ruby and Lloyd were no closer to discovering the truth about the man Vladimir claimed to have shot. No one had come forward with information and the trail seemed to have gone cold. Lloyd told Ruby to resign herself to never knowing, saying they couldn't keep asking in case their questions got to Vladimir's ears, but Ruby couldn't let it drop. She could smell trouble. Ruby hadn't been back to England, and was now only in contact with Cathy when she rang her daughter once a week, without fail. Cathy seemed yet more distant, more at home with her aunt and uncle, and Ruby could feel her slipping further away, which brought her fresh heartbreak every time she put the phone down after their calls.

Meanwhile, Vladimir seemed to be openly wooing Ruby now, though she kept reminding him that their partnership was only business. Every time they met, he brought fresh white roses, proof to her that he could never follow Archie in her heart as lilies were her favourite flower. Archie had bought her lilies every week and so their homes were always filled with them. He had known her so intimately, it was inconceivable to her to think any man could follow in his footsteps. Yet, the Russian did not give up trying. He was persistent, she could give him that.

'Dear lady, for you,' he said, stepping into the villa's atrium. Large earthenware vases with plants spilling over the sides lined one side. The floor was white marble and, overhead, an intricate chandelier twinkled in the sunlight.

'Thank you, you're too kind, as ever,' Ruby murmured, accepting the large bouquet of white roses, passing them to her housekeeper as she led Vladimir through the villa to the dining area. They had decided to go through their business for the day over a meal before Vladimir was due to fly to Moscow to meet contacts from further within Siberia, to discuss a possible new opportunity to extend their market into the frozen wastelands, a place once inaccessible due to local warring gangs. One of the gangs had approached their cartel, and they had decided to negotiate a deal to sell coke from the Ural mountains and beyond into Siberia.

'Could this mean that by extendin' through Russia, we could eventually break into China?' Ruby said as a maid brought through a gazpacho for the starter.

She placed the soft, white linen napkin onto her lap, and spooned a ladle of the cold soup into the Russian's bowl.

He didn't reply straight away. She looked up to find him frowning, adjusting his shirt collar. 'Sorry, Ruby, I felt a little unwell for a moment. I'm sure it is passing.'

'Are you OK, Vladimir?'

The ladle clanged down against the large bowl containing the soup as Vladimir clutched his left arm, his face twisted with pain.

'Ruby, you must get me help,' he managed to say before collapsing off the chair and onto the floor.

'Call an ambulance. Now!' Ruby shouted to the staff who were hovering nearby. 'Get help, fast!'

She ran around to where the Russian lay and undid the top buttons of his shirt. He was panting and his face looked pale.

'Hurry!' she yelled as she carefully placed him in the recovery position and grabbed a throw from a sofa to cover him.

Within only a few minutes, the sound of sirens blasting their way towards them could be heard.

'Go and let them in!' she shouted again. A minute later, a private medic was crouching on the floor by Vladimir's prone body. Ruby stood back, watching the scene, wondering what she should do. Another paramedic examined Vladimir before gesturing to the other to grab a stretcher. Vladimir's prone body was manoeuvred onto the fabric and carried swiftly to the waiting ambulance.

'I'll follow in my own car,' she said in Spanish, running for her bag and keys.

Minutes later, she was following the vehicle as it screamed through the streets of the small harbour town. They pulled up outside the emergency department of a large hospital and Ruby slammed on her brakes and ran out to follow them. Something, some instinct, told her to keep close. She fumbled inside her handbag for her phone and called Lloyd.

'Ruby? You OK? You sound out of breath,' Lloyd said.

'Listen. It's Vladimir. I think he's had a heart attack. He ain't well at all and I've come with him to the hospital. The paramedics had to work on him in the ambulance. He's alive but he'll probably need immediate surgery. If anythin' 'appens to him, what will it mean for the business?' Her voice was low as she paced, waiting for the hospital trolley to arrive.

'Forget that for a moment, Rube, just make sure he's OK and he gets what he needs. Keep me posted. If he dies, then we'll deal with it as and when it 'appens. All right?' Lloyd's voice always kept her steady. Sometimes she could hear Archie's voice in his dad's, calming her down, returning her focus.

'Ruby?'

'Yes, yes, sorry, Lloyd. I'm listenin'. Look, the porters 'ave arrived. They're takin' him to the private medical wing. I'll call back when I know more,' she said, ending the call abruptly.

Seconds later, her heels clattered across the shiny corridor floor as she pushed through the doors to the private accommodation. There were large bunches of flowers in the nurses' station, porters in spotless white uniforms and the sound of classical music playing discreetly in the background.

'And this is . . .?' A brusque matron stepped towards Ruby.

'Vladimir Ivanov. I think he's had a heart attack. He wasn't well at all, came over all peculiar while we was eatin' our lunch,' Ruby replied.

'And are you Mr Ivanov's wife?' The Spanish nurse looked up from her notes, an eyebrow arched.

Ruby stared back, momentarily taken aback by the direct question. She had to think fast. If she told them she was merely a business associate, she'd be kicked out. She nodded. 'Yes, I'm Vladimir's wife. Will he survive?'

The nurse held her gaze. 'The surgeons will do their best for him. He's gone straight into theatre.'

Ruby watched them roll him away.

'You can wait in his room. It is freshly prepared. There is a full concierge service, so if you need anything, please ring us. I will send some fruit and water to your room in the meantime. Please don't worry, your husband is in the very best possible hands. Our surgeons are extremely experienced.' The matron touched Ruby's shoulder in a small, soothing gesture.

Ruby walked down to find the room, wondering what on earth would happen to their empire if one half of it died suddenly. It had survived Archie's death. Would they be so lucky this time? She had no idea if Vladimir's networks would stay loyal to them, so they had to be prepared.

She switched the TV remote from channel to channel, sighing, as people came and went. Eventually, she turned it off.

She called Lloyd. 'They've said it might be a long wait. A surgeon came in saying Vladimir has definitely had a heart attack and he's 'avin' emergency surgery. What if he don't pull through? Ya need to shore up our contacts, make people aware. We need to know who they're loyal to. Call Alfie and get him onto it as well. If Vladimir dies, our territories will be threatened. Tell our men to arm themselves and be ready,' Ruby commanded, 'and one other thing. Send me men. I need guards 'ere. One of Vladimir's enemies might take this chance to finish him. He needs protection, and so do I.'

'It's as good as done, Rube. I'll send men now from the villa. Are you armed?' Lloyd said.

'I am,' Ruby answered.

'Good,' Lloyd said gruffly before hanging up.

Ruby looked down at her phone. The next few hours would decide the fate of her family – and possibly their entire empire – yet there was nothing she could do but wait.

Four hours later, a surgeon knocked at the door.

'Come in,' Ruby called, standing up to see who it was. She put her hand inside her handbag, touching the cold steel of her gun. She felt safer knowing it was there. Would she have to use it?

A man wearing full surgical scrubs opened the door and walked in, making Ruby start. She knew the risk they faced; chancers with a grudge against Vladimir or her could come in any guise, and the word might already be out that the Russian was sick. Who knew whether there were informers from other gangs working inside this hospital, exclusive as it was?

'Hello, Mrs Ivanov, I'm Dr Garcia and I've been operating on your husband. I'm happy to tell you that his condition is now stable, though we had to perform open heart surgery on him.'

Ruby gasped.

'Don't worry, Mrs Ivanov, it sounds more dramatic than it is. These days we make only a small set of incisions in order to graft a new artery as a way of bypassing the blocked one. He has been transferred to the Intensive Care Unit as a matter of caution, though there is nothing to indicate any problems. He'll be brought here tomorrow morning. You are welcome to stay, but if you wish to return home, that would probably be better. You can come back in the morning and be here for his transferral down to the ward.'

Ruby nodded.

'Thank you, Doctor, but I won't leave until I know he's safe. He's a prominent figure. He needs protection. His bodyguards are on their way. I'll leave as soon as they arrive.'

The doctor nodded.

Once Vladimir's guards were in place, Ruby called her chauffeur and was driven back to the villa, where she spent the evening calling Lloyd and Alfie. It looked like Vladimir would be OK, but they had to be ready if not.

The next morning, Ruby arrived with two security guards in her wake to add to those now posted outside Vladimir's room. He'd been transferred from ICU in the early hours. The two henchmen who'd guarded ICU overnight were now stationed outside the door of Vladimir's private room. The guards she brought with her would take their places inside. One of the guards pushed open the door and Ruby walked inside. Vladimir lay semi-conscious in his hospital bed, tubes coming out of his chest and IV lines snaking from his arm. Various monitors flickered and bleeped.

Vladimir's eyes opened and registered Ruby's presence. He smiled, and when he spoke his voice was throaty and slurred.

'They told me my wife was here. I could not guess it was you, dear Ruby . . .'

Ruby smiled. 'Save your breath, Vladimir, I'm just glad to see ya lookin' so well, under the circumstances.'

He seemed to drift off, but then a few minutes later he spoke again. The words were thin and reedy, and Ruby had to lean closer to the stricken man to hear him.

'I did it for you, my darling Ruby . . .'

Ruby stared at him. Something told her a bomb was about to go off. Her instincts were screaming at her, though she kept her voice calm and soft.

'Leave us,' she told the guards.

When they'd stepped out closing the door so it was only Ruby and Vladimir in the room, she spoke.

'Did what, darlin'?' she muttered, holding his hand, gazing into his now-clouded blue eyes. He swallowed. She saw his mouth was dry and so she reached for the glass of water nearby and wetted his lips.

'Killed Archie, of course. Didn't you know? It was me who hired the gunmen, me who bribed your security guards, which was too easy, by the way. It was me all along . . .'

Shock hit Ruby. For a moment she thought he was delirious, but when she searched her feelings, the reticence she'd held towards this man, she realised he was telling her the truth she'd been searching for all this time. Of course, it had been Vladimir! Who else was so powerful they could pay big money to order away guards who knew their lives were endangered for ever as a result? Who else could command men to do this? Yet, how hadn't she guessed this? Had his attractive persona, his charm and eloquence, been the most effective mask for his motives?

Though her insides were frozen, Ruby managed to whisper.

'But they were goin' to kill me . . .'

She thought Vladimir hadn't heard, but eventually he smiled.

'My dear lady, they had strict orders not to harm a hair on your beautiful head. I love you, Ruby. I have loved you from the moment we met in your villa. I was looking at your exquisite painting . . .'

Struggling to contain the feelings that now roared in her chest, Ruby urged him to keep talking. However painful, however much she wanted to kill this man who presumed to love her, who'd killed the love of her life, she needed him to tell her everything. Only then would she know what to do next.

'Go on,' she uttered, trying to keep the shock from her voice.

She gripped his hand tightly as if to reassure him.

'Why won't you say yes to me after everything I did to get rid of Archie? I thought when he was gone, you'd be mine . . .'

Ruby kept the smile on her face though she fought the desire to rip the lines from his body, to see his blood. There was silence now, apart from the bleep of the machines.

Eventually, she said, in a voice like honey, 'Did you do all that for me? I had no idea.'

Vladimir tried to nod but he was already slipping back into unconsciousness as another jolt of morphine pumped through his veins with a click from one of the machines.

Ruby sat back in her chair. Watched him sleep his narcotic dreams.

She looked around the room. There was a large spare pillow by the bed. It would take but a minute to pick it up and place it over the Russian's face. He might try to struggle but she would overpower him, and then he would be sent to hell where he belonged, that special place for traitors and crooks, for those who betray the honour of their dark profession. He would be dead within seconds.

But that felt like an easy way out.

He must suffer like Archie did. He must know pain and horror, just like Archie did . . . she thought to herself.

As Vladimir slept, she plotted. She watched over the man who'd destroyed her world, who'd taken everything away, and slowly, slowly she hatched a plan. Nothing less than complete revenge would do.

She had to be careful, clever. They didn't want any retaliation from Vladimir's men. It would need to be meticulously done. Her brain whirred but by the time the matron came to check on him an hour later, she knew what had to be done.

CHAPTER 9

'She's arriving today?' Cathy asked Belle, who was pouring a glass of orange juice for her niece in the kitchen. It was a grey, drizzly early spring day in Chigwell, and both women were due at work, Cathy to the bar and Belle to do some volunteering at a local art college.

'She is. She says she's got some news, wouldn't tell me on the phone. She wanted to speak to you, really, love . . .' Belle looked over at Cathy, who was sitting on a bar stool gazing out at the miserable weather.

'Cathy? You're miles away!'

Cathy started. 'Sorry, Aunty Belle. Yes, I know I should've spoken to her but I was tired; it had been a long shift. Thanks for covering for me.' She smiled apologetically at her aunt. Belle had said Cathy was asleep when Ruby rang to say she'd be coming over for a special visit. It had been months since they'd seen each other, and they hadn't left things on the best of terms last time, so Cathy was feeling worried at the prospect of seeing her mother again.

'Why is she coming over? I guess she'll tell us when she's here,' she said at last, yawning and stretching. She hadn't left The Locksmith until almost 1 a.m. last night. Some new punters had come in and hadn't left until after closing time, which meant it was late by the time she'd cashed up and made sure the place was clean and ready for the next day.

She wasn't complaining, though. One of the new group had been a very attractive guy, called Levi. From the minute he'd stepped into the bar, he'd made a beeline for her – smiling and flirting with her all night. A lot of the clientele did that; it was part of the job, and most of the time she found it a bit of a chore, but Levi had seemed different. He'd had a twinkle in his eye and he'd made her laugh, which had been a refreshing change.

In her thoughts, she was still in the bar, soaking up his attention, but she knew she had to get a grip and make sure she was ready to greet her mother.

'What time will she be arriving? Will she stay here again?' Cathy yawned.

Belle tutted. 'That job really is too much for a young woman. I'll speak to Bobby, see if he can't cut your shifts down a bit.' Belle frowned, looking her niece up and down.

'No, no, it's all right. I'm fine, honestly,' Cathy said, thinking of the dimple that had appeared on Levi's cheek each time he'd smiled at her, that mesmerising green of his eyes as he'd winked at her. She shivered, which Belle caught sight of, thinking her cold.

'Go and put a jumper on. Your mum will be here at lunchtime. I've told Bobby you won't start work till later today. And no, she won't be staying here.' At this point Belle bit her lip and looked away. It definitely hadn't gone well the last time Ruby had stayed with them. It was best they all had some space between them if this trip was to go better than the last.

'OK, so she'll be staying at our old home . . .' Cathy said.

Belle cut in hurriedly, 'She will, but you don't have to go there. I'm sure she'll understand. Now, drink this, get some breakfast inside you and get yourself ready because she'll be here in a couple of hours.'

'Thanks Aunty Belle,' Cathy said, walking over to her aunt and kissing her cheek. 'I'll grab some toast after my shower.' She walked upstairs, thinking about her mum's visit. She must have something important to tell her if she was flying here with hardly any notice.

She hummed to herself as she turned the shower on, hoping fervently that her mum's trip was simply a long-overdue family reunion.

Two hours later, Cathy waited by the lounge window until she heard the sound of the Bentley bringing her mum to their door. She stood at the doorway as Ruby stepped out, her high heels appearing first and then her slender form in her Chanel suit and, finally, her long black hair and expensive shades. Ruby looked so much younger than her forty-one years. She never failed to amaze Cathy with how youthful she still looked. As Ruby stood on the driveway, there was a slight hesitation, an awkwardness in her approach. Cathy felt that familiar mix of happiness, love and nervousness. Her mum exuded power, a power that Cathy had learned was gained from being at the pinnacle of the criminal world. When her father was murdered, she'd discovered the truth. The money came from importing and exporting drugs. It was a world away from her naive assumptions that they were rich because of a 'normal' family business. She'd assumed their armed guards and security men were just the trappings of wealth, protecting them against kidnappers like any rich family. She didn't realise they were also protecting them against other cartels and the violence and killing that were an integral part of their dodgy trade.

It had been a shock, but one that was swamped by the sheer force of her grief and the trauma of seeing her beloved father shot in front of her eyes. She'd found some kind of peace here in England, but no relief from the nightmares that began plaguing her in the days and weeks following the robbery. Coming on top of her fragile recovery from being raped by Uncle George, it had been a further, devastating blow. She'd struggled to sleep, tossing and turning for hours and then waking bolt upright in the early hours, screaming and crying. Belle, who had since taken to sleeping in Cathy's room, would run in and hold her tight, feeling the sobs shake her body, soothing her, shushing her, until they too subsided.

Night after night, the dreams woke Cathy. She saw George, felt him pawing at her, scratching her, hurting her as he panted, his face twisted because he was high on drugs. Just as she couldn't take any more, it would switch to her dad, her beloved father as he yelled at her mum not to open the safe. 'They'll kill us all!' he would shout over and over in her dreams, then, just as she knew the robber would turn his gun on him and blast him into his grave, she would wake up, covered in sweat, with tears rolling down her face, her bedsheet coiled around her, and her mouth open as she screamed and screamed.

She hadn't told her mum about the night terrors, and she'd begged Belle not to say a word either. She knew her mum was struggling with Archie's death as much as she was, and she couldn't bear upsetting her further. If she was honest, it wasn't just that, though. Cathy's world had collapsed entirely that day; her dad was dead and her mum was revealed to be the head of a drug cartel, leaving the young woman unsure whom she could trust, or feel safe with. Even though her mum's quick actions had saved her life, she could never see her the same way. That gun had blasted away the lies and secrets of her family's business, just as it had killed Archie. She'd reeled from the truth, the shock of this new knowledge, and she'd wanted to run as far away as she could, not just from the gunmen, but, to her shame, from her mother too.

She knew Ruby had picked up on this, and was trying hard to reconcile with her daughter, but Cathy almost recoiled at the sight of her: her luxury, her wealth, her humble beginnings and the criminal path that made their lifestyle possible. She'd seen it all in a new light, and she wasn't sure she liked any of it.

'Darlin', it's so good to see ya,' Ruby said, now holding her arms out for an embrace. As she did so, something winked from her hand, catching what light there was. When Cathy glanced down, she saw a new ring, a huge emerald surrounded by diamonds, but it took her a moment to realise it was sitting on her mother's left hand, where her engagement ring from Archie used to be.

'Mum?' Cathy asked.

Cathy loved her mum, but her tough exterior, her wily business instincts and her ruthlessness left her daughter almost scared of her now. Belle was softer, gentler, and, though she was ashamed to admit it, more of a mother in many ways to Cathy than Ruby was.

That's why, when Ruby held out her arms, instead of running into them as she would've done as a child, even as a young teenager, Cathy stopped herself, held back, self-conscious. Ruby lowered her arms, not saying a word. She smiled and stepped into the house, taking Cathy's arm. Cathy felt oddly formal, as if a visiting dignitary was passing through.

'You've noticed my ring,' Ruby stated once they were inside. She put down her handbag and turned to her daughter. 'I wanted to tell ya in person rather than on the phone, which is why I've come. There's no other way to say this but with the truth: I've accepted Vladimir's proposal. We're gettin' married while I'm over 'ere. He'll join us once it's all arranged.'

Ruby looked almost nervous as she told Cathy. There was a pause after she'd finished speaking as she waited for her daughter's response.

Cathy looked down at the ring as if mesmerised.

'It's beautiful, Mum, I'm happy for you,' she said. It wasn't a surprise that Ruby had found someone new; she was a beautiful and powerful woman. It wasn't even a surprise that the new man was Vladimir, who reeked of charisma and wealth. What was a surprise was how soon after Archie's death it was; it had been just over seven months since they'd buried her dad. Surely it was too early for her mother to be thinking of marrying again? Emotions collided inside Cathy's heart. She wanted her mum to be happy and to be free of the terrible grief that had so overwhelmed them, but this was so soon, *too* soon. She didn't know what to say. How could her mum have moved on so quickly? It seemed unfathomable that Ruby had mourned Archie as deeply as Cathy had if she'd found the space in her heart to love again.

'I know it's quick, darlin', I know what ya must be thinkin'. It don't mean I didn't love ya dad, he'll always be the man of my life,' Ruby said, a sad smile on her face.

Cathy nodded, but she didn't understand, not really.

'But it's *so* quick, Mum. Sorry, I shouldn't say that. You are obviously over Dad, and I guess I should get over his death too . . .' Before Cathy could finish, Ruby grabbed her arms. This time her voice was urgent. 'I 'ave *not* got over your dad. I will *never* get over him, but I 'ave to move on, for the business, for our family. You 'ave to believe me. Can ya do that?'

Cathy didn't know what her mum meant, but she saw the pain on her face.

'OK, I can try.'

'Thank you, darlin'. I know this is a shock. I wasn't expectin' it myself, but the situation arose and . . .'

'And?' Cathy asked. Her mother's face seemed to withdraw, shut down like a veil had passed over it.

'Nuthin', sorry, I meant nuthin'. Vladimir and I, we want a quick weddin'. No fuss, just family and a meal somewhere lovely. I promise I'm doin' this for the right reasons.'

Cathy had no idea what her mum meant, but she knew Ruby would go her own way, do her own thing, and there was no stopping her once she'd made her mind up.

'All right. We'll go dress shoppin', 'ave a day out in the West End. We'll go up Bond Street and then Selfridges, with lunch somewhere very expensive!' Ruby giggled, though her face still looked sad.

Cathy made herself smile. 'Whatever makes you happy, Mum,' she said, hiding her hurt and confusion. Her mother was asking her to trust her judgement, but could she do that ever again?

'Well, the ring is gorgeous, and so expensive. Vladimir must really love you, Mum.' Cathy tried harder to keep the pain out of her voice.

'He does, darlin', I'm a lucky woman,' Ruby said, though she'd turned away and Cathy could no longer see her expression.

'We'd better find you a dress then ... Mum,' the teenager added, hoping Ruby wouldn't notice her slight hesitation before saying the word 'Mum'.

Just then a key turned in the front door and in walked Belle, back from her volunteering.

'Oh,' she said, looking momentarily flustered before recovering herself.

The air was suddenly frosty as the two women came face to face.

'Hello, Belle, it's good to see ya,' murmured Ruby politely. 'Don't worry, darlin', I'm not stayin'. I just wanted to say hello to my beautiful girl and tell her the good news about me marryin' Vladimir.'

Ruby held out her hand. The emerald contrasted with her creamy skin.

'My goodness, this is a surprise. We've been wondering why you needed to come in person, and now we know.' Belle's voice bordered on unfriendly. Cathy hated seeing her mum and aunt like this.

'I'm pleased for Mum,' she said firmly. Belle looked at her niece quizzically but Cathy said nothing more.

'Of course. Well, congratulations, Ruby,' was all the art teacher managed to say.

There was a brief pause as the three women digested this strange new situation.

'Thank you, Belle. I apologise for rushing off, but I want to get settled into my place and, well, I've got a weddin' to plan.'

'I'll help you, Mum. When shall we start?' peacemaker Cathy said, smiling now. She hated feeling at odds with Ruby.

The next day, Cathy stepped into the gleaming chauffeured car and allowed herself to be whisked to the best shops in London. They ate lunch at the Ivy, after spending a fortune in Selfridges, and for a short while the pair were reconciled and happy in each other's company. By the time it was getting dark, they had a green dress with matching heels and pillbox hat and veil for Ruby and a soft pink Chloé dress for Cathy. Ruby had booked Claridge's for an intimate wedding and by the time they got back to Chigwell, both were tipsy on the free champagne they'd been liberally offered in each store and at the hotel.

They were both surprised to see a Porsche, almost the same shade of red as Archie's, on the driveway at Ruby's where the women were heading to try everything on before dropping Cathy back at Bobby and Belle's.

For a moment, neither of them spoke. Cathy's heart lurched when she saw the car, almost as if she expected her dad to step out of it, his linen shirt immaculate, that look of happiness on his face at the sight of his 'gorgeous girls'.

Instead, Vladimir stepped out.

Cathy swallowed back the emotion. It wasn't Dad. It would never be Dad ever again – and somehow, she had to get used to it.

'Dear ladies, I am sorry to surprise you both like this, but I couldn't stay away,' the Russian murmured as he took Cathy's hand and kissed it.

For a moment, she thought she saw her mum's face harden, but looking back, Ruby was as composed as ever, a smile on her face as she greeted her fiancé.

A trick of the light, thought Cathy, turning back to the man who would now be her stepdad.

As if reading her thoughts, Vladimir kept hold of her hand.

'The real reason I have come is because I wanted to reassure you. I know it has not been long since your dear father was taken from us. A sad day, a very sad day.' Vladimir's face looked wolflike in the gloom as he shook his head, his teeth white, his eyes piercing. *Another trick of the light?* Cathy thought, but couldn't suppress a shiver. Ruby had always said her daughter had inherited her gift, the legacy of her Gypsy blood that meant she could feel things, sense things, that others couldn't. Cathy had always denied it, in truth was wary of it, thinking it a burden, but sometimes it crept up on her like a gentle breeze, reminding her to stay vigilant. *I'm just tired. All that Gypsy stuff is complete nonsense*, Cathy thought to herself, but she realised the Russian still had hold of her hand. He clearly had more to say.

'Dear Cathy, you know I will never try to replace your father, a man I too loved dearly,' he said, 'but I have fallen in love with your mother, and I count myself the luckiest man alive to become her husband. I promise I will protect and care for you both,' he finished. She gazed at him, seeing a handsome man with high Slavic cheekbones and dark hair shot through with silver which was expertly cut. Though she wanted to believe him – she always wanted to see the best in people – she found she couldn't. Something about him troubled her. He was *too* perfect, *too* loving towards Ruby. *Too eager . . .*

Cathy didn't reply straight away, not wanting to give him any indication of her thoughts, and hoping desperately that she was wrong.

Three weeks later, and the deed was done. Ruby looked ravishing in the green dress that perfectly matched the shade of her eyes. Vladimir looked immaculate in a tai-lored grey suit. Alfie had flown back from Bolivia and so with Lloyd, Belle, and Bobby they sipped champagne and toasted the nuptials.

As they raised their glasses, Cathy spoke.

'If only George could be here,' she said lightly.

If there was a single heartbeat before everyone agreed, Cathy didn't notice it. She didn't see the glance her mother threw at Lloyd before she answered.

'Yes, darlin', if only . . .'

Cathy didn't notice Belle's shudder, and how the champagne seemed to turn sour on everyone's lips. Vladimir didn't notice either.

CHAPTER 10

Ruby stretched out a long leg and pointed her pedicured toes, stroking her foot up Vladimir's calf. She peered over her shades at him. He lay next to her on the huge lounger aboard the cruise liner on which they were honeymooning. They'd spent a month touring the Caribbean and were now heading home to Spain. He looked tanned and handsome in Gucci bathers and sunglasses. Nothing more had been said about Vladimir's confession in the hospital. Ruby had watched her husband closely in the days and weeks afterwards, and was convinced he hadn't remembered telling her the news that would seal his fate.

'Babe, I've been thinkin' . . .'

'What about, my darling wife?' Vladimir replied, openly admiring her in her white bikini which showed off her newly tanned skin.

'I don't think I can ever go back to that villa, not after what 'appened with Archie. And now that I've remarried, well, it don't seem right.'

Vladimir nodded slowly. 'My darling, anything you want is yours. If you don't want to go back there, then we won't. We'll live in my villa; it is more than big enough for us. I will make it into a palace for you, and you'll never have to worry about the memories associated with that place ever again.'

Ruby smiled, leaned over and kissed her new husband on the mouth – a slow, sensual kiss. She could feel his desire stirring, but she needed him to agree to something else.

'Ruby,' he whispered throatily as she moved her face away from his.

'We need to sell it. We need to sell the villa and be done with it. The memories of Archie's death are too raw. Can we do that, babe?' Ruby knew that Vladimir hated any mention of her first husband's name. She was banking on this to make him agree to her request.

Vladimir shrugged. 'I said anything you want, and I meant it. As soon as we're back, put it on the market and we will get you the best price. You never have to step foot inside that place ever again, and you never need to remember those times. They are gone, we move forward with our life together. I am your husband now, the past is over.' He moved closer to her, holding her waist to him, nuzzling his head into her chest. She felt his hot breath on her skin and knew she'd won a small victory.

'Oh, Vladimir,' Ruby sighed, knowing he was desperate to take her back to their suite for an afternoon of lovemaking, 'how can I thank you?' She batted her eyelashes, inwardly laughing at the effect it had on this cartel boss, this man who could have her murdered in a second if he knew what was to come. He was hers. He was weak when it came to her, and she was relying on this for what lay ahead.

Back in Spain, the villa was put on the market immediately, and within days had sold to another English expat, a blagger from the Midlands who needed to put his cash somewhere, no questions asked. There was no need to perform many of the administrative details, and a date for the handover of the keys – and cash – was agreed upon without troubling solicitors or the authorities. Two days before the completion date, Ruby received a phone call.

She had only just got out of bed as Vladimir was proving an insatiable husband. His desire for her seemed only to increase as the days and weeks passed.

He was showering as she answered the call in his master bedroom's en suite, a room covered in honey-coloured marble. She heard him turn off the shower, and seconds later he walked out, drying his hair on a white towel, still naked, as she rang off.

'Who was that, my darling?' he said immediately, walking over to her and wrapping his arms around her waist, planting soft kisses down her neck. Despite his attentions, he said again, 'Who was it? I am your husband, my darling, and I should know everything.' He continued to kiss her, his arms holding her tighter as he spoke, his voice a caress, but behind it, Ruby knew there was a steely edge.

Ruby had noticed that Vladimir was possessive of her to the point of intrusion. He continually asked who she was doing business with, and where she was going. Even when she'd just popped out to one of the cruise hair salons, he'd wanted to know. She made a point of smiling sweetly each time he asked, and kissing him tenderly on the lips, promising to be back quickly. Despite this, he always accompanied her, saying he wanted to be in her company, but she wondered if there was more to it. She'd agreed every time, but she knew her patience was running out. He seemed to want to control her every move. Ruby, who was wearing a silk dressing gown covered in exquisitely stitched flowers, which Vladimir was now pulling off her, turned to him and kissed him hard on the mouth.

'There are a few last-minute issues to sort at the villa. That was the estate agent on the phone. He wants to meet me there today. Can ya spare the time to come with me?' As she spoke, her gown slid to the floor and Vladimir bent his head lower, pulling her to him, his lips never leaving her skin.

'Of course, I will come. I don't want you to ever leave my side now, my darling.' He drew her back towards their bed.

Two hours later, after they'd made love again and Ruby had finally managed to dress and eat a hastily prepared salad for lunch, the pair set off in Vladimir's armoured, blacked-out Range Rover. He always drove. He wouldn't let her do a thing now they were married. Ruby played along, but she had a plan – and it was time to put it into action.

*

Ruby's heart swooped down to her stomach as they pulled into the gated entrance of her and Archie's Spanish home. Despite this rush of emotion, she gave no indication of her feelings, knowing Vladimir wouldn't approve. Instead, she smiled at him as he stopped the car. Everything looked the same, even though she hadn't been there for months. Outside, there was a smiling man carrying a brochure for a similar villa development, and some paperwork.

'The estate agent,' murmured Ruby as she stepped out and offered her hand to shake.

'Mrs Ivanov, Mr Ivanov, it is a pleasure to meet you both at last,' said the Spanish man. He was in his early thirties with trendy stubble, a relaxed white shirt open at the neck, expensive jeans and leather slip-ons. From the tail of her eye, Ruby saw Vladimir frown as the young man took her hand and kissed it. Inwardly she laughed, though of course gave no sign of being flattered by his attention. She'd chosen well: he was handsome and flirtatious – in other words, the most likely candidate to rile her new husband.

'Please come this way, we have some last-minute paperwork to sign,' the man, whose name was Mateo, smiled, his eyes twinkling at Ruby as he took the villa keys from his pocket and, with a hand on her back, led her into the atrium, leaving Vladimir to follow behind them.

Ruby shot a look back at her husband, knowing he would be fuming inwardly at the disrespect shown him. On the surface, he remained as charming as ever.

'We really don't have much time for this, we are newly married and have other . . . pursuits . . . to enjoy,' Vladimir said brusquely, walking to Ruby's side and taking hold of her waist.

'Of course, of course, congratulations to you both. I'm so sorry to trouble you with this, but Mrs Ivanov must sign these papers to make the sale legal. It is a mere formality, and I thought she might like to see the place before it is sold.'

Vladimir nodded, but said nothing.

The place was empty. The security guards had been placed at her husband's palatial villa. Her staff were all now engaged there too, except for those who had chosen to leave.

'Can I 'ave a last look around?' Ruby said after she'd signed the documents.

'Of course, madam, this is still your property after all,' Mateo replied. If he noticed Vladimir's deepening frown he didn't give any indication.

Ruby walked down the corridor, white marble underfoot making her heels echo in the empty space. She came to the double doors that opened into the large, lavish lounge and she pushed them inwards. She gasped. Vladimir and the estate agent were beside her. All three turned to see two masked men brandishing guns, pointed at their faces.

Before anyone could react, the men sprang into action, shoving Vladimir into a chair by the huge window and tying his hands behind his back with cable ties. The other stood pointing his gun at Ruby while he handed the estate agent a suitcase. In Spanish, he said, 'You were never here. Tell no one. Now, go!' He moved his gun's aim to the estate agent's head. Mateo, stunned by the scene unfolding around him, seemed to jolt into action. He didn't need telling twice. He took the case and fled. They heard the main entrance bang shut behind him and his handbrake crunching before his car squealed out of the driveway.

The main gunman now tied Ruby up roughly, making Vladimir spit with rage. 'You fucking bastards. Take your hands off my wife. You don't have a clue who you're fucking dealing with. Untie her immediately.'

Neither gunman reacted except to laugh.

'Now. You come.'

The men took hold of Ruby, kicked Vladimir off the chair so he staggered into a standing position, and shoved them out of the room and towards the back part of the villa. They frogmarched them to an open door which led from the kitchens to the storage area. Vladimir tried to break free but his struggles were easily overwhelmed.

Outside there was a van with its back door open.

'Get inside,' the Spanish gunman said.

'Where are ya takin' us?' said Ruby as she stood in front of the open vehicle. The van smelt of tobacco smoke and was visibly dirty, with several filthy blankets on the floor.

'Shut up, bitch,' was the reply.

'Get the fuck inside. Now!' The man squared up to Ruby's face but she didn't flinch. She'd seen the business end of a gun before. She knew what it felt like to know she might be seconds from death. She stared back at the man as if they were enjoying cocktails on the manicured lawns.

Vladimir's reaction was a different story. He was incandescent with rage.

'You don't fucking speak to my wife like that!' he shouted. 'Whatever you're being paid I will double it! Now set us free.'

The gunmen laughed again as they shoved him inside the van, a dark streak of engine oil smearing Vladimir's suit. 'You miserable fuckers. I will kill you both. You have picked the wrong people to fuck over!'

'Vladimir, darlin', you 'ave to calm down, or they will kill us. Shoutin' at them will only make it worse. We 'ave to roll with this, see what they want, then find out their price. Every man can be bought, every single one. Just wait, babe . . .'

'I am sorry, my darling. I cannot bear hearing these bastards speaking to you like this,' Vladimir said before swearing in his native language. 'I will burn them for this. I will cut them open and burn them for daring to touch you, for daring to do this to us.' His face was demented with rage.

'And you will, my darlin', of that I 'ave no doubt,' Ruby said soothingly, her voice a whisper so the men wouldn't hear them. 'We 'ave to hold our nerve, don't show them we're rattled. We'll get out of this, I promise ya.'

Vladimir nodded, but it was clear he was fighting himself on this. His instincts were to blast them both:

kill first, ask questions later, but that wouldn't get them anywhere.

'We 'ave to get out of this alive,' Ruby finished as the Spanish gunman jumped up into the back and the door was slammed, plunging them all into darkness. Ruby was grateful for the dark, for the gloom inside that van. If it had been lit, if there had been natural light, then her husband might have seen her expression. She wasn't smiling, but there was no fear on her face, no terror nor panic. Instead, there was a look of grim satisfaction, entirely at odds with the scene unfolding around them.

As Ruby's eyes adjusted to the gloom, she saw that the man was pointing the gun towards them. He was chewing gum, looking between them both through the holes in his black balaclava.

They were silent as the van rode roughshod over the land and down the winding track to an exit at the far end of the estate. The other gunman, the one who hadn't spoken a word, was driving.

Eventually, the van appeared to reach its destination, careening to a halt. Ruby knew that this would be the crucial moment. This might be the point where they took them out in a deserted field or warehouse and shot them. This could be the place they both died.

Ruby could feel Vladimir's fear rising. She tried to keep eye contact with him, to show him they must remain calm, must be ready for anything. He blinked back at her, his blue eyes wild.

Suddenly, the door was opened by the second, silent, gunman, and they were bundled out. Vladimir exclaimed, 'But this is my villa? What the fuck is going on?'

There was no time for answers. Neither gunman seemed to want to explain as they marched them past Vladimir's Range Rover, the one they'd used to drive to Ruby's villa.

Vladimir tried to break free again, but this time, the gunman slammed the handle of his gun against his face, cutting his lip. Blood seeped onto his white shirt, but Vladimir wouldn't stop now. 'Where the fuck is my security? What the fucking hell is going on? How did you get my car here?' He tried to wrestle with the talkative kidnapper, but the man was too strong for the Russian and Vladimir was pushed towards the open front door.

'Inside. Now!' the gunman screamed in Vladimir's face, grappling him into the main entrance. Inside the lounge, Vladimir was hustled over to a chair that appeared to be waiting for him, and forced to sit, the silent man's gun pointing at his forehead.

Ruby was pulled inside behind her husband. Her cords were untied, her hands freed. She rubbed them as they were sore. The ties had been tight enough to leave red weals on her wrists. She looked around the room. There were no others, just Vladimir, her and the two gunmen. They were alone.

The Spanish robber walked slowly towards her. Even though she couldn't see his mouth, he sneered, 'Open the safe, bitch.'

CHAPTER 11

Ruby turned to face the intruder.

There was a moment's silence. The gunman looked back at her. There was a second of pure understanding, a moment dispelled instantly by the sound of her husband shouting.

'Don't open it, they will kill us anyway! Give them nothing!' yelled Vladimir from the other side of the room.

She glanced at him. Blood still oozed from the cut on his lip, making livid red marks on his shirt. His eyes were wild. He struggled against his ties, but it was futile; he was bound as securely as Archie had been. Ruby stared again into the balaclava-clad robber's eyes. This was all so familiar.

The man's gun pointed directly at her face, his eyes bright behind the mask. It was as if time had stood still and she was back in her villa all those months ago, with Archie tied to the chair and Cathy witnessing everything. Back then, she had been swamped with the fear and adrenalin that coursed through her body, every sense on high alert. Her mind had whirred with questions, asking how the gunmen had got past her security, how they'd managed to overpower her husband, and whether they would live or die. She'd known then that a single mistake would mean death for them all.

Now, things were different. She hadn't expected to feel that adrenalin rush again, but, back then, it had been her beloved Archie who was in danger. Her beautiful daughter had been in peril too. She had to remember: Archie was dead. Cathy was safely in England.

The seconds ticked past.

Vladimir squirmed in the chair. 'Let me go. Fucking let me go. I'll pay you ten times what you're being paid, just don't harm us, please don't harm us.' He was starting to beg. Archie would never have stooped so low.

Both gunmen ignored him. Their eyes were on Ruby.

She felt her blood surge through her veins, the muscles and sinew supporting her, the breath coming in and out of her lungs. She drew herself up to her full height. She felt strong this time, assured.

'We're running out of patience,' the Spanish robber said in heavily accented English. He turned to the other man and nodded, giving some kind of instruction without words.

The second intruder responded by turning to her husband and, without warning, slamming his fist into Vladimir's face, finishing the work the handle of the gun started earlier. Vladimir's nose exploded in a mess of blood and the Russian shrieked in pain.

Ruby said nothing, did nothing. She knew what would happen next. She knew to stay calm, to stay in control. She realised she was enjoying seeing her first husband's killer writhing in agony. She felt strangely calm. But the show wasn't over yet.

'Give. Us. The. Money.' The man stepped closer, his gun almost touching her cheek now.

Ruby imagined it was becoming obvious to Vladimir that the staff had all disappeared – bribed or threatened, he might guess – and they were completely alone in the mansion with their assailants. She looked over at him. Vivid red blood contrasted with his face, pale despite his tan.

'All right. I will do what you . . . *gentlemen* . . . ask of me,' she said quietly, as she had the other time, the time she lost Archie, and she nodded at them.

This time, the gunman nodded back.

Vladimir was too terrified and injured to notice. He groaned as thick red blood poured from his broken nose, and muttered curses in Russian, his head hanging over his chest.

'I'll give ya the money.' Her voice was steady as she spoke. 'The main safe is behind that paintin', but there are other safes in the villa,' she added, not looking at her husband though he stared up at her now.

'No! Ruby, they'll *kill* us as soon as you hand over the money. Listen to me, Ruby! Don't tell them anything!' Vladimir tried to shout but his voice was hoarse. He spat out the blood that had filled his mouth.

Ruby didn't look at him; her attention was wholly on the gunmen. How could Vladimir not have guessed? How could he be so ignorant, so stupid, not to have worked out what was really happening? Surely this all felt familiar to him, too? She'd overestimated him. He didn't have a clue. He hadn't realised what he'd said in that hospital bed. He hadn't guessed that her feelings towards him were of revulsion, not love. He hadn't worked out that Ruby's heart was cold as steel, and that this was all her plan.

The thought made her despise him all the more. She turned and began to walk towards the large Gainsborough painting that hung on the wall of the room, one of three reception rooms in the villa. The painting was an original, of course. No crook ever bothered to hide their artworks deep in underground safes. They were, after all, the people other art lovers feared, the ones who would steal a picture like this, worth several million dollars.

The sun shone into the room. A fly buzzed at the glass, tapping against it, trying to fly free, not understanding yet that it was trapped.

Ruby's heels clacked against the ceramic Italian tiles that Vladimir had imported at great expense from Tuscany. The sound filled the room, distracting her from the noise of her husband panting, his breathing short and strained as the blood in his nose began to clot and he struggled to draw in air.

What Vladimir couldn't see was the smile that now crept across her face.

She walked slowly, buying time, feeling the echo of the past in her controlled steps. As she reached the painting, she again turned to the gunman who had followed her, his gun now held to her back.

'I'll get yer money if ya put yer gun down. You're makin' me nervous and I might forget the combination.' Her words were a parody of the ambush in which Archie died, an exact copy of what she'd said. Again, she wondered if Vladimir noticed. She felt a strange sense of calm as the words moved through her lips, and couldn't resist a glance at the man who'd been responsible for her losing the love of her life. A thrill went through her. Vladimir looked at her, quizzically. Something had clicked, and not just the gun.

Revelling in his confusion, Ruby staged the last act of this piece of theatre, this retribution she'd planned all along. She took hold of the picture, which was a land-scape – dark trees against an arching blue sky dotted with creamy clouds – and with a single gesture, rolled it to one side. The mechanism worked seamlessly and without effort, revealing a large metal safe.

'Don't do this, Ruby. Listen to me. They will kill us both as soon as you hand over the money. Ruby?' Vladimir pleaded with her now, but was he pleading for their lives or for her to stop this charade? She heard the pain and frustration, the terror in his voice, but there was some-thing else, some new knowledge perhaps.

Not enough, Vladimir, not nearly enough pain yet, she thought as she reached for the dial.

Then, a gunshot echoed around the room.

Vladimir cried out in agony.

She didn't need to look. She knew already. Her husband had been shot. He screamed this time.

'Stop! Stop! Don't fucking do this!' he cried. She looked around, past the barrel of the gun that now pointed at Vladimir, and saw that the second attacker had shot him through the foot. Blood gushed from the wound.

Another shot and Vladimir yelled a guttural sound as the bullet went through his knee, shattering his patella, his kneecap. He was weeping now. The floor was wet with his thick, red blood. Ruby nodded at the sight. Calm, measured.

She turned back as his moans filled the room, their sound amplified by an expectant hush as she took hold of the dial. The two men were breathing heavily inside their balaclavas. Vladimir coughed as he slumped now on the chair; a broken man.

Her mind sharpened as she turned it.

Click. Click. Click.

'No, don't do this. Ruby, I beg you . . .' Vladimir's voice was as weak as a child's. His face was white, as if he had already died. In her mind, she was taken back to this point, all those months ago. She'd been facing two gunmen who, just like now, had ordered her to open the safe and hand over the money inside it. Instead, she'd reached for the gun she knew was hidden there, grabbed it and pulled the trigger, shooting one of those intruders in the face. Sprayed in his blood, she'd heard another shot ring out. Time had stood still. She'd looked over to that second gunman and had known before her eyes caught up: he had shot Archie. His blood already pooled under his body. Without hesitation, she'd turned her weapon on that gunman, the only one still living, and she'd emptied the round into him, carrying on shooting him even after he was dead. Then she'd run over, slipping in her husband's blood, to cradle him in her arms as police sirens sounded and her world crumbled completely.

This time was different. For a second, she'd been back there, in her villa, as her murdered husband lay in her arms, horror and grief smashing into her like ocean waves. But this wasn't then. This was now – and she had to finish what she'd started.

'Ruby, I beg you . . .'

She knew in that instant that he'd guessed, or was beginning to. He would die knowing she had set him up. She wanted him to suffer the pain of his wounds, and her betrayal. Only then could she let Archie's death rest.

The safe was open, but she took nothing out. Instead, she turned back to face all three men. Vladimir looked up, bewilderment and knowledge colliding on his face.

Ruby stepped towards him, away from the open safe, to stand beside the gunmen.

All three moved closer to the Russian. They stood over him, surrounding him.

'What the fuck have you done—' he started to say, but was interrupted by the intruder who had, so far, remained silent.

"Allo, Vladimir, fancy seein' you 'ere,' Alfie's voice came from inside the balaclava, which he proceeded to rip off his head, revealing his menacing grin.

'What? What is this? Ruby? Ruby, what is happening?'

'Oh, I think you know, husband? Took ya a while to work it out. I'm surprised at ya, you're an intelligent man after all. I thought you'd like our little re-enactment. Wasn't it you who ordered my Archie's death, makin' it look like a robbery? Don't even think of lyin' to me, I know everythin' because you told me yerself.' Ruby's voice was cold as she stepped closer to Vladimir and leaned over to meet his terrified gaze.

She stood back to watch the impact her words made upon the man she'd taken to her bed, the man she'd set up all along.

'First we did some diggin' and we couldn't find no Alec Rumanov. We realised you hadn't been entirely honest with us.'

'Not honest with us. A terrible mistake, Vlad,' echoed Alfie, who was pacing around the captured Russian, holding his gun aloft.

'But at the time, we thought that perhaps he'd slipped our radar, was too deep inside the KGB to be traced, so we let that go. I knew, though, Vladimir. I knew deep down that it was you all along, so when ya confessed me to me in hospital, high on morphine after your heart operation, I wasn't surprised.'

'Wasn't surprised at all, ya fucker,' said Alfie, grinning maniacally.

'Ruby, please . . . I'm sorry. Ruby, I love you . . .'

Ruby shook her head as Vladimir begged, tears streaming down his bloodied face.

'My Archie would never 'ave begged to no one. He was a *real* man, a proper man, not some snivelling traitorous little bastard like you,' Ruby said, smiling. 'You told me everythin' in that hospital bed: how you'd wanted me all along, how you'd planned the attack to look like a robbery. You squealed like the pig you are.'

'I . . . I . . . I would never have hurt you, Ruby, my darling. You have to understand. I had to have you.'

Ruby paused for a moment.

'You could never 'ave me, Vladimir. I was never your "darlin"'. You could never 'ave replaced my Archie. No man could,' she said eventually, considering each word, wanting him to know how deeply she scorned him.

'So, when ya told me the truth, I wanted you to suffer just like my Archie did – in fear and pain. Don't get me wrong, you was a dead man from the second you opened ya mouth, and I could've killed ya then. I could've stuffed a pillow over yer face and done it that night after the operation, but I wanted my revenge, you see. You do see, don't ya, Vladimir?'

Ruby's face was millimetres from the Russian's, her green eyes wide as she relished her retribution.

She saw the effect her words were having. Vladimir began to cry, to plead with her. He shook, his face a mess of blood and bone, his leg bloodied and broken.

'Don't do this, Ruby. Please, don't kill me. I did it for you . . .'

Anger surged in Ruby's heart, breaking through her cold demeanour.

'You did it for *you*!' she shouted back, finally letting her grief show, the grief that had been hidden from view for months. 'You did it so you could take what wasn't yours. You did it to get rid of my husband. You traumatised my Cathy; you deprived her of a father and me of an 'usband. You will burn in hell for that, I'm sure of it. It is your turn to die but I wanted your last breath to be taken knowing how much I despise ya.'

Vladimir sobbed. Ruby looked down on him, almost pitying him. Almost.

'Do it,' she ordered. 'Kill the no-good piece of filth.'

Alfie raised his shotgun and pointed it directly at Vladimir's head.

'It's your turn. You will suffer the same fate, in exactly the same way,' she whispered, a slow smile spreading across her face. 'You 'ave been set up, my love. You 'ave been duped by the wife you profess to love so much. Well, this is what ya get for lovin' me.'

With that, she turned away, signalling to Alfie she was done.

BANG!

It was over. She didn't need to look to know that Vladimir was dead, his skull blasted to smithereens. She'd seen the horror on his face and that was enough to satisfy her. She glanced back at Alfie, who awaited her next command. Ruby didn't speak. She nodded – a pre-agreed gesture. Alfie knew what to do. He turned to the Spanish gunman and shot him twice in the chest. He fell to the ground heavily. Ruby nodded to Alfie.

'He had to die; I had to kill him. It has to look like another robbery. Make sure the Chief of Police gets double his money.'

Alfie nodded. Ruby looked around the room, taking in the carnage: the dead bodies, the bone and gristle, the smell of cordite from the weapons and the sharp metallic tang of blood. It really was over.

She picked up her phone and called the local police. 'A robbery has taken place. Two men 'ave died – there was nuthin' we could do. My husband is dead.'

'Another funeral,' stated Alfie.

She nodded. 'I will play the part of grieving widow to perfection, then I will return to England. My business in Spain is finished. You can 'ave the villa, Alfie. Stay and oversee the company from 'ere. Find someone else to oversee our contacts in South America – I want you close from now on. Keep things steady over 'ere while the shock of Vladimir's death sinks in. Speak to his networks, reassure them that all is well, and we carry on as before. We'll make sure his funeral is lavish.'

Alfie nodded. He had been all too glad to avenge his brother's death. When Ruby had told him of her plan, he'd wanted to pull the trigger. He'd wanted to end it, and so he had.

In the distance, they heard the sirens.

PART 2

BETRAYAL

Flying back to England,
July 2012

CHAPTER 12

'It's over, Rube,' Lloyd said, handing her a glass of champagne.

Ruby accepted it, putting the glass to her lips and raising her short black veil to take a sip of the ice-cold bubbles. She leaned back in her leather seat and pulled off her black pillbox hat with its fine mesh used to hide a widow's grief and threw it onto a nearby seat.

'Good riddance,' she said fiercely, clinking her glass with her father-in-law and turning to look out of the window of their private jet as it soared through blue skies, away from Marbella.

Lloyd was sitting opposite her on the plush white leather seats, looking relaxed and smiling at Ruby. Ruby had tussled with the idea of leaving for England straight away, but knew she had to 'look the part' of a grieving widow, so had stayed in Spain for the funeral. She knew it was the right decision. They had to maintain the story that she was a love-struck new wife, and her husband was the victim of a robbery that went wrong, so that the

Russian's extensive web of loyal contacts, runners, cartel members and drug lords carried on dealing with Alfie and the family. If they suspected that it was, in fact, Ruby who'd ordered the killing, there could be retribution and, at the very least, it would shake the foundations of their enterprise. She knew that Vladimir's men were loyal to him, and she'd gained their trust because of their faith in him. She couldn't reveal the truth, no matter how tempting it was to show the world how she'd avenged Archie's death.

Alfie had spoken to Vladimir's contacts at the funeral, reassuring them that everything would stay the same. No one had questioned the Russian's death. Robbery, theft and violence were occupational hazards in their game, and even though his death had come as a shock, it wasn't entirely unexpected. Like any gangster, Vladimir had enemies. If anyone had noticed the similarity between Archie's death and Vladimir's, they stayed silent, helped by the bribe of a million dollars paid into the Chief of Police's account the evening of the faked robbery. Once the police had been paid off, Ruby knew that the matter would be dead and buried under Spanish bureaucracy and there would be no comeback from that quarter.

The wake had taken place at Vladimir's huge villa after a short service at a local church. Ruby knew that the sight of so many mafia and cartel henchmen dressed in black suits and dark glasses would draw attention from reporters and photographers, and so guests were invited to the private wake only. Ruby ensured there was plenty of champagne for the crooks who came from all over the globe. Most were contacts from Russia and the Baltic States, the epicentre of Vladimir's supply network. She made sure she looked every inch an oligarch's wife with sunshades to hide her eyes even behind the small veil, and an immaculate dress suit from her beloved Chanel. She'd descended the sweeping staircase clad entirely in black, the very picture of a grieving widow, yet one who had an empire to run; still beautiful, still dangerous.

Lloyd nodded discreetly at her entrance. They wanted all eyes on Ruby as the beautiful widow, to deflect from any awkward questions asked about the manner of Vladimir's death.

The mansion heaved with their networks of hardened criminals, who all graciously kissed Ruby's hand and told her they were sorry for her loss. Ruby dabbed a handkerchief to her eye to mop up fake tears, looking for all the world like a woman bereft of the man she loved. Lloyd and Alfie circulated, shaking hands, accepting condolences, but the real business of the day was to ensure that everyone stayed loyal to them. They wanted Vladimir's men to switch allegiance to Alfie, to stay with them in the months ahead as they shored up their supply chains from South America. Promises were made, huge sums of money discussed, and by the end of the day, all three were sure that the crooks who'd flown in from across Russia and Europe would see that sticking with their cartel made sense.

Of course, Ruby had discussed none of this with her family back in England. As she sat in the jet with her glass of vintage fizz, she recalled, with that familiar mix of guilt and love, her phone chat with Cathy, breaking the news to her that Vladimir had been killed.

'Darlin', how are ya?' she'd begun, her heart hammering in her chest. Lying to her daughter was worse than facing the most hardened of crooks with her pretend grief, fake tears, fake heartache. When it came to the prospect of endangering her relationship with Cathy, she felt out of control and out of her depth. It wasn't a feeling she liked.

'Oh, I'm OK, Mum,' Cathy replied on the other end of the phone.

It was the day after Vladimir had been shot. Ruby was sitting in her lounge. The bodies had been removed by the police and the place scrubbed clean. It looked like nothing bad had ever happened there as the sun streamed in through the large villa windows in the place she'd shared with her husband only twenty-four hours previously.

'That's good, darlin'' Ruby continued, 'Listen, I 'ave somethin' I need to tell ya, and it might upset ya.'

There was silence at the other end of the phone. Then Cathy called to Belle, 'I'm on the phone to Mum, I'll be there in a minute.'

'Sorry, Mum, I have to go soon. Belle wants me to help her in the kitchen. You were saying?'

Ruby was thrown for a moment but she gathered herself.

'Listen, Vladimir is dead. He was shot by a robber at the mansion. I'm fine, honestly I am, but I wanted ya to know.'

Ruby waited for her daughter's response.

'Christ, Mum, oh God, what happened? Are you safe? Mum, you have to leave that life, you're in danger!' Cathy sounded both shocked and concerned, making Ruby hate herself for the lies she was about to tell.

'It's all right, I promise ya. It's all sorted and dealt with. We found out who it was and it's sorted. I was never in any danger,' Ruby replied, hoping Cathy wouldn't ask any more questions.

'Sorted? What does that mean? How can you possibly be safe when this keeps happening? And God, you went through again what we went through with Dad . . .' Cathy's voice broke a little. Ruby could hear Belle's voice calling for Cathy again. This time Cathy ignored her.

'I know, and I'm dealin' with it. I promise ya, I'm fine. But I'm leavin' Spain for good. I'll be back with you as soon as the funeral is over.'

Ruby hoped that her daughter wouldn't notice the lack of genuine grief in her voice, and how she was glossing over the events of the previous day.

'You're coming back?' Cathy said, seemingly oblivious, 'When?'

'The funeral is in five days' time. When it's done and I can leave Alfie 'ere, then I'll be on that plane. I won't ever come back to Spain.'

'Why is Alfie there? I thought he was in Bolivia?' Cathy said after a short pause.

Damn, muttered Ruby to herself; she'd forgotten that Alfie wasn't meant to be there. She said hastily, 'Oh, yes, darlin'. I called him straight away and he flew over that night. I needed him 'ere.'

'Of course,' Cathy replied. 'Look, Mum, I'm sorry. You must be devastated. I'll tell Bobby and Belle that you're coming home, but don't you want us to come for the funeral? They'll be so worried about you.'

Ruby paused, knowing she had no choice but to keep up the pretence. The less Cathy knew about any of this, the safer she was.

'No, darlin'. Don't come. I don't know if it's safe yet; we've got to sort out a few more things 'ere. With Vladimir gone we may 'ave trouble on our 'ands with his business, and we want to make sure it'll carry on runnin' smoothly. Listen, things will be chaotic for the next few days, so tell them not to worry. Lloyd is on his way 'ere to help me. I've got support, so stay where you are and I'll see ya soon, all right?'

'All right, Mum,' Cathy answered. 'I love you.'

'I love ya too, darlin',' Ruby replied a heartbeat later, taken aback by Cathy's words, feeling again that loathing for the secrets that seemed forever to be a part of her life; secrets that piled up and up, like the bodies.

As soon as she could slip away from the wake, Ruby took her chance. She'd already sent her bags ahead to the jet, so with her handbag, her gun stashed safely inside it, and her passport, she stepped into a black limousine waiting for her outside, and allowed herself to be taken to the private airport, appreciating the cool air conditioning after the sweltering heat of the day. Lloyd followed an hour later, once the last of the deals had been negotiated, leaving Alfie in charge at Vladimir's villa, his new business empire stretching out before him. When Ruby had taken her leave of Alfie, he'd smiled at her, and had looked for all the world like his twin, making Ruby's heart twist with longing.

'Bye, Rube. Ya did well, very well. No one would've thought you was anythin' less than a grievin' widow,' he said, his voice strangely soft. She saw tenderness in his eyes, something she had never seen before except perhaps during that first meeting when he and Archie had sat with her in the Spanish café all those years ago. He'd looked scary but he'd been a gentleman, gentle with baby George and courteous with her.

'We did it, Alfie. I couldn't 'ave got through today without ya.' Ruby felt oddly unsettled, feeling like this was goodbye to so much more than Spain. It was the end of an era. Her score with the Russian was settled. Archie could now rest in peace. That life for her was over. With sadness in her heart, she reached up and kissed Alfie on his cheek.

'Be good,' she said. 'Keep those Russians on their toes.'

He nodded.

'Bye, sis. Give my love to Cathy and the others.'

She waved to him as she left. He stood and watched her depart. A look of understanding passed between them.

'Drive,' was all she said to her chauffeur, and soon, Alfie disappeared behind the high walls of the estate as the driver pulled away. Everything was tied up nicely now. Any legal entanglements following the Russian's death could be ironed out by a series of expensive lawyers which Ruby now had working for them permanently. It was time for a fresh start, away from Archie's place of death, away from her revenge on Vladimir. She wanted to leave it all behind. Only Lloyd, Alfie and Ruby knew the truth, that Vladimir killed Archie, and that she'd taken her revenge by copying the way her love had been killed.

Now, as she sipped her champagne on their private plane, Ruby searched her feelings. She discovered what she already knew; that she felt no remorse for her Russian husband's violent end. In fact, she felt a grim sense of satisfaction to have pulled it off. In her mind's eye, she relived the moment Vladimir's panic switched to horror when he realised what was really happening. She saw him beg and plead, which made her more ruthless, colder, towards him. He'd disgusted her in life – and even more as he approached his own death. It had been worth every embrace she'd suffered, every kiss and stroke from her Archie's killer's hands. It had been worth hiding her disgust behind tender smiles and faked passion. Her heart had grown colder as his had become enflamed for her. As he'd barely let her out of his sight, she had waited patiently, plotted with Alfie and Lloyd as he lay sleeping, and now, she was free at last.

'You OK, Rube?' Lloyd asked drowsily as he leaned back in his chair and grinned at her.

'Never better,' she replied, clinking her glass with his, a smile spreading across her face at the thought of being home with Cathy at last.

'To the future,' Lloyd said, smiling back at her.

'The future.'

CHAPTER 13

Cathy sat in her bedroom, hands placed on her flat stomach, as she waited for her mum to arrive from Spain. She couldn't feel anything yet, she was hardly showing, but the thought that a tiny baby was growing inside her filled her with a mix of joy and trepidation. She'd told Levi at the weekend. He'd picked her up from work and taken her to a local beauty spot in his BMW. Hardly a glamorous date, but Cathy had been too dazzled by his good looks, his husky voice, to object – until now.

He'd parked and turned to her, had begun kissing her neck. It was dark outside and there was no one about but Cathy suddenly realised she didn't like having to meet like this. Perhaps it was being pregnant that made her keen to be looked after, protected.

'Can't we go to your place?' she asked.

'My place? I can't take ye to mine, I'm sorry, baby. It's a traveller site and they don't like strangers goin' dere. Ye understand, don't ye . . .' It was a statement rather than a question. His voice was low and his Irish accent pronounced, and usually it made Cathy giddy to hear it, but tonight was different. Things had changed. She wanted a cosy bed to make love in away from prying eyes, not a car, though it was a high-spec one with blacked-out windows for privacy.

'I've told you, we have Romany heritage so why can't we go to yours? It'd be comfier than here,' Cathy grumbled as Levi's hands moved down from her neck. He kissed her passionately, but she felt distracted. She'd only known about her pregnancy for a few hours, and she wasn't sure if it was too early to tell him. As his kisses grew more urgent, she decided she wanted him to know he was going to be a father. She wanted to celebrate together, for him to be as happy as she was.

'Baby, I've got something to tell you,' Cathy started to say as she tried to push him back from her, but he was insistent.

'Mmm, what's that, baby?' Levi began to undo her blouse. He'd courted Cathy for months after he first walked through the door of The Locksmith. He'd gone to the bar every night to flirt with her, begging her to go out with him. She'd held off, unable to believe that a man so charming, so handsome, could have fallen for her. By the time she'd relented and let him take her out, she was besotted. She could hardly believe this man with his razor-like wit and cheeky smiles could want to be with her.

'Baby, stop. I really need to tell you something!' Cathy said, more sharply than she'd intended. Levi sat back, ran his hands through his dark hair and fumbled in the pocket of his leather jacket for his tobacco and Rizlas.

'Go on, what is it ye want to tell me that's so important?' He glanced sideways at her, then took a pinch of baccy out of the pouch and, using the thumb and middle finger on each hand, expertly rolled it in a cigarette which he then lit. Inhaling deeply, he blew the smoke out of the part-open window and then turned to face Cathy.

She felt suddenly exposed, and nervous. Until that moment, she hadn't considered that he might not want the baby. She realised in that second that she really knew very little about him. He'd appeared out of nowhere, an Irishman with all the chat, who lived on a traveller site in Basildon. She'd never been there, she'd never even asked to go there, and for all Cathy knew, he might already have a wife and kids tucked up in a trailer somewhere. This new thought made her suddenly nervous.

'Go on, baby, spill the beans. What do ye want to tell me?' Levi was studying her face and his voice was gentler, though his dark eyes were narrowed. Cathy coughed a little as the fug of smoke filled the car, then, realising it was bad for the baby, she pressed the button hurriedly for the window to glide down. Levi arched an eyebrow then flicked his rollie outside.

'Cathy, are ye goin' to tell me what's up?'

She took a deep breath, then said, 'I'm pregnant.'

It was Levi's turn to cough.

'You're what? Baby, I thought ye were takin' summat to stop that happenin'.'

Cathy looked at her boyfriend. He looked like she'd announced she was an alien – his handsome face was aghast. He ran his fingers through his hair again and turned to look out of the BMW, though it was pitch black outside. She saw his reflection in the darkened window, his high cheekbones and tanned skin making him look unnerving in the bleak overhead light.

'I . . . I thought you'd be happy,' she said quietly, 'I know we haven't been together long, but we love each other, don't we? Baby, talk to me, please . . .'

'Jesus Christ, Cathy, I thought ye were on the pill or somethin'. I had no idea this could happen.'

This wasn't the reaction Cathy had been expecting. In her naivety, she'd thought Levi would be over the moon in realising their love would result in a baby. She felt bewildered. Hadn't he been telling her she was the love of his life? Hadn't he told her they'd be together for ever? She wondered, briefly, if everything he'd ever said to her amid their frequent lovemaking was a lie. For a moment, Levi said nothing, then he turned back. 'It's late. I'll drop ye home now. We'll speak tomorrow.'

He drove her back to Bobby and Belle's in silence. Confused and afraid, Cathy said nothing either, but as she opened the door to leave, Levi stopped her by placing a hand on hers.

'Sorry, baby. It came as a shock. I'm happy, so I am.' Her fears melted away. She kissed him, then skipped inside.

Everything was going to be OK. Levi had just freaked out a bit. Lots of men did that when they learned they were going to be fathers, didn't they? Cathy saw her dad Archie in her mind's eye. She couldn't imagine him 'freaking out', especially over a child with Ruby. She shook her head to try to clear her thoughts. *You're panicking – it's all new and strange. Levi said he's happy. Perhaps we'll even get married earlier now,* Cathy thought to herself as she undressed and got into bed, taking care not to make a noise and wake her aunt and uncle. It was big news. No wonder Levi had reacted strangely. It was all going to be fine – more than fine; it was going to be wonderful. Cathy smiled to herself as she drifted off to sleep, with Levi's baby in her womb and only a hint of the worry that had overtaken her still remaining.

Cathy hadn't yet told Uncle Bobby and Aunt Belle that she was seeing the charming traveller guy who turned up at the bar each night. Somehow, she'd managed to keep her relationship with Levi a secret, saying she was going out with friends after her shifts. She'd told herself it was because she didn't like everyone knowing her business, and because things were still so new, but if she was honest with herself, it wasn't any of those things. She was in love with Levi but she knew that her family might not approve of him. He was confident to the point of cocky, something she knew her mum would hate. He was a traveller, but as she had Gypsy blood from her great-grandmother Ruby, she felt he was a kindred spirit, and her family couldn't object to that, could they?

Over the next few days, as they waited for Ruby to confirm the date she would return, Cathy tried to find a moment to tell her aunt and uncle, but each time there was a lull in the conversation, she chickened out and said nothing. Perhaps it was because she hadn't seen Levi since she'd told him about the baby. He hadn't come to the bar for the past few nights, though he had texted her to let her know he was busy until the weekend. She tried to feel reassured, but this was precisely the moment she needed him to be around, to support her as she shared their news with her family.

Belle had asked her several times if she was OK.

'You seem distracted, Cathy. Is everything all right?' But Cathy had fobbed her aunt off, saying she was tired or had a headache. Then Ruby announced she was flying home straight after Vladimir's wake, and somehow it seemed wrong to tell Belle and Bobby before her own mother, when her mother would be here so soon.

'Cathy, love, I think she's arrived. Why don't you go down and greet her? She'd like that,' Belle called up the stairs.

'All right, thanks Aunt Belle,' Cathy replied. She took a deep breath. Telling her mum made her feel anxious. How would Ruby react? Would she be pleased for the couple? Where was Levi, anyway? He'd said he was away working, but where? Why wasn't he here with her enjoying this precious news?

Cathy walked down the stairs. Every time she saw her mum, she experienced that strange mix of love and resentment. She also felt guilt for her closeness with Belle. She was angry at Ruby for lying to her for years about the nature of the work she did, and, in Cathy's eyes, for putting it before her and George. And, despite George's terrible crime, she was resentful that Ruby hadn't brought him back to the family, and had let her dad banish him. She hated to admit it but she was also jealous of Ruby. Her mum attracted respect and admiration from those around her. She was strong and, at times, ruthless: a woman who was the equal of anyone. Cathy was softer, gentler, perhaps weaker than her mum, and sometimes she yearned to be like her, to command people's admiration. When she saw Ruby step out of the car, wearing black from head to toe, it was love that overwhelmed her. For the first time in a long while, Cathy ran up to her mum and hugged her.

'I'm so sorry for your loss, Mum. I can't imagine how you must be feeling.'

If Ruby was taken aback by this display of affection, she didn't show it. Instead, she closed her arms around her daughter and held her, sensing there was more to this than met the eye.

Lloyd stepped out of the other side of the car. 'Let's go inside, shall we?' he murmured, ushering them quickly into Belle's home in Chigwell. They had no other security with them except for the guns carried by the chauffeur. All of their chauffeurs had a similar pack with them, hidden in their SUVs, so they were never without firearms once they'd stepped off a plane.

'Thank you, please leave the bags in the car,' Ruby called back to the driver, 'we'll only be an hour or two 'ere before goin' back to my house.'

'I won't stay this time, Belle,' Ruby said as they walked inside. 'The place looks lovely, though.'

'Thank you,' Belle replied. 'Tea or coffee, or something stronger? We're all very sorry for what happened. So strange coming so soon after . . .' Belle didn't finish her sentence. Bobby strode in and over to Ruby and enfolded her in a bear hug.

'We're all pleased to see ya back where ya belong, in England,' he said, more loudly than perhaps was appropriate. Ruby looked over at Belle. Belle looked back at her, her face pale. She looked mutinous, like there was something she wanted to say. Ruby didn't let her gaze drop and, eventually, her sister-in-law looked away.

'I'll get some drinks and something to eat. You must be famished after the journey,' Belle said, retreating into the kitchen.

'Cathy, why don't ya come with me back to the house and we can catch up together while I get out of my widow's weeds,' Ruby said confidentially.

Cathy, who hovered by her mother, trying not to place her hands on her non-existent bump, nodded. 'I'd like that, Mum.'

'Sorry, Bobby, would ya tell Belle we're goin' to head back. It's been a long day, I'm sure she'll understand . . .'

Bobby nodded. The tension between Ruby and Belle was palpable. He wasn't the sharpest tool in the box when it came to understanding the strong undercurrents of emotion that swept through his family, but this time it was unmissable. Cathy followed Ruby to the car, leaving Lloyd to call for his own driver to take him to central London. He had a meeting later with one of the crooks he'd met at the funeral and there was already the new promise of a deal to export coke into Eastern Europe.

Once they were both in the back of the vehicle, Ruby put a hand on Cathy's arm.

'Mum?' Cathy said.

'What's wrong, darlin'? I can tell you've got somethin' on your mind.'

Cathy smiled. The car moved off, making the short journey back to the mansion which had been transformed by a well-known interior designer.

'I know ya don't like comin' back to the house, but I've had it all changed. It's all brand new and I hope it'll bring a new start for us all,' her mum continued. 'So, tell me, what is goin' on?'

Cathy saw that she couldn't hoodwink her mum. Ruby's famous sixth sense was on good form, and she'd sussed out that something was up.

'Mum, I'm pregnant.'

There was no point beating about the bush.

'You're what, darlin'?' Ruby's face was almost as thunderstruck as Levi's had been.

'I've been seein' this guy. He's a traveller just like Great-Granny Ruby and we love each other.' Cathy hoped the edge of defensiveness in her voice hadn't been detected by her mum. Ruby gave no sign she'd heard it.

'Darlin', this is all so quick. I don't believe it. Are ya happy, really?'

Cathy nodded, though her heart was beating furiously. Why did she feel like she was lying to her mum? Why did she suddenly feel so alone? Levi would do the right thing and look after her and the child, wouldn't he?

'We're both really happy, so please be happy for us?' she said, looking pleadingly at Ruby. 'We've talked about getting married. Well, that was before I told him, but he just needs to set up his tarmac business and get some money coming in, then he's said we'll be married.'

'He has, has he?' Cathy's mum said, smiling now. 'So, where is he? Will he come over and meet the family? I want to meet the man who's givin' me my first grandchild.'

Cathy plastered a smile on her face in response. 'Oh, he's away doing stuff to set up the business but he should be back this weekend.'

'Does he know he's a very lucky fella?' Ruby said softly. 'And what's this lucky man's name?'

Cathy beamed now as she spoke of her boyfriend, letting her fears trickle away.

'He's called Levi and he lives on a traveller site in Basildon. He's gorgeous and funny, so funny. I love him, Mum,' she finished, gazing over at Ruby. As she spoke, the car came to a halt outside the main entrance of the mansion Ruby had been left by her friend and mentor Charlie Beaumont, a man who knew how to live lavishly. The front of the building had been painted a fresh white and the arched entrance now boasted two large earthenware pots each side of the large doorway containing small palm trees. A clematis had been trained over the archway, creating a beautiful exterior. Cathy looked up at the house.

'Mum, it looks so different, it's gorgeous.'

Ruby nodded, but she was still giving her daughter an unreadable look.

'Please be happy for me, Mum, it's all I've ever wanted,' Cathy said as the driver unloaded the baggage from the boot. Ruby took hold of Cathy's hand. It seemed so delicate and frail.

"Course I am, darlin', I'm thrilled for ya . . . both. When he's back this weekend, I'll get to meet him?'

Cathy noticed the pause before Ruby said 'both' and wondered what she meant. The car door was held open for her and so she stepped out. This was the place that her Uncle George had forced himself upon her – high on crack, sweating and swearing, pulling at her clothes and ripping down her jeans. This was the place she returned to in her night terrors. Cathy shivered but forced herself to step inside.

It was just as her mum had said. Nothing looked the same. The designer had worked magic and the place now exuded a classic country house style, though with a contemporary Shaker kitchen and the latest technology. She walked through the newly extended kitchen to the bifold glass door that stretched across the back of the house.

'It looks amazing, Mum,' she blinked.

'You 'aven't answered my question, darlin',' Ruby said, smiling at her daughter's genuine astonishment. She'd blown a fortune on the upgrade, trying to make all memories and associations of that awful night when Cathy was raped disappear under a sea of glass, marble and luxurious velvet.

'He'll be back on Saturday night,' Cathy said, whistling when she saw the new cinema room Ruby had commissioned. 'I'll tell him to come to The Locksmith and meet us there.'

'All right, darlin', though there's one thing I will insist upon: you and the baby 'ave to come and live with me 'ere. I know it has bad memories for ya but I want to keep an eye on ya. And now it's all done up nice, it won't be so bad, will it?'

Cathy looked back at her mum. She felt a surge of shame. She hadn't even asked how Ruby was feeling to be widowed again, to have gone through another robbery. She'd concentrated on her own news, when Ruby had been through so much. Perhaps Ruby needed her as well.

'Deal?'

'Deal, Mum.'

CHAPTER 14

A young man, barely into his twenties, walked into The Locksmith. No, he swaggered into the room, tipping his cap at Bobby, who was helping Cathy that night. He had jet black hair under his hat, and tanned skin from working outdoors, which highlighted his cheekbones, square jaw and sensuous lips. Oh, he was a looker, all right, and Ruby knew this had to be Levi as soon as she set eyes on him. She carried on watching him from her vantage point, seated at a bar stool at the far end of the bar so she could chat to Bobby and Cathy in between them serving punters. Ruby was dressed to kill with a black figure-hugging dress and sky-high heels. It was a glamorous joint now, after all. Her hair hung in a glossy sheen down her back and she wore a discreet chain of diamonds around her neck.

Cathy looked radiant. Bobby and Belle had been delighted at her news, and if they'd had any misgivings about the father, they'd remained silent. Ruby had watched Belle as she'd pulled Cathy into an embrace, her shock at the announcement quickly becoming delight, and felt envious again of the easy nature of her relationship with Cathy. There seemed to be none of the nagging resentments or expectations she shared with her daughter. Belle and Cathy loved each other dearly, that much was obvious, and even though Ruby knew she should be pleased her daughter had such caring people around her, she couldn't stop the jealousy rearing up each time she saw them together. *You're back now, Ruby*, she'd said to herself, *me and Cathy will be right again, it just needs a bit of time.*

Ruby watched Cathy now as she set eyes upon Levi, and something about her reaction made her shiver. Her daughter's face was alight with love as she rushed over to greet him. She saw Levi wink at her and pull her to him for a kiss, but she also saw him glance quickly around the room, sussing out who was there, during their embrace, which made her heart sink. There was something not right about him. Yes, he was cocky, but that wasn't it. Yes, he was clearly very charming and good-looking, and none of this was any different to her first impression of Archie, but something nagged at her. Though she'd had but a brief glance at the father of her grandchild, she sensed something insincere.

'I just 'ope I'm wrong,' she muttered under her breath. Cathy didn't appear to notice. She clung on to him, her head on his shoulder, as he came towards the bar. Ruby's gaze didn't falter as Levi's pals followed behind him, rowdy, clearly drunk, and laughing. The young man slung his arm casually around Cathy's shoulders, introducing her to some of the boys, clearly the leader of the pack. *He fancies himself, does this one*, Ruby thought, sipping her chilled glass of Chardonnay.

Bobby called his niece back to the bar to help out with serving, and Ruby saw that her daughter's eyes never left the handsome figure, even as she pulled pints of expensive lager and uncorked champagne bottles.

'So, it's him who we 'ave to welcome into the family, is it?' Bobby grimaced as he came to stand where Ruby was sitting, polishing a champagne glass with a cloth.

'It is, Bobby, and I don't like it one bit,' replied Ruby slowly.

'He's been hangin' around Cathy for ages. Been in the bar most nights, so I gather,' her brother continued. Ruby nodded, looking over her shoulder at the man who'd stolen her daughter's heart. At that moment, Levi glanced round. He had an unlit hand-rolled cigarette between his teeth and he was grinning. He checked out Ruby watching him before flitting his gaze back to his mates.

Ruby didn't bother trying to introduce herself. He'd find out soon enough who she was. Cathy, who had come back round to stand with him like a magnet drawn to its opposing pole, brushed her hair back and giggled. She was in love – Ruby could see that a mile off. Did Levi feel the same way, though? He seemed to be making a good show of adoring her, but why then did his eyes wander off to other women in the bar? She'd caught him doing it a couple of times, sliding his gaze to an attractive brunette sitting at a different table with another young woman. *This one needs watchin'*, Ruby thought, though she knew she was probably being a harsh judge of character because it was her daughter – and grandchild – at stake. She hadn't even met the man yet. Perhaps it was time to change that. Ruby stood up and smoothed down her dress. At that exact moment, he looked round at her again. Was he eyeing her up? She walked up to him and held out her hand to shake. He turned to her, a sly smile spreading on his face.

'And who do we have here, den?' he said, confidently. So sure of being irresistible to women.

'We 'ave Cathy's mother 'ere. I wanted to say 'ello, Levi,' Ruby's face was impassive. Her hand remained steady. Levi almost choked on his ciggie. Cathy clearly hadn't warned him that she was there that evening. He took her hand and shook it, dropping it as if she was scorching hot.

'Well now, Cathy didn't tell me she had a mother like . . . like . . .'

'Like me? She does, Levi, and her mother would like to meet ya properly. Come and sit with me,' she beckoned. Levi looked stunned momentarily, then quickly hid it, feigning a cheeky smile, his eyes flashing as he strode to where she'd been sitting. If he knew she'd set him up for that one, he didn't let on.

Had he been flirting with her? Ruby knew she had to knock that on the head and show the boy the right order of things. She waved to Bobby. 'Bring Levi a drink, he looks like he needs one.' Ruby leaned towards the young man, could smell the old tobacco smoke on his breath.

'You're the man responsible for my grandchild,' she said, her tone colder. She crossed her legs, picked up her drink and took a sip.

'Well, so Cathy says . . .' Levi shrugged, slugging back the whisky Bobby had placed in front of him.

'And if my daughter tells ya she's the mother of your child, then that child is most definitely yours. My daughter is one of life's innocents, Levi. She don't 'ave a bad bone in her body. We're so very unlike each other, if ya get my drift.' Ruby paused. 'D'ya understand me?' She stared straight into the liquid brown eyes that her daughter found irresistible. There was something behind them, something she felt wary of. She had the feeling this man was always looking out for the next opportunity. It was hard to tell with such a short acquaintance, but what was becoming clear already was that this man was not someone she felt she could trust. Not at all. This felt like the old way her instincts had worked. Something had gone awry at first with Vladimir – perhaps because of her grief, and the sense of exhaustion around it, the need to push on and keep business running. But here, now, she wasn't doubting herself that she could sense something off. But she still needed to give him the benefit of the doubt, for her daughter's sake.

Let's see how he acquits himself at a family dinner.

'I hear ye've got Romany blood, Mrs . . . er, what do I call ye now? I know ye've recently been made a widow.

Sorry for your loss,' Levi murmured, not sounding sorry at all. He was looking Ruby up and down, taking in the glittering necklace, her Louis Vuitton bag, the Cartier watch on her slender wrist.

'You can call me Ruby, and I thank ya for yer condolences. Yes, my granny was a traveller. Some said she had the sight, and that I inherited it as well. It means we know things, Levi. We know people even if we've just met 'em,' she said lightly, giving him a trace of a smile.

'She died giving birth to my dad because she wouldn't go to an 'ospital. Cathy will 'ave the very best of everythin'. She'll 'ave that baby in the best clinic with the best nurses, I will make sure of it. She's my jewel, Levi, and if anythin' or anyone ever hurts that jewel in any way, I can't say what I'd do.' Ruby put down her drink and looked over at Bobby, who stared back at her. He knew what she was doing: protecting Cathy, making sure everyone knew where they stood. Only Ruby had the authority, the force of personality, to square up to this young Romeo. Bobby was too soft to do it. He'd believe everything anyone said and then buy them a drink. And Alfie and Lloyd would go in too heavy. So it had to be her. Levi smiled in response, but his eyes were hard.

'Cathy is a jewel to be sure. She's *my* jewel, and she's havin' *my* baby, so she says, and so you say now, so we'll all be one big happy family, so we will.' He drained the last of his shot. 'I'll be thankin' ye, Ruby, for the chat and the drink. I'll get back to my mates now, if ye don't mind, but it's been a pleasure makin' your acquaintance.' Levi began to move away but Ruby shot out a hand and held onto his arm so he was forced to turn back to her, his eyes refusing to meet hers.

'Come for dinner. Meet the rest of the family. The men in particular are all dyin' to meet ya.' She smiled at him, though her eyes were cold too. Levi nodded, and gently peeled her hand from his arm. Now he would know they were watching him, and that if he took one step out of place, he'd find himself in trouble. What struck Ruby, though, was the fact he didn't seem to care. He doffed his cap at her in an exaggerated way, kissed her hand, and sauntered off back to his pals with that grin plastered on his face as if he'd just met the queen rather than a woman who could make him disappear in a heartbeat. Ruby finished her drink and motioned to Cathy that she was heading home.

'An early night and a bath will do me the world of good,' she said, reaching for her bag.

'What did you think of Levi?' Cathy said, her face beaming with happiness. For a second, Ruby wondered how on earth she and Archie had made such an unworldly, tender girl. It seemed almost unbelievable, considering the world she'd been brought up in. But she had been sheltered from it. *Perhaps too much*, thought Ruby as she pondered how to answer.

'He's a very handsome man, and I'm lookin' forward to knowin' more about him,' she replied eventually. 'Listen,

I'll see ya later and we'll talk more. Levi will come to ours for a meal. We can get to know him properly then.'

As Ruby walked out, Levi caught her eye and watched her as she went. He still grinned. She felt a shiver down her back as she stepped into her Bentley. The car moved away and she looked out of the window, seeing none of the streetlights nor passers-by, her head sorting through the events of the evening. Ruby had that strange, undefinable intuitive sense, that thud of knowledge she couldn't explain. She knew in her gut that Levi was bad for Cathy and bad for the baby. If what people said was true, that her gran had the sight, then she knew she had it too. It didn't come always but when it did arrive, she couldn't ignore it. Mulling it over, Ruby saw his face, wolfish in the low lighting, his arm around the daughter she loved with a primal force.

You might swagger now, Levi, but you'd be a fool to mess with my family, Ruby thought as the car travelled through the night.

CHAPTER 15

'Mum, I've said I'll stay at Bobby and Belle's tonight as they want to go up to the West End with me tomorrow,' Cathy panted as she grabbed a piece of toast from her mum's plate on her way through to the front door. She was late for work again. 'They're going to help me choose some bits for the nursery. Is that OK?'

Even though she was only around three months gone, she was already struggling to sleep each night. She would lie in bed, thinking of the baby and Levi, trying not to wonder where he was each night, trying not to wonder why she couldn't be with him, when she loved him so much. After a few hours of tossing and turning, she'd fall into an exhausted doze and then sleep through her alarm clock. The situation had been made worse by the fact that Bobby had promoted her to bar manager, which meant she started earlier in the day.

'Don't rush, darlin', you'll do yerself an injury. Think of the baby, ya need to be nice and calm,' Ruby called from the kitchen.

The Game

'I'm fine, Mum, don't fuss!' Cathy yelled as she picked up her bag and keys to the new Mini Cooper her mum had bought her upon her return from Spain. Ruby had seen straight away that Cathy needed her independence, and it also meant it wasn't always Bobby or Belle driving her around.

'Make sure ya eat somethin' proper when you're at the bar. It ain't just you now darlin', you've got to keep ya strength up.' Ruby's words were lost as Cathy dashed out, banging the front door shut behind her, knowing Ruby would be tutting at her from inside. She grinned as she turned the key in the ignition. It felt good to have a taste of freedom, to come and go as she pleased. Staying at her mum's seemed to be working out well so far, yet in her heart, Cathy felt her home would always be with Bobby and Belle. It had been where she'd felt safe after George's attack, then later after Archie's brutal murder. This mansion, though originally her home, was more of a show house now, and paint and new furnishings couldn't completely cover the memories of that dreadful night. No, she had been happy at her aunt and uncle's, in a house that was never gleaming and immaculately tidy like Ruby's. It was cosier, with decorative shawls and incense everywhere, books piled on tables, paintbrushes and paints stacked here and there. Even though it was cluttered, it felt like a haven from the world her mum inhabited, and any excuse she got, she still stayed with them.

*

Cathy was so busy that the day passed quickly. She was thrilled when she caught sight of Levi's cap as he walked into The Locksmith.

'Levi!' she blushed. He always made her feel a little nervous.

'Baby, it's good to see ye,' he winked, sauntering up to where she was taking a stock check behind the bar. He pushed back his cap, pulled her to him by the waist and gave her a long, lingering kiss.

'Levi!' She pushed him off though she felt weak at the knees every time he embraced her. 'You can't do that here, someone might see.'

'Who'd be lookin' at us, eh? Not your uncle. If he starts lookin' at us while we're gettin' it on, then he's the one wid a problem.'

'Levi,' Cathy hissed now, her voice low. 'Bobby'll be here any minute. He won't like hearing you say something like that. Stop now.' But he didn't stop – and Cathy, after a slight hesitation, didn't either. She found she had little or no defences against his amorous advances.

'Ahem,' came Bobby's voice from behind them. 'I see you're visitin' Cathy again, Levi,' Bobby said, without smiling. 'She's got a lot of work to do, and I'd be grateful if ya didn't distract her.' For a brief moment, Cathy caught sight of the boy who'd grown up surrounded by crooks in Star Lane, and saw how he'd survived. Bobby, who looked older than his years because of his time spent in prison, had squared up to Levi, his bulky frame looking almost menacing. Cathy only ever saw the soft side of Bobby, and it was a surprise to see him as he was: a toughened man with a criminal past. Levi turned around. Eyeing up Bobby, he smirked, touched the front of his cap then turned back to Cathy and kissed her slowly, prolonging the moment. Then he stepped past Bobby and said, lightly, 'I'll be seein' ye, baby. I've got some business to do tonight. Tomorrow, I'll be in wid the lads for sure.' He walked past Bobby.

'Is that your tarmac company, Levi? When's that goin' to be up and runnin' so ya can support yer baby, eh?'

'Bobby! Don't push him. He's sorting it, he's promised me,' Cathy began to say, but Levi just laughed, saluted at Bobby and said, 'You heard her, it'll be sorted.'

Once he'd left, Cathy realised she was furious at her uncle.

'How could you say that to him? That's the man I love, the father of my child. If he says he'll sort things, then I believe him.' She bit her lip, fighting back tears. Bobby instantly dropped his hard-man demeanour.

'Sorry, darlin'. I was just stickin' up for ya. I'll leave him be next time, I promise.'

He seemed distraught by Cathy's distress.

'It's OK,' she replied, turning her back on him. 'We've got the stock check to do. Let's just get back to work.'

Bobby worked beside her all afternoon. That night, the bar wasn't busy and he decided to leave early to check over the accounts at home. Cathy had said very little since Levi had left. She knew Bobby was looking out for her, but she hated how interfering her family could be at times. What she hadn't yet admitted to herself was that Bobby was only saying what she'd wanted to ask her boyfriend. When would Levi get his business set up? When would they get married? If she wasn't allowed to visit his traveller site, then how on earth would they ever live together with their child? Her thoughts ran wild as she worked, and it was a relief to shut the place just after 11 p.m. and head to her aunt and uncle's place. She knew they always waited up for her, so she'd have their company – and probably a hot dinner – before heading to bed. She'd managed to convince herself that all would be well once the baby came. She hoped the minute Levi set eyes on his son or daughter, he'd be smitten and they'd become a proper family. With that on her mind, she hummed to herself as she drove back to Chigwell. Pulling up in the driveway, she saw the lounge lights were on behind the curtains.

'It's just me,' she called as she turned the key in the lock.

Once inside, the first thing that struck her was the sound of raised voices from the kitchen at the back of the house. So, they hadn't seen her car lights or heard the engine as she'd arrived. Cathy stepped towards the door to announce she was there.

'It's me, Cathy. Aunt Belle? Uncle Bobby?'

Their voices were louder. It was a humdinger of an argument. Cathy felt torn. Should she try to creep upstairs and pretend she hadn't heard them, or should she carry on trying to alert them to her presence? The decision was taken out of her hands.

Clear as anything, Belle's voice thundered at Bobby.

'I don't believe Ruby wasn't involved in Vladimir's death. She's killed before, why not now?'

Cathy froze where she stood, with one hand poised to grip the door handle. She'd been about to open it, to go inside and show them she'd arrived. Her heart pounded in her chest, blood rushed to her ears, and her stomach turned queasy as she stood stock still, waiting for what came next. She'd never heard Belle shout before. Cathy was unable to move away. She heard every word.

'Of course, she bloody didn't!' Bobby yelled back, defending his sister. 'Yes, she's killed before, but that was necessity. She had to do it!'

Cathy tried to swallow but found her mouth too dry. She wanted to leave. She wanted to flee in case her beloved aunt and uncle thought she was spying on them. But she couldn't move an inch. Belle snorted loudly, a bitter laugh filling the room.

'Necessary? That woman does nothing unless she gets something from it. She's a killer, a monster, and now she's killed off Vladimir and you're too blind to see it.'

'You're overreactin', Belle. She loved Vladimir, why would she kill him?' Bobby sounded calmer now, but his voice was still loud enough for Cathy to make out each word.

'Nothing stops your little sister, nothing. She's ruthless. She loved your brother George but she killed him!' Belle screamed. Cathy leaned hard on the door handle and yanked the door open.

'What are you saying? Mum killed my uncle? Tell me the truth!' Cathy saw that at the moment she'd interrupted them, Bobby was gripping Belle's wrists as his wife had been screaming furiously at him. His face was a picture of concern, and then horror, as he realised they'd been overheard. Belle flopped back, seemingly spent from the fury she'd unleashed. She looked over at Cathy with her face twisted, then she seemed to go calm.

'You heard everything?'

Cathy nodded, looking wildly between her uncle and her aunt.

'I heard everything, and now I want answers,' she said, her voice trembling: a mixture of rage and disbelief.

'Ruby, your mum, shot George. She killed him in the office that used to be in the garden before they bulldozed it to hide the evidence,' Belle said bitterly. Bobby sank down into a chair and put his hands over his head.

'Don't say any more, Belle, you've said enough.'

'She needs to know. I'm glad she's finding out who her mother really is.' Belle turned back to her niece. 'The night George attacked you, your dad and Alfie found him and dragged him back to the house. He'd been taking more drugs; crack cocaine, I think. He must've been in a terrible state. They took him into the office, and all I know is that, in that office, your mum took her gun out from her handbag and she shot him in the head. They disposed of his body, then they lied to you; we've all been lying to you. George was never in America. They'd never have let him walk free because in Ruby's world it's the law of the jungle. No one gets out alive . . .'

Bobby began to moan.

'Stop it, Belle. Stop!'

Cathy was stunned. In her heart, she realised she'd known the truth all along. Suddenly it all made sense. Being fobbed off by her mum each time she'd asked her to find George and bring him home. The evasive answers. The strange atmosphere every time George's name was mentioned. How foolish she'd been, how naive. All along, the people she most trusted had been lying to her, over and over again.

Suddenly, Cathy registered the fact her uncle was dead, and had died at her mother's hands. She doubled over in pain, and started to scream and scream.

'I loved him, I told her I would've forgiven him. I told her!'

Belle saw the impact the revelation had on Cathy and stepped towards her, crushed by her reaction. Cathy backed out of the room, shaking her head, tears streaming down her face, though her cries had stopped.

'You lied to me, you all lied to me. He was never in America. You told me he was, you all kept telling me he was travelling when you all knew . . .'

'Cathy, love . . .' Bobby moved towards her, following her into the living room, but she shook her head again.

'Get away from me, both of you. Don't come near me ever again.' Her distress was making her pant. 'You have blood on your hands, all of you. I'll never trust any of you again.'

'Look what you've done, Belle, look what you've done,' Bobby cried angrily to his wife, who was deathly pale in the yellow overhead light. Cathy's aunt said nothing. Tears ran from her eyes as she stared back at the niece she loved. Any rage she had felt had gone now, replaced by remorse. Cathy looked between them. She felt an urge to hurt them as deeply as they'd hurt her.

'I don't know who any of you are. You're not my family any more. I'm finished with you all,' she said slowly, relishing the pain she could see she was causing them.

Bobby looked up, his face a picture of despair.

'But we love ya, Cathy.'

Cathy ignored him. She turned slowly, picked up her shoulder bag, and strode towards the front door without another word, leaving Bobby and Belle staring after her.

Cathy knew they'd pick up the phone the minute she left to call her mum. She slammed her car into first gear, her tyres screeching as she drove off. She had no idea where she would go or what she would do, but she knew one thing: her life with her family was over. Her family was dead to her, as dead as George was. She choked back tears as she drove, knowing her old life was finished.

'Don't worry, little one, I'll take care of you. We're finished with them all,' she murmured, focusing on the child in her womb, praying that she'd find the strength to go on.

CHAPTER 16

Cathy was almost surprised to find herself outside her mother's mansion. She stopped the car, wiped her tear-stained face with the back of her hand, and sat for a moment, breathing heavily, contemplating what to do next. It was pitch black except for the security lights that switched on the minute her car drew into the long drive-way. They cast a ghostly blue over the house and gardens, making sinister shadows of the trees and plants. There was a single light on downstairs. Cathy knew that her mum would be awake as Bobby would've called Ruby the minute she left. How could she face the woman who had killed her own brother? How could she step foot inside the home of a killer who happened to be her own mother?

Cathy shivered despite the warm summer night. She knew her mum would try to talk her round. But the thought of even seeing Ruby sickened the young woman. She stayed inside her car, listening to the low whirr of the engine. She placed her hands on her stomach; the small bump was warm against her hands. The last thing in the world she wanted to do was confront Ruby, but there was no other way. Cathy had to collect her things and get the hell out of this life, this disgusting lawless world where people could kill without censure, where murder was part of its very fabric. Anger rose as bile to the back of her throat. She had to face her. She had to say what she needed to say, and then go. Cathy hadn't called Levi yet, but she'd texted him.

Call me. Urgent. Love you baby XXX.

When the 'message sent' sign had appeared, she'd drawn in a long breath. For the sake of their baby, she had to do this. Cathy slammed the car door shut, liking the sound – it echoed her fury. The front door was already opening as Ruby must've heard her arrival and seen the security lights spring on. She stormed in, almost pushing past the woman whose face was white and shocked. Ruby stepped towards her daughter, but Cathy, standing in the large atrium surrounded by plants and beautiful paintings, put out a hand. So much beauty. So much sheer ugliness. All of it meant nothing to her any more.

'Don't come near me. I know what you did. I know everything, and I can see that Bobby's told you,' she spat.

'He was worried about ya, darlin', I'm worried about ya,' began Ruby, who wore a long silk dressing gown over her negligee, but Cathy interrupted her with a laugh.

'You're worried about me? That's a joke, Mum. A really, really shitty joke.'

Cathy couldn't remember the last time she'd sworn at anyone; it wasn't in her nature. But these were different times; something in Cathy had broken free of her mum's grip, and it felt like there were no rules any more. The freedom born of her anger made her giddy and afraid all at once.

'Tell me what Belle said,' Ruby commanded, her voice low. It was the kind of voice her mum used to elicit respect from her henchmen. Well, she was used to hearing her mum's orders. This time, Cathy's rage gave her the strength to ignore her, to turn around and march upstairs instead.

'I'm collecting my things and I'm going. I won't ever be back.'

Cathy banged open her bedroom door, seeing all her usual clutter, her belongings sprawled across the room. She reached for a suitcase at the back of her wardrobe and started shoving clothes and shoes into it furiously. Ruby had followed her up the stairs. She stood in the doorway.

'Cathy, please, don't do this. You 'ave to listen to me. What I did, I did for love of George . . .' Ruby was pleading now. She'd never heard that before.

'For love? Don't make me laugh, Mum. You don't know what love is. You don't know the meaning of the word. Everything you've ever done was for you and you alone. I hate you. Don't you understand? I never want to see you again.'

Cathy turned to Ruby and saw the effect her words were having. Tears slid down her mother's face. She'd

only ever seen Ruby cry when she'd held her dying husband, Cathy's dad, in her arms.

'You're to blame for everything. If you weren't so power-
hungry, so obsessed with your business, Dad would be
alive today, and so would George.'

Ruby's face changed. She bit back. 'That's not true!
Your father was up to his neck in crime when I met him.
We were a team. The business was ours, and we both
wanted to make it big. Everythin' we did was to protect
our family, and make us untouchable. Everythin'!' Ruby
sounded outraged. How did she have the nerve?

'Untouchable? So, how did that work out, Mum?' Cathy
sneered, pulling her underwear from a drawer, throwing
in make-up and books, her credit cards and jewellery. She
reached up for the baby supplies that Ruby had already
bought and stashed away.

'No! Don't take those, ya 'ave to believe me. Cathy, yer
dad and Alfie would've tortured him for what he did to ya.
It's how it works in our world. We deal with things our
own way, and it would've been terrible for George, terrible,'
Ruby's voice cracked. 'The only way I could end it was to kill
him myself, quickly and without him knowin'. He didn't
feel nuthin'. It was the kindest death. Please, Cathy, listen
to me!' Ruby beseeched her daughter.

Cathy looked round at her, knowing the sight of her
packing nappies and tiny babygros had made Ruby realise
she meant what she said: she'd never be back, and Ruby
would never know her grandchild. For a moment, the two

women stood and stared at each other, Ruby with eyes that begged her daughter to stay, Cathy with a face that showed pure revulsion. Cathy took a deep breath, knowing that what she was about to say would hurt her mum deeply. It would break their family for good. For a second, she teetered on the edge of a chasm, knowing she wasn't sure who she really was without her family – her mum, Lloyd, Alfie, Bobby and Belle – knowing that she would wreak damage it was impossible to repair. Her voice was calm when at last she spoke.

'I'll never speak to any of you ever again. From now on, I don't have a family. You're not my mother and I don't want anything to do with you. You're a monster, Mum. Say goodbye to your grandchild, because you won't ever see them. I won't ever be back. And when my child is older, I'll explain to them how I had to leave you all behind because to stay would've been impossible. I'll teach them to trust no one except me and their father.'

Ruby's face fell even further. She gripped the doorway for support. Cathy thought she might fall, but Ruby stayed standing, her eyes filled with tears.

'All right, Cathy, all right. Go, if you must, but know that I love you and I love your baby more than you'll ever know. I've lied to you, and I'm sorry. I'm so sorry, darlin'.'

For a moment, Cathy felt an intense desire to run into her mum's arms, for Ruby to stroke her hair and soothe her, telling her it was all OK. But it wasn't OK, it would never be OK again.

'Goodbye, Mum,' Cathy finished, picking up the suitcase.

Ruby resisted the urge to help her daughter carry it, and instead watched as Cathy bumped the heavy case down the stairs and out across the drive and into her car.

Cathy put the key in the ignition, as her mother got in her final words, 'I never meant to hurt ya.' Cathy put the car in reverse and drove out of the driveway and away from her mother, her family and her security, and into an unknown world where she'd have to look after herself. As she drove down the street, she glanced in her mirror and caught sight of something she'd never forget: Ruby, crumpled to the ground, her sobs making her body shake. Cathy almost turned back, almost. Instead, she squealed away, not knowing where she was going, or what she would do, but knowing she had to leave before she, too, crumbled. She had to be strong. She had to get away before her anger turned to sadness, in case she gave in.

After a few minutes, she started to shake violently, the shock of her departure sinking in. She pulled over at the roadside and leaned her head on the cool leather of the steering wheel. Where could she go? Who was she now that she wasn't her mother's daughter? With trembling hands, she picked up her phone and dialled Levi's number. It was almost 1 a.m., and though it was late, she knew he kept strange hours and might be hanging out with his mates or making late-night business deals. It rang and rang. When he didn't pick up, she ended the call and tried again. Still no answer. With a heavy heart, she knew she was utterly alone. For the first time in her life, she had no one to turn to and nowhere to go. The realisation was like a great void opening up in her mind, a place of darkness that scared her.

All her life she'd been surrounded by family, and now she'd discovered it was her family she should fear and hate the most. Her Uncle George was dead and the thought of him being shot played over and over in her mind. Grief swelled and crashed through her with oceanic force. What a trusting idiot she'd been to believe her mum's lies. For years, Ruby had fobbed her off, told her he'd gone to America and wasn't welcome back, and he'd been dead all along. She felt chilled to the bone though it was a warm August night.

Even Belle had lied to her. In a way this hurt more. Belle had been Cathy's confidante, her escape from the world her mum lived in. Her aunt had been more than her uncle's wife, she'd been a mother figure. Belle had been there for her in practical, normal ways, helping her through the months after being raped, talking with her on the phone every night and taking her in after Archie was killed. With Bobby and Belle, she'd found comfort and safety, and now even that was gone. The loss felt like a crater beneath her feet, a wound that would never heal.

She felt like she was falling into a deep pit and had no idea how to dig herself out. It was her aunt she had turned to when George disappeared. It was Belle's betrayal that felt like the noose around her neck. The thought of never being hugged or comforted by her ever again felt like a death in itself. And had she been right? Had her mother killed Vladimir as well as Uncle George? Was Ruby so mired in the criminal world that she'd lost any humanity, any human feeling? Was her mum just a hardened gangster now, a woman so cold and ruthless she'd kill anyone who got in her way, even her new husband? And how many other bodies were there along Ruby's path? How many more had she killed in cold blood? Cathy had no answers as she sat in the darkness, the car's internal lights having switched off, leaving her alone in the night, her thoughts racing and nausea rising in her belly.

All she had was the father of her child. She tried not to think about where he was or what he might be doing, as it made her more anxious. *He'll be sleeping*, she thought, *fast asleep, with no idea of what I've been through. But he'll take care of me, I know he will.* With that thought in her head, Cathy pushed the car seat back and tried to curl up on her side. She'd have to spend the night in the car. She didn't want to find a hotel at this late hour and have to explain why she needed a room, and anyway, she had no idea of knowing who was in her mother's pay and who wasn't. There was nothing else to do but wait for Levi to return her calls.

Cathy spent the next few hours trying to sleep, confused, grieving and filled with a sense of horror that wouldn't abate. She held her stomach, and took comfort from the new life growing within her, yet she had never felt so bleak. She had lost everything.

CHAPTER 17

'Lloyd, get yer best men onto it. I want Cathy followed night and day. I don't want her to do nuthin' or say nuthin' that we don't know about.'

Within minutes of Cathy's departure, Ruby, who had sunk to the ground in shock and despair as she saw her beloved daughter walk out of her life, had pulled her mobile from her bag, fumbling as the shock set in. The first person she called was Lloyd, who by now knew everything from Bobby.

'Ruby, ya sound dreadful. Look, darlin', I'll come over. Ya can't be left alone like this,' he said.

'Just 'ave her followed, that's all I need now, Lloyd. She's carryin' my grandchild, *our* grandchild, the last link to Archie. I want to know where she is, what she's doin', if she's eatin' – everythin'.'

Ruby started to cry again now. The worst had happened. Cathy had discovered her secret, and their relationship was broken, perhaps for ever.

'Ruby, please, ya need someone wiv ya,' Lloyd pleaded. He couldn't see her shake her head.

'No, just do what I ask of ya. Cathy doesn't realise that none of us is ever safe. Just because we ain't in Spain no longer, don't mean that anyone with a grudge, anyone who might suspect what really 'appened to Vladimir, could come over and retaliate; take their revenge on my daughter. She needs protection. She's never lived alone before, and I can't see how she thinks that Levi will step up for her. She's on her own. She'll be frightened and distressed so I want her watched. Can ya do that for me?' Ruby wiped her tear-stained face.

"Course I can, Rube. I'll find her somewhere to live, a flat with security somewhere decent. I'll call her and sort everythin'. She'll talk to me, at least I hope she will.'

'Just make sure she's safe,' Ruby finished, ending the call, the horror of the evening washing over her once more. The tears came again, and this time she didn't try to stop them. Her life, her business, it all meant nothing without Cathy. Ruby sank down to the floor, barely noticing the plush carpet beneath her. She lay there, sobbing, her whole body heaving with the pain of the revelation.

After some time had passed, she pulled herself up and walked to the kitchen, and flicked on the kettle. She had to stay calm. She couldn't give in to her emotions. Surely she'd learned that by now? Cathy would be on their radar. That, at least, gave her hope. She wouldn't lose her completely, and she would make sure that her daughter and grandchild were watched, for their own safety. As for Bobby and Belle, well, she'd always known it was a risk trusting them to keep her secret. Both were too soft-hearted, too 'normal' for this game, and Belle in particular had always struggled with it. She'd threatened to tell Cathy many times, but Ruby had always managed to silence her. If Belle had deliberately told Cathy, then the situation might be different. Ruby would be on the warpath. But she hadn't. It was just bad luck that Cathy overheard them rowing. There was nothing Ruby could do about that, though she was still angry at Belle for forcing the issue with Bobby.

When Bobby had rung his sister that night, Ruby had thought it was them who needed help. She'd picked up her phone, half asleep.

'You OK, darlin'?' she said, leaning over to check the time, which was just past midnight.

'She knows,' Bobby said, his voice strangled in his throat. 'She knows, Rube, about George's death, and that isn't all . . .'

Ruby sat up immediately in her bed.

'Who knows? What are ya on about? What's goin' on?'

'Cathy knows. She knows everythin'. Belle and me were arguin' and she walked in. We didn't hear her. I'm sorry, I'm so sorry.' Bobby's voice trailed off as he wept openly.

For a moment Ruby was too shocked to answer. Her heart raced and her mouth felt dry.

'What else? Ya said there was somethin' else? What could she possibly know that's worse than that?' Ruby shot back at him, angry now.

'Oh God, sis, I'm sorry, ya know what Belle's like. She suspects everythin'. She'd got it into her head that you killed Vladimir, and that's what the row was about. I'm sorry. She's bang out of order.'

Ruby paused. She couldn't believe what she was about to say. It was like the dam had burst, and all her secrets were flowing out, enough to engulf them all.

'She's right, Bobby,' Ruby said quietly, 'I did kill Vladimir.'

Bobby stopped crying as her words hit home. He'd been stunned into silence, so Ruby continued.

'I set him up. He was behind the robbery in which Archie was killed so I did the same to him. I married him so that I would have the perfect disguise as his lovin' wife, and also so we wouldn't lose his empire once he was dead. Belle was right. I had him murdered and I don't regret it at all.'

'Christ, Rube . . .' Before he could finish his sentence, Ruby heard Belle's voice in the background. 'What? What is it, Bobby?'

'Belle, just leave it,' Bobby snapped at his wife. 'Listen, sis. My guess is she's comin' over to yours now. She's in bits. Try and stop her leavin'; try and stop it, Rube. You 'ave to make good the damage done. I don't care what ya did to Vladimir, but make it OK wiv Cathy, that's all that matters.'

With that, Bobby rang off, no doubt to tell his wife that her instincts were correct, that everything she suspected about Ruby was true. Ruby didn't care. She pulled on her dressing gown and ran down the stairs, hearing the crunch of tyres on the gravel as she opened the front door.

Ruby tried not to think of the next few moments – now, as she made her coffee – the minutes that had ripped apart her family: watching Cathy pack, seeing the look of pure anguish on her daughter's face. It was something Ruby would never forget – along with the fact it was her who'd caused it. The sight of Cathy driving away had left a hole in her heart so vast, she could hardly breathe. Yet, despite the night's events, deep down she knew she had to keep going. Life went on, especially when there was a criminal empire at stake, no matter how bad things were. She couldn't slack off. She couldn't retreat into the darkness of her feelings. Any lapse might be the death of them all. One mistake, and she knew her empire could collapse. She had to pull herself together, try to put Cathy to the back of her mind, now that she knew she was being watched over, and carry on. In a few hours, Ruby and Lloyd had important business to see to, and she had to look the part. She couldn't show any weakness, any tiredness or emotion. It was 2 a.m. by the time she headed back up to her bedroom, knowing she wouldn't sleep another wink. She carried her coffee and a magazine, hoping to distract herself during the long hours until daylight.

*

'Rube, I didn't think ya would come, after everythin' that's 'appened?' Lloyd was surprised to receive his daughter-in-law's call. It was just past 7 a.m. and Ruby had managed to doze off for a couple of hours.

'Of course I'm comin', Lloyd. This is important. I need to see if this warehouse is big enough for the doublin' of supply we're experiencin'.'

'I know, Rube, but are ya up to it?' Lloyd's voice was all concern. He was continually surprised at how Ruby could change her skin: heartbroken mother one minute, ruthless businesswoman the next.

'I'm fine, Lloyd,' Ruby said firmly, shutting down his question and stifling a yawn. 'We 'ave to do this, and ya know me, I always like to see the place and the people guardin' it in person.'

'All right. I'll pick ya up in an hour and we'll head down there,' Lloyd said, ringing off.

Ruby sat on her bed. The memory of the first ever job she and Bobby did together suddenly returned. She'd insisted on casing the joint, just as she was doing now. Back then, when they lived in Star Lane in Canning Town, she did it because she didn't trust that oily weasel Freddie Harris who was stealing the heist from under Charlie Beaumont's nose. Ruby had taken charge of the deal, agreed that Bobby would disarm the security system at the site of the robbery and break open the safe for Freddie. Ruby remembered the moment when she agreed to the job; that new, intoxicating feeling of power. Everything was at stake: their family, their home, their lives – yet Ruby, even then, had realised she was born for this. It had been the start of everything.

She took their baby brother, still in his pram, down to the wharfs of Milwall Docks, to check out the security system and the exit routes. Flanked by the River Thames, she looked up at the wharf, huge cranes overhead and chimneys spewing out thick smoke, and felt undaunted. She agreed they'd do the job. A few days later, Bobby dressed all in black, with gloves and a balaclava and his 'twirls' as he later called them, and set out to begin their life in the underworld, the first step down a difficult and dangerous path.

Even as she'd now survived the worse night of her life so far, Ruby knew she'd never have chosen different. This work, these risks, were in her blood, as much a part of her as her pounding heart and the blood in her veins. She dressed carefully, pulling on her sunglasses, this time to hide her swollen eyes.

When Lloyd's Bentley drew up, she stepped inside, her cream-coloured trouser suit setting off her black shining hair. She thought again of that young woman wearing clothes from Rathbone Market pretending to be a normal young mum as she eyed up the security systems and plotted Bobby's escape routes. Her life was a far cry from that these days. She smoothed down her Stella McCartney jacket, pushed her hair back from her face, feeling its thick, glossy weight, and looked down at her Chanel clutch bag, knowing that what she was wearing cost more than she would've made in years as an office girl. Lloyd nodded to her as if reading her thoughts.

'Let's go,' he said to the driver.

Arriving at the warehouse on the south bank of the river, they were met by the owner, a man in his fifties, wearing a dark T-shirt, jacket and expensive jeans. He showed them round and they talked business as they went. Lloyd looked over at Ruby, trusting her instincts.

'We'll take it,' she said, 'for the right price.'

'Of course, let's talk money. I can move everythin' out by tomorrow and the place will be yours. I won't ask questions. I don't want to know what you want it for, but I want money for six months' rent up front.'

Ruby nodded. The place wasn't damp. It was hidden away from the main roads inside one of the railway arches but there were several exits out through smaller roads. There was enough space to unload a lorry, and, best of all, there were no questions being asked.

'Agreed,' said Ruby, 'and we'll 'ave our men 'ere from midnight tonight. We'll bring the money then.'

'Thank you for your time. Good to strike a deal,' Lloyd murmured to the man, shaking his rough hand. Ruby threw him a smile, withdrawing to the car for the journey back to Chigwell.

'Good work, Rube. It's perfect for the deliveries. We can get the first truck there tonight, and the London boys'll 'ave somethin' to sell. The demand for coke is sky high right now,' Lloyd said in the back of the car.

'And the price,' grinned Ruby. 'And did ya get on top of the other matter, watchin' Cathy?'

'I'm on it but we've had a small problem . . .'

'What? You 'aven't lost her, 'ave ya?' Ruby jumped onto Lloyd's words.

'We 'ave to find her first. She didn't go to the traveller site. I've got men out there casin' it. She didn't go to a hotel as I've had someone checkin' them all across London and Essex. I've got a bent copper checkin' the police files to see if she's been nicked anywhere, and one of my guys is ringin' all the hospitals. My guess is she spent the night in the car and is tryin' to get hold of that bastard Levi.'

Ruby took off her shades, revealing her panicked expression.

'Don't worry, Rube. She won't 'ave gone far. I've held off callin' her as she was so angry. She might need to hear a familiar voice by now so I'll try her number. I will find her.'

Ruby nodded.

'And get your men to trail Levi as well. I don't trust him. My gut tells me he needs watchin'.'

The rest of the drive back was tense. Ruby couldn't relax, knowing they'd lost Cathy, even temporarily. Lloyd made several calls on his phone but no one had seen her.

'Call her now,' Ruby said as they pulled into her driveway.

Lloyd shook his head.

'Later, when she's had time to realise she needs us. Let me handle this. You need a break, Rube. Take some time to yerself today. The warehouse is in hand. I'll 'ave the truck unload overnight. I'll make sure one of my men goes wiv the cash. There's nuthin' more for ya to do.'

Ruby nodded reluctantly. As she went into the house, she felt her emotions overwhelm her again. She was glad Lloyd wasn't there to see her tears, the tears that wouldn't stop coming.

She took off her jacket, threw it over the banister, then spotted a letter on the doormat. She picked it up. She'd recognise that handwriting anywhere. Scrawled in writing that was like a child's, but written by a woman her own age, was her name and address. Next to it was a stamp. Holloway Prison.

Sarah, what 'ave ya been up to now? Ruby sighed, wiping her eyes. She kicked off her heels and padded to the kitchen to turn on the coffee machine. Tearing the envelope, she saw a letter from the girl next door in Star Lane, where she'd grown up. Sarah had been Ruby's best friend. And as a girl, Ruby had envied Sarah. Her dad was a blagger. He robbed banks and spent the cash lavishly, buying everyone in the pub drinks and bringing home all the latest gadgets. Sarah always had new clothes and the latest tape recorders or video machines, but then it all came crashing down when her dad was banged up for a long stretch, and when, shortly afterwards, her mum was nicked for theft.

Sarah was left to bring herself up, and so naturally she went completely off the rails, hanging out with bad men, shoplifting for numerous boyfriends, and taking drugs.

Ruby's heart sank now. How could the two women, who'd grown up side-by-side, have led lives which were so different? She felt the familiar pang of guilt and frustration as she read the words. Guilt because she'd never been able to help Sarah, frustration because her friend was too easily swayed by a handsome face or a promise of affection.

Ruby, mate. You won't believe it, but I've been nicked for dealing. You know how it is, I met this guy and he was all right though he was heavy with his fists sometimes. He got me into it, and so here I am. Will you come and visit? There's a VO in here. Please come, love Sarah xx

Ruby sat down heavily at her pristine work surface, in her immaculate kitchen with all its technology and the huge range at which her chef worked. She saw Sarah in her mind's eye, shuffling in the canteen lunch queue, locked away overnight in a cell she shared with other women. Life was so unfair. She sighed, tucked the letter behind the clock on the mantelpiece. Ruby would go and see her, of course she would. She was loyal to her friends, always, but something niggled at her. Sarah knew her better than most people, even though they'd grown apart – and so she would guess that something was up. Ruby knew she wasn't ready to talk about Cathy. Would she have to lie to her friend, too?

CHAPTER 18

Cathy awoke with a start. The first thing she noticed was how cold she felt, shivering a little even though the sun was warming the day up. For a moment she was confused at waking in her car, then she remembered, and it was like an excruciating physical pain through her heart. She scrabbled in the glove box for her phone. Levi had called back and she'd missed it. She tried his number again but he didn't pick up. She ran her fingers through her hair and checked her appearance in the rear-view mirror. Her hair was a bit messy but otherwise she looked surprisingly OK. Her skin was still pink and luminous, though she had dark shadows under her eyes; and her eyes, though swollen, were still startlingly green. Her stomach rumbled and Cathy realised she couldn't remember the last time she'd eaten. Luckily, she'd parked on a leafy suburban road and so no one had bothered her or tried to break into the car. She looked around. There seemed to be nobody about.

I must feed you, my darling, she whispered to her unborn child. *Mummy's hungry and I guess you are too. It will all be OK, little one. We'll find somewhere to get food and it'll work out from there.* Cathy felt a sliver of optimism. She'd lost everything that had meaning in her world, except for her baby and her boyfriend. Together, they'd work it out, they'd be OK.

Just as she was about to turn the key in the ignition, her phone rang. Without looking at the name that flashed up, assuming it was Levi calling her back, she answered it.

'Baby, oh God thanks for calling. Something has happened . . .'

Lloyd cut across her before she could carry on talking.

'It's me, sorry Cathy, it sounds like you was expectin' someone else. Listen, don't put the phone down.'

Cathy had already reached for the off button, but his words stopped her.

'Granddad, what do you want? I won't go back to Ruby, it's finished, I'm finished with her,' she said stubbornly.

'It's all right, Cathy darlin', I'm not goin' to talk ya into anythin', but tell me first, are ya OK? Where are ya now? Are ya safe?'

Lloyd's caring voice almost undid Cathy. She took a deep breath.

'I'm OK, and the baby's fine, we just need some breakfast is all. I'm sure once Levi gets back to me he'll sort everything. He'll look after us,' she said, though her words sounded uncertain.

If Lloyd picked up on her hesitancy, he didn't mention it.

'That's good to hear, Cathy, really good. Listen, I might be able to help ya get started. I might 'ave a flat for ya – and Levi, of course, somewhere nice for the baby to grow up. I won't tell yer mum where it is, only that you've got somewhere to live. How does that sound?'

Cathy paused. Could this be a trap? Was this Ruby's idea, getting her to an apartment, then turning up? As if reading his granddaughter's mind, Lloyd added, 'Ruby won't know a thing. I won't tell her where it is, I promise. Please just come and meet me. I'll buy ya breakfast, the baby must be starvin'.'

'OK, but if Ruby is there, I'll never trust you again, and I'll leave straight away. Just me and you, Granddad,' Cathy agreed reluctantly.

'Just me and you, darlin'. Good. I'll see ya at the fish stall in an hour. I love ya, darlin'. It'll all be OK, I promise ya.'

Lloyd's words echoed her own, yet his reassured her in a way she couldn't reassure herself. Perhaps things would work out. Perhaps Levi would bring their wedding forward and they'd be a proper family. Perhaps she didn't need Ruby or Bobby or Belle in her life after all. As she drove, she tried to ignore the lump in her throat.

An hour later, Cathy was sitting at a wooden table outside the front of Lloyd's favourite pub in Epping. At the side of the attractive building decorated with hanging baskets that spilled summer flowers was Debbie's Fish Stall, a place where Londoners came to enjoy traditional jellied eels, oysters and mussels. It was also the place where dodgy deals were done, where members of the shady underworld met, away from prying eyes.

Lloyd's Bentley drew up in the car park. Cathy checked her watch; he was half an hour late and she was ravenously hungry.

'Sorry darlin', I had some calls to make first,' he smiled as he ran over to her in his designer suit and smart Italian leather shoes.

'Business with Mum?' Cathy said, her lips drawn tight.

'Yes, darlin',' Lloyd said smoothly, 'of course it was business involvin' yer mother. Now come on, what d'ya want to eat? I fancy the chilli mussels for a change.'

Cathy half got up to go to the stall to choose and pay for her meal, but Lloyd stopped her.

'Sit down, darlin'. This is on me. Tell me what ya want, and just don't disappear before I'm back. Do we 'ave a deal?'

Lloyd looked at her over his shades. Cathy shrugged.

'OK, I'll 'ave a bacon and scallop roll and coffee, thanks.'

'Comin' right up,' Lloyd said and walked over to the stand where the stall owners greeted him with handshakes. The family was well-known – and wherever they went, people wanted to say hello. Cathy could hear the greetings, knowing that her family commanded respect in this part of the world. Would it always be this way?

Would she ever properly break free and live a normal life, away from gangsters and drug money? Cathy shivered again, drawing her cardie around her body though it was already getting hot. Her phone rang. It was Levi at last. She glanced over at Lloyd to make sure he wasn't coming over any time soon.

'Baby, I can't believe we're finally speaking. It's been hell.'

'What's goin' on, like? Ye called me overnight, I've been worried about ye, so I 'ave,' Levi answered.

At the sound of his soft Irish voice, Cathy melted. Of course he loved her and the baby. How could she ever doubt him?

'I can't speak now. Please meet me later, baby, and I'll tell you everything. I must go. I love you,' she whispered into her phone hurriedly before ending the call. She'd spied Lloyd making his way to her with a mountain of food on a tray. She wasn't sure why she felt she had to hide her phone call with the father of her child, but she did, and it confused her.

'Here ya go, darlin'. Two large rolls, that's for you. I'm 'avin the mussels. Here's ya coffee, love.'

Cathy murmured her thanks. She was so hungry. She dived in, chomping on a bacon and scallop roll as if it was the first meal she'd had for a very long time.

'Hungry, were ya?' Lloyd smiled, making his eyes crease. He didn't look like your average granddad. He had silver streaks in his expertly cut hair and blue eyes peering from his tanned face. Archie had looked so much like him: the same high cheekbones, the same way of making every person in the room look at him. Cathy thought of her dad, and her heart lurched. She must've shown something in her expression as Lloyd stopped digging out his mussels with his fork and looked over at her.

'Are ya OK, really, Cathy?'

She sighed.

'I'm fine, it's going to be fine,' she said without conviction. 'I don't want anything from any of you.'

Lloyd nodded, and took up his fork again, his face unreadable.

'I know ya don't, sweetheart, I know. But there is somethin' I want to give ya, and I won't take no for an answer.'

'What's that, Granddad?' Cathy said, chewing on a mouthful of her second roll.

'You definitely was famished!' chuckled Lloyd, then his face became serious. 'Listen, darlin'. I've found ya somewhere to live. It's away from yer mum and the rest of the family. It's a lovely flat in a nice part of Woodford. It's close enough to The Locksmith if ya want to carry on workin' there . . .' Cathy shook her head in response.

Lloyd continued anyway. 'What the baby needs is somewhere safe and nice to grow up, and you need a home. Am I right?'

Cathy looked mutinous but eventually she nodded her head. Lloyd reached into his pocket.

'I own a few flats in a very nice apartment block. It's near a park and there are good local schools. Listen, I sound like an estate agent now,' he grinned. 'The baby will love it, and I'll be happy knowin' you've got somewhere decent to live.'

He placed a set of keys on the table between them, pushed them towards his granddaughter. Cathy looked down at them.

'Take 'em, please, Cathy,' Lloyd said softly. 'I promise yer mum won't know where ya are. She won't come to ya. She'll leave ya in peace. Do we 'ave a deal?'

Cathy nodded.

'Listen, darlin', what yer mum did was wrong, I'm not excusin' her for it. Killin' is killin' whichever way ya look at it, but believe me, she did it for love of her brother. I know it's hard to understand, but what George did to ya, well, he was dead meat; a dead man walkin'. This is the way of things in our world, and yer mum knew that, which is why she had to act first or they'd 'ave ripped him to bits.'

Cathy was silent as she listened. She looked away at the trees that surrounded them, seeing nothing. She blinked away tears, wiping her face with the back of her hand in a childlike gesture.

'I don't want to talk about it,' she said stonily.

'But ya must, Cathy, or it'll destroy ya. I know our world has come as a shock to ya—'

'*Your* world,' she interrupted. 'All this – the people, the respect, the money, the cars – all of it is *your* world, not mine. I don't want anything to do with any of it. I hate that world. It's based on lies and violence. It's Mum's world,' she said bitterly.

'You're right, Cathy, it is Ruby's world, and it does 'ave different rules, and sometimes killin' is justified. That's the truth of it. I might as well tell ya straight. George had to go. Ruby was the one who was brave enough to do it. We do things differently and I'm sorry it's so distressin' to ya, I really am. Ruby always said you were made of better stuff than us, like an angel come to earth, and she was right. I'm not sayin' ya 'ave to agree with our methods, I just want ya to understand them. This stuff can eat ya up from inside. It'll take any happiness ya might 'ave, so don't let it. You 'ave to grow up now, Cathy. You say ya want nuthin' to do with us; that's your choice, we won't stop ya. But ya 'ave to know what that means. It means you'll 'ave to take on the world without our help, without our love. Is that what ya really want?'

Cathy stood abruptly.

'That's exactly what I want,' she said fiercely. 'It should've been me who decided George's fate, not you, and definitely not my mum. I would've forgiven him; I would've said we should let things lie. How dare you all lie to me for so long. I can't trust any of you again,' she finished bleakly.

Lloyd joined her in standing up. He reached an arm out to her, but Cathy stepped back.

'Your mother was protectin' ya, and believe it or not, she was protectin' George.' Lloyd's voice was harsh now.

'Your dad would've ripped him to bits if she hadn't 'ave shot him. It was a mercy killin'.'

There was silence now between them.

Cathy shook her head; a single tear slid down her face which she wiped away roughly.

'I have no mum now. I don't want anything to do with a world where people are killed no matter what they've done. I would've forgiven him and you didn't give me that choice.' She lay a protective arm across her belly.

Lloyd could see that he had lost her, that she was about to walk away.

'Just take these. It's ready for ya. I've texted ya the address. I've spoken to the concierge and they're expectin' ya. Do this, take the flat, and we'll never trouble ya again.'

It was Lloyd who turned away first, who walked to his car and with a beep of his key fob, got inside and drove away. Cathy stood, tears now streaming down her face, her hands closed around the set of keys. She realised people were looking her way, could see her distress, and so she gathered up her bag and, with an apologetic smile, walked hurriedly to her car. She fumbled with the gears, crunching into reverse and then driving away at speed.

Later that day, the buzzer in her new apartment sounded. Cathy had gone to the flats and been shown to her apartment on the first floor. The flat was painted in neutral colours and was furnished with expensive-looking items, a brand-new kitchen and views out onto the countryside. She'd walked around it, marvelling at her new-found independence. The fridge and freezer were stocked up with food and there were two bedrooms, just enough for the three of them. After the emotional turmoil of the past twenty-four hours, Cathy was relieved and amazed to find herself in a sunny, warm space, her baby growing inside her and her lover coming to see her. He couldn't refuse to live with her now – they'd be away from the traveller site in their own little world, happy together.

Cathy was cooking a stir fry when the buzzer went, announcing Levi's arrival. She let him in, beaming as she opened the door. He took off his cap and gathered her in his arms to kiss her, biting her ear as he whispered, 'So, where's the bedroom, darlin'?' Cathy giggled.

'I'll show you, but first we need to talk. Baby, I've left my family.'

'What d'ye mean by dat, eh?' Levi said, still kissing her neck.

'I found out something, something that was so awful I told them I don't want to see any of them ever again. It's just you and me now, Levi – and our child.'

Levi pulled back.

'What?'

Cathy turned and walked into the kitchen. Levi followed, his eyes darting around the space.

'Nice place ye got yerself here. How did this come about, eh?'

'My granddad Lloyd got it for me. It's his place but he says it's now mine, *ours*,' Cathy said. 'Last night, I got back from the bar and I heard my aunt and uncle fighting. Belle was screaming at Bobby.' Here, Cathy took a deep breath.

'Go on,' said Levi, leaning towards her. He'd plucked a grape from the fruit bowl and was chewing on it.

'She said that Mum killed her husband Vladimir, but more than that, Mum had been the one to kill my Uncle George, the one who attacked me. She shot him in the head and then lied to me, saying he was sent away to America. So, I went to Mum's and confronted her. It was all true. So I left, and I'll never go back.'

Levi whistled a long, low sound, his face alight with an emotion Cathy couldn't name.

'So, she killed them both. That means . . .'

'That means what?' Cathy said. She didn't like his sudden interest.

'Oh nuthin', nuthin' at all. So, baby, do ye want me to make ye feel better?' A sly grin appeared on Levi's face.

'I want you to move in with me here so we can be together at last,' Cathy said.

Levi moved round to her, turned off the hob, took hold of her hand and led her into the main bedroom.

'Oh, I want dat too,' he reassured her, pulling off her cardie and top. 'Yes, I want dat, darlin',' he said as he kissed her.

Cathy felt powerless to resist, yet she managed to say, 'So, is that a yes? Are you moving in here with me?'

Levi had broken off from her to undo his jeans.

'Darlin', I want the best for ye and I want to do this properly, but like I told ye before, I need to set up the company first and make sure I can support ye both, but there's been a hitch, like . . .'

'A hitch?' Cathy asked as Levi pulled her back on the bed.

He gave her a long, lingering kiss, but Cathy insisted. 'Tell me, Levi.'

Her boyfriend looked away then said: 'Look, darlin', we need capital. We need an investor to put money up front, but like I said, it's nuthin' to worry ye.'

Cathy pushed him off her, interrupting their love-making.

'How much do you need?'

Levi coughed.

'Two hundred thousand pounds, baby. Now where on earth can I get that kind of money?'

CHAPTER 19

Sarah looked gaunt and bruised, sitting across the table from Ruby. She fiddled with the cuff of her hoodie as she grinned at her friend. Ruby looked around the visiting room of Holloway Prison. It was a surprisingly light and airy space with a few pot plants here and there, and books for young children.

'How on earth did ya end up 'ere again?' Ruby sighed. She was exasperated with Sarah for getting herself into trouble, though she also saw a woman who'd had a hard life. Though they were the same age, the pair couldn't have looked more different. Ruby looked ten years younger than her age, the very epitome of a wealthy woman, with sleek hair, manicured nails, a designer outfit and Louboutin heels. Her teeth were white, her skin flawless, and she wore just a smattering of make-up: a slick of lip gloss and mascara.

Between Sarah's smiles, her expression fell into disappointment. Her skin looked grey, due to lack of sunlight, and she had lines around her eyes and mouth, signs of a hard life. Her blonde hair was scraped back in a ponytail, but she wore a good-quality tracksuit, one that Ruby had mailed to the prison for her.

'You look gorgeous, Rube,' Sarah said enviously, looking her friend up and down.

Ruby smiled back at her, wondering if she should take any of the blame for Sarah's inability to make a life for herself. Though they'd grown up living beside each other, their worlds were galaxies apart. Should she have done more to help her friend? *Could* she have done more? Ruby waited for Sarah to speak. The woman sighed, rubbed her sleeve cuff against her chin.

'Got into a fight with one of the girls in 'ere,' she said, explaining the livid purple bruise above one eye. 'She tried to nick my ciggies. Well, I gave her a pastin' she won't forget, though I've got to go in front of the board for my punishment.'

Ruby nodded. She knew this probably meant that Sarah would have to serve longer behind bars as a result. Somehow her friend never seemed to get a break.

'Why are ya in 'ere? It ain't the nicest place to end up,' Ruby went on.

Sarah fidgeted again.

'Drugs, weren't it. I always said I'd never do heroin, but along came Terry and before I knew it, we was doin' it together. Then he wanted me to sell it, not big-time dealin' but just to a few mates, and I got caught.'

That would explain the amount of weight Sarah had lost. She was hardly more than skin and bones.

'So, where's this Terry now? Is he standin' by ya?' Ruby said, but regretted it instantly as she saw the shadow pass over Sarah's face. Of course he wasn't. Men like him rarely did. He'd be off somewhere, if he wasn't banged up, picking another vulnerable woman, someone who would do anything he asked for whatever it was he offered that passed for love. Ruby felt a sudden lump in her throat. She saw how different she was to her friend, how she would never have let a man take her power in return for, what? A few hollow words and a bit of comfort?

Well, Sarah was paying for her naivety.

"Course he ain't,' the prisoner said. 'There ain't no happy endin' for my story, unlike you, Ruby Murphy.'

Ruby smiled at the use of her maiden name. It had been a long time since she'd been called that.

'Happy endin's. They're in short supply at the moment, Sar,' Ruby replied. It was her turn to look sad.

'You look tired though, Rube. Not sleepin'?'

Sarah emphasised 'you' as if Ruby was a woman who skirted all bad luck, who attracted only good fortune: gold coins and rainbows.

'Oh, it's nuthin'. Had a bit of trouble with Cathy, but nuthin' I can't sort . . .' Ruby's voice trailed off. She felt an immediate desire to open her heart to her friend, pour out her woes and tell her everything. It was only her hard-won conditioning that kept her emotions in check. Despite this, Sarah was looking at her now as if for the first time. Her head was cocked to one side.

'Rube, I know ya think I'm the stupid one, but I ain't so thick as ya think.'

'It's fine. I can sort it,' Ruby replied defensively.

Sarah looked at her oldest friend.

'Are you sure about that?' she said.

Disconcerted by the feeling of exposure, Ruby was glad when the visit ended. She hated seeing her friend in prison but, sadly, it had been as inevitable as rain. Sarah never learned when it came to men. Ruby had waved goodbye to Sarah, but hadn't looked back. As she stood at the visiting room door, there came a sudden swooping in her stomach and she felt momentarily dizzy. *This place feels bad, I don't like it*, she thought to herself. Shivering, she looked around. The walls seemed to close in. It was a warning, perhaps, a portent, like her grandmother used to get. For a second, Ruby thought she was going to faint, then, just as a cloud moves to reveal the sun, she suddenly felt brighter. The feeling disappeared, though it left behind a strange trace.

As Ruby drove back to Chigwell, her phone rang. She looked at the screen in her car and saw it was Cathy's number. Heart beating furiously, she pressed the hands-free.

'Oh, darlin', I knew it'd all be OK and you'd be back in touch. Are ya safe? How's the baby? I miss ya so much.'

There was a pause, then she heard Cathy's voice, which was cold and distant.

Instantly, Ruby realised this wasn't the reconciliation she had been praying for each night.

'I need money,' is all Cathy said. Ruby nodded to herself, biting back her feelings.

'Ya need money, darlin'? Of course ya do. Ok, well we 'ave plenty of that. How much d'ya need?' Ruby tried to keep her voice calm, tried to think of this as being like a business deal, but her usual restraint had vanished. She was desperate to know where her daughter was. Lloyd had told her she was safe in one of his apartment blocks in Woodford but he hadn't told her which one. When Ruby had demanded he spill the beans as she had a right to know where Cathy and her grandchild were living, Lloyd had held both her shoulders and looked into her eyes.

'I promised her I wouldn't tell ya. Leave it for now, Rube. Nuthin' good can come of ya turnin' up. She might run again, and we can't risk losin' her. This way we know she's surrounded by our men, and she won't come to any harm.'

Ruby had been devastated.

'How dare ya, Lloyd? I want to know where my daughter is. You 'ave to tell me!'

Lloyd had smiled sadly. 'I can't Rube. Leave it, now. It's for the best.'

Ruby had to be content with that, though it pained her to know that Cathy hated her so much she'd made her granddad promise not to give her the address.

'I need two hundred thousand pounds.'

The huge sum of money made Ruby jolt back to the present. She swerved the car to the side of the road, pulling over from the traffic. Her head rang. She was disconcerted after seeing Sarah, and now this. What on earth did Cathy want that kind of money for? The answer came to Ruby straight away: Levi.

'Darlin', that's a lot of money. Can I at least ask what this money is for?' she said, trying to stay reasonable, trying not to say the words, to beg Cathy to come home.

There was a pause on the other end.

Ruby thought she heard whispering, but it could've been the connection.

'It's for Levi's business. He needs two hundred thousand and then he can set up the tarmac company. Once he's got it all up and running, we'll be a proper family with no secrets and no lies.'

Ruby winced at this. Cathy's voice was filled with resentment.

Somehow, Ruby managed to keep her voice light, though she was desperately hurt by her daughter's coldness, and the anger that still lay beneath it.

'That's a lot of money, darlin'. Does he really need that much to set up?'

Cathy's fury exploded out now. 'Yes, he does, Mum, though I wouldn't expect you to understand. You don't have to help us. We can find someone else or do it ourselves!'

'Cathy, darlin', I'm only askin',' Ruby said, her voice pleading. She hated hearing herself this way, but her daughter meant everything to her, and the loss of Cathy was destroying her, even though she'd faced so much already and kept her head held high.

'That's a lot of money, but of course you can 'ave it. Let me come over. I'll bring it with me and we can talk?'

Ruby heard the whispers again.

'No, Mum. You're not coming anywhere near me or my baby. If you want to help us you'll have to get the money to Levi. Do we have a deal?'

For a moment, Ruby heard the echo of her own voice, with Cathy knowing what she wanted and how to get it. She stared out of the window as the cars moved past her.

'All right, darlin', all right. I'll arrange a drop to Levi. One of my men will be in touch so text me Levi's number and I'll get onto it,' Ruby gave in, her voice flat. She put the phone down and sat for a while, her brain whirring. Had Cathy told Levi their secrets? Had she wept in his arms and told him about George and Vladimir, how Ruby had killed them both? Is that why Levi felt confident in getting Cathy to ask for a large sum of money? Somehow, Ruby already knew the truth. Immediately, she rang Lloyd's number.

Eyes narrowed, she said, 'Check out Levi for me, will ya? 'Ave him tailed. See if ya can dig out whatever there is to know about him. He's just asked for two hundred grand.'

Lloyd whistled.

'He's probably just a gold digger who's seen his chance with Cathy to make a few quid,' she said, 'but I want to know for sure. Can ya do that for me?'

"Course, Rube. I'll get some of my guys onto it today. I'll make sure he's followed day and night,' answered Lloyd.

'I think he knows why Cathy left. I think he knows our secrets.' Her voice was low as she spoke. The thud of intuition in her gut was unmistakeable.

'Ah, that would make sense. Oh, Cathy. Why trust a guy like Levi, all charm and not a lot else? Don't worry, Rube. He's just a small-time crook, nuthin' for us to worry about, I'm sure of it,' Lloyd tried to reassure her.

'Even so, I want information.'

Two days later, Levi let himself into Cathy's apartment at 6 a.m. carrying a large black holdall. Without a word, he marched into her bedroom, waking her up.

'God, you frightened me!' she exclaimed, then saw the huge smile on her boyfriend's face and realised what must have happened.

'Did she give it to you?' Cathy sat bolt upright, looking expectantly at the Irish traveller. He nodded, his eyes shining and his smile wide.

'She sure did. Ye hit the jackpot there, my angel. Baby, there is two hundred thousand nicker in this bag. Do ye want to see it?'

Cathy nodded, her eyes wide. Levi put the bag down and carefully unzipped it. He picked it up by the ends and turned it on its head so that the bed was immediately covered in notes rolled into thick bundles.

'Oh my gosh!' shrieked Cathy, running her hands over the money as if she'd never seen hard cash before.

'You've done well, baby, very well,' Levi leaned over and suddenly his face became a sly grin. 'And I know exactly how we're goin' to christen it, like . . .'

Cathy looked puzzled. Carefully, he got onto the bed, kneeling on the notes.

'Come on, baby,' he whispered through his teeth as he pulled off her nightie and proceeded to make love to her, rolling her across the pile of money, Cathy giggling in his arms, her giggles turning to happy sighs.

After they'd finished, Cathy turned to him and said, in all seriousness, 'So, there's enough money there to start your business. That means we can get engaged. There's more than enough to buy me a ring.'

Levi hesitated for a split second.

''Course, baby,' he said, nuzzling her neck, 'I'll find ye the finest ring that's ever been made.'

Cathy lay back contented in his arms. He loved her. The baby was well. They had the money. Life looked good.

'I've got to go, baby. Sorry, it would've been nice to be here all day but got to get this business up and runnin',' Lloyd said, jumping off the bed and dressing quickly. He gathered up all the money and stuffed it back in the holdall, turning to throw one of the rolls to Cathy. She caught it deftly, but she watched him, knowing he always found a reason to leave. Perhaps when the baby came, those reasons would vanish. She had to trust that they would. He was everything to her now. She had no one else, except perhaps for Lloyd, but she had to keep him at arm's length in case he led Ruby to her.

Cathy didn't want Levi to see her scowling before he left so she plastered a smile on her face.

'When will you be back?'

'Not until I've got all the boys on board. A couple of days, maybe longer.' Levi seemed distracted already.

Cathy sat up, pulling her knees into her chest. Seeing her look of disappointment, the one she was trying – and failing dismally – to hide, Levi relented. He reached over and kissed her on the forehead.

'I'll be back as soon as I can.'

'I love you,' Cathy called after him but the slam of the door told her he'd left. She looked around the room. Her few possessions lay scattered. The flat suddenly seemed silent, too quiet, and the day stretching before her was too long. She looked down at the roll of money.

Perhaps I'll go and buy some bits for the nursery, I wonder if Belle is free . . . Cathy caught her thoughts. How could she have forgotten that her aunt and uncle were no longer part of her life? The casual thought about seeing them only served to deepen the sense of isolation that hovered in her empty flat.

PART 3

REVELATION

Chigwell, England,
October 2012

CHAPTER 20

'Alfie, darlin',' Ruby turned her face to receive his kiss.

'How are ya, Rube?' he said, smiling. His face looked tanned and he looked the happiest she'd seen him since Archie had died.

'South America suits ya,' Ruby said as they walked towards a wooden table outside Debbie's Fish Stall. It was a glorious early autumn day and people were already arriving for the lunchtime rush. Several shady-looking guys nodded to them, and Alfie nodded back. He wore a white linen shirt and designer jeans with a heavy gold necklace around his neck. On his wrist was a Patek Philippe and he had on Dolce & Gabbana shades. Ruby was also glamorous in sky-high Louboutins and a Chanel suit with the Prada sunglasses she wore no matter what the weather was like. They both exuded wealth and danger. No one walking into Debbie's could mistake the smell of hard cash seated at its tables. Though the fare was simple East End food, the clientele looked like they wouldn't be out of place at The Ivy.

'It does, but you've called me back to England for a reason. So, what's the problem?'

'Grab me a coffee and I'll tell ya,' Ruby said over her shades.

The weakening sun was still warm on her face and for a brief moment she almost wished she was back in Spain, though that thought ended as soon as she caught it. She waited for Alfie to reappear with their drinks, her hand gripping her mobile phone. Even though she knew in her heart that Cathy wouldn't ring, she still couldn't put her phone down. Part of her still hoped that one day she'd call.

'Spill the beans then, sis. I've travelled a long way to be 'ere and I must say, I don't care for the weather much,' Alfie said grumpily, shivering. He placed the hot coffee down in front of Ruby. She lifted off the polystyrene lid and sipped it.

'It must be swelterin' over there,' she said.

Alfie grinned.

'Humid, too, at least when you're close to the rainforest.'

Before he could expand on the differences in the Bolivian and London climates, Ruby cut in.

'All right, listen. Of course I've called ya back for a reason but I didn't want to say nuthin' on the phone. We 'ave to be careful who might be listenin' in these days.'

Alfie nodded. Sensitive information was best kept to face-to-face meetings. It was the surest way of avoiding any leaks.

'Last week's shipment of coke, the largest so far, went missin' the day after clearin' customs, on the road from Dover to Glasgow. The driver of the lorry says masked men stopped the truck in Grays and it was hijacked. He was badly injured. They beat the crap out of him.'

Alfie frowned.

'Go on,' he said, taking a sip of his drink.

'The story seems kosher but I don't buy it. The driver was too eager to talk. He was beaten up but he didn't need an 'ospital. It was like his injuries were done so they looked bad but weren't serious. He's already back behind the wheel, sortin' out another run, but somethin' tells me not to trust him. I think there's a grass among my men. It probably sounds silly to ya,' Ruby finished, looking over at her brother-in-law.

His eyebrows shot up. 'I won't lie and tell ya it's a rational thing to hear but I know your gut, Rube, and if ya say you're worried then I'll do everythin' I can to help ya.'

'Thanks, Alfie. All I know is that we've lost a massive cargo in this hijack. The whole shipment was taken, so it must've been planned. Ya don't just walk up to a lorry and demand they hand over cocaine worth millions. Ya need transport. Ya need men and guns. It all strikes me as a planned job and so there must be someone on the inside workin' with whoever nicked our gear.

'But what sticks out is that, despite the efficiency of the hijack, the driver managed to escape, and to me, that's just dodgy. Any gang wantin' that shipment would kill him first. They wouldn't let him get away.'

Alfie considered this.

'What about the Old Bill? Anyone there got a grudge who might decide to take our product and make sure we can't complain about it?'

Ruby shook her head.

'At first, I wondered that, but we pay them too much to upset the apple cart. I'm also pretty sure it weren't the bonded warehouse either because they'd lose our very lucrative business for ever. It can only have been one of two things: chancers, though I think this is unlikely, or a set-up by another gang,' Ruby said, thinking aloud now. 'Get onto it, Alfie. We've got people at customs and across the supply chain. Speak to them. My gut tells me the driver ain't as innocent as he looks, despite the black eyes.'

Ruby's phone rang. She scrabbled for it, and her face must've registered her disappointment when she saw Lloyd's number.

'You thought it might be Cathy . . .' Alfie murmured, sitting back as Ruby picked up the call. She didn't look over at him because to do so would confirm how right he was.

'Meet me at Debbie's,' Lloyd said. 'I've got information.'

'You're in luck, Lloyd. I'm already 'ere and I've got a guest with me,' Ruby smiled, glancing over at Alfie.

'Has Alfie arrived? Good. We need him 'ere. I'll be there in ten minutes,' Lloyd said, ringing off.

*

Before long, the sound of Lloyd's Bentley purring into the car park made his arrival known. The cartel boss stepped out of his car and walked over, nodding at those who greeted him while heading straight to Ruby's table.

'Son, get me two coffees, won't ya,' he said, kissing Ruby on each cheek.

''Course Dad. Two? Are ya sure?' Alfie got up and started walking towards the counter.

'I'm expectin' a guest,' Lloyd called over to his son, then, turning to Ruby, said, 'He'll be 'ere any minute.'

Almost as soon as he finished speaking another, this time nondescript, car pulled in.

''Ere he is now, bang on time.'

Ruby looked quizzically at her father-in-law, the man she turned to most, who was her rock in Archie's absence. They'd grown closer – in business – since her husband's death and they were fast realising they made a great team; him with his experience and steady hand, her with her sharp business sense and the intuition that served her so well.

'How are ya, Rube?' he said, looking at her with concern.

'I'm fine. No word from Cathy, but that's to be expected,' she said, shutting down that conversation. She didn't want to be distracted from business, but despite that, her mobile was back in her hand. Lloyd nodded as if he understood. Alfie joined them, carrying a tray with two coffees, spare milk cartons, and a freshly cooked roll.

'They said it was your regular, so they sent it over – for free,' Alfie said, placing it in front of his dad. Lloyd looked over at the counter and waved to signal his thanks.

'They know me, they're discreet,' Lloyd said approvingly as he bit into his bacon and scallop roll.

Ruby looked up as a man walked over from the grey estate car that had pulled in moments earlier. He wore dark sunglasses, a black hoodie and jeans. He nodded by way of a greeting and stood beside Lloyd.

'Sit down, 'ere's ya coffee. Rube, Alfie, this is one of the men I've had trailin' Levi. I won't bore ya with his name or details, but he's been in charge of followin' Cathy's boyfriend and reportin' back on everythin' he sees. Well, we was chattin' this mornin' – but I'll let him tell ya . . .'

Lloyd nodded at the guy, who sat down next to his boss. He looked shifty. He didn't make eye contact with anyone and he fidgeted as he spoke. He had a cockney accent like theirs yet he looked Middle Eastern.

'As Lloyd says, I've been trailin' Levi. We can't get access to the traveller site in Basildon but we've staked it out and we can see everyone who comes and goes. Levi lives there but he leaves, mostly at night, to go and see your daughter or to meet with his mates and go out drinkin'.' At this point, the man looked at Ruby as if he'd just noticed her, then dropped his gaze again and carried on. 'We know everywhere he goes, who he sees and what he does. What we don't know is whether he has a family on the site or whether he lives alone.'

Ruby nodded.

The man paused as if he knew that what was coming next would upset the attractive woman sitting in front of him.

'I can tell ya that his visits to your daughter are 'appenin' less. When we first started followin' him, he went most nights after her shifts at the bar. Now, he's goin' once or twice a week at most.'

Ruby felt a pang of concern for Cathy. It seemed obvious that Levi was losing interest. Except, of course, when he needed cash.

'Go on,' Ruby said, pulling up her glasses so she could try and scrutinise this man's eyes through his shades. She needed to know for sure she could trust him, and you could learn a lot by a person's eyes.

'He doesn't stay all night. He leaves around 3 a.m. He used to stay until the morning but even that's stopped. We've been watchin' him especially closely after the money drop.' So, Lloyd had told him about the two hundred grand. Ruby didn't like having to tell someone outside of the family, but they needed answers.

'And what did ya find out? Has he blown the lot on gamblin' or whores?' she said, her eyebrow raised.

'Well, we think we've discovered what he's doin' with the money. It ain't gamblin' but it's heavy stuff . . .'

At this point the crook looked at Lloyd, who said, 'We want to 'ear it. Tell us everythin' ya know. We'll make it worth yer while.'

The man gave a half-smile and continued. 'He's bought up a whole load of coke from one of your runners, and seems to fancy himself a dealer.'

'He's done what?' Ruby exclaimed, almost laughing. 'He can't be so stupid that he'd buy up coke from one of our men?'

'He don't necessarily know that sellin' coke is our game. Let's face it, Rube, we don't know what this Levi knows, or what he don't,' Lloyd said.

'What about the business he's tellin' everyone he's settin' up?' Alfie added, looking between them all. 'What's 'appened to that idea?'

The man shrugged. 'There ain't no tarmac business, not from what we can see, anyway.'

'And does he know that the contact for the coke is ours?' Ruby asked, her attention now fully on the man bringing her this information.

The man shook his head.

'No, I don't think so. From what my men are tellin' me, he's puttin' most of the gear up his own nose instead of sellin' it on.'

Ruby looked over at Lloyd, whose face was stern.

'This is serious, Rube. That's a lot of cocaine and we don't want him edgin' into our business, even if he's usin' some himself. And it don't bode well for him as a father, neither. He also don't know what he's doin' and could cause us trouble with other suppliers and dealers. He should never 'ave been sold the product in the first place.'

'Agreed,' said Ruby, 'get rid of that runner. He'll 'ave gone to ground, so find someone to dig him out sooner rather than later. We can't 'ave suppliers sellin' elsewhere, it don't look good on us. As for Levi—'

Lloyd stopped her. 'Levi needs to learn his lesson. He's puttin' Cathy at risk if he's a dealer, and he's also playin' a game he don't understand.'

Ruby shook her head.

'I knew he was a shyster. I knew he was lyin' to Cathy, and now, at least, we 'ave proof.'

Her brain was whirring. Should they confront Cathy with the truth? How would she feel knowing the father of her child was getting his hands dirty, selling her mother's cocaine on the streets? What if Cathy chose not to believe her? If so, for all Ruby knew, the information could drive a bigger wedge between them. She bit her lip. It was a risk too great to take as things were.

'We need to warn him off. Alfie, 'ave a casual word with Levi, no violence, just a friendly chat. Tell him he's stepped onto our territory. Threaten him with tellin' Cathy. With any luck, he'll give up dealin' and do the right thing for her and the baby.'

Both Alfie and Lloyd looked doubtful.

'I know it might not work but we 'ave to give it a go. If we tell Cathy she'll think we're stitchin' him up, lyin' to her to try and get rid of him. We 'ave to go easy on her and let the land lie. It's Levi who needs a quiet word put to him. Let's give him a chance to sort this out himself.'

Ruby looked at the three men. They each nodded, and the Middle Eastern guy took his leave of them and drove off. Ruby kept her face impassive until he'd left but as soon as he'd gone, her mask crumbled.

'Cathy is alone, I can't bear it.' Her voice cracked.

'Rube, you 'ave to stay strong. We're goin' to sort this. I've got the best men on this. It'll be OK,' said Lloyd.

She nodded, though his words didn't make her feel any better. The thought of Cathy sitting on her own in the flat, waiting for Levi to visit, holding on to his empty promises, would haunt her.

Ruby took a deep breath. The air was warm though the evenings had that bite of autumn chill. She straightened her back. Perhaps she should be grateful that this charmer with his good looks and lilting Irish accent was mostly staying away from her daughter and unborn grandchild. It was cold comfort, though, knowing how much pain his absences would be causing Cathy. She thought about what her father-in-law had said. Lloyd was right; she couldn't falter now. Levi was in their sights. He was a marked man. If he put a foot out of place from now on, he could very well be a dead man. The thought reassured her.

'Keep tailin' him. Let's not warn him off just yet. There must be more goin' on, so we'll keep a very close eye on him,' she said, her expression grim.

CHAPTER 21

'It was the fuckin' driver,' Alfie swore on the phone to Ruby. 'He was paid off by a London gang. We've never had dealin's with these bastards before. It looks like they saw a chance and took it.'

Ruby held the phone away from her ear and stared through her bifold kitchen doors at the garden where workmen were digging up the area intended for a heated swimming pool.

'Rube? What d'ya want me to do?'

'Nuthin' yet, Alfie,' she replied. Ruby didn't ask how Alfie knew what had taken place. She didn't want to hear the sordid details; which men he'd tortured to get this information, which contacts he'd bribed. The most important thing was protecting their empire from enemies, big or small. So, it had been some kind of local gang who'd seen a chance and hadn't thought much past the cash they'd make selling on her coke. They would soon learn the rash nature of that decision, but how best to teach them? If Alfie had managed to discover the truth, then it was out there, and her cartel would look weak if she didn't retaliate. But it had to be done properly. They had to send out a strong message, that you should never fuck with them, and Alfie was the best person to do it.

'Tell the driver we believe his story that the lorry was hijacked and ask him to do another run,' Ruby continued. 'Let's gamble on his greed.'

'He'll do it,' Alfie said a couple of days later, 'and my man 'eard him boastin' in the pub about the "stupid bastards" who'd believed him.'

'Good, he doesn't suspect, then,' Ruby replied. 'Get everythin' in place. He won't be boastin' for much longer. The shipment comes in tonight. Make sure the driver is at Dover waitin' for it.'

'Listen, Rube, now we're in England we can't sort this ourselves; it's too dodgy and we might get noticed. I'll phone the rubbish collector, a guy called Kurt, and he'll sort it.'

The rubbish collector was the hit-man Alfie used. He would do everything, from bugging the lorry cab so he knew when to strike, through to killing all those involved and taking back the shipment.

'Make sure our man at customs knows to wave through the goods,' Ruby finished. 'Call me when it's done.'

Crooked customs officers on their payroll would know to look for their cargo. The drugs were hidden in all sorts of ways, but this time they were coming over in crates filled with boxes of fish food. The lorry would be loaded with the hidden coke and transported to the point where the fake hijack would occur. That's when the plan would come into force. The driver didn't know what was about to hit him.

Ruby spent the rest of the day speaking to the project manager at her home, making sure all the small details of her pool were in place. She wanted the letters R&A inscribed on the bottom of the pool, a tribute to her late husband. Around the pool in summer would be love seats and four-poster daybeds, like she'd seen on the cruise when she was stringing along Vladimir. It amused her to have a memento of that time, and they'd looked so exotic and expensive she had to have them. When the workmen had all left the site, she walked the perimeter of the pool, imagining the parties she'd have there and trying to picture her grandchild playing in the water in Cathy's arms. Tears came suddenly to her eyes, and she realised she was tired, though it would be a long night ahead.

The weather was closing in now. Autumn was well and truly under way as the days moved onwards. Ruby had become accustomed to the weather in Spain, so she was beginning to dread the impending winter cold, the rain and grey skies. It had never bothered her growing up, when Star Lane and the streets around it were her world. She only really remembered hot summers and cosy nights in with her family; her dad Louie cleaning his boots, her mum Cathy doing something in the kitchen, Bobby sneaking out for a pint with his mates on Sunday lunch-times, making Cathy cross when he was late back for their traditional roast. Somehow, she never noticed the chill of the sleety rain, the wind that seemed to whistle across her land in Chigwell. Perhaps because she had more space, more grounds, a bigger house, she was more aware of the seasons as they changed.

Bobby had popped round earlier in the day for a coffee. Their relationship was fragile, their conversation stilted, but at least he'd made the effort. Belle didn't show her face, and whether that was because she was mortified at the anguish she'd caused, or grateful that Cathy knew the truth, Ruby couldn't be sure. Bobby had fudged his answer when she'd asked why his wife hadn't come.

'Sorry Rube, she had a headache,' he said weakly, 'it's nice to see ya though.'

For a moment, there had been silence.

Ruby knew Bobby didn't dare ask whether she'd seen Cathy. It was the looming elephant in the room. Her brother fiddled with his mug; picking it up and putting it down, until Ruby couldn't bear it a moment longer.

'I haven't seen her. I've heard nuthin', well, except for one phone call.'

Bobby looked up. 'She rang ya?'

Ruby nodded. There was no use hiding it. Especially now she'd learned that Cathy hadn't been in touch with her aunt and uncle either. This showed how angry she was.

'She did,' she sighed, 'to ask for money, a lot of money. Levi wanted two hundred grand to set up a business. Apparently, he's told her he'll marry her once it's up and runnin'.'

'Bloody hell, Rube. What's he playin' at?' Bobby looked stunned. She could see that with his tender heart, he had convinced himself that Levi and Cathy were happy together, and that Levi would do the right thing by her. For such a big, burly man, Bobby was surprisingly naive.

'Don't worry, we're on to him, he's in our sights. So, how's Belle?' Ruby said, changing the subject abruptly away from Levi. She couldn't resist asking.

Bobby looked down.

'She blames herself for what 'appened. She's sorry for it, Rube, she really is.'

'Are ya sure she's not just sorry for Cathy runnin' off? Didn't she always want the truth to come out?' Ruby added, with the sensation of having shown her claws.

Bobby's eyes met hers. 'She did want Cathy to know what really 'appened, but not like that, never like that. She ain't rung us. Belle is devastated. Honest to God, I wish we'd never had that fight!'

Ruby felt like hugging her brother; his expression was utterly bereft. Cathy had been like a daughter to them, a fact that had always given Ruby pain and comfort in equal measure. Ruby knew exactly the grief they were both feeling, because she felt it too.

As Ruby made a solitary supper later that evening, and settled down in front of the TV, she heard Bobby's words in her head again, saw his distress. She could only imagine Belle's upset, and the thought of it gave her no pleasure at all. Her brother had left shortly after that conversation. Ruby had been glad of it. She had to be sharp for tonight, and the rush of emotion that had accompanied his visit disturbed her. She'd kissed him goodbye, and her heart had sunk to her boots. When would their family be back to 'normal'? Would they ever be? The thought of losing Cathy for ever was too painful to bear, but the thought crept in whenever Ruby's defences were low.

You're tired, Ruby. Get some sleep. Alfie will handle things, and you'll know about it soon enough if he doesn't, Ruby tried to reassure herself, *and ya won't get Cathy back by worryin'.*

Hours later, Ruby realised she'd dozed off. She checked her Cartier watch. It was almost 2 a.m. and she would hear from Alfie very soon. She tidied up her supper plate and switched the coffee machine on, then looked at her phone. No missed calls, which was good. The event must be going to plan. About twenty minutes later, as she sipped her fresh coffee, Alfie's number flashed up.

'Sis?'

'Yes, Alfie. Is everythin' all right?' Ruby said.

'It's done. Smooth as clockwork,' Alfie boasted.

They had followed the plan exactly. In her mind's eye, Ruby went over the details, imagining the revenge they'd plotted. The driver would've checked the cargo, then rung the gang to tell them he'd got the load and the next heist was on. Big mistake. Kurt, the hit-man, would've heard every word through the bugging devices on board. As the driver passed through customs, their contact at border control would've distracted him, taken him inside to confirm the documents for the cargo. That would've given Kurt a two-fold advantage. He would've had time to get inside the back of the lorry with two Serbian henchmen, all carrying guns. Also, the driver would've been frightened by the rigorous checks, or 'shitted up', as Alfie would put it. Then he must've driven off to the same spot in Grays where the first robbery took place. Another mistake. Any gang worth their salt would know to do things differently.

As two masked men jumped out of the shadows from a ditch at the side of the road, their guns held up to 'rob' the truck, Kurt would've been prepared and waiting, inside the hold.

As soon as the back of the lorry was opened, Kurt would've opened fire, gunning down the robbers. Jumping out of the back, he would surely have seen the driver trying to leg it, realising they'd been caught out, and that's when Kurt's henchmen would've shot him dead too.

The hit-man had orders – Ruby's orders, told to him by Alfie – to drag the driver's body next to the other two slain men, the three corpses left in the open as a message to the underworld: Don't fuck with Ruby. Don't fuck with this cartel. If you try, you're a dead man walking.

'And did it go as we said it should?' she asked.

'Exactly as you wanted it,' replied Alfie, hanging up.

Ruby held the phone to her ear for a second, relishing the feeling of control she had now exerted over the gang who'd betrayed them. Alfie's men wouldn't stop there. They'd hunt down every last man in that outfit and make them pay, too. They had to send a strong message – and they'd done it their way, with bloodshed and violence.

"Ave ya seen this?' Lloyd threw a copy of the newspaper to Ruby. She sat at her garden table on the decking that now stretched along the back of the kitchen and its bifold doors. It was the day after the shooting and Ruby sipped freshly squeezed orange juice while her chef prepared eggs with smoked salmon.

'Care to join me?' she smiled as she picked up the local rag from Romford. The front-page headline screamed *THREE DEAD IN TRAFFICKER GANG WAR*.

'Where'd ya get this?' she nodded, scanning the story.

'One of my men drove it over to me this mornin'. It's a good result, Rube,' Lloyd said.

'The Old Bill 'ave been quoted as sayin' they think it's traffickin'. No mention of drugs, no one to link it to us at all. The rubbish collector did well.'

Lloyd pulled up a chair and sat beside Ruby, reaching for a piece of toast and proceeding to butter it liberally.

'That's very good,' said Ruby. 'And it sends the right message to that gang and anyone who might've thought they'd try it on with us. They'll know – or guess – what really 'appened. And the cargo?'

' . . . is safe at the warehouse. All sorted and probably already bein' sold across the West End as we speak,' grinned her father-in-law.

Ruby put the newspaper down and sat back in her chair, eyeing up the man who'd started the drug cartel all those years ago in Spain. Once she'd married his son Archie and brought her tough negotiating skills and class to the operation – something that had been sorely lacking without a woman at the helm – the company had grown, absorbed a rival operation, and expanded across Eastern Europe and into the far reaches of Russia. They'd done what they'd set out to do, and a new thought was forming in Ruby's mind.

'Lloyd, I've been thinkin'. Perhaps it is time to stop all this, to retire? I've been thinkin' more and more about it recently, perhaps since Archie's death. We've been in this game for a long time, Lloyd, and it don't get any less dangerous . . .'

'You goin' soft on me, Rube?' Lloyd said, winking at her. His face changed as he saw her expression, though. It was obvious she was serious. He put down his piece of toast and looked around the garden, which would soon be an oasis. Ruby had commissioned a garden designer to create a classic English garden with wafts of bushy lavender, earthenware pots spilling over with the last of the summer's flowers and tangled roses that had blushed pink and red earlier in the season. The pool with its day beds would be the last of the additions.

'It would be nice to appreciate the finer things,' Lloyd admitted. 'And ya might 'ave a point, Rube. I've been thinkin' the same. I want to enjoy my retirement, mostly by being alive and not lyin' dead somewhere. It's gettin' more dangerous by the day, new gangs operatin' in new ways.'

'We always 'ave to be ahead, and I love every minute of that, but with what's 'appened with Cathy, and Archie before her . . . I don't know, it's somethin' that's been on my mind.'

Ruby looked back at the workmen, who were whistling. This game was a part of her. She'd fought for her position in this man's world. She'd had to be smarter, colder, more ruthless than any of them to survive. What was it all for, though, if she couldn't enjoy the rewards with her family? She'd done it all for them. When she was young, she'd gone against every instinct in her body and soul to create herself as a woman to be reckoned with. Had the sacrifice of all she'd been brought up to believe been worth it? At that moment, Ruby had no answer.

CHAPTER 22

'Miss Willson, you're carrying twins.'

The sonographer smiled over at the young woman lying on the hospital bed.

Cathy thought she'd misheard. She looked into the kind face of the forty-something medical professional and couldn't think of what to say. Stunned, she finally blurted out, 'Twins? Are you sure?'

The nurse laughed.

'Yes, I'm absolutely sure. Listen, there are two heartbeats.'

With amazement, Cathy looked at the wiggling shapes on the screen, listening as two tiny but loud hearts pounded through the speaker.

Tears sprang to her eyes.

'I don't believe it,' she said at last, feeling overwhelmed at the same time as grateful that both seemed healthy and strong.

'Are there twins in your family?' the sonographer asked as she wiped the jelly off Cathy's growing belly.

'Yes, yes there are,' Cathy whispered as tears now flowed down her face. Why hadn't she thought that twins could be a possibility? It was obvious now that she thought about it. After all, her dad had been a twin.

'I'm sorry, dear. Did I say something wrong?' The woman stopped and held Cathy's hand, looking at her with real concern.

She shook her head. 'No, of course not. It's just that my dad was . . . He died, though . . .'

The woman nodded, still gripping Cathy's hand.

'I'm sorry to hear that, dear. Pregnancy brings up lots of emotional things, especially with families. It's quite normal to feel sad, even with such happy news.'

Neither woman said anything while Cathy digested her words.

'Dad won't ever get to meet them,' she said slowly, as if this thought was new too. A feeling of intense loneliness stole over her, prompting a sudden urge to go home.

Cathy gently freed her hand. Levi hadn't shown up. He'd missed the scan, saying he was running late. And this was after she'd continually rescheduled waiting for him to be free. She tried not to feel upset, but she wondered what on earth was more important than attending your baby's scan. She felt exhausted – and very alone.

'Thank you, I'll be off now. Thank you for being so kind.' Cathy stumbled over her words as she grabbed her bag and took off the hospital gown that covered her top half. She pulled on her T-shirt and jacket, and fled.

At home, she flopped onto her bed, burying her face in the pillow. She was having twins, as her dad and Alfie had been. She'd have two babies to feed and care for, two little ones to love and bring up. Would she be doing that alone, too? As she felt her heart sink, her phone rang. She sat up and hunted through her bag. It was Levi. For a moment, she considered whether or not to answer it. He'd let her down badly. It kept ringing and eventually she relented, pressing the green button to take the call.

'Baby, I'm so sorry I missed the scan. I got held up with a meeting, like, and ye know how it is . . .' His voice oozed with regret and that characteristic charm. Yet, strangely, it had little effect on her this time. Cathy didn't reply.

Levi carried on speaking. 'So, what did they say? Are we havin' an alien wit green eyes and huge feet?'

Cathy couldn't help herself. She giggled.

'Or is it a wee devil inside ye. It must be, eh, if I'm the father.'

'Levi how could you not come? I was waiting for you but eventually I had to go in or I'd have lost the appointment,' Cathy said, her voice halfway between pleading and anger.

'Baby, I've said I'm sorry. It's business, like. Things don't always go to plan and I just couldn't get dere.' His voice sounded wheedling. At least he'd called. He must care, to be finding out what happened. Mollified, Cathy replied, 'It was all fine, but there is some news . . .'

'What's dat, den? Is it a boy? I knew it was,' Levi began but Cathy interrupted him.

'I didn't ask about the sex of our babies.'

She let that float in the air for a moment, wondering if he'd pick up on the plural version of the word. He spluttered, and she realised he had.

'Babies? What d'ye mean? How many have ye got in dere?' He sounded playful but Cathy knew that beneath it he was shocked.

'We're having twins, baby,' she said simply, relishing the surprise. That would teach him not to show up.

'Twins?' Levi said and let out a long, slow whistle. 'Twins are hard work, so they are,' he continued. 'That'll be difficult for ye.'

'For us,' Cathy said firmly.

As she was talking, she caught sight of herself in the bedroom mirror. Her long honey-blonde hair hung down her back. She was still tanned from the late summer sunshine and her face looked flushed – with both excitement and nerves. She saw a young woman with her whole life ahead of her, who would soon have two young babies to care for, and for a short moment, she was flooded with happiness. The babies were healthy. That's all that mattered. Her bump was showing now, and there were two tiny souls forming in there. For a moment, she was cast into the wonder of the new life they'd created.

'Levi, I'm so happy,' she said, cutting across something he was saying. She hadn't been listening.

'Oh, OK, babe. Look, darlin', I'll come and see ye tonight, but I need ye to do me a favour first.'

'What's that?' she said absentmindedly.

Cathy stared back at herself: a woman in the process of becoming a mother. She looked like any young mum doing it for the first time; a mix of worry and excitement on her face as her hands clasped the soft skin of her growing belly.

'Cathy, baby, are ye listenin' to me? This is important,' Levi said sharply.

'Sorry baby, I'm listening now,' Cathy said, her focus pulled back to the conversation.

As quickly as he'd snapped, his voice changed back to liquid honey.

'Baby, I can't tink of anytin' better than comin' to see ye tonight but I need ye to do one small ting for me. Can ye do that for me?'

'Will you promise to come tonight?' Cathy murmured, 'I miss you, and so do the babies.'

'I promise. Now, I need ye to pick up a delivery for work for me. I'm out on a job with my cousin and I can't get dere, so it'd be a big help if ye could go to this address and pick up a bag for me.'

'What's in the bag?' Cathy asked but she wasn't concentrating. A shaft of sunlight streamed into the room and she felt sleepy.

'Oh, nuthin' to worry about. Boring work stuff like tools. Just write down this address, will ye?'

'OK, let me grab a pen.' Cathy padded off, searching for a pen and something to write on. When she put the phone back to her ear she caught the tail end of Levi's conversation, presumably with his cousin.

'Don't worry, she won't . . . Oh, are ye back, baby?'

'She won't, what?' Cathy said, suddenly alert.

'Oh, nuthin' to do with ye. We're talkin' about someone else, baby.' Levi sounded strange. 'OK, here's the address.'

The road a few streets down from Star Lane where Cathy's mum and Uncle Bobby had grown up. She felt strange at the prospect of revisiting their neighbourhood without them knowing.

'OK, I'll have some lunch then go afterwards,' Cathy replied, looking down at the address. Shrugging, she shoved the paper into her bag and said to herself, *At least it's a trip out. And by the time I'm back, Levi will be here. Perhaps he'll be so grateful he'll stay a few days.* Cathy hated how Levi snuck off in the middle of the night. 'It makes me feel like a prostitute, and an unpaid one at that,' she'd grumble as he'd drop a kiss lightly on her forehead and tell her to go back to sleep. He always justified it, saying he had to pick up some of the lads early and be back at the site by 5 a.m. to go off to work, but Cathy hated him leaving. It felt too much like she was his mistress or he was ashamed of her. He'd always soothe her, saying, 'How could I be ashamed by a beautiful woman such as yerself, baby,' or, 'I hate leavin' ye, I promise I'll be back,' but somehow as time moved on, and her bump had grown, the doubts kept forming, and each time he left in the early hours, she felt worse.

'Actually, Cathy, would ye go now and get lunch later? I wouldn't ask, but it's urgent.' Levi cut through her thinking. He rarely used her name, so it surprised her when he did.

'OK, I'm on my way now,' she said brightly, eager to help. Perhaps whatever she was picking up was part of his tarmac business, which is why it couldn't wait. He must be as eager as she was to set up their life together.

Humming to herself, she got into her car and drove from Chigwell down to East London. As she got closer to her destination, the familiar streets were replaced by roads with denser housing, miles of concrete pavements and blocks of council flats, some daubed with graffiti.

She pulled over, checking the address she'd written down on the back of the envelope. This seemed to be the right street. She drove slowly until she found the number of the house, a particularly run-down Victorian terrace which was clearly divided into flats as overflowing bins with each resident's flat number were lined up along the path. She parked a few doors down and, with a feeling of trepidation, walked up the path, her nose wrinkling with the smell of rubbish.

Levi had told her to ring the bell of number three and wait. They'd come to her. All she had to do was collect the bag and take it back home and wait for Levi to show up. The black front door, which had peeling-off paint, opened and a man appeared out of the gloom. He wore a black T-shirt with a large skull on the front despite the cold, and when he smiled at seeing the young woman, Cathy shuddered.

'I've come to collect something for my boyfriend,' she said, feeling uncomfortable under the man's gaze.

'Have you now? He's a lucky man. He didn't tell us nuthin' about you.' The man grinned as he spoke and leaned back against the doorpost.

'Please, I've come for the package and I have to get back to him,' she said.

The man nodded, then slowly reached behind him and brought out a large black holdall.

'Make sure you keep that safe, girl,' he said, dumping it at her feet.

'Thank you,' Cathy managed, and lifted the bag. It was surprisingly heavy, and for a moment she panicked, wondering if it would hurt the babies to carry something so big, but when she realised the guy was hanging out, watching her, she decided it was better to leave quickly, and so she half-dragged it to her car. The man kept his eyes on her as she went, that grin never leaving his face. He didn't offer to help. She loaded the bag into the boot, slammed the driver's side door shut and reached into her handbag for her phone.

'I've got the bloody bag, but how could you let me come to this place? And the bag was heavy!' she sobbed to Levi as soon as he picked up.

'Baby, ye've done amazing. Just get yerself home now and I'll be there as soon as I can.' Levi's voice was soothing. He was obviously delighted in her.

She sniffed and placed her phone back in her bag.

Let's get home, little ones, she muttered to her bump. *I don't want to stay here a moment longer.* As she drove off, she glanced in her mirror. The man still stood there, smiling that strange smile. *What on earth is he grinning for?* she thought to herself and shuddered. Something about him didn't feel right. Perhaps it was the intuition she'd inherited from her mother, or perhaps it was just common sense, but Cathy couldn't get home fast enough.

As she drove, Cathy turned her music up to full volume and sang as she went. Life looked good again as soon as she was clear of the pickup. She'd helped Levi and now she could look forward to a cosy night together. In her bag was a picture printed off the scanner, two sets of tiny heads and limbs picked out in white against a black screen.

Your daddy will meet you both tonight. He'll see a picture of you and we'll be so happy, she said out loud, her eyes flicking to her rear-view mirror as the blue lights and screaming sirens of approaching police cars flashed behind her. She slowed down to let them pass and was astonished when, instead of rushing past, they stopped, screeching one in front of her car and one behind. She braked hard to avoid colliding with them, and sat, stupidly, wondering what the hell was happening. Two armed officers leapt out. One sank to his knees, pointing a gun at her car, while the other ran over to her.

'What's going on?' she called out, bewildered by the terrible mistake they were making. The person they were chasing would've fled by now.

'You've got the wrong person!' Cathy shouted, trying to be helpful.

'Open your boot,' was the reply.

Cathy looked at the officer, her mouth gaping open.

'Open your fucking boot! Now!' the officer ordered, breaking the spell.

Terrified, Cathy scrambled out of the car and walked in a daze round to the boot.

'But there's only some of my boyfriend's work stuff in here,' she started to say as she wrenched the boot open.

'Put your hands up and step away from the vehicle!' shouted the standing officer. He too was pointing a gun at her.

He stepped over as she raised her hands and roughly pinned her to the car, shackling her with handcuffs.

'What's happening?' Cathy cried. 'Be careful, I'm pregnant!'

Everything seemed to go in slow motion. Another police car arrived, its lights turning, its sirens shrieking. More officers seemed to appear from nowhere. People looked out of their cars to see what the commotion was. Cathy thought she might die of shame.

Just as she thought it couldn't get any worse, she realised she was being read her rights.

Shock hit her in waves.

'I'm pregnant, what are you doing to me?' she wailed, as a female officer told her to get into a waiting police car.

'But there's only work tools in there. Just something I had to pick up for him today . . .' she cried but no one seemed to be listening.

Seconds later, she was bundled into the back seat, but more gently this time. The female officer got in beside her. Her face was grim. Cathy shrank from her, realising any dreams of a cosy night with Levi were completely quashed.

She looked out of the window and saw a policeman walking towards his car with the black holdall in his grip.

CHAPTER 23

'Interview commencing at 3.05 p.m.,' said the female officer into the recorder. It was a different woman than had accompanied her in the police car. This one was aged about thirty-five, had blonde hair tied back in a severe ponytail and wore a smart navy suit. A male officer sat next to her. His arms were folded in front of his chest as he sat back, staring at Cathy.

Cathy was bewildered. She had never been inside a police station in her life, and especially not inside an interview room. There was nothing in the drab room except for the table and three chairs, plus the recording equipment. At the end, facing Cathy, was a large black window. She'd seen enough cop shows to know this was a one-way sheet of glass so she was probably being observed by more officers behind it. The thought of her every move, every action and facial expression being watched made her shudder. By now, tears streamed down her face. She held her rounded belly as if to protect the children growing inside her.

'Cathy Willson, you have repeatedly refused for a solicitor to be present.' Cathy nodded. She hoped this was just a stupid mistake and she'd be set free, so she'd refused any representation. She also knew that if she asked for the family lawyer Rupert Smithers, her mum Ruby would find out she'd been arrested.

'Two kilos of cocaine with a market value of quarter of a million was found in your car boot. Can you tell us how it got there?'

Cathy looked blankly at the woman police officer who stared coldly back at her. She was becoming numb with shock, unable to take in what they were saying. She said nothing in response. For a moment, she thought she'd misheard. There was cocaine in her car? How on earth did it get there?

She thought, for a moment, that the guy at the house in East London must've picked up the wrong holdall to give to her. This was obviously just some big mistake and they'd realise soon, wouldn't they?

'Did you understand the question, Miss Willson? Where did you get the drugs from?'

Cathy shook her head. Her voice, when it came, was a whisper.

'I don't know anything about drugs. My boyfriend asked me to pick something up for him,' she stammered. 'He said it was equipment for work, I think. I can't really remember, sorry. He gave me an address in East London which I've already told you, and so I went there.'

The male officer leaned towards the young woman.

'We know everythin', Cathy. We know it all. The runner you bought the cocaine from told us everythin'. He's been under investigation, and luckily for us, we'd started surveillance on him, which is how we picked you up.'

Cathy looked at him blankly. The officer sighed.

'All right, Miss Willson, I'll spell it out for ya. The runner tells us you've been buyin' coke from him regularly. He tells us you're makin' a name for yerself dealin' the cocaine, sellin' it in London and Essex.'

'What? That's a lie!' Cathy was stung into defending herself. She was sitting up straight now, her face flushed, her heart beating against her ribcage.

'You mean you've never met him? You're not dealin'? Don't make me laugh, Miss Willson, we've got you on film today pickin' up your latest supply.'

'I'm not a dealer! I don't know anything about drugs or cocaine! My boyfriend asked me to go and pick up something for work and so that's what I did . . .'

The officers glanced at each other. They obviously didn't believe a word she was saying. Cathy looked between them, frantically.

'You have to believe me. I'd just had the babies' scan, and we were meant to spend the night together. I don't understand why this is happening.'

'What's your boyfriend's name, Cathy? Perhaps he can come 'ere and tell us all about it, clear your name . . .'

Cathy looked at them. She saw the cynicism written on both officers' faces. She knew that they weren't taking her seriously, and she also guessed that Levi wouldn't thank her for naming him in case he really was caught up in this. She hesitated unsure what to think, unsure what to say. Her instinct was to protest her innocence, tell them everything about Levi and his instructions for collecting the bag. She wanted to show them that she had nothing to do with any of this, but something stopped her. Her love for the father of her babies stopped her, and so she ignored her gut feeling. She said nothing.

'Tell us his name and we'll ask him. If he loves ya then he'll want to clear this up for ya, surely?' The woman officer leaned forward, grinning.

Cathy shook her head.

'I made a mistake. I'm innocent, that's all I'm saying.'

The cops glanced at each other. Cathy saw their look. She saw they didn't believe her. She saw their triumph, perhaps in catching a member of the notorious Willson family. She saw she was screwed. That's when she burst into tears. The female officer reached for the recording.

'Interview paused at 3.15 p.m.'

The male officer got up and yawned. Before he left the room, he turned to Cathy, almost as an afterthought, and said, 'Erm. Can I get ya anythin'? A tea or a coffee?'

Cathy nodded, though she couldn't speak because the emotions were tumbling through her. She knew in her heart she couldn't grass on Levi. He wouldn't like it. His community definitely wouldn't like it, and if she was ever to become his wife, she had to keep them sweet. There had to be a way out of this, but she couldn't fathom what it might be. Eventually, she nodded.

'Tea, please. One sugar, thank you.' Her natural politeness and eagerness to please was evident even now. She eased herself back in the uncomfortable chair, her hands holding her bump. *It's going to be OK*, she crooned softly under her breath, as if telling her unborn children, or trying to convince herself. But the situation didn't look good. It didn't look good at all.

Ten awkward minutes later, the policeman reappeared balancing three polystyrene cups of tea.

'Ready?' The woman officer said, this time more gently.

Cathy nodded.

'Interview recommencing at 3.40 p.m.,' she said.

If they were playing good cop versus bad cop roles, then it was the man's turn to grill her.

'A colleague of mine has spoken to the runner you bought the cocaine from. He's in the same nick, you might be interested to 'ear—'

'I didn't buy anything,' Cathy interrupted. The sweet tea had given her a temporary lift.

'We've spoken to the runner,' the cop continued harshly, speaking over her, 'and he says it was always you that collected and paid for each shipment. He says there's no boyfriend. No one else involved at all. What do ya say to that?'

'Oh my God, why would he say that?' Cathy exclaimed. 'He's lying! I'd never met that man before. It was the first time I'd ever been there. There's been a terrible mistake!'

But even as Cathy said the words, she had a growing sense of unease, a realisation that perhaps her boyfriend and that man, whoever he was, had cast her adrift, and were leaving her to face this. Surely Levi wouldn't be so cruel? He loved her and their babies, didn't he? Cathy couldn't believe that the man she'd given her heart to would deny her, or slip away like mist over the Thames, leaving her to face this alone. There had to be an explanation. But why would the runner say he didn't know Levi? The questions were beating inside Cathy's brain and there were absolutely no answers to any of them. It was all so confusing.

The male officer sat and stared at Cathy. It was obvious he didn't believe her story at all. Almost as an afterthought, he added, 'Listen, Cathy, we know who your family are. We know your name. We know you're related to Lloyd Willson and the twins Archie and Alfie. The name Willson is known to everyone in the drug squad, though as ya know we've only managed to pin down Lloyd in the past and that was for robbery, not drugs.

'We ain't stupid, though. We know the Willson family are up to their necks in the cocaine business. We've just never been able to pin anythin' on any of them – until now.'

Cathy looked up at him and to her horror, saw something on his face which alarmed her. She saw a grim determination. Perhaps he was now determined to nail this Willson, the one who, somehow, had walked straight into their hands. Perhaps she would pay for her family's crimes – despite the fact that all she'd wanted was to get as far away from her family name as possible.

There was a short silence as Cathy digested what she'd heard. How ironic it was that she, who'd known nothing about her family's trade, their cartel, their runners and dealers, was now the one going down for it. She saw that, somehow, to the police, she'd become a sacrificial lamb. Ruby and Lloyd, and Archie too, were so clever, so ahead of the game, that they would never leave a trace to be picked up, no evidence, no scent for the police to follow. They knew their rights. They had the best lawyer in the country behind them. They were untouchable.

'I have to pee,' Cathy said dully, arching her back. Her bladder seemed so sensitive to any liquid these days. The officers exchanged an exasperated glance.

'Interview suspended at 3.44 p.m. Miss Willson, if you'll follow me,' the woman said, getting up and holding the door open. Cathy followed, her head whirring. The same questions kept beating at her brain. Why was the man in East London lying? Why was he saying he didn't know Levi? Most puzzling of all was this man's insistence that she'd been there before. Was he confusing her with someone else, or, worse, was he protecting her boyfriend at her expense? She had to speak to Levi. He was her only hope in clearing this up. She had to make the police understand that she wasn't involved even though it was obvious now, because of her family name, she was a marked woman.

Cathy sat down heavily on the loo and waited for the trickle of urine. The female officer stood in front of the slightly ajar toilet door. It was degrading having to wee in front of this woman who was obviously the senior officer on this case. When she'd finished, Cathy shuffled out, throwing the officer a filthy look, then allowed herself to be led back to the room. The interview started again.

'Listen, I need to speak to the dealer guy. He'll explain everything,' Cathy pleaded, 'This is just a big misunderstanding. He'll tell you that I've never been to that place before, and I had no idea there were drugs in that bag. He must've confused me with someone else, it's the only possible explanation.'

In response, the male policeman leaned forward again, his elbows on the table, his hands clasped together as if in prayer, and, in a voice that was surprisingly gentle, he said, 'Cathy, you do know you're in a lot of trouble. We know you went to the dealer's address and you picked up a bag containing a large amount of cocaine. You was caught on camera. We've got the evidence, so make life a bit easier for yerself. Tell us how many times you've been there. Tell us where you're supplyin' the coke, and perhaps we can cut a deal . . . Cathy, ya need to come clean. If ya tell us everythin' now we can try and help ya.'

The distraught young woman looked between the police officers. This was like a nightmare that didn't seem to end. She couldn't get through to them.

'I don't understand,' was all she could say in response. Tears sprang to her eyes again. This time she didn't bother wiping them away. Levi had given her the address; he'd got her to write it down. He hadn't texted it to her. There was no proof of his involvement at all. She could tell them that Levi had wanted big money from her mum, and got it, so had the means to buy cocaine, but where did that leave their love for each other? She had to keep quiet and hope this all blew over, though she couldn't imagine how. Her natural loyalty and her love for Levi stopped her naming him. She could tell them everything she knew about him: which traveller site he was based at, which bars he drank in. But she realised again she actually knew very little about this man. It was a strange feeling, carrying her lover's children yet knowing almost nothing of real value about him. Had she been swept off her feet? Did he mean everything he'd said about their future together? She had to trust someone, and she'd made the decision that it was him. So she continued to say nothing. She couldn't nail her own boyfriend to the cross. She had to believe this was just a ridiculous mistake, that, admittedly, was getting out of hand.

'When did you start dealing? Who have you supplied?'

'I don't know. I promise, I don't know what you're talking about!' Cathy wept openly now. The officers were unmoved by her plight. They'd seen it all before. Cathy was starting to realise that she was just one more person protesting their innocence; one more person they didn't believe.

'Give us the information and it might go better for ya. They'll throw the book at ya, you do realise that. Because of yer name, because of yer connections. They'll make an example of ya unless you play ball with us. Give us the names of the scum that sell you the coke. Give us all of them, and ya might get off, if not lightly, then with a reduced sentence,' the male officer finished. He sat back in his chair as if he'd dealt the winning card in this game. He was a muscular-looking guy with hair shaved close to his head and an uncompromising expression. Tears rolled down Cathy's face as she looked back at him. Did he mean she would be sentenced? Did that mean they were going to send her to prison? None of it made sense, yet she understood that she was in deep trouble – and there was no one who could bail her out.

Eventually, she shook her head.

'That's all I know.'

The officers glanced at each other again. The woman was the first to speak.

'Cathy Willson, I'm charging you with possession of two kilos of cocaine with the intent to supply.'

CHAPTER 24

Ruby stepped out of the shower. Her long black hair dripped on the Italian tiles. She reached for a fluffy white towel, wrapped it around her, and swept into her bedroom. Her phone was on the dressing table, and it wasn't until she sat down to blow dry her wet mane that she saw the twelve missed calls from Lloyd.

'What's 'appened?' As soon as her father-in-law picked up her call, Ruby got straight to the point.

'Rube, it's serious. It's Cathy,' he answered quickly.

'Is it the baby? God, tell me what's 'appened? Is Cathy alive?'

''Course she's alive – and the baby is fine, so far as I know, but listen . . .'

Ruby was grateful she was sitting down as her legs felt weak enough to crumple.

'What is it, then?' She regained control of herself almost immediately.

'She's been nicked.'

Ruby hadn't expected that.

'Arrested? But why? For what?' Ruby asked, her heart beating faster. Yet, somehow, she already knew why. A tingling sensation ran down her spine.

'Levi . . .' she breathed. 'Lloyd, tell me everythin'.'

'Well, one of the coppers in our pocket at the nick called an hour ago. A young woman called Cathy Willson was brought in for questionin' yesterday afternoon. Her notes say she's pregnant. She has to be our Cathy.'

Ruby held the phone away from her ear. She couldn't bear to hear what was coming next.

'Go on,' she said eventually.

'Rube, she's been charged with intent to supply.'

'Oh my God, that bastard Levi has set her up!' Ruby exploded. 'I'll bet you any money he's the one responsible for this. My innocent girl would never be caught up dealin'. Oh Lloyd, it must be the coke he's been buyin' with the money I gave him. How could he do this to her?'

'Hold on, Rube. We don't know the circumstances yet,' Lloyd tried to reassure Ruby, but to no avail.

'It's him. That rotten bastard, I'll kill him for this.' Despite not knowing the facts, Ruby was damned sure she knew what had happened. She could feel it in her gut – and, unlike her daughter, she always trusted her instincts.

'Listen, that isn't all, Rube. My men are sayin' that Levi has vanished. He's either hidin' out at the traveller site or he's been smuggled out of the country. No one's seen him for days.'

'Perhaps he left before the shit hit the fan.' Ruby was a classy lady but this was too much, even for her.

'We don't know that either, Rube,' Lloyd interrupted her train of thought, slowing her down. 'He might've got lucky and been away on whatever business he's up to. All we know is that they 'ave Cathy. My source said there's been no arrest of anyone with the name Levi.'

'Surely they'll find the scumbag and arrest him instead?'

Lloyd didn't answer straight away.

'Rube, prepare yerself for the worst. If Cathy is still loyal to Levi, and what we think about him dealin' is true, then she'll be protectin' him. She won't say a word.'

'Then she's in big trouble,' Ruby said simply. In that moment, she knew that if she set eyes on Levi again, she'd kill him. 'Get Rupert Smithers down there now. She needs representation. We need to know what 'appened,' she commanded. 'And we need to find that shyster boyfriend, and fast.'

'He'll know the Old Bill 'ave Cathy by now. He'll 'ave gone to ground, until he finds out either way if the cops are after him,' Lloyd predicted. 'They found two kilos of coke in the boot of Cathy's car. I'm bettin' she was asked to do a drop by that bastard Levi, and I bet she didn't 'ave a clue what she was doin'.'

'He's a dead man, whether he's set her up deliberately or not,' Ruby said with venom. 'He's a dead man walkin'.'

If either of them remembered that this same death wish had hung briefly over George's head then they didn't say. Levi, like George before him and Vladimir too, had crossed a line. There was no going back. Ruby was on the warpath.

Ruby ended the call. She held the phone to her chest for a moment, breathing hard. Shock threatened to overwhelm her. She needed to think. The first thing to do was to get down to the police station and see what she could find out. In the meantime, Lloyd was going to hunt down Levi using his network of contacts. She needed to act, so why did her body suddenly feel weighted down? Her limbs moved through thick molasses, heavy with disbelief, as she pulled on clothes and then picked up her sunglasses and handbag as she made her way downstairs. There was no time to eat. No time for coffee. She had to get to where Cathy was being held, though she had no idea what she would be able to do when she got there. A feeling of despair started to settle on Ruby, and though it was so unlike her to succumb to it, she couldn't resist. She'd known Levi was trouble and yet she hadn't done enough to persuade him that seeing her daughter wasn't an option. She should've warned him off, got Alfie onto him. As she screeched her car out of the driveway, she knew in her heart that she was to blame.

The police station was only a ten-minute drive away. Ruby parked haphazardly and almost ran inside, her high heels clicking on the concrete slabs. She wrenched open the door and saw there was already a short queue of two women in front of her. Ruby wasn't used to waiting in line. Her life involved first-class travel, premium access to anything she wished for, and it had been like this for a long time. She didn't like to have to stand there, helplessly looking on, while the clock ticked and goodness knows what was happening to her daughter. The wait was excruciating. She was impatient to speak to someone, anyone. Both women in front of her looked downtrodden; one wore skinny ripped jeans and had greasy long brown hair, the other stank of cheap tobacco and was covered in tattoos. Both looked Ruby up and down, taking in her expensive clothes, her glossy hair – though it was still wet from her shower. Ruby stared back at them. She wasn't intimidated. She knew these girls, because she almost became one of them. They looked like they'd had hard lives, had always just scraped by, like her friend Sarah. They were probably here to chase up dodgy boyfriends or wayward sons, to plead to see them, like Ruby would be doing for Cathy. Why was the world so cruel to women? Why did they continue to love the ones that hurt them, or abandoned them? Ruby didn't have an answer, but she knew that having loving, straight parents in her childhood had given her something these girls would never have: a solid sense of herself, and a true knowledge of what being loved felt like. It was like a kind of glow – a mysterious protection from the outside world, an inner strength that was priceless.

'I want to see him. Why don't ya let me, just for a moment? I ain't goin' until ya let me,' the woman in front of her said sullenly. The one wearing skinny jeans had slunk off, leaving the woman with tattoos and Ruby standing in front of a high desk, behind which sat a female officer. Her expression was unyielding. She was very obviously unmoved by the woman's tears.

'Madam, I've told you I can't help you. The first court hearing is in two days. You can attend that if you wish.'

For a second, Ruby felt the woman's powerlessness. The impotent rage when faced with uncaring authorities. She knew what it was to come from one of the poorest parts of East London. She knew how people like her, and this woman, were nobodies to these desk clerks and lawyers, the officers, judges, barristers and detective inspectors. They didn't land on the radars of these people, their lives were inconsequential – and one thing was for sure, they'd never beat the system. The system always, always beat them, and she was watching one small example of it now.

Ruby felt mounting anger as she heard the defeat in the woman's voice.

'Please, I need to see him.'

The desk clerk didn't even look up from her computer as she replied. 'That's not possible, sorry.' For a moment, Ruby wondered what the woman would do.

'Thanks for fuckin' nuthin',' came her answer. 'Bitch,' she grumbled under her breath as she walked off, throwing Ruby a hard stare as she went.

Ruby didn't recoil. She'd seen her brother Bobby go down for a robbery, standing in front of the powers-that-be, knowing everything was against him. She knew that people like them, even with the money and power they had, were nothing in this system. How could this woman, with her poverty, her inability to pick a decent man, the wounds from a life where she could never get ahead, ever stand up to the law? It was inconceivable. Yet, now it was Ruby's turn. As she approached, the desk clerk flicked her eyes up, noting Ruby's expensive clobber, before losing interest again. Ruby might not have been the typical punter seen across that desk but, like the other women, she was still on the wrong side of it.

'I'm 'ere because you're holdin' my daughter, Cathy Willson. I want to see her.' Ruby didn't beat around the bush. *And I ain't goin' to beg to the likes of you*, she thought to herself.

The clerk tapped on her keyboard and looked up at her screen. She was attractive, with dark brunette hair pulled back from her face and large brown eyes.

'She was charged last night. You can't see her but she should have a solicitor, she's up in front of the magistrates tomorrow.'

The desk clerk looked away as if that concluded the matter.

'My daughter is pregnant. I want to see her, please, and make sure she's bein' properly cared for,' Ruby said, keeping her voice calm, though she could've stamped her feet in frustration.

'I can't help you. Sorry, love,' the clerk said without looking up.

'Listen, whatever they think she's done, she's innocent. They don't come more innocent than my daughter.' Ruby's voice was pleading now, something she'd vowed never to do, but this was worth more than her pride. She was desperate to see Cathy, whatever it took.

The young woman looked up, checked out the Gucci bag, Prada sunglasses and Bentley car keys, which seemed to give her a moment of interest, but, as before, she looked away.

'Next, please.'

For a moment, Ruby didn't realise she'd been dismissed. No one would dare do that to her in her world. She had to swallow down her temper. Turning round, she walked slowly to the doorway, her heels making a hollow sound on the vinyl floor as she went. She fought the urge to shout or cry. The frustration she'd felt when she'd realised they were making an example of Bobby and sending him down for a long stretch reared up again, though it had been years ago. She knew then, as she knew now, that the gulf between herself and 'those' people – lawyers, the police, court judges – was unbreachable. Her kind might bribe or threaten their way to achieve power and money, but at the end of the day they'd always be scum to the authorities, they'd never win. Ruby was deflated as she walked out of the police station. Despite the sunshine, she felt the chill of the autumn air that set in once the sun went down, a foretelling of the long winter ahead. Yet again, she couldn't help her loved ones once they were inside the system. The thought almost broke her.

Back in her car, she dialled her lawyer's mobile number.

'Rupert Smithers . . .'

'Rupert, it's Ruby. It's about my daughter Cathy,' she said.

'I know. Lloyd called. I'm in court but I'll be there as soon as I can,' the family lawyer said in his cut-glass accent. 'Don't bother waiting, there's nothing you can do at this stage. I'll call you when I've seen her.'

Ruby drove home, wondering how on earth she would get through the next few hours waiting for news. The rest of that day, she couldn't settle on anything. She paced the house, unable to concentrate, picking up a magazine and then discarding it after a few words, unable to take anything in, unable to think of anything but Cathy's predicament.

Finally, at 7 p.m., her phone rang. It was Rupert.

'Tell me,' Ruby said.

'I'll be frank with you; it doesn't look good. She was found with two kilos of cocaine in her boot. She says she has no idea whose it is. The police had mounted a sting against the dealer she picked up the drugs from. It was unlucky, more than anything. The police had just started staking out that building and so they have video evidence of her collecting the bag containing the drugs.'

'What can we do?' Ruby felt like begging. To lose her brother to jail for ten years was hell enough, but for Cathy to be locked up – it was unimaginable. Bobby was very different to her daughter. He'd grown up in poverty and he could handle himself, even though at heart he was a softie. To those outside of their family, he could present a formidable front. Cathy, by contrast, had grown up with every luxury, and had been protected from their world, possibly too well. She would be lost in prison. She would be brutalised. They had to find a way to sort this.

'Ruby, I'm sorry to say that there's nothing you, or anyone else, can do. I know you're a woman with wealth, and I know that some of your business is, shall we say, outside of the remits of the law, which is none of my concern of course, but there are procedures to follow,' her lawyer said. 'She's been caught red-handed, with an awful lot of cocaine. Officers were staking out the house that day, and they have a witness who says she bought it regularly, though they have no evidence of that apart from the dealer's claim. Steel yourself, Ruby, because I'm afraid they might make an example of her.'

'An example of her?' Ruby said, her voice choked.

Rupert coughed.

'Look at it from the court's point of view: she's a young woman who's had the best education and life afforded her by rich parents, and still she breaks the law on a staggering scale. And it isn't just that. She comes from a family with well-known nefarious connections. Her grandfather was jailed for robbery, and so the Willson name has, ahem, a *reputation . . .*'

'I see,' said Ruby. She couldn't argue with that. 'So, what can we do?'

Rupert Smithers paused. His reply, when it came, was measured. 'Unless we can find out from her what really happened, whether perhaps she was acting upon another's instructions, and prove that this was the one and only time she did what she did, then I'm afraid things don't look good.'

Ruby almost threw down her phone in frustration. She stared out her window, the light from the outside lamps shining on her immaculate lawn with the new planting all taking shape, the new pool and sun loungers covered now the season had changed, and she wondered, for the briefest of moments, what the hell all this had been for.

'How can we do that?' she said bleakly. 'My gut tells me it's her shyster boyfriend Levi who's set her up, but he'll never admit to the Old Bill that he's the dealer because he'd go down for a long stretch,' she said, her brain running ahead of her. 'He's not stupid. He charmed my daughter, got her pregnant and now he's nowhere to be found. It ain't like he's 'ere by her side. He's done a runner, I know it. And in doin' so, he's leavin' Cathy to the wolves.'

Ruby couldn't say any more because she felt the sudden urge to burst into tears.

It was Rupert who cut through her thoughts. 'Find me evidence to prove that Cathy wasn't involved except as a mule for this man's drug trading, and there might be hope. Until then, I'll do what I can, which – to be honest, Ruby – isn't much.'

Ruby ended the call. In her heart, she knew Cathy was lost. Who on earth would take the rap for a drug bust if they didn't have to? Not Levi, she suspected; not many men, now she came to think of it. Cathy had been naive, and had put her trust in someone who was about to let her down spectacularly, or so Ruby's instincts told her. The pain this gave her almost choked her. Despite her feelings, she hoped desperately she was wrong. After all, she had no evidence of any of this. They didn't know what had really happened and would only find out once Cathy came to court. She hoped fervently she'd misjudged Levi, underestimated his affections for Cathy, and he would give himself up and do the right thing by his pregnant girlfriend. Ruby sat down heavily, staring at the bedroom wall, not seeing it nor any of her plush surroundings.

She should've acted on her instincts about Levi sooner. Cathy was a sweet girl who had been grieving her father and uncle when Levi came along. Her relationship with him should never have got this far, whether he did the right thing now or not. It just shouldn't ever have got to this point. Ruby should've stepped in months ago, but she'd failed. She'd left her daughter to fend for herself, up against an uncaring system, abandoned – or so Ruby suspected – by the father of her child. Ruby saw very clearly that she only had herself to blame.

CHAPTER 25

Tearful and scared, Cathy sat in the back of the police van as it pulled off the road and into the precincts of Holloway Prison. Past the threshold, the large wooden gates slid shut, grinding as they moved. Nausea rose within her as the van doors were opened and she stepped out.

'This way,' said the guard curtly as Cathy followed behind her with two other women. No one had spoken on the journey. They'd each stared out the blackened windows, lost in their own fears and problems. What she first noticed inside were the sounds: indistinct shouting, the jangle of keys and doors banging.

'I shouldn't be here,' Cathy said to the receptionist, who barely looked up from behind the thick toughened glass screen.

'Of course, love, you and everyone else. Just sit over there and I'll get to ya,' the woman replied, an eyebrow raised.

'I'm innocent, I really am,' stuttered Cathy, this time to the guard who was gesturing for her to take a plastic seat, which was bolted to the concrete floor. She was beginning to feel something beyond fear or anger at being locked up. It was a sense of profound panic in the face of absolute disregard. Somehow, she had to make these people see that she shouldn't be here, even if they could do nothing about it. She didn't understand why that felt so important, it just did.

'Yes, they all say that,' the guard replied, crushing Cathy's spirit and making her realise that she truly was stuck in this place, at least for the short term.

An hour later, Cathy had been strip-searched and now sat in the holding room with all the girls who were fresh in or back from court. Cathy hardly dared raise her eyes from the floor. The atmosphere was tense, and there was some bickering now and then, or raucous laughs and nudges, most likely at her expense.

One of the women, who was around the same age as Cathy, but sporting a tracksuit and smudged make-up, her hair scraped back in a high ponytail, leaned towards her and said, 'What you in 'ere for?' As she spoke, she eyed up Cathy's clothes, her expensive jeans and T-shirt, her designer trainers, with undisguised envy.

'Nothing. I'm innocent,' Cathy replied, holding her bump, dropping her gaze back to the floor.

The woman snorted as if this was the funniest joke she'd heard that day.

'Oh yeah, you and me both, love, you and me both.'

This prompted a chorus of sniggers from a couple of the other girls who were fidgeting and pacing the room.

'She's the Virgin fuckin' Mary, I'll bet ya,' said another girl with dyed red hair and a short skirt with ripped leggings.

'No, she ain't. She's fuckin' pregnant!' laughed another, turning away from Cathy to try and ponce a ciggie.

Cathy kept her eyes downcast, hoping and praying they'd leave her alone.

The girls quickly got bored of taunting her, and instead turned to each other.

'Got any baccy? Or a fag?'

'What you in 'ere for, then?'

'Those fuckin' judges and their snooty, shit-fer-brains barristers. They don't 'ave a fuckin' clue what it's like bein' me.'

Eventually, a guard appeared and gestured for the women to follow her.

Cathy filed in at the back, wondering what on earth was happening now.

The screw eventually got to Cathy after allocating cells to the other new girls. 'This is yours,' she said. Cathy stood with three other girls: two Jamaican women and a small dark-haired Scottish woman. Inside were four small beds, all with stained mattresses, lumpy-looking pillows and a small pile of bedding. The guard handed each woman a toiletry pack with basic supplies: a toothbrush, tooth powder, flannel and a small bar of soap.

Once the door was clanged shut and locked, the women sat down on each bed and stared at each other.

'Anyone got a fag?' asked the Scottish woman.

They all shook their heads.

'Girl, you look good. Nice threads,' one of the Jamaican girls said.

'Is that a Rolex?' said the other, her eyebrows arched.

Cathy nodded uncertainly.

'I think so,' she said, her voice barely above a whisper.

The woman who'd spoken first, whose name she gave as Lisa, whistled.

'She don't even know if it real or not!'

'So, Little Miss Rich Girl, what you in here for?' The other Jamaican girl said, her eyes sliding over Cathy.

'I'm innocent, they got me by mistake for drugs. I didn't know what I was picking up,' Cathy said dully, her heart aching as she navigated away from the thought that her boyfriend might've had a hand in it. She couldn't bear to think that, even sitting here in a prison cell.

'Leave her alone, she's probably the only one in here who actually hasn't done what she'd been banged up for,' the Scottish girl said. 'I'm Maggie. Shoplifting.'

'Drugs,' Lisa said in her sing-song voice, lying back on the bed and folding her arms behind her head. Both Jamaican women had long nails like talons, decorated with crystals. Despite herself, Cathy felt a hint of fascination. She'd never met anyone like these women before. The girls talked among themselves, but it was all too much for

Cathy. She got into the hard bed and pulled the blanket around her, her back to the women as they bickered and chatted until late into the evening. Her whole world had collapsed, or so it felt. Closing her eyes, she hoped she would never wake up.

The next morning found Cathy staring blankly at the wall of the cell. She had been unable to sleep, unable to think clearly or understand what had led her to this point. All three of the other women seemed to have slept soundly. One of the women had snored loudly through the night, but the sounds of her sleeping hadn't masked the unfamiliar and frightening noises made by women down the corridor of the Reception Wing. Cathy was being held on remand, but she thought she had descended into hell. All night there had been the sounds of women shouting at each other or talking, some crying while some howled. The noises were strange, echoing around the corridors, scaring the young woman who lay awake, listening, as tears rolled down her face onto the lumpy pillow.

Now and again, someone would lift the hatch and ask, 'You OK?' But what could she say? She was in shock, devastated at this turn of events, unable to pick through the details that had led her here. The cells that lined the corridors were filled with girls who, like her, were waiting for their court hearings. She lost count of the times she heard different voices shout, 'I'm innocent!' She also lost count of the number of times she heard women yelling at the prison guards, 'You fuckin' bastards!' and 'Get me the fuck out of 'ere!' As the night stretched on, Cathy began the impossible task of sorting through the events of the past few days. The questions piled up. Had Levi known about the contents of that bag? Had he deliberately led her into danger? If so, why? At the very least, he'd played Russian roulette with her safety, and that of their babies. It was still unfathomable to her that Levi might have put her in harm's way.

Cathy heard his voice in her mind on the day he rang and asked her to go. He had sounded genuinely sorry for missing the scan, or was that just a ruse so she'd do his bidding? When she conjured up an image of him, she saw the big brown eyes that made her melt, felt the heat of his body against hers, and the agony of not knowing if the man she loved had betrayed her rushed in again. Worse, though, was the fact that he hadn't come forward. He must know by now that she had been arrested. Surely, if he knew the guy who'd given her the bag, then he'd know he'd been arrested too? It was all so confusing.

Cathy started to wonder if the pregnancy was messing with her brain. She started to question if she'd even gone to the right address. She wanted to believe this was all a terrible mistake, but she remembered the gleam in Levi's eyes when he'd brought round the money Ruby had given them. In his eyes was something she now reluctantly identified as greed. Had he started dealing? Had he used her as a drug mule? And if he had, could she actually judge him for doing what she now knew was the trade of her parents, her family? She'd grown up surrounded by the trappings of wealth accumulated by this drug trade, albeit at the very top end. She'd lived off dirty money for years, though she didn't know it at the time. How harsh could she be with Levi when she knew her beloved dad was the joint boss of a drug cartel with her mum and granddad? It had all come as an almighty shock and yet there had been signs, which she'd ignored, so naïve and trusting was she with her family. Her parents were glorified drug dealers, and everything she owned came back to selling cocaine or robberies. How could she judge Levi for trying to do the same thing?

At the same time, a single question kept beating through her skull: *How am I going to survive this?*

At 7 a.m., a prison guard banged on the door.

'Wakey, wakey, rise and shine.'

The hatch opened and the same voice said, 'Time for breakfast. What do you ladies eat?'

Cathy, disorientated for a moment, stammered, 'Erm, bacon, eggs, mushrooms . . .'

The voice laughed, 'Don't be funny. I mean are ya veggie or normal?'

'Normal, I guess,' Cathy replied, before a blue plastic plate was shoved through the open hatch. On it were two thin slices of streaky bacon and a slice of cheap white bread with a knob of margarine. Cathy took the plate, staring down at it. She saw now why the prison guard laughed at her description of a proper breakfast. The other girls yawned and shouted back 'normal' as a chorus, and they received their meagre offerings.

'This isn't no hotel. You eat when they say, and your bairns won't thank you if you don't. You've been given two rashers as you're pregnant, so eat up quick, the others only get one,' Maggie chided, seeing Cathy's grimace at the sight of her plate of food. 'Go for the porridge tomorrow. They make it with actual milk. I worked in the kitchens last time I was in, so I know,' she added. Cathy looked at the young woman, who couldn't have been much older than herself, and wondered at her acceptance of all this. The matter-of-fact way she spoke about being here was so alien to Cathy, who had spiralled into deep shock. If she'd have been in her right mind, she might've wondered what Maggie's life had been like – and why she kept ending up behind bars. Before Cathy could think any further on this, the voice from behind the latch added, 'You're bein' let out today.'

'Let out?' Cathy's face lit up. Instantly, she thought that Levi must've done the right thing. He'd told the cops that she was innocent! Her face must've lit up with delight, which made the screw laugh.

'Not out, out! Out in the wing,' the voice laughed as if this were all a joke. 'You can go and 'ave a wash, then later, eat your lunch with the other girls.'

Cathy's heart sank.

'Oh,' was all she said, as the hatch slammed shut, leaving them alone again with the sad, greasy-looking food and a hollow feeling in Cathy's heart.

As she sat on her bed, yawning, Cathy managed to eat a little of the unappetising meal. As she chewed the bacon rind, she thought of Levi. She missed him, though he had put her and their babies in danger. She missed his voice, his touch, the dreams she'd had for them becoming a family. She wanted desperately to believe in someone, and who else could it be but Levi? It must've been a terrible mistake, she concluded. Levi can't have known there was coke in the bag. The dodgy guy at the address must've mixed up the bags. It was the only explanation that made sense to her right now. After all, he was the father of the children growing in her womb.

No, he can't have let me down; there must be an explanation, she thought as she pushed away the plate. *I love him and he loves me. This will all be OK. He'll realise what's happened, that I picked up the wrong bag, and he'll make it right. Then we'll get married and have a family.*

Maggie was watching Cathy, almost as if she could guess what was going through her mind. Before anyone else could speak, the voice came again.

'All right, time for your wash. Don't mind the other girls . . .'

Cathy barely noticed the warning. She hung back and let the others go first, though Maggie held back too, waiting for her. Maggie was small but wiry, and wore faded jeans with a pink sweat top. Her dark hair was pulled back off her face with a bright pink scrunchie. Despite her rough appearance, she had a kind face.

'Hen, you don't look like you've slept at all. Look, it's not so bad. You'll get used to it,' she said with a smile.

Cathy shook her head.

'I won't get used to it. My boyfriend will get me out of here as soon as he realises the mistake,' she replied more firmly than she felt.

Maggie just looked at her. If there was a hint of pity in her eyes, then Cathy refused to notice.

''Course he will, hen. Come on, let's go and see what other delights are in store.'

Gripping the toiletry pack she'd been given, Cathy stood for a moment, wondering what she was going to meet when she stepped outside. Suddenly, ironically, the cell felt like the only safe place in the prison. Head down, her heart pounding with terror, Cathy walked along the corridor to the bathrooms, following the line of women who were catcalling to each other or arguing. Several women shoved into her deliberately, knocking her into the wall as she went, but she kept her eyes low, and her pace steady, not meeting their eyes, hoping she would blend into the furniture and they'd leave her alone.

They'll get me out soon. This will all be over when they realise I'm innocent, when Levi gets me out, she repeated to herself, fighting back tears.

'Won't be needin' that clobber in 'ere girl,' laughed a screw, which only made Cathy blush and dip her head lower. They'd spotted her designer clothes, the discreet logos on her jeans and T-shirt.

'She's goin' to need hardenin' up,' said a woman with a shaved head, arms filled with tattoos and a nasty smile who blocked her path.

'Outta the way, Jones,' said the prison guard lazily. 'Leave the girl alone, she ain't used to scumbags like you.'

'Oh, isn't she? Well, she'd better learn to get used to "scumbags" like me, eh, beautiful,' the woman said nastily.

'Just let me pass. There's been a mistake and I won't be here for long so please leave me alone,' Cathy whispered. She couldn't help it: the tears were coming now. They felt hot against her flushed cheeks. Everyone was looking at her; the new girl, the soft one. Cathy had never felt so frightened, nor so alone. Maggie had seen that Cathy was attracting unwelcome attention. She walked back and took Cathy's arm.

The screw said, now with more authority, 'Go on, leave her be. She's used to better than us. Move along, Jones, she's new, she'll toughen up.' There was an air of suppressed tension, hostility, which Cathy realised must be there all the time.

Women banged up, tempers fraying, the boredom and isolation making them hanker for a fight. Cathy couldn't blame them, she just didn't want to be anywhere near them.

The woman with the sneering expression blew Cathy a kiss, which made the others in the queue all laugh, then moved aside, reluctantly, allowing her and Maggie to pass.

'After you, m'lady.'

Cathy hesitated, unsure whether to walk past her tormentor, before being given a shove by the girl behind her.

Clutching her washbag, she stepped past, praying with all her might that she'd be released soon.

CHAPTER 26

An hour later, Cathy had managed to wash and had also been seen by the prison doctor, who confirmed her pregnancy for the prison files and told her she would leave for the mother and baby wing as soon as there was space. She was back in the cell, listening to the other girls bicker over a packet of fags, when a screw put her head round the door.

'Cathy Willson. Someone to see ya. Follow me.'

Cathy followed the guard down to the waiting room, where she was frisked before being led into yet another bleak-looking room with bolted-down plastic chairs.

'Oh my God, is it Cathy?' said the woman she sat down heavily next to. Cathy turned to her, but before she could say a word, the woman broke into a smile.

'Oh my God, it is you. Your mum gave me a good description. She was right, your eyes are almost as emerald green as hers!'

'How do you know my mum?' Cathy replied, puzzled. Strangely, there was something familiar about the older woman who now gripped both of her hands. The woman was thin and scrawny-looking, with missing teeth and greasy brown hair, but her face was kind and she seemed overjoyed to see her.

'Your mum Ruby and I go way back. We was best mates at school. I'm Sarah.'

With that, the woman, whose name Cathy recognised as her mum's childhood best friend, drew Cathy into a bear hug. Sarah smelled of old tobacco and cheap deodorant, but her grip was the tonic Cathy desperately needed. The embrace prompted a further outburst of weeping.

'There, there, Cathy. It ain't so bad. Honestly, you'll get used to it. And I'm 'ere to protect ya. I'll keep an eye on ya – Ruby asked me to.'

Cathy immediately pulled away.

'My mum knows I'm here?'

Sarah looked shifty, wouldn't catch Cathy's now-fierce gaze. The woman shrugged, eventually.

'Yer mum knows a lot of things, Cathy. She's worried about ya. She says it must be your boyfriend who's done ya over.'

In that moment, Cathy realised Ruby had probably told Sarah about their troubles. She felt sick all of a sudden. Was there no place her mother would not find her? Not even in jail was she free of her.

'Don't speak to me of my mum,' Cathy hissed. 'You don't know what you're talking about. My Levi would never hurt me, or our babies. He loves me. My mum knows nothing, and you can tell her from me: if she ever, ever tries to hurt him, then she'll never know her grand-children.'

Sarah stared back at her, then dropped her gaze, fidgeted.

'Listen, Cathy, I understand you're angry. I'll tell her what ya said, don't stress. She won't touch this Levi. Whatever you think of yer mum, right now, you need her help – and mine. You can hate her when ya get out, but until then, take whatever help you're given,' Sarah said, sitting back in her chair and biting the skin above her bitten-down thumbnail. In an instant, the fight drained from Cathy. She felt exhausted, scared, desperate. She didn't know whom she could trust, and to whom she could turn, and this thought, combined with the lack of sleep, floored her. Tears leaked from her eyes again, which she wiped away on her sleeve, a childlike gesture that revealed more of her confusion and upset.

'Cathy Willson?' The guard returned.

Cathy stood up.

'That's me.'

'Come through.'

Levi was sitting at the table. His large brown eyes looked up as Cathy walked in. She stopped for a moment, unable to take him in. He'd come! He'd come to get her out!

'No touching,' the guard said, standing behind them, as if she'd just read Cathy's mind. She longed to run into Levi's arms, to be held by him. Instead, she sat down awkwardly, not taking her eyes off him.

'Baby, I don't know what to say. I don't know what happened there, like . . .'

Cathy scanned his face. He looked gorgeous. His skin was tanned from working outdoors. He wore a flat cap perched on his head, jauntily. His eyes were filled with tears as he looked at her, making her stomach flip over. His voice a whisper, he said, 'Baby, I don't know what's goin' on. Some fucker must've set me up, like. Baby, I'll be here every day until we get you freed.'

Cathy nodded, unable to speak. There was so much she wanted to say, so many questions to ask him, but she couldn't find the words, especially not in front of the prison guard. She looked up, realising that he hadn't yet asked about the babies.

'Don't you want to know about our children? They're growing, I can feel it,' she sniffed, her throat croaky.

''Course I do, babe. How are they? Are ye eatin' enough, like?'

Mollified by Levi's renewed interest, Cathy smiled and smoothed her hands over her larger belly.

'Well, they won't get much bigger if I stay in here. The portions are tiny, the food is disgusting.'

'Ah, ye not used to goin' hungry, but you'll be OK,' Levi said, smiling, leaning towards her as if he knew the effect he was having on her.

Cathy was sleep-deprived, exhausted and horrified by the turn of events, and his attention was like a drop of water to a thirsty plant. She beamed back at him and nodded.

'They'll get me out of here soon, once you explain everything.'

'Sure I will,' Levi said, not quite meeting her eyes. 'Though, baby, I've got to get off, like. I'll be back tomorrow, I promise ye.'

'I love you,' Cathy said almost desperately as he winked at her and she was led away. If she noticed he didn't return her words, she quickly shut down that thought. She had to stay focused. Levi would tell the truth, tell them he'd been set up, and then she'd be free at last.

The next day, one of the screws stopped Cathy while she was shuffling to the toilet block.

'You'd better tidy yerself up, love, you've got your hearin' this mornin'.'

'My hearing?'

'Were ya born on another planet?' jeered the woman with tattoos from further down the line. 'Little Miss Precious don't know a fuckin' thing about what's 'appenin' to her!'

'Shut your mouth, Jones. It's none of yer business,' retorted the guard, who turned to Cathy.

'The magistrates. You need to scrub yerself up a bit. Go on, love. Get back in the queue.'

Cathy stumbled forward, her head spinning. She would face the next part of this nightmare. Perhaps they would listen to her and this whole ordeal would finally be over.

*

An hour later, the cell door was opened and the freshly washed Cathy was led through the corridors and out of the building. The journey to the court was short, and within minutes she was sitting inside another bleak-looking room, waiting for her turn. The time seemed to slow to a halt. Finally, her name was called and she stood up, unsure what to expect, knowing her lank hair and red eyes would reveal the level of her distress to anyone in there. Walking into the dock, she almost stopped dead at the sight of her mum, uncles Bobby and Alfie and granddad Lloyd sitting in the courtroom. Belle was the only family member who wasn't there. Ruby stood up at the sight of Cathy, her face bleaching pale. Shocked at the sight of them all, Cathy faltered as she stepped into the dock. She couldn't help the feeling of relief that flooded her body. And yet, these were the people who'd lied to her, had broken her trust. She hated them, didn't she?

Head swirling, heart frozen with emotions she couldn't name, Cathy held her mum's gaze. Ruby leaned forward as if she wanted to say something, but the usher called for silence and the moment was lost. Cathy looked away, feeling her cheeks burn. She hated herself for feeling so desperately pleased to see them all. She realised that someone else was missing. Levi wasn't there. Where was he? She looked frantically around the courtroom. Then, the magistrates entered and the court rose. The shuffling of papers and talking among the lawyers and ushers stopped instantly.

Cathy stared blankly at the people who would be part of the system that would determine her fate: two women and one gentleman, all elderly, all sharp-eyed and stern-looking, at this, her plea hearing. Then, as she stood at the dock, her hands gripping the bench to keep herself steady, she felt a distinctive kick in her belly. The babies were kicking! For a brief second, the courtroom vanished; the lawyers and people, her family, they all disappeared and she was suspended in wonder. She'd experienced fluttering sensations, but this was something else. The kick was strong. Her babies were strong. Cathy's reverie meant she almost didn't hear the command to stand, to confirm her name, to enter her plea.

She whispered, 'Not guilty.'

Her mum's lawyer, Rupert Smithers, was there. He was talking quietly to a colleague and glancing back at Ruby now and again. Cathy held her swelling bump protectively, retreating into her own mind as the proceedings continued. She didn't have long to wait before it was over. There was a discussion and her lawyer spoke but none of the words went in. The babies were well. Her family hadn't abandoned her, but perhaps Levi had? Again, just before she was led away, she looked around. Perhaps he'd snuck in after the hearing began? As she was looking, knowing her boyfriend wasn't there, she caught Ruby's eye again. Her mum looked immaculate as ever. Ruby looked like her sister rather than her mother. Her hair was sleek, her clothes understated but clearly designer. She was everything Cathy wasn't right now. Cathy knew she must look a sight. Her clothes were crumpled and her eyes were puffy from all the tears she'd shed. She'd pulled a brush through her hair but the shampoo she'd been given was cheap and cloying and made her hair dull and flat. Instead of her initial relief at seeing her mother, Cathy now felt a renewed surge of anger at her. The fact she'd come today meant nothing. She still couldn't forgive her mum for killing George, and then lying to her. Quickly, she glanced away, smiling briefly at Lloyd and Alfie but otherwise refusing to meet Ruby's eyes. How dare she come? What a nerve she had to walk in here in her sky-high heels, a renowned drug boss who was too clever to get caught! Cathy had a bitter taste in her mouth. She hated her. She never wanted to see her again.

The proceedings were short. Bail was refused despite representation by Rupert Smithers and the lawyer who had come to speak to her while was being held in the police cell. A screw she didn't recognise grabbed her arm, and said, not unkindly, 'Come on, love, yours is over. You go back to the prison now.'

Cathy looked over at her family, her face stony, tears gathering in her eyes.

'I love ya, darlin . . .' It was her mum's voice that followed her as she walked onwards. 'I love ya. We'll get ya out. I promise ya.'

Cathy gave no indication she'd heard her mother's words as she walked away.

*

Back in her cell, Cathy was alone for once. The other girls had presumably gone for their hearings. Cathy didn't know – and she didn't care. Just then, Sarah popped her head round the doorway.

'Time for lunch, babe. Thought I'd come and find ya. I won't be able to keep an eye on ya once they send ya to the mum and baby wing but I'll make sure the girls know you're with me. It ain't Marbella, or Chigwell for that matter . . .' Sarah snorted with laughter at her own joke but stopped as soon as she saw the crestfallen look on Cathy's face.

'What I mean is, I know the ropes, I know who to watch out for and who has more bark than bite. There are some in 'ere that'll make yer life a misery just because they think you've got a prettier face than them. I'll let the girls know you're with me and they should leave ya alone.'

Cathy nodded. She felt weary to her bones. In a million years, she'd never have thought her gilded life would lead her here. Sarah appraised her. She nodded as if she knew exactly what Cathy was thinking, which made the large gold hoops in her ears jiggle.

'You get used to it,' the older woman said softly. Cathy looked up, revealing her crumpled, tearful face.

'How?' she replied, bleakly.

'Come on, Cathy. It ain't as bad as all that. Yer mum will get ya out. Look, I've brought you a doughnut, left over from the officers' mess. Don't tell no one, it's a treat for ya.'

'Thank you,' Cathy replied politely, taking the cake. 'So, why are you in here?'

'Oh, usual. My boyfriend got me into sellin' gear for him.'

'Gear?' said Cathy, looking puzzled.

'Heroin, babe. God you are green, ain't ya!'

Cathy shrugged, then placed her hands on her bump.

''Avin' a baby in prison. That ain't easy, I'll give ya that,' Sarah said after a short pause.

Cathy didn't know what to say.

'Well, I'm sure Ruby will get ya released before its born . . .'

'Actually, I'm . . . *we're* having twins,' Cathy replied, smiling.

'Was it the guy who visited ya?' Sarah sat down on the hard bed next to Cathy.

'Yes, they're Levi's. We're going to be married. He loves me and he'll be trying to get me out, I'm sure of it,' Cathy said, though her voice trembled.

Sarah gave a tight smile. ''Course he will, babe. Now come on or there'll only be stew left.'

Cathy allowed herself to be walked to the canteen. She noticed how many of the women greeted Sarah with respect.

'Allright, mate. Listen, do me a favour and tell Jones that Cathy's out of bounds. Any more problems, she'll 'ave me to deal with.' Sarah got straight to it. Cathy smiled, sensing her troubles might be easing.

'Now, let's get those babies in yer belly fed.'

PART 4
RETRIBUTION

Traveller Site, Basildon,
January 2013

CHAPTER 27

Lloyd drew up outside Ruby's house. Ruby stepped into the Bentley; Alfie was seated on the back seat. He opened his suit jacket just slightly to reveal his gun in its holster. Ruby nodded.

A puzzle piece had fallen into place and they were on their way, finally, to confront Levi at the traveller site.

'Let's hope we don't need it, eh, Alfie?'

The journey took just over an hour. They pulled up at the gates to the site. The concreted area was filled with tidy-looking caravans and seriously expensive cars parked alongside some of them. A few looked scruffy with washing hanging outside and snotty-nosed kids playing, but the site mostly looked well-maintained, and even homely.

Ruby stepped out of the car. She was dressed to the nines in heels and one of her beloved Chanel suits, with a string of diamonds around her neck. She usually commanded respect dressed this way, but in this situation she couldn't be entirely sure. Beside her, dressed in designer suits, were Alfie and Lloyd. If they looked incongruous standing by the entrance, they didn't care. They were on a mission.

Eventually, a young guy sidled over, blatantly eyeing up Ruby. Before he got a chance to speak, she said, 'We're lookin' for Levi. He's the father of my daughter's baby, and we want to see him. We're not lookin' for trouble, we just want to speak.'

'Oh, yeh do, do ye? I don't know this *Levi*,' the young man said, grinning and emphasising the word in such a way that it was obvious he knew exactly who they were talking about.

Ruby stepped forward, her green eyes flashing. In a soft voice, she replied, 'Oh, I think ya do know who I'm talkin' about.

'We're not 'ere for trouble,' she repeated, holding the man's gaze until he looked away. A few men and women had started to gather, arms folded, staring at the three of them.

'Who's in charge?' Lloyd got straight to the point.

'We'd like to 'ave a gentle word,' added Alfie, grinning back at them.

'A very gentle word,' smiled Ruby.

Then, a large, rough-faced man walked up. The crowd parted as he came through so Ruby knew she was now encountering the man in charge. She stared straight at him and was surprised to see him looking back at her, his gaze direct but not hostile. His blue eyes twinkled, and he instantly gave a small bow and said, 'Open the gate, lead the lady in, though she can keep her henchmen here.'

'Not on your life, mate. Rube. We're comin' with ya,' Alfie said, biting back, shaking his head.

'That's right, Ruby. You ain't goin' in there alone.'

Ruby, whose gaze hadn't left the older man's face, quickly sussed out the situation. It was a risk, for sure, walking in alone. But what else could she do? She needed to speak to Levi; he was their only hope, apart from nobbling the jury, and that always came at a risk. No, this was something she had to do. The man smiled without malice. He wore a clean shirt and decent jeans and there was something about his expression she couldn't name, but she felt an instant warmth towards him. She made a quick decision.

'I'm goin' in and I'm goin' alone at this gentleman's invitation. I'm honoured to be invited onto your site,' she said, now directing her voice at the man. His smile deepened, and she stepped forwards and into the traveller site.

'Ruby, for fuck's sake!' swore Alfie.

She turned round to him and his dad. She saw the concern on their faces, but, surprisingly, she felt none, none at all. This was about her daughter, and she would take the risk, alone, as the head of the site wanted. She never balked at what needed to be done. There was no other way to earn the trust of these people. She had to be brave.

'I'll be fine. Wait 'ere for me. Don't try and come in. I know what I'm doin',' she said, then turned back to the older traveller.

'Lead the way,' she said simply.

As Ruby stepped across the tarmac, the crowd parting as she followed the man she'd easily trusted, she mused over the situation. She could see Alfie's blood was up. She knew that if Levi was hiding out here, then letting Alfie into the site would be a big mistake. He'd waited impatiently for this moment and, she now realised, he'd probably kill Levi if he saw him, and perhaps he'd be right to. But now was not the time or the place. Ruby saw the only card she had to play in this was her Romany grandmother. Would it be enough to gain this man's understanding and help? Would she be able to convince them to hand over Levi based on that distant connection? She and Lloyd and Alfie had assumed, of course, that Levi had been buying coke and used Cathy as a runner. But she'd hoped she'd been wildly wrong, even though her instincts told her she was straight on the mark. She'd held off, worrying that making a wrong move would mean losing Cathy for ever. But Lloyd had called her this morning, having heard from a contact that the bag of coke Cathy had picked up was from a new supplier, presumably someone Levi must have found after they'd ditched their runner.

So, it was confirmed. Levi was a shyster. She'd known it from the day she met him. He may have them over a barrel, but it was time for him to come clean and face up to what he'd done. And she needed this man in front of her to help them do that. Looking round briefly, she saw children running to and fro; men milling around while women stared at her clothes and belongings with undisguised envy. But there was no sign of the man she had come to see.

The traveller opened the door of the largest caravan on the site.

'Thank you,' she said as she stepped inside. The caravan smelt of polish and cleaning products. It was as neat and tidy as anywhere she'd ever been. He had a lounge of sorts with two armchairs and a small sofa, still wrapped in their plastic covers.

'Take a seat, please,' the man said with a small hint of an Irish accent. He had a freckled face and dark red hair. His skin was tanned from working outdoors and he had a robust, strong build.

'Listen, I ain't 'ere to cause trouble, but I am 'ere to ask for yer help,' Ruby began.

'With all due respect, why should we help ye? We don't know ye or your men outside. What business can the likes of you possibly have with the likes of us, Mrs . . . ?' He smiled. 'Can I offer ye a beverage?'

'No, thank you,' Ruby murmured. 'My name is Ruby Willson. You may 'ave heard of me and the business I run. My grandmother Ruby was a Romany from a site in Dartford. She died givin' birth to my father but his dad, my granddad, always kept him close to his roots.

'Your gran married someone who wasn't Romany?' whistled the man, who still hadn't given his name. He leaned back in the armchair opposite Ruby and stared at her.

'He did. And they loved each other very much; he was devoted to her. She wouldn't go to the hospital, though, and there were complications. It was a long time ago . . .'

'It was, but I'm sorry for your loss all the same.'

Ruby shrugged off his words. She wanted to get to the point.

'Ye still haven't explained why you're here today, Ruby Willson.'

Ruby looked up at him, pausing for a moment. She took in the gleaming surfaces of the modest home, the smell of polish, the feel of the plastic cover against her legs.

'I'd like to know who I'm talkin' to first,' she said, a small smile playing on her lips.

'Forgive my manners. I'm Joe. They call me Big Joe here, and actually I think I know why you've come. Ye see, my son is called Levi, and he tells me he might've got a young lady into trouble. Would I be right in thinkin' that lady is your daughter?'

'If you mean Cathy, then yes, he's got her into trouble. She's expectin' his baby, but that's not the "trouble" that brings me 'ere—'

Before Ruby could finish, Joe butted in.

'Ye mean, babies. Didn't ye know she's carryin' twins? It was a surprise to us all. We don't have twins in our family, like.' Joe's expression was unreadable. He didn't sound like a doting grandfather. He sounded businesslike, but that was beside the point. Ruby suddenly realised what he'd said.

'Twins! Oh my God, no, I didn't know.' Ruby felt a rush of tears, which knocked her off-balance. She fumbled in her handbag for a tissue. Emotions collided. She was deliriously happy, as it was just like her beloved husband Archie and Alfie all over again. She was also desperately upset that Cathy hadn't told her, and was facing this pregnancy, and possibly even the birth of the twins, in prison. It took Ruby a few minutes to compose herself. Big Joe said nothing. He didn't take advantage of her distress. He didn't try to avoid it or change the subject. He just let her cry. After a few minutes, Ruby took a deep breath and continued.

'You know about the twins, but did ya know about my Cathy bein' in prison?' This time, she stared back at Joe defiantly. She wanted to know if he was complicit in keeping the truth from the Old Bill.

Joe looked instantly puzzled. He shook his head. Now that Ruby was speaking, she couldn't stop.

'Your son used my daughter to collect a bag of drugs – cocaine, to be precise – from a dealer in East London. Well, the police were onto this bloke, and so she got clobbered. Caught, then arrested, and she's now in Holloway Prison waitin' for her next hearing, charged with dealin' thousands of pounds of coke. Your son was behind all of it,' she said. 'I think he tricked her from the start, Joe. I want your help. I want your son to confess what he done, make it right for her so she can get out of prison and come home. She has to 'ave the baby, those babies, at home with me where I can take care of her. Will ya help me, Joe?'

Ruby sat back, deflated. She wanted to weep. Her daughter was alone in jail with *two* babies growing inside her. Ruby had to stay strong, and she needed Joe's support, but would he give it to her?

The seconds ticked on. Joe stared out of the mobile home window. There was a selection of fake flowers in pots on the windowsill, without a speck of dust in sight.

Eventually, he spoke. 'Mrs Willson, Ruby . . . this is the first I've heard of this, like. I'm shocked, I don't mind tellin' ye.' With this, he stood up and walked to the kitchen area where he flicked the switch on the kettle. He was silent while the water boiled. Minutes later, he brought them both a mug filled with hot milky tea.

'There's two sugars in there. Best thing for shock,' he said simply.

Ruby accepted it and took a sip. It wasn't her usual drink. She preferred hand-roasted coffee these days, but it was a welcome boost amid this increasingly strange conversation.

'I want to speak to Levi. I want him to understand he has to give himself up to the Old Bill,' Ruby blurted out.

Big Joe nodded. He looked away again.

'Until I know the facts, I can't say what we'll do. If my son has put an innocent girl behind bars then he'll pay, don't ye worry about that.'

'But I want to see him. I want to be the one who confronts him, Joe . . .'

Big Joe shook his head.

'I can't let ye do dat, Ruby. It isn't our way. We deal with tings ourselves.' Abruptly, he put down his cup. 'Thank ye for comin' and tellin' us.'

Ruby stared back at him. Was he dismissing her? That never happened. She wanted answers, and she usually got them.

'Again, thank ye, now I need to speak to some people.' Big Joe got up and gestured to the door.

He *was* dismissing her. Ruby felt a surge of rage and upset. Hadn't he heard her? Hadn't he understood how important it was for her to tackle Levi? For a moment, she considered refusing to leave, but she knew it would be futile, and they would definitely not help her if she upset them. No, it was best to leave with some dignity and hope this man would do the right thing.

Ruby stood, and let herself be led out, but before she stepped back into the yard, she added, 'You're honour-bound to help us, Joe. We mustn't fail those children.'

Joe looked at her, and again she felt a strange pull to him. His face looked surprisingly kind, like he knew exactly how much this was killing her inside, what this meeting had cost her. Despite this, he said nothing.

The crowd by the door was even bigger now. She walked alone to the gate, leaving Big Joe and the other travellers staring after her. She could've wept at this, but instead, she kept her head high, her features closed. She didn't want that man to know how deeply she was suffering. Someone appeared and held open the gate for her.

She whispered her thanks, then shook her head at Alfie and Lloyd, who were pacing around the Bentley.

'Let's go,' was all she said, a single tear inching its way down her cheek.

CHAPTER 28

'I want to kill him,' Ruby said through gritted teeth. 'I want him dead, Lloyd. I can't bear knowin' what he's done to my girl.'

Ruby looked over at her father-in-law. He'd driven Ruby home, dropping Alfie off in town for drinks. He'd sensed that Ruby would need company after their visit to the traveller site. They were now in her kitchen.

'I know ya do, Rube, but it won't help. We won't get nowhere if ya do that. I don't want you up in front of a judge for murder because of that scumbag . . .'

Ruby smiled, though her eyes were still narrowed.

'I want justice,' she added simply. 'Good, old-fashioned justice. I want him to pay for this, Lloyd, and I won't stop until he does. Big Joe said they take care of things themselves but will he really seek the truth that could bring down his own son?'

'We 'ave to play the long game,' Lloyd replied, switching on the coffee machine. 'Listen, Rube, we're goin' to pay off the jury at Cathy's trial. We will get her free—'

'And the babies,' Ruby butted in.

'And the babies, of course. Then we can deal with Levi, if nothin's been done, but only then. Are we clear, Rube? I don't want ya callin' anyone. We're not in Spain. We 'ave to take it carefully now that our family is under the spotlight.'

The smell of the coffee as the dark liquid poured into one of Ruby's bone china cups was enticing. She took the proffered cup gratefully. The bitter taste and burning heat were a welcome distraction, though her head still whirred.

'Levi is no fool,' Lloyd continued, 'He knows that he's safe while Cathy is onside and 'avin' his children. He knows she'd never forgive us if we touched him. We 'ave to step back.'

'Yes, we do,' Ruby said angrily. She'd also discovered from Sarah that Levi had been visiting Cathy every day since her hearing. Ruby desperately wanted to see her daughter, but Cathy was keeping her away, and this knowledge broke her heart afresh.

'Rube, you're goin' to 'ave to accept that we can't do anythin' until after the trial. I know it hurts not bein' able to visit her . . .' Lloyd had guessed the source of Ruby's pain. 'She'll be free. We'll make it happen. Try not to worry, Rube; we'll get that bastard, have no doubt of that.'

Later that evening, long after Lloyd had left her, Ruby found she couldn't sleep. Tossing and turning, she ached for Archie, her dead husband. She knew if he'd been there he'd have known what to say, known how to soothe her. He probably wouldn't have said anything different to her father-in-law, but words coming from him always made a difference.

Oh, Archie, it's so hard livin' without ya, she whispered, over and over. *Why did ya 'ave to go and die? I still love ya, I always will.* Ruby sank back onto her pillows. Archie's face had faded from her mind over time but she could never forget his eyes, blue and piercing; she had always thought they looked straight inside her. Then, without warning, the eyes changed. Another face swam into her mind. For a moment, she was disorientated, wondering if she really had fallen asleep and was dreaming, but then she knew whose they were. Big Joe's eyes appeared, blue and twinkling. She'd sensed something today, some connection perhaps, or just a small scratch of attraction. She'd dismissed it – after all, they had business to complete – but his face came back to her and, without realising, she smiled into the darkness.

'Pack your stuff, Willson, you're off to the mum and baby wing,' the screw said as she opened the cell door.

Cathy looked up, realised she had to move quickly, and began to gather up her minimal possessions. Once she had everything, she turned to the other girls and, with a shy smile, said, 'Wish me luck. It was nice meeting you.'

Both Jamaican girls looked up lazily. They were gossiping together on one of the beds. They waved, but otherwise carried on talking. Cathy looked at Maggie, who by now was standing beside her. Maggie smiled, then hugged her.

'Good luck with everything, hen,' she said sweetly.

'You too, Maggie. I hope you get off this time . . .'

Maggie smiled, but it didn't reach her eyes. She shrugged.

'Och, well we'll see what the fockers do this time, eh. If it's the same judge as last time, then I'm screwed.'

Cathy didn't know what else to say. She picked up the plastic bag holding her belongings and walked out of the cell, following the same guard along the corridors and through locked door after locked door, over to the maternity wing.

'It'll go easier for ya 'ere,' said the screw when they finally arrived, and she gave Cathy an almost apologetic grin.

Cathy looked around. Women milled about, some heavily pregnant, some with newborns in their arms. They didn't seem to have to be in their cells. They were free to move about, chat together. Without realising it, Cathy exhaled. Her shoulders dropped and she felt the first sense of peace since the moment her car had been pulled over. Here, at least, she could concentrate on having her babies, on planning for a future outside this place. She was one of the lucky ones. She knew she had Rupert Smithers on her side and was being afforded the best legal representation, albeit by the family she despised. Standing there, seeing the reality of mothers giving birth in prison, starting their life as new mothers locked behind bars, Cathy realised she might be the only one in here with a real chance at freedom. It was weeks away. Her trial had been set for a month after the twins were born, but until then, she could begin to hope, to pray that a miracle would happen and she'd walk out of here and into Levi's arms.

Before she'd left, she'd spoken to Sarah about the prospect of becoming a mummy after her mum's old friend had popped by with a small gift of a cake from the kitchens. Cathy had got her appetite back, and the twins were ravenous, so she'd eaten the cake with relish as Sarah watched her. Sarah had a good heart – too good for this world, in many respects. Even Cathy, with her limited life experience, could see that what Sarah wanted – and lacked – was love. She'd had indifferent parents who were up to no good from the moment she was born, and older brothers who were also on the take. Poor Sarah had been well down the pecking order, or so Ruby had said several times in the past. The older woman grinned as Cathy finished the last crumbs.

'Hungry, were ya?'

'Starving! Thank you, Sarah.'

'That's allright. I'd do anythin' for Ruby's family. She's always been good to me. She sends me new clothes and money for fags. I don't 'ave anyone else who looks after me the way she does.'

There was an awkward silence as they both digested this. Cathy was overcome with sadness. She placed her hands around her bump, felt the movements of the twins inside her. Suddenly, Sarah spoke.

'I was born in prison, did ya know that? The only person who knows that, apart from my family, of course, is Ruby.'

Cathy took in the strange look on Sarah's face, partway between sadness and resignation.

'No, I didn't know that.'

The silence continued until, again, Sarah broke it.

'Yeah, they gave me a prison number and everythin'. I was born 'ere in Holloway, in fact. Weird, but it's the first home I ever had.'

'You were born here? In this prison? Oh my goodness, Sarah, that's awful. I'm so sorry. It must be really hard for you being here?'

Sarah shrugged.

Honestly, Cathy, I don't know no different. The screws were good to my mum and they must've looked after me OK. It's weird, though, ain't it? Bein' a prison baby and endin' up back 'ere again.'

Cathy shivered. She knew she'd give birth inside these walls but she hadn't thought her babies would have numbers, or have that shadow over them for ever, the way Sarah obviously had. She'd been so upset about being there that she hadn't given it a thought. The reality started to sink in.

'Oh my God, Sarah, that's awful. I don't want my babies thinking they're prison babies. I don't want them given a number, that's so inhuman!'

'It's the way it is, babe. You'd better get used to it. Anyway, you've got a proper family out there, though you 'aven't seen your mum for ages. Why aren't ya givin' her your visitin' orders, Cathy? What's she done to upset ya?' Sarah spoke softly. Cathy was relieved that Ruby hadn't told her the truth.

There was another silence, this time filled with unsaid words. Sarah nodded, as if she understood that Cathy couldn't – or wouldn't – tell her.

'My family is Levi now. When I'm free, we'll be together and be a proper family. The twins will never find out they were born in here. I'll never tell them.'

If Sarah was upset by Cathy's outburst, she didn't say. Instead, the older woman smiled sadly. 'Allright, babe. I'll catch ya later. Glad you enjoyed the cake. I'll try and bring ya two next time.' With that, she exited, leaving Cathy staring into space. Did prison babies always return? Was there some kind of curse on those born inside these walls? Would her children ever be free of Holloway? The unsettling questions had no answers.

CHAPTER 29

'I'm Kelly. You allright?'

Cathy looked over at the new mum sitting on the bed nearest hers. She couldn't have been more than nineteen years old, with a face hardened by poverty, her dark hair pulled back off her make-up-free face. She cradled her baby, giving the little girl a bottle with a beatific smile on her face. Then, the baby pulled off the plastic nipple and arched her back, letting out a juddering cry as she did so.

'Wind. Poor love. She suffers bad from it,' Kelly said, grimacing.

'Will she be OK?' Cathy said, alarmed, looking away in case she was the cause of the disturbance.

Kelly cast her a strange look, before replying, "Course she will. Babies get wind all the time. Don't worry, she'll be fine . . .'

Cathy nodded, aware of her inadequacy, her lack of knowledge about babies. She had been so caught up with the drama of her arrest, the shock of prison, the fear of staying here a long time, that she hadn't really thought about the actual presence and care of the little ones growing inside her. For a moment she felt like she couldn't breathe, so taken aback was she by this new reality.

Kelly smiled at Cathy, her baby slung now over her shoulder while she rubbed her back until the cries turned to whimpers, and then little moans, as she fell back to sleep on her mum's shoulder. 'Don't look so scared. It ain't all that difficult. They basically shit, eat and sleep – with a lot of cryin' and burpin' in between!'

Despite herself, Cathy giggled. She had been in the wing for a week or so when Kelly arrived back from the maternity area to become her new cell mate. Cathy saw the piles of cheap prison nappies, the babygros that had clearly been used before. She wondered if Kelly was a single mum and if that was why she didn't have any new stuff for the baby. Even the single teddy propped up on the cabinet was a bit lopsided and had clearly seen better days.

'Wanna hold her?' the young woman said, and before Cathy could object, Kelly handed the sleepy baby to Cathy. The little girl lay on top of Cathy's bump, which seemed to be growing hourly, and promptly fell back to sleep.

'She's lovely,' Cathy breathed, feeling tears well up in her eyes. She would have two of these to care for soon. How on earth could she do that when she knew nothing about caring for a child? Yearning took hold of her; she wanted Ruby, her mum, all of a sudden. The need for guidance from her mother overwhelmed her, and Cathy felt she couldn't breathe, it was so strong. Kelly watched her quietly, seeing that this was bringing up something for the pregnant woman. Eventually, the feeling subsided, but it left Cathy feeling bereft. She hated her mum – yet she needed her, and that thought was troubling and sad all at once.

'What's her name?' Cathy said eventually.

It was Kelly's turn to look away.

'I ain't givin' her a name. She's got a prison number, though. Shit start.'

There was a moment's silence. The little girl sighed and snuffled, shifting a little, her warm body smelling of milk and talcum powder.

'No name, but why?' Cathy blurted out, before immediately apologising. 'I'm so sorry. I don't mean to intrude . . .'

Kelly shrugged. She turned back to Cathy and there was a strange expression on her face, halfway between love and regret.

'I'm not keepin' her, so I won't give her a name. It ain't my place to.'

Cathy was horrified.

'Not keeping her? Why ever not? She's beautiful. She's your daughter. Surely life can't be that bad? You'll get out of here one day and have a life together.'

This was absolutely the wrong thing to say. Kelly, who up until now had been the stronger of the two women, suddenly burst into tears. Cathy didn't move to hug her, couldn't move, as she was cradling the little girl and didn't want to wake her. She had to wait until the tears had subsided. Sniffing, Kelly looked over at her baby and started to speak. Instinctively, Cathy knew to say nothing, to let this young woman she'd only just met say what she had to say.

'My mum and dad were junkies. I grew up not knowin' where the next meal was comin' from. They forgot about us for days. It was shit, proper shit. One time, Dad went nuts – he was takin' crack – and he set fire to the fuckin' furniture. All of it. Just threw it out the windows of our council house and set a match to it. We didn't 'ave much, but by the end of that we didn't 'ave nuthin'.'

Kelly wiped her nose with her arm, leaving a trail of tears and snot.

Cathy listened in a state of shock. She'd known she was privileged, had grown up with the best of everything, but she'd never known life could be like that. Even if she'd wanted to say something, she couldn't have.

'My dad was mental, a proper nutcase. We had social workers round all the time but they didn't do nuthin'. We was left to our own devices and when I was ten Dad OD'd and died anyway.'

'He overdosed? I'm so sorry, that's awful. I lost my dad too. Not when I was so young, but it still hurts. I don't know how you must've felt back then . . .' Cathy's eyes were filled with sympathy.

'It wasn't like that for us. We was relieved – but then Mum had loads of loser boyfriends who nicked her dole money and beat the crap out of her,' Kelly said, reaching out her arms for her child. Cathy gently handed the sleeping bundle back to her mum without a word. She could tell Kelly hadn't finished her story.

'So, what happened then? How did you end up in here?' Cathy said, almost as a whisper.

Kelly paused for a moment. The baby shifted in her arms, then started to snuffle again as she slept.

'Ended up livin' on the streets after Mum met this guy who tried to hit me as well as her. That was it. I was out. I had nowhere to go but it was worse stayin' there. Then I met Steve. He was stayin' in a hostel so we kipped there. He got me into drugs and that was that. I got nicked for supply. By then I was pregnant. Look, I ain't got no home, no family. I've got nuthin' I can give to her.' Kelly looked down at the bundle with her shock of thick black hair. 'I don't want her havin' the same shit life I did. It's better if she goes to a nice family somewhere better.'

Cathy was on the verge of tears. She swallowed hard as the new mum finished, and looked down at her bump. The birth was only a few weeks away, and she felt a rush of nerves thinking of what lay the other side: motherhood. The thought of giving birth was scary enough, especially knowing she wouldn't be allowed to have Levi with her, but the thought of having to bring her twins into this world as prison babies was terrifying.

'So, what about you? Sorry, I don't even know yer name!' Kelly smiled, though her face was puffy from crying.

'I'm called Cathy. I'm so sorry to hear about your life, I had no idea things could be like that.' She stumbled over her words, unable to think of anything to say that might help her new friend, or show in any way how much it had meant to her to hear that story. 'My life has been so privileged. I had no idea how much until I came here. I got arrested by mistake, though, for picking up cocaine. I was only meant to be collecting a bag of my boyfriend's work tools but the guy gave me one filled with coke. They'll let me out soon, I hope.'

Kelly raised her eyebrows at her. 'What?'

Cathy continued, not registering the look on Kelly's face. 'Yes, I got pulled over and arrested after picking up Levi's work bag. They must've given me the wrong bag because it was full of cocaine and now they think I'm selling it.'

'Are ya fuckin' serious?' Kelly blurted out. 'He's made a mug of ya! Your boyfriend ain't no Prince Charming. Babe, he's a drug dealer, and he got you to pick up his goods. Ya need to ditch him, and fast!'

Cathy looked at her, stunned. 'That's not true. Levi loves me. He visits every day. He's sworn to me he knew nothing about the drugs. He agrees they gave me the wrong bag . . .'

Another silence in the cell, this time an uncomfortable one.

Kelly was the first to speak.

'Allright, babe, you know him better than I do. I don't know yer business, but I'd be askin' him a few questions if I was you.'

Anger surged in Cathy. What right had this girl, who knew nothing about her situation, who'd never even met Levi, to say this to her? She turned her back on Kelly and lay on her side, staring at the cell wall. Why was everyone so against Levi? He had sworn to her that he'd done nothing wrong. Weren't his visits each day proof of his love for her and their babies? He'd never have used her as his mule, would he? She had to trust him, she had to. Who else was there? Cathy ignored the next thought that came into her head – her family – but it kept beating against her brain. Levi hadn't lied to her. He'd promised to speak to the police, to set them straight, and she had to believe him.

Another thought had crossed her mind. It had been stirring inside her for weeks now, but she was so confused she hadn't chased it down, examined it in the light. What if Ruby was to blame? What if she had tried to set up Levi by changing the bag? What if the guy at the place near Star Lane, the pickup address that was so suspiciously close to Ruby's childhood home, was actually one of her mum's runners, and she'd told him to hand over a bag stuffed with coke, thinking Levi was collecting his tools? Cathy knew her mum must be following Levi. She'd learned about her mum's methods since

Archie died and the truth had come out. If her family ran a large drug cartel, surely they followed people, intercepted their calls, watched them, all the time? It was hardly a huge leap in logic to think that Ruby, or Lloyd, or Alfie, might be watching him, knowing where he was going, listening in to his calls. Cathy had no proof of this, of course, but the more she thought about it, the more sense it made. Ruby hated Levi. She wanted Cathy back with her. Was she ruthless enough to do this to Levi? To try to get him banged up for dealing drugs? If that had been the plan, it had failed dismally, and, for the first time, Cathy was almost exultant that she'd been the one taken in. The plan had failed. Ruby could now watch in agony as Cathy stayed behind bars, away from her family, her grandchildren being born in the lowest place of all.

'Your legal guy is 'ere, Willson.'

The screw barely put her head round the door. Cathy pulled herself up and, without a word to Kelly, shuffled down to the rooms used by lawyers to meet the inmates. Rupert Smithers was sitting inside one of them. Cathy walked in and sat down, conscious of her bulk in the small space.

'I'll get straight to the point, Cathy,' the lawyer said, 'Your trial is set for a month after the twins are born. You must plead not guilty, otherwise you'll be given a hefty sentence for a crime you didn't commit.'

Cathy nodded. Of course she would plead not guilty, because she wasn't!

'Another thing, and sorry, I have to dash as I'm due in court this afternoon – you'll have to say who gave you the address. You'll have to tell the judge and jury that it was Levi who called you and told you to collect the bag.'

There was a pause. Cathy's expression was decidedly frosty. She shook her head.

'I can't do that, Mr Smithers. I won't do that.'

'You have to,' he replied simply, looking up from his papers. 'Think it through, Cathy. Your mum, your family, are all behind you. They'll deal with any problems arising out of this – ahem – situation, but you must tell the court.'

'You're not listening to me. I won't tell them. They'll arrest Levi and they'll think he's a drug dealer. I won't do that to the father of my children.'

Cathy and Rupert stared at each other for a second. The lawyer sighed.

'You have to. We'll speak soon. I must run, sorry.'

Cathy watched him go, her heart set. She wouldn't grass on her Levi, whatever anyone said. He was all she had in the world.

CHAPTER 30

'She said what?' Ruby couldn't believe her ears.

'Cathy won't incriminate Levi. She says she won't tell the court he told her to collect the bag. I'm afraid, if she doesn't, she won't have any defence to speak of,' Rupert Smithers.

'I'm sorry, Ruby, there's very little I'll be able to do . . .' the lawyer said. 'Is there no one who can speak to Cathy, make her see sense?'

For a moment, Ruby could hardly breathe. Yes, there was one person, the very person who might then end up being arrested and charged with the crime he was most likely guilty of. That meant there was no chance. No chance at all.

'There's only Levi. He's the only one she's allowin' to see her in prison. He's the only person she seems to care about – and he's the very person who's done this to her.' Ruby could have cried with frustration.

'I'll do my best to persuade her, but there's very little hope without her boyfriend confessing, or at the very least, telling the police what really happened, if indeed it was a case of mistakenly being given the wrong bag.'

Ruby snorted. 'He's guilty as hell,' she said bitterly, 'and one day, I'll make him pay for all this.' She ended the call.

She rang Lloyd, who listened silently as she explained.

'Listen, Rube, don't worry. We'll nobble the jury, it'll go our way. She has to plead not guilty – and we'll do the rest. I promise ya she'll be out. Leave it to us.'

'I hope you're right, Lloyd,' Ruby answered, thoughtfully. 'If they find her guilty after she's pleaded not guilty, they'll put her away for longer.'

'That won't happen, Ruby, you 'ave to trust me.'

After the calls, Ruby sat for a while. She was in her office surrounded by the white lilies that Archie would always lavish on her. Their potent sweetness carried across the room. This was the life she'd chosen. This was the deal. If you played with fire, sometimes, just sometimes, you got burned.

The days and weeks passed, and Cathy grew close to her time. Her relationship with Kelly had improved, as they had bonded over being first-time mums. The day came for Kelly to hand her daughter over to the adoption agency. Before she left, the two women sat in their cell, the little girl staring up at them from her cot, her eyes beginning to droop after her feed.

'I'm sorry I questioned yer boyfriend. I can see ya love him. He's a lucky man. I hope he deserves ya,' Kelly smiled, her eyes filled with tears.

'Thanks. I hope your daughter has a good life with good people, and I hope she thinks of you one day. You never know, she might try to find you . . . I hope she does, Kelly.'

There was nothing else to say. Kelly gathered up the few bits she had for the baby, then cast Cathy a last look as she scooped the child into her arms.

'Listen, if I was goin' to name her, I'd call her Cathy, after you. You're the kindest person I think I've ever met. I just wanted ya to know that,' Kelly sniffed. The tears were rolling down her face. Cathy watched her, feeling this young woman's agony, desperately wishing there was something she could do. Knowing there was nothing.

'They're sendin' me back to the general prison after, well, after this, so I wanted to say goodbye, for now anyway.'

'I'll see you every day in the exercise yard, at least,' Cathy said, unsure what else to say. A gulf had opened up between them that felt so vast, she couldn't hope to cross it. What could she say to Kelly to ease her pain? She had never considered having to give up her children after they were born. The realisation that, sometimes, women not so different from her would have to send them away to a better life was almost too much to bear. For the first time, Cathy saw that the future of her babies was uncertain. They couldn't stay in jail with her if she was sent down for a long time. If that happened, who would be there to look after them? Would Levi come through for her, for their children? Uncomfortably, she realised she wasn't sure.

The next day, Cathy was thrilled to see Kelly during their exercise hour, until she saw her red, swollen eyes. It was disturbing enough that the pregnant women were made to take exercise at the same time as the rest of the inmates, but to have gone through what Kelly had and be back in the main prison seemed, to Cathy, to be heartless.

'How are you?' Cathy made a beeline for the girl, who stood away from the other girls.

Kelly shrugged, and in that one movement, Cathy saw her sense of defeat. It chilled her to the bone, but she wasn't sure why.

'How did it go? Oh, Kelly, I wish I could help,' Cathy said. As she spoke, one of the women traipsing around the depressing space suddenly started yelling at another woman.

'Don't fuckin' look at me, you bitch!'

'I ain't lookin' at ya. Why would I look at such an ugly cow?'

'Fucksake!'

Before anyone could react, the woman who'd shouted first launched at the other girl, punching her in the face and sending her flying. Two more girls threw themselves in. The yard was like a tinder-box, one spark and the whole place ignited. Fights would kick off regularly as the mounting tensions inside the cells and the corridors found release in the grey concrete space. Amid the screams and shouts, the catcalls and whistles, Cathy and Kelly were shoved apart. Cathy's last glimpse of Kelly's face revealed she was sobbing as the guards rushed in and everyone was sent back to their cells.

It'll be OK, I'll see her tomorrow and I'll comfort her. It'll be OK for Kelly, she'll get through this, she's strong . . . Cathy thought to herself as she was herded off, back to the mother and baby wing, her stomach in knots, her heart beating out of her chest. Kelly would be all right, wouldn't she?

Cathy barely slept that night. Her bump was uncomfortably large now, but that wasn't what made her toss and turn. She couldn't get the image of Kelly's tear-stained face out of her mind. The usually dreary exercise hour the next day couldn't come fast enough. Cathy looked around the yard, but Kelly was nowhere to be seen. Sarah caught her eye. She had an odd expression on her face.

'Where's Kelly? Is she OK? Have they sent her to another wing?' Cathy's voice rose an octave as she spoke. It was as if, suddenly, she *knew*. Sarah had walked the length of the rectangular stretch of concrete, surrounded on all sides by towering red brick walls. Her face looked anguished.

Then Cathy realised that all the girls were subdued today. People wandered around listlessly. A couple of the women were crying. There were no raised voices, no shoves or punches or fights to break up.

'What's happened? It's Kelly, isn't it?'

Sarah nodded. Tears now streamed down the older woman's face. She seemed to be struggling for words.

'Tell me,' Cathy said, simply. She held Sarah's left hand. 'Tell me, please . . .'

They found her last night. She'd taken shitloads of pills. I don't even know what they were or how she got hold of them. Kelly was dead when the other girls in her cell came back from dinner.' Sarah tried wiping away the tears, but they kept coming.

Cathy felt like her body had frozen, her heart had stopped beating, and the blood was slowing in her veins.

'They're sayin' there'll be an inquiry but that don't mean nuthin'. She's dead and they should've known she'd do somethin' like this. She'd given up her baby. They should've known, Cathy.'

By now, Cathy was bent double, with pain rising inside her. She wanted to scream. She wanted to cry out, but she could barely breathe. Grief smashed into her. It filled her up, overwhelmed her. Her friend, albeit for only a few short weeks, had gone. No one had helped her. No one had seen the depths of Kelly's misery. She had been failed, as she had been all throughout her life. Would anyone care? Would anyone mourn for the girl who had no family, no friends, no child? Cathy sobbed, but had no recollection later of the events that followed. As Cathy bent over – with Sarah, pale, supporting her, shouting for the guards – her waters broke. The pains became the surges of childbirth, and Cathy was taken into a different realm, a place where the pain of losing her friend was overtaken by the very real contractions that meant her babies were coming.

*

'Ruby, it's Cathy.' Sarah's voice was urgent.

'What's happened? Is she OK? Are the babies OK?' Ruby knew instantly this call was important. Sarah's voice, her tone, the fear underneath it, told her, without any need for explanation.

'She's havin' the babies. She's been rushed to Whittington Hospital. Listen, Rube, she's had some bad news. A friend of hers overdosed last night. The shock started her labour. She's not in a good way, ya need to get down there.'

Ruby was already reaching for her keys, handbag, her jacket. Lloyd, who was with her as they'd been going over the details of some new contacts in Mexico, grabbed his jacket without saying a word. He could see Ruby's only thought now was to get to her daughter's side. They drove in silence, knowing they didn't have long before Cathy would be taken back to the prison. This was a small window of opportunity, perhaps a chance to see Ruby's grandchildren, Lloyd's great-grandchildren, before the jail swallowed them up.

At the hospital, they half-ran to find the maternity ward. Then, just as abruptly, Ruby stopped. The sound of her high heels clattering across the polished floor immediately ceased. It was him. Levi. Walking towards her, that familiar grin on his face. It was obvious he had already been in to see Cathy and was on his way out.

Ruby couldn't move. She couldn't breathe. Anger rose within her with startling force. Burning, raging, slicing anger. She opened her mouth to say something, to let him know that they knew. They had no proof. They had no evidence to show that Levi was buying cocaine and letting his pregnant girlfriend do his dirty work, but she knew – and she wanted him to know this too. Ever cautious, Lloyd put an arm on Ruby's shoulder, a warning gesture. It stilled her, reminded her that this was a long game. She might not be able to do anything now but, in the fullness of time, she would find a way to avenge her daughter, to make Levi understand. You don't fuck with Ruby. You definitely don't fuck with Cathy. The time would come, and Cathy would see him for who he truly was, and Big Joe would have no choice but to step aside. She breathed in deeply, held her smile on her face and waited until Levi had sauntered past, bobbing his cap to her as if she was the queen.

'The babies are beautiful,' he smiled, his teeth bared.

Levi walked straight past as if he had every right in the world to be there.

'Little shit,' muttered Lloyd. 'Come on, it's Cathy and the babies that are important now.'

'I know, Lloyd. I know,' replied Ruby.

The door to the ward was shut. Ruby knocked on it and an overweight screw with a surprisingly kind face opened it.

'Sorry, no visitors allowed,' the guard said, though she smiled in a friendly way.

'Please, I'm Ruby Willson, Cathy's mother, and this is her granddad, Lloyd. We're desperate to see Cathy. I know it's not allowed, but please can we see her for one minute?'

Ruby smiled back at her. She spoke from the heart. There was no anger, no forcefulness in her voice. Just a simple, plain, heartfelt request. The screw looked at her, then she nodded, and Ruby knew she'd struck gold.

'A couple of minutes. I can't give you any more than that or we'll be in trouble.'

'Thank you, thank you so much.' Ruby was almost in tears.

The screw led them at a slow pace, due to her wide girth, through the ward. They reached a separate room at the end. Knocking, she pushed open the door and Ruby stepped inside.

What she saw shocked her.

Cathy's wrist was shackled. A chain ran down the side of the bed. Her daughter looked up, her face a picture of surprise.

'Mum? How did you get in here?'

Ruby felt tears, hot and salty, run down her immaculately made-up face. She couldn't help it. Years of facing down hardened gangs and crooks hadn't prepared her for the emotional onslaught of seeing her beloved girl chained to her bed after giving birth.

'The babies?' was all Ruby could say. She felt Lloyd's arm around her, fatherly and protective, and she broke down.

Both Cathy and her granddad stared at each other. They'd never seen Ruby lose control like this. They waited until she'd scrabbled in her Prada handbag for a tissue before Lloyd spoke gently.

'Can we see the littl'uns? Babe, it's so good to see ya. We love ya, Cathy, and we'll get ya out, I promise.'

Cathy, who also looked stunned, pointed to the cot where both newborns lay swaddled, one with a pink cap and one with a blue one.

'Oh my God, a boy and a girl!' Ruby cried, stepping over and gazing into the little puckered faces.

'You've got one more minute,' the screw said from the doorway. 'We've gotta get you outta 'ere. If they find out we let you both in . . .'

"Course, sorry, and thank you again,' Lloyd said smoothly, not taking his eyes from the sleeping babies.

'Can I hold one?' Ruby sniffed, looking over at her daughter and smiling almost shyly.

'Sorry, Mum, they're asleep,' Cathy replied awkwardly, not catching her mum's eye.

Ruby nodded. She sensed that she shouldn't push things, even though she ached to feel the weight of her grandchildren in her arms.

"Ave ya decided on their names?' Ruby said in a whisper.

Cathy nodded.

'Kelly, after my friend in the prison who died, and Levi, after their dad.'

Ruby nodded in reply. Her throat felt tight, but she managed to say, 'That's lovely, Cathy, lovely names . . .'

'Time's up,' the guard said abruptly.

'Cathy, we will get you out,' Ruby said with urgency. 'You'll be home safe and sound. We're doin' everythin' we can . . .' she started to say. Cathy's face shut down, her emotions closed off. Ruby didn't know what she'd said wrong, but she could see the resentment against her was still strong, still raw.

Without a backward glance, Ruby let herself be led out of the hospital. Back in the car, she turned to Lloyd, and said bleakly, 'I don't think I can bear it.'

'Listen, Rube, you 'ave to trust me. We'll get Cathy out of prison. There's an order to everythin', Rube, you know that. Gettin' Cathy free is the priority. Gettin' the babies back, then we'll sort Levi. It's a done deal. That fucker's time is limited.'

CHAPTER 31

Cathy smiled as Levi walked into the visiting room, though it was an effort. Ever since the birth of the twins, she'd been feeling strangely disconnected and low, like she was going through the motions in life. Giving birth while shackled to the hospital bed had affected the young woman deeply. She felt she had failed, somehow, as if her life as a mother was now worthless. Seeing her mum and granddad appear not long after the births had knocked her as well. She'd been surprised at her yearning to be held by them, to be loved. As they crept in – as she saw their shock, and felt her own – she wanted to hate them fiercely, as she had done for so long now, but she found she couldn't. In that moment, she realised how much she missed them and needed them. The realisation depressed her. After they left, she felt like a balloon losing its air, deflated. In her heart, she'd wanted them to stay, to make it all better. But it wouldn't be better. She couldn't trust them. She was stuck inside a jail with two beautiful children who only made her want to cry every time she looked at them. She was grieving for her friend Kelly but was also dealing with the aftermath of giving birth. Her body was still sore, her emotions unbalanced.

Cathy hadn't confided in anyone. She pretended she felt OK, smiled at the screws, did what she was told, but inside she felt like she was unravelling. Perhaps if Kelly were still alive, she'd have told her how she was feeling. Her friend's death was a source of immense grief, and Cathy couldn't bear to think of her, because if she did, the big black hole that seemed to have opened inside her might swallow her whole.

'Baby, how are ye? How's the twins?' Levi said, winking at Cathy as he sat down.

She held out their boy, who yawned, his little face screwed up.

'I want to call him Levi after his daddy,' she said, almost as an afterthought. She'd assumed he would be thrilled. His face told her otherwise.

'No, babe, not Levi,' he replied instantly, shaking his head.

'But why?' Cathy stuttered.

'Well, ye know, I just never liked it. You pick a name, baby. He's a handsome boy, though.'

Cathy stared at her boyfriend, then shrugged.

'I like your name, but of course, whatever you want. I think I'll call him Archie. So, Archie and Kelly. I'll get them registered this afternoon.'

'Make sure I'm named on the birth certificate, won't ye,' Levi said, shooting Cathy a glance over Archie's head.

'Of course, why wouldn't I?' Cathy said. Kelly squirmed in her cot, as the next feed was due. Distracted by her daughter, she didn't see Levi nod to himself. With an awkward gesture, he went to hand Archie back to her, though she had reached in to pick up the little girl.

'Sorry, babe, got work to do. Ye know how it is.'

For a moment, Cathy almost, almost replied with a sharp, 'Do I?' but something stopped her. Instead, she turned to look at Levi.

'Before you go, just tell me how the new business is going? Are you doing the tarmacking? Is it taking off? Now you've got the money, it must be up and running?'

Levi shifted in his seat and cleared his throat. He held Archie out again and she took the baby. He stood and stepped over towards Cathy, a smile curling on his lips, and said in a gentle voice, 'It is, baby, sure it is. I'll tell ye all about it when I next see ye.'

At that moment, an argument broke out. The inmate nearest Cathy started effing and blinding.

'You fuckin' bastard. I knew you was screwin' her. I fuckin' knew it. She's a cow, what the hell d'ya see in that manky bitch, eh?'

'Don't fuckin' call her that, you cunt!' shouted the guy who was clearly her partner – or had been, anyway.

Before Cathy or Levi could respond, a polystyrene cup filled with hot vending machine coffee was flung across the room, narrowly missing Archie and almost splattering across Kelly's cot.

'Oi, you fucker, that's my babies in dere. Keep yer fuckin' problems to yerselves.' Levi moved towards them, looking like he would land a right hook on the woman who'd thrown the coffee.

'Oh, go fuck yerself,' she screamed as several screws ran towards her, shoving Levi and Cathy out of the way and grappling with the now-hysterical woman. Cathy recognised her from the mother and baby wing. She'd been aggressive and sarcastic with everyone and so Cathy had steered well clear. She had her own problems, so hadn't wanted to get involved.

The whole place went up. Girls were shouting and laughing, and the visitors were just as bad. Cathy started to shake uncontrollably, and barely managed to keep hold of Archie in her arms. Levi was oblivious. He was still trying to front up the bloke. It took a few minutes for the scuffle to die down. The man was herded out of the visiting room, while the woman, still swearing and hollering, was led back to the cells with her baby in her arms. Cathy stared after them, shock hitting her in waves, unable to take in the scene that had erupted so quickly and violently. There could be no worse place for her children to be born into.

Finally, Levi turned to Cathy and saw the look on her face.

He paused for a moment, then said, 'I've an idea, baby. Listen, the babies aren't safe here. Ye can see it, I can see it. Now, you're goin' to get them registered today, so I'll officially be their dad, so I will.'

Cathy nodded vacantly. She felt like she was sitting inside a goldfish bowl, watching her partner, the father of her children, talk and smile at her, and she had no clue what he was actually saying.

'Cathy, are ye listenin' to me?'

'Sorry, baby,' she replied, 'of course I am, go on.'

'The twins aren't safe. They nearly got hot coffee all over them and this would've been a trip to the hospital. I don't want that, and I know that you definitely don't. Listen, wouldn't it be better if I took the babies? If I looked after them until the trial, until you'll be able to come home and we'll be a family? It'd only be for a couple of weeks.' His voice was wheedling, but Cathy appeared not to notice. She felt even more deflated and also defeated. She looked at Levi. He wore his cap at an angle, and a waistcoat and T-shirt that showed off his lean, muscled arms and tan. She felt a small shudder of desire for him, though her weariness soon stopped that. It was good he was showing an interest in being a daddy. It was amazing to hear him talk about them being a family. So why did she feel so sad?

'I can stay at the flat with Archie and Kelly until you're home and then we can start our lives again. What d'ye reckon? It's a good plan, baby,' he finished, sitting back and winking at her.

Cathy found herself nodding.

'OK, yes, I see the babies are best off if they're out of here. They gave them prison numbers,' she said, tears hovering. She blinked them away. 'Prison numbers . . .' Her voice trailed off.

Levi looked at her quizzically now. He nodded again.

'Yes, they did, baby. But we can get dem outta here. Will ye help me? Will ye do the forms today and then I will look after them until ye're free?'

Cathy gazed at him. She loved him with all her heart, didn't she? So, why did she feel so distanced, so distracted? This was an important decision.

'I'll take care of dem, baby. I'll keep dem safe and away from headcases.'

'OK,' Cathy said at last, feeling the heavy warmth of Archie against her. He was wriggling now, too. They needed their feeds or soon they'd be bawling.

'I have to go and feed them, but yes, OK. I'll tell Rupert Smithers. He'll sort everything.'

Levi smiled a long, triumphant smile.

'Ye won't regret it,' he said, as Cathy turned away from him, not looking back.

'She said what?' Ruby thought she'd heard the worst, but this was too much.

'I had a legal visit with Cathy today and she says she wants Levi to have custody of the twins until she's freed. She's registered the births and put his name as the legal father. She has every right to do this.' Rupert Smithers spoke quickly, knowing Ruby would want all the facts straight up. She hated anything less than direct speech – and action.

'I don't believe it. I just don't believe she's done this.' Ruby said. She was in the bonded warehouse with Lloyd, checking over a shipment that was due to go out that night. 'Why can't *I* take the babies if they're so unsafe in there? Why hasn't she asked me to keep them 'ere? They'd lack for nuthin'. They'd have everythin' they needed. What is Cathy playing at?'

'I believe it was Levi's idea. He's convinced her that the babies are better off with him at their flat. She's adamant they're to go with him and she wants me to organise it. I need your instructions,' the lawyer said brusquely.

'Can I fight him?' Ruby said simply.

'You mean, try and get custody?' Rupert replied.

'That's exactly what I mean. Can I get custody of them through the courts to stop that shyster from takin' my grandchildren?' Ruby didn't bother to conceal her anger.

She'd determined that the coke in the warehouse was good quality – and it looked like the majority of it had got through, so it had been a good day, until now.

'What's goin' on, Rube?' Lloyd interjected. He walked over to his daughter-in-law.

'It's Cathy. She wants Levi to 'ave custody of the twins. If we allow it, we could lose them for ever.' Ruby's voice broke. She felt like she'd been punched in the stomach.

'Calm down, Rube. Let me speak to Rupert.' Lloyd took Ruby's phone. For once, she was so shocked she almost couldn't breathe.

'Rupert, it's Lloyd. What's all this about?'

The lawyer repeated what he'd told Ruby.

'Did Cathy say why?' Lloyd said.

'She thinks the babies are in harm's way, and I'm inclined to agree with her. Prison is obviously no place for newborns. If she can have them looked after, and the court agrees, then it'll be better for them.'

'So, what can we do about it? Can we fight him? Can we go for custody instead?' Lloyd and Ruby exchanged a glance. Their thinking was always the same. How could they get back on top of the situation? Who would they need to bribe or bully? How could they turn this round so they got what they wanted – in this case, the twins.

Rupert sighed down the phone.

'Yes, like anything, you can fight it, but what you need to understand is that you'll be fighting Cathy. It's Cathy who is pushing for this and it'll be her application to the court. You can, however, launch a case against Levi, but it would possibly mean months of legal entanglement and it could turn Cathy against you even more. I cannot advise you either way, it's your decision. It's Ruby's decision.' He paused. 'What do you want to do?'

For a moment, Ruby couldn't speak. Struggling to gather herself, Ruby took the handset, her hand trembling.

'Let me talk it through with Lloyd,' she said dully. 'For the moment, take Cathy's instructions. I don't see that we've got a choice, but if we change our minds, I'll let ya know.'

Ruby ended the call and almost dropped the phone. She felt faint. Was she about to lose her grandchildren for ever? She knew that once they were in Levi's clutches, that might be the case. Would she ever hold Archie and Kelly in her arms again? Tears slid down her face. Lloyd walked over, and without a word he put his arms around her in a fatherly embrace. He waited until Ruby had stopped crying. One of the warehouse men walked in without knocking.

'Fuck off outta 'ere,' Lloyd barked back at him, making the man freeze before turning swiftly round to depart.

'It'll be OK, Rube. It'll be OK,' he said as he held her.

Ruby shook her head.

'I don't think it will,' she wept.

CHAPTER 32

Cathy kissed Kelly's head for the last time before they had to go. She stroked Archie's as she looked down at them both. The babies were asleep in their cot, blissfully unaware of what would happen next.

'It's time to go,' came a screw's voice from the cell doorway.

Cathy nodded, saying nothing in return. Tucked inside the twins' bag were the mittens that covered their tiny hands, the mountain of cuddly toys Ruby has sent, the babygros and nappies, and the creams and bottles that were the detritus of motherhood. The young woman paused, taking in the scene. The twins snuffled peacefully together, swaddled and cosy in the cot. The bag was packed. She leaned over and inhaled their warm, milky scent, drawing it into her lungs as if it was the last time she'd ever smell them.

It will all be OK, she thought to herself. *Levi is their daddy. And he's right, prison is no place for them. They need to be kept safe.* Cathy ignored the lump in her throat, the aching in her heart, so she could follow through on her decision. She hadn't discussed this with anyone, not even Sarah. Every day that went past, she withdrew more and more into her shell. She seemed incapable of knowing what the right thing to do was, and so she had decided to trust Levi, to let her babies go to him to live in her flat until she was released. She just had to have faith that the jury would believe her story. She didn't have long before her trial, a matter of days, and perhaps it would be best to be clear-headed, get some sleep, leave the care of her children to their father. Levi had promised that he'd return the next day, and every day she was in prison thereafter. She trusted him, didn't she? It would all be fine, or so she kept saying to herself.

As they walked, Cathy still said nothing. She kissed the top of her little girl's head, her lips brushing against the fuzz of her hair. It seemed impossible to hand them over, but she knew she now had no choice. Rupert Smithers had sorted the paperwork, and the court had accepted that the father should have custody while she was banged up. Now, she would meet Levi in one of the legal rooms and they'd do the handover in front of the lawyer. As she walked, passing through gates, hearing the screech of the metal grids as they opened, and keys turning in the locks, numbness came over her. She could feel the baby in her arms, but it was like holding a dead weight, a bag of potatoes. Her heart beat, but it felt like someone else's body was moving ever forwards to the room where Levi would be waiting.

'Baby, it's good to see ye.' His words sounded like they came from far away though her boyfriend stood right in front of her, Rupert Smithers by his side.

'Cathy, I have some papers for you to sign, please take a seat,' said the lawyer efficiently.

Cathy sat down. The screw handed Archie to his father. Levi seemed to be a natural, taking hold of the baby, supporting his neck. He'd obviously been around children, Cathy mused, though none of this was of any interest as her depression crept in and settled over her. The room was small, with two chairs and a Formica desk. The walls were a dingy yellow colour and there was a single, half-dead pot plant in the corner. It couldn't have been more bleak. Cathy took the pen that was held out to her and signed her name. She didn't bother reading the papers. She didn't raise her eyes to see Levi's gaze moving between her and the lawyer. She looked down at her child, who was already making those little mewling noises and sucking motions with her mouth to show she was rooting for another feed.

'Take them. Look after them. Tell them I love them every day and bring them in to see me as soon as you can,' Cathy said, wiping her leaking eyes.

'Course I will, babe. I'll bring the babies tomorrow, don't ye worry. Well, if dat's everyting, I'll be saying thank ye to ye, Mr Smithers. Tomorrow, baby, I promise.' Levi winked as he placed Archie and then Kelly into the double pram he'd wheeled to the doorway of the cramped space. Cathy watched him, stuck to the seat as though with super glue, unable to move, unable to think. She stood up as Levi turned to go, and almost cried out, the sudden pain of her babies' departure breaking through. The lawyer saw her reaction.

'Are you OK, Cathy?' he said gently. 'I can call him back. You can say goodbye properly?'

'No, no, thank you. It's OK, it's for the best. I just never thought anything would turn out this way. And after all, Levi said he'd be back tomorrow, so I'll see the twins then.' She paused. Then she heard more words come from her mouth. 'And my mum, did she say anything about Levi having the babies?'

Rupert gave her a sad look.

'She was confused, perhaps, and upset, naturally. She'd have liked to take the babies herself and look after them for you. She loves them, Cathy, she really does.'

Cathy looked away. The kindness on his face was too much to bear.

'It's best they're with their father,' she said, though the sinking feeling in the pit of her stomach told her otherwise.

'She could've fought Levi for the children,' the lawyer persisted, 'But she decided not to, for your sake. It broke Ruby's heart to let Levi walk off with her grandchildren.'

'They're his children, they're not my mum's,' Cathy retorted, though her voice sounded weak.

'Yes, they're Levi's children, but your mother is a for-midable woman. She felt strongly that the babies should be brought up with her, with your family, the people who love you. They would've had everything they needed, until such time as we can get you released. She could've launched a custody battle that would've dragged on for months, but she chose not to. It almost broke her . . .'

Cathy looked at Rupert Smithers. He stared back at her over his glasses, frown lines on his face. He looked older under the stark fluorescent light. There, again, was that unmistakeable yearning for her mum. It almost overwhelmed her, and for a moment Cathy felt dizzy. Already, her arms ached for her babies. Would Levi know to give them a feed when they cried? Would he love them the way she did? In Cathy's heart, she knew she couldn't be sure, and that fact gave her pain that went almost as deep as the emptiness she now felt.

Cathy was moved back to the general wing once the twins had been taken. With a cruel irony, she realised she was occupying the cell her friend Kelly had died in. She lay down, too weary to take it all in. She kept starting, thinking, *They need a feed, why are they so quiet?* Then she'd remember, and slump back down onto her hard bed.

'Babe, how are ya?' Sarah's voice came from the doorway.

Cathy didn't bother to rouse herself, to look up. She felt unbelievably sad and tired.

'Hey, Cathy, I know it was today, givin' the twins to Levi. I spoke to Ruby on the phone. She's worried about ya . . .'

Still Cathy stayed silent. A single tear trickled down her face. Sarah walked over to the bed and sat at the end. She chewed her nails, her face a picture of concern.

'Cathy, talk to me. It's OK. It'll all be OK, I promise. Your mum'll get you out, she as good as told me.'

'Yeah, by bribing or threatening the jury, I expect,' Cathy butted in.

There was a pause. Sarah shifted on the blanket.

'So, Mum will pay the jury off and I'll walk free, then everything will be fine. Is that what she told you to tell me?' Cathy sat up now, anger spurring her on.

'Listen, Cathy, I don't know what your mum will do but I know she'd do anythin' to see you're OK. Why do ya hate her so much? What's she done to ya? Everythin' she ever does is for you . . .'

'It's complicated,' Cathy said, dully, and tried to roll over to stare at the other wall.

'Talk to me, Cathy. Tell me what's botherin' ya. Perhaps I can help. I'll try, anyway.'

'You can't help me, Sarah. I can't tell you what's wrong, but I can't trust her – or any of my family – any more. I know you speak to her regularly, so the next time you do, tell her if anything happens to Levi, anything at all, she'll never see her grandchildren again. If his blood is on her hands, I'll never speak to her, never set eyes on her. I mean it, Sarah,' Cathy said, vehemently.

Sarah sighed and shook her head.

'What 'ave you both done that's so awful, so bad, that you'd risk never seein' your own mother again? I just don't understand ya, Cathy, you've got everythin' – and take it from me, who has nuthin'. You 'ave a lovin' family, two beautiful children, and one day, you will leave this place, however it happens, and you'll never look back. People like me don't get to leave, or if we do, we're back, same old trouble, same old problems, never gettin' ahead in life. I'm sorry for ya if ya can't see that.'

Sarah spoke from the heart, her words gushing out of her. As she stood up to leave, thinking Cathy a lost cause, two women shoved open the cell door. One had jet black hair pulled up into a high ponytail, the other had red hair worn the same way. Both wore large, flashy, gold hoop earrings and expensive Nike tracksuits.

'Ye fuckin' whore,' the dark-haired girl spat, aiming her insult at Cathy, who jumped up off the bed and stared at them in shock. The redhead was waving a letter about.

'Who the fuck are you?' Sarah instantly bit back. 'What the fuck are ya doin' in 'ere. It's polite to knock, or didn't ya know that?'

Both women ignored Sarah completely. They seemed beside themselves with fury.

'So, this is da little bitch who's taken our mate's husband? She's nutin' to look at, jeez, ye think Levi could've chosen better than this piece of drab,' the red-haired girl sneered.

Cathy looked between them in complete bewilderment.

'How do you know Levi?' she stuttered.

Sarah stepped in front of the one who spat, but the other woman turned, putting her face right up to hers.

'She's under my protection. Now what the fuck is this about?'

'We don't give a feck whose protection she's under, she's ours to deal wit. She stole our friend's husband, it's all over the grapevine. Levi's girlfriend was so stupid she got herself caught wit the coke, and so now everyone knows, even his wife in Ireland . . .'

There was the briefest silence. Then, all three women instinctively turned to Cathy, who gawped back at them, uncomprehending.

'His wife . . . ?' she said at last.

'She didn't feckin' know? Feck, what a sap!' The girl with black hair grinned from ear to ear, enjoying this revelation and the effect it was clearly having on the young woman.

Sarah stepped forward again. Her voice was low, menacing.

'Fuck with Cathy and ya fuck with me. You don't want to do that. Now you miserable cunts get outta 'ere. Come 'ere again, and I'll make your life a livin' fuckin' misery.'

Neither woman spoke, they just grinned back. They dropped the letter on the floor and sauntered out, throwing Sarah a last look – a mix of hate and triumph.

'Don't read it,' Sarah cautioned, but Cathy had already picked up the sheet of paper. The handwriting was looping and childlike but there was no mistaking the words. Cathy scanned it, gripping the page, her heart freezing inside her chest.

The bitch that tried to steal Levi is now in your prison. Go see her and tell her from me what a manky cow she is . . . She deserves everything she gets. You can tell her my husband was just screwing with her, wanted her money, then she goes and fucks it up by getting caught. She owes us. She owes me.

Cathy almost dropped the letter. She was breathing hard now, shock waves pounding through her. He was married. Perhaps they'd mixed her up with someone else? But the more she read, the more she knew. He had lied to her. The man who now had their babies had cheated and stole her mum's money. Cathy's world began to crash down, her heart breaking with every word she scanned.

The little kiddies miss their dadda. I hope we'll see him now his conniving bitch is out of the way and banged up . . . The words went on but the letter slipped out of Cathy's hands.

'What does it say? 'Ere, give it to me.' Sarah snatched the paper before it fell to the floor. Cathy's face was deathly pale.

'He already had children. I wonder if that's why he wouldn't let me call our boy Levi? Perhaps he's already got a son with that name?' Cathy felt sick. She retched and ran to the steel toilet in the corner of the room. Gripping the sides, she vomited violently into the bowl.

Sarah stood in the doorway, reading the letter to the end. She saw that Levi wasn't just a husband who'd betrayed his wife to screw Cathy out of her family's money, but he was already a dad, already had kids of his own, a fact that had hurt Cathy most of all.

'Cathy . . .' she started to say but was interrupted by the cell door being kicked open. The two women had returned, this time with two others, presumably as back-up.

'What the fuck?' Sarah shouted, but the red-haired woman was swift. In two paces she was at Cathy's side, dragging her up and slamming her fist into her face.

'Ye're a feckin' slag!'

Cathy fell to the ground, whimpering. The dark-haired girl began to screech. Sarah took her chance, grabbing her and slamming her face-first into the wall. Blood spattered everywhere as the girl's nose broke. The two other women leapt on Sarah, pulling her off. Sarah kicked and yelled. Within seconds, the corridor alarms were triggered and all hell broke loose. More women joined; then several screws, brandishing batons, ran in and started to pull the women off each other.

Cathy lay on the floor, sobbing, heartbroken, knowing she'd been lied to, knowing she'd been a pawn in Levi's ambitions to become a drug dealer. How had she been so blind, so naive? Cathy could barely feel the pain in her jawbone, the blood running from her nose and mouth. All she could feel was the searing pain of Levi's betrayal, the complete devastation of the truth. Had she known it all along? She wasn't sure. All she could feel was a kind of horror. This was the reason he never took her to his traveller site, the reason he never moved in with her, and why he avoided talk of marriage. She'd been such a fool – and worse, her mother had been right all along. Now, he had their babies, and she didn't know where he was or what he was doing with them. She'd given the man everything: her heart and soul in the form of Archie and Kelly. Was she even more naive than she'd thought? Had he stolen her children as well as her peace of mind? If so, she'd walked willingly into this, too blind to see any of his betrayals. Would she now pay the ultimate price and lose her babies to him too?

CHAPTER 33

'Where is he? Levi said he would come?' Cathy asked the screw who was moving on to the next cell. 'He told me he'd come . . .'

'Sorry, Willson, he ain't 'ere. No one for ya today,' the woman said brusquely as she went. Then, Sarah appeared.

'You OK, Cathy?' she said, seeing the look on the young woman's face.

'He said he'd bring the twins, but he didn't come yesterday, and he hasn't today. I've tried calling his number but it says it doesn't exist any more.'

Sarah took in Cathy's tear-stained face, her crumpled clothes, her lank and greasy hair. She looked like she hadn't washed for a couple of days.

'Babe, ya need to be patient. Perhaps he's lost his phone. He might be tryin' to get hold of ya. And didn't ya say that prison wasn't the place for the babies? Perhaps he's bein' a gent and not wantin' them to come in 'ere. It ain't the best place, is it?' Sarah knew she was mollifying Cathy, but what else could she say? Despite his promises, and the affection he'd apparently shown the children, the stark fact was that since the day he'd left with them, Cathy had not seen or heard a thing from him.

Cathy's impending trial was nothing compared to the desolation she felt in not being able to hear Levi's voice or hold her babies. She woke up each night, thinking they were in their cot, waiting for them to call out for food, but they weren't there. She had no idea where her children were now. Since Cathy had discovered that the man she'd given her heart to had lied to her, she had become frantic. She wasn't sleeping, wasn't eating. Every day that passed, she asked whether he was coming, desperately hoping he'd prove her wrong and appear – but he hadn't. Where were her children? Were they even safe? Cathy felt sick to her stomach and all she could do was pace her cell, night and day, hoping against hope that she was wrong and he'd appear, his eyes twinkling at her, his voice lilting in his soft Irish accent, and he'd bring her treasures to her. By now, three days after he'd taken them, she was beginning to realise this was a fantasy.

'He's taken them, Sarah. He's stolen our babies. He lied to me. He was just after the money; we saw it with our own eyes. He's left me and he's taken Archie and Kelly . . . I know now I should never have believed Levi or trusted him.' She put her head in her hands. 'I really loved him, but he can't have ever loved me – and he never will. And now I've let my babies go. What kind of mother am I? What kind of pathetic loser mum does that? I hate myself, Sarah, not him. I didn't see it, but everyone else did. My mum was right. She's always right. Why can't I be more like her? I'm so weak, so stupid . . .' Cathy started to sob. She sank to the ground, and Sarah rushed over to her, to try to catch her before she fell.

'There, there, darlin'. Don't talk like that, Cathy. You've made a few mistakes but it's not over yet. You've got to calm yerself down. Don't talk like that, neither. There's nuthin' you can do right now except get ready for the trial. Look, I've bought ya a doughnut, and on a proper plate too, like the lady you are. Don't worry. Rube will find that fuckin' scumbag if he's done a runner with the babies. She'll send hell-fury down on him. Please don't worry, shush, Cathy.' She stroked her hair. 'You've got to be strong now, it's your trial tomorrow. You've got to get ready . . .' Sarah's voice trailed off when she saw the look of utter despair in Cathy's eyes. 'It'll be OK. I promise ya, it will,' Sarah finished, holding the crying woman to her.

Sarah had called Ruby each day to give her an update. Sarah had cautioned her old friend to wait until the third day, to see if it was just Levi being unreliable. Now, it was the day. It was time that Levi was brought to heel – and there was only one woman who could do it.

Ruby pulled up at the traveller site. Her patience had run out. Alfie was with her, sitting in the passenger seat, his craggy face thin, his expression as dark as it got.

Ruby walked over to the gate. She didn't attempt any niceties this time. 'I want to see Big Joe. Now.' Alfie stood beside her, his sharp Westwood suit contrasting with the casual clothes of the travellers who were gathering in front of them. For a moment, no one moved, then the people parted and there Big Joe stood, a frown on his face.

'I think ya know why I'm 'ere,' Ruby said sharply, though she felt a small thrill in her heart at the sight of Levi's father. In another time, in another world, perhaps there would have been something between them. Big Joe returned her gaze, steady and direct. With a gesture from him, the gate was pulled open and both Ruby and Alfie walked through. Big Joe looked for a moment like he would try to stop Alfie, before thinking better of it. This time, the knives were out. There was no pretence of conversation. They followed Big Joe to his caravan, and sat down at the table while the man flicked the switch on the kettle. They waited, silent, for it to boil.

'Where is he?' Ruby said when the mug of tea was placed in front of her. She didn't look down to it, didn't touch it. Joe sipped his drink, said nothing. Alfie flexed his fingers, put his chin on his folded hands and stared at Levi's father without blinking. 'So, ya know where he is then,' Ruby continued as if this was a perfectly normal chat over coffee.

'It so happens that I do,' Big Joe replied, turning to stir more sugar into his tea. Ruby leaned forward across the table, locking eyes with the man who had the information she required.

'You know my family history. You know we have Romany blood. So, now we need to cash in on that connection. D'ya understand me?'

Joe said nothing. He watched her, his expression neutral.

'You are honour-bound to help us. Levi has taken my grandchildren – your grandchildren – and he's left, ain't he.' It was a statement rather than a question. There was no point tiptoeing round this. Ruby's patience had dissolved. 'Levi used my daughter. He took our money and he bought drugs, which Cathy got busted for. I don't know if that was deliberate; it doesn't really matter. It don't change nuthin'. My daughter was nuthin' but a cash cow for your son. I know he didn't want those babies. We know he's already married and has a family of his own. We know my Cathy's babies were a nuisance – at first.' She took a breath. 'That feelin' didn't last long, did it? He saw an opportunity, didn't he? He saw that the babies could be quite good for him, but only if he got control of them. Am I right?' Ruby paused, but seeing that Joe's expression was unchanging, she continued regardless.

'So, what does Levi want? That's why we're all 'ere, ain't it? He's taken the babies and he wants somethin' in return for his trouble. So, spit it out, what does your son want from me that he can't get otherwise? Is it money? Because we 'ave money, more money than you can imagine. So, I want to know, and I want to know now.'

Alfie yawned and stretched back. He exuded menace. A wiry but toughened man, his muscles lean, his expression inscrutable. He was the hard man Ruby knew she could always rely on. Big Joe stared at them both, then finally, he nodded.

'I know where my son is. He isn't here, by the way. No, he's in Ireland. And yes, he's got the babies. They're a lovely pair of littl'uns. They look so much like Levi, don't they?' Joe answered.

Ruby could feel her anger mounting. Even though, strangely, she trusted this man, she knew that, whatever happened, they were on different sides. Her family had left behind their Romany roots. It was only a small thread running between them, but she had to milk it for all it was worth. She had to find out where Archie and Kelly were, for Cathy's sake, for all their sakes.

'Go on . . .' she commanded.

Joe smiled. His eyes were an intense blue. In the dim light of the caravan, Ruby's emerald-coloured eyes looked back at his; their gazes were locked.

'Ye won't find him – unless he wants ye to. He's safe with his own folk, so there's no point tearing across the country lookin' for him. He did leave ye a note though. Now, where did I put it. He knew ye'd come lookin' for him.'

Joe made a show of scrambling through a drawer in the built-in cabinets, but sure enough, he pulled out a note inside an envelope. Ruby took it without a word. She opened the paper and read the words it contained. Unsurprisingly, there it was. He wanted 'compensation' for the return of the children. He called it a financial settlement, and the figure of £1 million was demanded in scratchy, childish handwriting. Ruby passed the note to Alfie, who yawned again, and nodded.

'I must say I'm disappointed in his lack of imagination,' Ruby said eventually. She stood up, leaving her tea undrunk. Alfie joined her, standing at her side, his face a grimace.

'And if we don't agree? If we decide we'll do better to hunt down the fucker you call a son by ourselves? What will he do then?' She needed to know the real terms of this agreement. Would he do something to the children? Was he capable of even worse crimes? Ruby had to be sure she knew what she was dealing with. She'd faced up many a hard man who just wanted to earn a quick buck, but now and then, she saw men who would do anything – and it was those men she had trained herself to recognise, to spot. There was only one man whose true intentions had slipped past her for too long – Vladimir. But he'd paid hard for hoodwinking her. Was Levi one of those who'd stop at nothing? Or was he just a lucky chancer who'd seen his way to making a million pounds?

The atmosphere inside the caravan was tense. Alfie's eyes glittered dangerously. He cracked his knuckles in a display of raw male hostility. Joe looked them both up and down, and almost reluctantly said, 'He says he knows some things about ye, and he tells me that if ye don't agree to his terms, he's to say the word "George" and ye'll know what he's implyin'.'

Ruby tried to hide her shock. So, Cathy had told him. She'd sensed Levi had something over them. At least now she knew what it was, but she could've wept over Cathy's naivety, her trusting nature, so unlike Ruby's. She exchanged a grim look with Alfie. She nodded.

'So, it's blackmail, is it? At least I can understand that. Tell him I'll pay what he wants, but I insist on seein' him, and I want a guarantee that he'll never come near Cathy or the babies again.'

'And if ya don't, then I'll burn this shithole to the ground,' Alfie growled.

Big Joe nodded, looking entirely unconcerned. Ruby caught his gaze and for a moment, neither of them looked away. Something nagged at her. Somehow, she didn't buy into Joe as a hard man. There was something softer about him, she could feel it. Was there more to Levi's father than met the eye? Her instincts were rarely wrong, but she had no evidence to say he was any different from his shyster son.

Joe nodded as if he'd read her thoughts.

'We'll be in touch.'

CHAPTER 34

There was a knock at Ruby's door. It was the first day of Cathy's trial and Ruby was dressed head-to-toe in black: a skirt suit, a pair of heels and an oversized coat. Lloyd was due to pick her up in half an hour. The evening before, Lloyd had assured her that once the jury was sworn in, they'd be nobbled, and so the outcome was a done deal. Today marked the beginning of the process of bringing Cathy home, though the trial could take three weeks or more. The next thing they had to do was get the babies back, but that could wait – for now.

Ruby had been checking her handbag for her keys and mobile when the door sounded. Opening it, she saw a policewoman standing on her doorstep next to a man in a black suit. Ruby stared at them, and their sombre expressions. She was momentarily taken aback at the sight of the Old Bill so close to home. It was raining, and already the pair looked soaked through.

Even before she spoke, she knew.

'Can I help ya?' Ruby managed. She was used to fronting up dangerous crooks, so she didn't show her sudden
fear, the jolt of expectation for what news they might bring.

'Mrs Ruby Willson?'

'Yes, that's me, officer.'

'We have to talk to you. It's about your daughter,
Cathy. Can we come inside?'

The world stopped. In that second, Ruby knew that her
life would change for ever. She opened the door as if in
a daze, and said, 'Of course, do come inside.' As she led
them to the plush living room, she felt like she was moving through treacle. They sat down, awkward. There was a
short silence. The man in black cleared his throat.

'I am the governor of Holloway Prison. I am deeply sad-
dened to inform you that your daughter, Cathy Willson,
died in her cell yesterday evening. She was discovered by
an inmate, a friend of hers, Sarah, who immediately alerted
staff. There will, of course, be a full inquiry . . .'

Ruby looked up at the stranger, who had given her the
worst possible news. She nodded.

'And will that bring my daughter back?' she said quietly.

'It won't,' the governor replied. 'We are deeply sorry for
your loss.'

'How did it happen?' Ruby said, her voice harsh now.

The officer looked at the governor, who shifted uncomfortably on the velvet seat.

'It appeared she had cut her wrists, though we won't
know the full picture until the coroner's report.'

'Cut her wrists?' Ruby uttered. 'And how did she come to 'ave anythin' that could be sharp enough to do that? I thought knives and blades were forbidden?' Tears now ran down Ruby's face, though she couldn't feel them. Her entire body had gone numb.

Again, the man cleared his throat.

'We don't know for sure, but a broken plate seems to have been the – erm – implement used to do the damage.'

'A broken plate?' Ruby echoed. 'But why did she do it? Didn't anyone realise she was strugglin'?'

The officer glanced again at the governor.

'We cannot comment on the details of the incident. Until the post-mortem has taken place, there is nothing else we can say. I'm sorry, but if there is any support you need, Mrs Willson, then we have officers trained to deal with this kind of incident. Can we send someone to you?' Her voice was gentle, her manner soft, but she wasn't going to be drawn. Of course, Ruby knew why. She knew that Cathy had discovered Levi's infidelity in the worst possible way. She'd found out he'd been using her all along – and now he had their children. No person could cope with all that. Ruby had known Cathy would crumble, but she'd hoped her daughter would make it to the trial because from then onwards, everything was in place for a not guilty verdict. The prison had a duty of care, but they'd failed her, just as Levi had, just as Ruby had. None of them was innocent – they'd all played their part in Cathy's demise. This wasn't something Ruby was going to say, so she shook her head.

'Thank you, I don't need no one, just my family,' she replied, not returning the officer's gaze.

'Then we will leave you with our condolences, and this . . .'

The officer handed Ruby a letter addressed to her. It was Cathy's handwriting. Ruby had always been so proud of how neat Cathy's writing had been. She'd been educated in the best international school and it showed. Her accent was worlds away from her mum's rough East End dialect, and her writing was immaculate. All that education, all those opportunities and all that privilege – and for what? A life cut short. A grieving mother. Two helpless children who would grow up without knowing her, without feeling Cathy's arms around them, her light kisses on each of their crowns. They would all have to find a way to live without her – but how? How on earth would that ever be possible?

Ruby took the envelope. Her hands shook.

'Thank you,' she said, standing up. The meeting was over. She wanted them out of her house, out of her private space, so she could meet the grief head on. Already, she felt like she was drowning.

The door clicked shut. Ruby sank to the floor. Opening the envelope, her hands wouldn't stay still. She was trembling, and cursed her clumsy hands. This letter, these words, were all she had left of Cathy. What would her daughter say? Would this be more pain heaped upon the deluge already flooring her?

Mum,

I'm sorry. I know I'm a disappointment to you. I trusted Levi and he let me down. I helped him to take all that money, and now he's taken my babies and I don't know what to do. The pain is too much, Mum, which is why I'm writing this. The trial is tomorrow, and I can't face it. I know Levi has left me and I'm sure he's going to try and blackmail you for more money or just take them away from me for ever. That's something I can't handle, Mum, I hope you understand. I can't see any future for me. I've lost your grandchildren. Please forgive me. Please tell Archie and Kelly that I had no choice, and that I'll love them for ever even though I won't be there to see them grow up. They deserve better than me. I've let everyone down. I couldn't see that you were all trying to protect me and I gave away our worst, our darkest secret. There have been so many secrets and I was so naive. I deserve to die. I can't give the twins a proper mum, one who does the right things and is capable of looking after them. So, I wanted to say that, if you manage to get them back off the man I trusted with my whole heart, then you must bring them up. Love them for me, Mum. Keep them safe, as I can't. They are better off without me. And please give Kelly the middle name Sarah. Sarah has been so good to me. She's looked after me in here and I don't know how else to thank her. I have to go now. I love you, Mum.

Cathy xxx

By now, Ruby was sobbing. When she'd finished, she held the paper to her chest and moaned, 'Why did ya do this, Cathy? You had everythin' to live for . . . you were goin' to walk free. I should've told ya about George, about me killin' him. I should've told ya all along. It's my lies that 'ave got us 'ere. It's my fault, all my fault, that you're dead.'

Cathy's funeral was a blur. Lloyd and Alfie had wept and raged when Ruby had made the call to them just after reading the letter. At first, Lloyd refused to believe it, while Alfie had punched a wall and thrown a chair before collapsing. Grief consumed them all. Telling her brother Bobby and his wife Belle was the hardest of all. Ruby hadn't spoken to them for a while, and the rift in their family had just got wider.

'Rube!' Bobby had said when he picked up her call. 'It's been ages. How are ya? Don't worry, we're comin' to the trial, we wouldn't miss bein' there to support Cathy.'

'It isn't about the trial, Bobby,' Ruby said, the love for her brother and the terrible sadness she was about to force on him making her throat ache.

'There won't be a trial today,' she said. Ruby had called them straight after Lloyd and Alfie. She wanted all her family around her on the day of this horrific news. She wanted them to be at her house, in their bubble, with all the previous worries and problems behind them, reunited for their love of her daughter.

'No trial? Fuck's sake, they 'aven't put it off, 'ave they? Poor Cathy . . .'

'No, Bobby, they 'aven't postponed it. I've got some news and I want ya to promise me you'll sit down. This is the worst thing I think I'll ever say to ya, but I 'ave to tell ya.'

'What is it, Rube? What's goin' on? You don't sound like yerself. Is there trouble? Can I help?' Bobby sounded confused. It was so like him to want to help her even though they'd fallen out when Cathy learned the truth about George's death during her aunt and uncle's argument.

Ruby drew in a deep breath.

'Cathy is dead,' she finally said, her voice wobbling. 'She's dead. It looks like she killed herself, Bobby. Our beautiful girl is gone.'

There was a moment's pause, then a strangled sound at the other end of the line.

'She's dead? I don't believe it. Oh God, no.'

'The worst thing is, Bobby, she would've walked free. Lloyd had sorted it: he was going to fix the jury. Cathy didn't know. We couldn't exactly go into the jail and tell her, but she would've come home to us. And now she's gone for ever and I don't know how to live without her.' Ruby broke down again. Tears streamed down her face.

'But the twins?' was all Bobby managed to respond.

'Levi has them, but we're goin' to get them back – and finish this once and for all,' Ruby replied grimly. She wasn't going to share the details, but a plan was forming in her mind. She just needed to speak to Big Joe. In her heart, she knew that once he learned that the mother of his grandchildren had killed herself in desperation, he would help her. She had to believe that, as the whole plan rested on it. Somehow, she had to get him onside. She had to take revenge on Levi, Big Joe's son or not, and finally, she knew a way to do it.

Ruby murmured to the guests at Cathy's wake, on autopilot, making small talk with the crooks they called their friends who had come to pay their respects. Alfie and Lloyd were with her, as were Bobby and Belle. They'd all been staying with Ruby at her Chigwell mansion in the days following Cathy's death. When the verdict of suicide came in, they cried and hugged each other, knowing they were all complicit. They'd all played a part in their gorgeous girl's desperation.

'She was the best of us,' Ruby said, her eyes glazed with tears.

'So sorry for your loss', 'Our condolences to all the family', 'She was a diamond, a true diamond', and so the tributes went on.

When Belle stepped in front of Ruby, the women held each other's gaze in a way that was both direct and knowing. They hadn't had a chance to really speak, even though they'd all been together. There was too much to arrange, so many bouquets to arrange in vases, cards to open, documents to sign. Now there was just the pair of them, as if alone, despite being surrounded by well-wishers, crooks and robbers.

Belle was crying. She took hold of Ruby and embraced her.

'I'm so sorry, Ruby. It's all my fault. If she hadn't heard me and Bobby arguing, this would never have happened.'

Ruby choked up. She appreciated her sister-in-law's honesty, her direct words.

'No, Belle, I should never 'ave lied to her. I broke her trust. But if we blame anyone, it's that bastard, Levi. He broke her heart and that was that. From the moment she found out about his wife and kids, that was it. Sarah told me she never really recovered. It was as if part of her had already gone.'

'What will you do, Ruby?' Belle said, pulling away from Ruby's arms as if she sensed danger.

Ruby didn't say a word. Her eyes narrowed. Belle stared back at her, almost recoiling. Without a word passing between them, they both understood.

Bobby appeared at Belle's arm.

'I need to go. Sorry, Rube, it's all too much. Are Lloyd and Alfie stayin' with ya?'

Ruby smiled sadly, her mood shifting, the tension dissipating.

'Yes, they are, Bobby. Don't worry about me. Get yerselves home. We all need our own beds tonight. Thank you, both of ya,' she murmured, 'I don't know how I would get through this without ya.'

'Cathy was our special girl too. We loved her as if she were our own,' Belle said as the tears started to flow again.

Ruby watched them depart, saw that Lloyd was drawing the event to a close. She walked up her palatial staircase, kicking off her heels as she went, not bothering to pick them up. She reached for her phone. It was time for business. The only part of her that felt alive still was the burning hatred she had for Levi. Yes, they were all guilty, but some were more guilty than others. Levi. It was his turn for justice – and by God, Ruby would deliver it.

CHAPTER 35

Ruby sat down wearily on her bed. She wanted to lie back and close her eyes, let grief wash over her, but she couldn't do it yet. There was work to be done.

She drew her phone out of her bag and dialled a number.

'What is it?' Big Joe didn't wait for niceties.

'It's Cathy,' Ruby said, her voice low, controlled. 'She's dead.'

There was a brief silence, then Joe spoke.

'There were rumours, but we didn't know for sure. I'm sorry for your loss. I'm sorry for the twins, they've lost their mammy,' he replied softly.

'Did those rumours say how she did it?' Ruby went on. She couldn't stop. She had to tell him the truth.

'They didn't, Ruby. So, why don't ye tell me.'

Ruby took a deep breath.

'She smashed a plate and used the sharp edge of one of the shards to cut her wrists. They found her alone, blood soaked in the bedding and the mattress, all over the floor. The last thing she did was write me a letter to say it was better if she wasn't around.' She paused. 'Joe, your son did this. He might not 'ave been there, holding the broken plate, but he did this, all right. He took everythin' from her. She was an innocent; my beautiful girl was an innocent in this world and he destroyed her.' Ruby began to cry. She didn't try to stop the tears, the sobs that shook her body. Unselfconsciously, she wept, and Joe stayed on the line, listening and waiting. When, eventually, the weeping subsided, Joe spoke again.

'And so ye need my help?'

'I do,' Ruby replied, wiping her eyes, knowing her mascara was smeared over her face, not caring at all how she looked.

'Leave it with me,' Joe said, before hanging up.

Two days later, Ruby's phone rang. It was an unknown number.

'I have the drop-off details. Ye'll need to get to Ireland today. One of our associates will meet ye there.' It was Big Joe's voice.

Lloyd and Alfie were with her, all ready to leave at a moment's notice. Ruby had a hunch that Big Joe would do the right thing and help them get the babies back. She didn't know for sure. There was a lot at stake, not least the strict codes among traveller communities that excluded outsiders, even ones with distant Romany ties.

'Was that him?' Lloyd said. He sat at her dinner table sipping an espresso.

'Yes, it was. We're goin' to Ireland.'

Running in, a sweat-drenched Alfie appeared in the doorway. 'Fuckin' bring it on,' he said, clearly having heard their conversation. Ruby turned to him, saw the look of total determination on his face and, not for the first time, she thanked her lucky stars she'd met him and his brother all those years ago. Her life had pivoted from one path to a new one that moment in Spain when Archie spoke to her. It had been her passage to the big league, to the dizzy heights – and terrors – of running a cartel that spanned several nations. It had also been the point at which she had stepped out into the world, ready to become the ball-breaking, confident woman she was meant to be. Ruby had a strange sense that it had all led to this moment. She now needed to be that person more than ever. She needed to focus like she never had before. Her plan was in place. The deal was struck. Vengeance was waiting for her, she just had to reach out and take it.

'Good, you're back. Did ya get the money?'

'It's safe. We can get it from the lock-up on our way. A million in notes, just as you asked.' Alfie wiped his face.

'I'll grab a quick shower. Give me ten.'

The journey passed uneventfully. The cash was safe in a sports bag. Lloyd drove them to their private aircraft, and they embarked, all three wearing Prada sunglasses. All three exuding power, danger.

Big Joe was as good as his word. A blacked-out Mercedes was waiting for them at the other end. Its engine purred as it pulled out of the small airfield, and it was soon on its way. The driver didn't say a word, neither did Ruby or the others. They were tense, expectant. Ruby wasn't stupid. She knew they could be walking into a trap. Who was to say that Levi wouldn't kill them all and take the money? If the thought had crossed Lloyd and Alfie's minds, they said nothing. This was too significant. Getting the twins back was the only thing that mattered. It was more important than any fears about what lay ahead.

The car had been travelling for a couple of hours, and now splashed through country lanes. Just as Ruby was wondering how much longer they had to travel, they pulled to a halt in a lay-by seemingly in the middle of nowhere. They were surrounded by trees, still dripping after a rain shower earlier, and fields, and little else.

"Ave ya got a gun, Rube? Ya might need it,' said Alfie, his gaze darting everywhere.

'I won't be carryin' a gun, Alfie. I don't want to risk the twins gettin' hurt, assumin' Levi actually intends on handin' them over to us,' she replied.

Alfie nodded. She knew he and Lloyd were carrying guns under their Savile Row suits. Almost as an afterthought, Ruby touched the rough, thick material of the bulletproof vest she wore under her Lacoste coat. They'd come prepared for anything. They'd learned their lesson after being set up by an Albanian drug gang many years ago, and it was only the bulletproof vest that had saved Archie at the time. Ruby tried not to think of that. Her focus had to be absolute. Would they all get out alive?

They waited. Still, the driver said nothing. They stared out of the windows, through the thickened dark glass. The rain started to drizzle again.

'What a fuckin' country. Never stops fuckin' rainin',' snorted Alfie, which made Ruby smile.

The minutes passed and nothing happened.

D'ya think they're comin'?' Ruby said softly.

'I think they are. They're just bidin' their time, hopin' to rile us,' replied Lloyd, checking his Rolex.

Alfie lit a cigarette as the seconds and then the minutes ticked on. He buzzed down the window and exhaled the smoke outside. Then, they heard the sound of a vehicle approaching, its tyres splashing through puddles made in the uneven track.

'Stay in the car. If they shoot, then get the fuck out of 'ere. Don't worry about me, save yerself.' Alfie didn't mince his words.

Ruby nodded, knowing it was the way of things, the law of the jungle. Get the fuck out if you need to. Better one of us gets out alive than all are killed.

A tatty vehicle pulled up.

'It's him,' Ruby murmured, and she could feel the heat of her anger rise within her. She had to remain calm, keep her cool. This was going to be the hardest thing she would ever have to do. Everything had led to this. Every decision. Every risk, every gamble. It had all led here, to this moment. Ruby blinked. She breathed, trying to still her heart, which was now pounding. Two men got out of the car – one was Levi, and the other, a surprise. It was Big Joe. Was this a good thing? Had Big Joe betrayed her? Was he siding with his son, going in on the money? Would Joe help his son, kill them and take the cash? In that moment, Ruby honestly didn't know. She glanced at Lloyd, who looked back at her steadily.

'Stay calm, Ruby,' he said, though the strain showed on his features. His hair, previously speckled with grey, was now almost entirely silver; his cheekbones were still high but his face looked drawn. They'd been through so much tragedy, so many deaths. Was this their final moment?

'You're a long way from home, Joe,' Ruby said pointedly as she stepped out of the Merc.

'So I am, Ruby. It's good to see ye,' Joe replied.

Ruby stared at him for a moment, but her intuition told her nothing. She had no idea what would happen next, whose side Joe was on. His involvement was critical. If he was there to defend his son, then they were all fucked. She had no choice but to trust him to keep to their plan, to keep going, whatever the cost.

Levi took a few steps forward and squared up to Ruby. She wasn't fazed. She held his gaze until he looked away, giving her a disproportionate sense of exultation. She could do this. She could see this through. He was nothing but a shyster coward who'd manipulated her daughter. Well, he couldn't pull the wool over her eyes. She almost laughed but contained it. Any wrong move could be the end of them all.

'Have ye got the money, bitch?' Levi said lazily.

'Don't disrespect the lady,' murmured Joe, though his son ignored him.

'So, *bitch*, show us the cash.' Levi emphasised the insult. Ruby could feel Alfie's hackles rise. She willed him to stay focused, stay calm.

'We've got your money, but I want to know when I'll see my grandchildren. If you've harmed a hair on either of their heads, you're a dead man,' Ruby said almost politely in response. She nodded to Alfie, who walked round to the boot of the Mercedes and took out two large bags, which she knew were stuffed with rolls of notes.

'Did ya know that Cathy's dead?' Ruby added as her brother-in-law placed the bags down on the ground halfway between them, as if an afterthought.

Levi slouched forward and picked up the bags, shooting her a look of pure menace.

'So what if I did know. The silly cow didn't need to do dat, but then again she missed me . . .' Levi grinned. A big mistake. Ruby felt her anger begin to overwhelm her. Levi carried on, seemingly oblivious of the effect he was having. He unzipped both bags and whistled.

'Jeez, look at all this money, Da, won't ye? It's a feckin' fortune. I told ye I should've asked for more. These rich bastards can afford a bit of blackmail, am I right?'

Levi winked at Ruby who, by now, was having to breathe through her rage.

'Where're the fuckin' twins?' Alfie cut to the point. Perhaps he could sense Ruby's distress, her failing will-power. Ruby started to tremble. She was looking at her daughter's killer – or that's how she saw it. This was too much, way too much.

'Tell us where the twins are or we'll make ya,' Lloyd said, pulling out his handgun.

Levi laughed, so sure of himself. So cocky to the last.

'Don't ye worry about your precious babies. They've been looked after by kings, but ye won't get to enjoy them for long. No, they'll be whisked off into care before ye can blink—'

At this point Big Joe, who had remained almost silent until now, interrupted Levi.

'What are ye talkin' about? The deal was you take the money, I bring the twins back to England. Nice and clean, all settled, so everyone can get on with their lives . . .'

Levi laughed triumphantly.

'Dat was your plan, Da. It weren't mine. No, as soon as they're back across the water, I'll be makin' a little phone call to the police. I know all your secrets, ye know. I know ye killed George, your own brother. I'm goin' to shaft yous all. The police will surely know everyting now.'

Big Joe shook his head.

'No, son, that's not what we agreed. I won't let ye do dat.'

'Ye can't stop me,' sneered Levi, 'I can shaft dat silly cow's mother, and I'll 'ave destroyed the Willsons. I knew when I met dat girl she'd be a fuckin' goldmine – but I had no idea it would work out as well as this.' Levi's eyes were gleaming. He seemed almost high on something, he was so reckless, so candid. The veins in Alfie's neck pulsed as he struggled to contain his anger. Lloyd held his gun up, pointing it directly at the young man who held all the cards – or so it seemed.

'Don't worry, Da, dey won't shoot me, like, because dey won't get the twins if they kill me.'

'Is dat right, son?' Big Joe said, his voice shaking.

And before any of them could move, before they could blink, Joe pulled out a handgun and stood in front of his son.

'I knew ye was a waster from the moment ye was born. I knew ye were a bad'un, but I never thought it'd be as bad as this. I'm ashamed to call ye my son. Ruby was right. Dat girl, dat ye call her, dat girl Cathy was the mother of your twins!'

Joe turned to his son. He now stood right in front of him, close enough to land a kiss or a punch.

'She's dead, and Ruby's right, it was your fault. Ye treated her like dirt, and ye might as well have held that shard to her wrist and cut it yerself. You're a murderer, son, and ye know what we do with those, eh?'

For a moment, Levi blinked, unsure where this was going. He clearly hadn't expected his father to say anything. Ruby and Lloyd exchanged a look. This wasn't the way this was supposed to play out.

Big Joe stepped forward again, nose-to-nose with his son. He has already stepped forward, above?

'You're no son of mine. Ye should've died when Cathy did. Those twins deserve a better life, one without ye. Think of what I'm about to do as just a formality. Ye should've died along with dat girl, as ye called her.'

With that, before Levi could react, Joe pulled the trigger.

Blood splattered across the wet grass, the muddy tracks, covering Joe from his head to his boots.

'Fuck!' shouted Alfie, holding his gun up, unsure what would happen next.

Levi's body slumped to the floor. Joe stood, swaying for a moment, then turned round slowly. His face was pale. His eyes deadened.

'He was mine to kill. Mine. It couldn't have happened any other way. Now get the fuck outta here and I'll be in touch about the babies.'

Ruby looked mutinous. She didn't care that Levi lay dead. She wanted her grandchildren. After all, that was the only reason they were there.

She opened her mouth to argue but Joe's look – a haunted, desperate look – stopped her.

Lloyd half-pulled her back to the car, her heels sinking in the quagmire as the rain fell heavily now. Head spinning, she let herself be led to the car. The countryside flashed past, but she didn't see it. All Ruby could think of was Levi's body, covered in his own blood, slumped on the ground at Joe's feet.

CHAPTER 36

The trip back to England was a sombre one. However much Ruby had hated Levi, and vowed she would avenge Cathy, his death played on her mind. She'd killed before. It wasn't the shock of it, it was the sadness that stayed with her. She felt nothing towards Levi's life having ended – it was Joe who filled her thoughts as Lloyd drove across country. She knew what it was to kill a member of her own family. She remembered holding the handgun to George's head while he'd wept and shook in her arms. She'd promised him he wouldn't be hurt, and in her eyes, she'd kept that promise. She'd ended his life swiftly and painlessly – a mercy, a blessing for him, almost. Cathy hadn't seen it that way when she'd found out, but it was the truth. In Ruby's world, mercy wasn't measured in forgiveness.

'You OK, Rube?' Lloyd said as he drove. They'd arrived in Chigwell and were minutes from home.

Ruby looked up at the man who had meant so much to her, and to Cathy. A man who had been at the helm of their lives for so long now. She couldn't imagine what life would've been like without him. It was fate, or chance, that had brought them together. It was her destiny, she saw that now, despite the deaths, the grief, the immense sadness that had piled up over the years. She'd lost her beloved husband Archie. She'd killed her brother. She'd now lost Cathy, too. It was almost unimaginable not to have them all in her world, yet she had to carry on. The twins, should they be sent to her, would need her strength, her love, from now on. She would, at least, have a reason to keep living.

'Yes, I think I'm OK,' Ruby replied. She turned her head to smile at her father-in-law. She was in the passenger seat while Alfie lay asleep in the back. Ruby had wanted to beg Joe to hand over the twins, implore him to tell her where they were, but Lloyd had taken charge, got her and all three of them out of there. Ruby remembered looking back as the Merc sped off, seeing Joe sink to the ground, his head in his hands, weeping beside his dead boy.

'Rube, we've talked about retiring. It feels like a million years ago now, but it's the right thing to do. If all goes well, you'll 'ave yer hands full with the twins. We 'ave to get out of this game. We've lost too much,' Lloyd said.

Ruby could see he was serious. She took in a long, slow breath. In her mind's eye she saw the anguish on Joe's face as he turned to her after shooting Levi. She saw, as one parent to another, the agony of a child's death. He'd been honour-bound to do it. She could tell he was a man who lived by his own code of honour, and Levi had breached it again and again. The ending had been inevitable, she reflected, but she was sure it didn't hurt Joe any less to know this. Joe's suffering only galvanised what Ruby had been pondering for a while; giving up this game, settling down and living quietly, creating a straight life at long last. A life in which the twins could grow and thrive.

'It's time to get out,' she agreed. 'Alfie can run the whole business, if he wants. He can bring in his own men from South America, or he can hand it over to someone else. After all, he's been runnin' Vladimir's side successfully. He's more than capable. I agree we should take the money and leave, put the word out that we're done with it all. We've got more than enough cash. I think you're right, Lloyd, it's time to leave all this behind while we still can.'

Ruby knew then that they'd come to the end of a very long road, one which had spanned decades. She'd made difficult choices as a young woman. Ruby and her brother Bobby had had to find a way to make ends meet, put food on the table and hold their heads up high. The only choice in the East End at that time had been a life of crime. They'd been brought up straight, but the temptation for easy money to pay the funeral bills and keep their baby brother fed was too much. Bobby had been the brawn while she had been the brains – and look where it had got them: a life undreamt of, a journey littered with death and mayhem, and power and riches they would never otherwise have experienced. Had it all been worth it? Ruby didn't know. She didn't like to look back. What was done was done. The past was the past. They had to keep moving forward, and not dwell on things. It was hard, though, damned hard.

'I just want Archie and Kelly back. I want them now. Why didn't Levi bring them with him?' Ruby said, feeling the physical ache for them as she spoke.

Lloyd couldn't answer that, but he did say, 'I'm glad they weren't there, Rube. I wouldn't 'ave wanted them to witness that even if they're too young to understand. Listen, you 'ave to trust Joe. He said we'd get the babies, so we wait. There's nuthin' else we can do.'

Ruby sat in silence, praying that Joe would be as good as his word, and would return the children to her. She didn't know what she'd do if he didn't. It would break her heart for good, that much was sure.

Ruby's phone rang. It was Rupert Smithers.

'Ruby, its Rupert. Are you home yet? I have a special delivery for you,' the lawyer said.

Puzzled, Ruby glanced at Lloyd, who shrugged. They were just turning into Ruby's driveway. Before she could answer, she spotted Rupert's gleaming black Aston Martin parked up in front of her house. Rupert, looking casual in jeans, loafers and a shirt, was holding his phone to his ear. He looked up and saw them, put his phone in his back pocket and waved.

'What now?' muttered Ruby. What she wanted more than anything was a hot bath and her own bed.

Lloyd pulled up and wordlessly got out of the car. Ruby followed him. Then, she saw something in the car which made her stomach turn over. She started to walk faster, reaching the car in only a few strides despite her sky-high heels. Her hands trembled as she wrenched open the back door. When she saw the two sleeping babies she cried out with complete delight, absolute contentment.

'Archie! Kelly! My darlings, my beautiful babies!'

'Shh, I've only just got them to sleep. I was phoned by someone who called himself Big Joe. I don't know how he knew my number, I don't think I'd like to know, but he told me where the babies were and that I should go collect them.' Rupert grinned as he saw Ruby's delight and the tears of joy that swiftly followed her discovery.

'Levi must've given his dad your name when Cathy signed over the twins to him. That's how they had your number. Makes sense—'

Ruby couldn't finish her sentence. A sob rose in her throat. She wanted to pull the twins out of their car seats and hold them to her, breathe in their baby smell and promise never to let them go. She couldn't, of course. They were both snuffling gently as they slept, oblivious to the swirl of emotions around them.

'You've come home to Nanny. You're goin' to 'ave such a good life. We'll talk about your mummy every day. We'll do all the things she loved to do. We'll go for ice cream and play in the park. We'll have a happy, simple life: free from drama and problems. You've got so many people who love ya. There's Bobby and Belle, and your great granddad Lloyd and Great Uncle Alfie. We'll all look after ya both. We'll protect ya, now and for ever.'

With that, Ruby eased Archie's baby seat out of the car and gestured for Lloyd to take Kelly inside once she'd opened up, fumbling for her keys in her happiness.

'And that's not all,' the lawyer added as he slid back into the driver's seat of his Aston Martin.

'Oh, what's that?' Ruby called from the doorway, mascara running down her cheeks, happy tears gleaming in her eyes.

'You're their legal guardian. I got word from the judge this morning. It's all settled. They're yours. Congratulations.' Rupert sped off, and, without being unkind, Ruby hoped fervently that it would be the last time she'd ever need his services. The future looked bright; it looked glorious, at long last. She'd never get over the death of her daughter, but she'd find a way to create a good life for her precious charges.

'My mum, your great-nanny Cathy, always said to me and Bobby when we was little, "A straight pound is worth three crooked." I promise ya both now, cross my heart and hope to die. I'll do it properly this time. You won't ever 'ave to look over your shoulders. I'll raise ya both straight, just as my mum and dad wanted for me and Bobby. We'll do it right this time.'

ACKNOWLEDGEMENTS

Thank you to my wonderful agent, Kerr MacRae, for all your support, insight and belief in me and my stories.

It took a whole team to make this book a reality and I want to say thank you to everyone at Welbeck. Jon Elek, Cathryn Kemp, Rosa Schierenberg and Rachel Hart for helping me bring all these characters to life. You are all absolute stars. Thanks also go to James Horobin and his incredible team of amazing sales, marketing and PR experts, especially Nico Poilblanc, Annabel Robinson and Rob Cox. The hard graft from this team has been second to none. Also, huge thanks to Alex Allden and the brilliant art team for the cover. I'm not sure I told you, but: 'I love it!'

And a special thanks goes to my dear friend Martina Cole, my inspiration and guide. You have supported my books from the start, but more than that, you have been a brilliant friend. Thanks again for everything!

ABOUT THE AUTHOR

'The first time I held a gun, I forgot to breathe'

LINDA CALVEY has served 18 years behind bars, making her Britain's longest-serving female prisoner. She moved to 14 different prisons, doing time with Rose West and Myra Hindley. But prison didn't break her. Since her release, Linda has become a full-time author. Her fascinating memoir, *The Black Widow*, was published in 2019 and her runaway fiction debut, *The Locksmith*, in 2021.

WELBECK

PUBLISHING GROUP

Love books? Join the club.

Sign up and choose your preferred genres to receive tailored news, deals, extracts, author interviews and more about your next favourite read.

From heart-racing thrillers to award-winning historical fiction, through to must-read music tomes, beautiful picture books and delightful gift ideas, Welbeck is proud to publish titles that suit every taste.

bit.ly/welbeckpublishing

WELBECK

ANDRE
DEUTSCH

MORTIMER

MORTIMER

WELBECK

OH!